Magical Cosmic Collection
Book Three

I0586402

CAITLIN II
MASQUERADE
MAGIC

Debbie Behan

Copyright

Dedication

To all those who crossed my path and inspired me to keep writing,
this book is dedicated to you.

Thanks for the memories.

CHAPTER ONE

Earth's Disarray

Caitlin looked deep into Melita's eyes. She was Jett's wife, and to their subjects, she was their queen. Melita was a proud woman and much loved by all, but today she was unsure, shaken and sad. Her weakened state was enough to grip the insides of Caitlin's stomach with shame. She was aware Jett was having trouble, but Axon had led her to believe her friend was only missing her and was quite capable of handling the pressure of his new position as the King of the Dwarf Planets. She could now tell her unintentional abandonment for so long had caused both Melita and Jett unnecessary suffering.

Melita sat next to Caitlin on a bench seat and pleaded with her as a friend, to help her husband. Her eyes were red from tears, and her voice quivered with sadness as she spoke.

'Since we saw you last, souls are escaping from the underworld and causing us some serious problems. Jett can't be in two places at once so has had to put his royal duties to the Dwarf Planets aside. There are some who don't believe he should have been given this title and have made it known. They threaten to go to war if he doesn't stand down. Current rulers are not happy that he never has time for them, and some are talking about joining this rebellion, denouncing him as their King.'

'Did he tell Axon this?' Caitlin fidgeted, uncomfortable with this news.

'Yes, several times. I was the instigator of many of the calls. I heard him ask for you. He even begged once or twice. But due to the difficulty of the mission you were on, his requests were denied. Now Jett is beginning to withdraw as he did before he met you. It's not only from his family but from me too. The underworld is reclaiming him. The Jett you know and love has reverted to his former self, Hades. For centuries, he lived with a cold heart in a cold world, without feelings for humans, or life. Your Jett has gone and so has my wonderful life with my happy husband.' Melita began to sob, pulled out a tissue and patted the tears. 'He has all but given up on everything. I know you have a whole universe to look after, Glow. Our world is just a little dwarf planet. But you must understand that I had to come here today to beg, on my hands and knees if I must, and plead my case for the man I love.' Melita cried in her arms for a long while.

Her hurt hit Caitlin hard. Melita sobbed, telling of her heartache, how Jett had retreated so far that she was unable to reach him. While Melita wiped her eyes and calmed, Caitlin was baffled why Axon hadn't discussed this with her. For two years, she had worked relentlessly beside Jett and Calyx. She'd helped and supported Jett while he renovated the castle. She'd worked beside him as King of the Dwarf Planets, and together they joined many Home Worlds to his Kingdom. All the while she continued to perform her regular duties as a Cosmic Rider, so was mystified about Axon's reluctance for her to be involved. To allow her two best friends to be left tormented and without support was ludicrous and unconscionable.

Melita's voice brought her back from deeply anguished thoughts. 'He sits all day in silence and rarely answers if spoken to.' She continued to weep. Her soft lashes lay wet and clinging to her pale cheeks. Her short dark hair was messy from stressful hands moving nervously through the ends.

Caitlin finally found her voice and pulled out a clean hanky, which she handed to Melita. 'I don't understand. Jett knows he can come and see me anytime he wants. If he hasn't come to me, maybe it's not me he needs.' Her soothing voice calmed Melita a little.

'He didn't want to go against Axon's wishes to disturb you.'

'Melita!' Caitlin shook her head. 'You should have come sooner. My work lately has drained me and I'd be no good to Jett the way I feel now. Axon was wrong keeping this from me, and I will deal with him later, but I just don't know what I can do. The mission I'm on is worse than ever. Earth is dying, and I can't put that right, so I can't see how I could be of assistance to a friend, never mind a King in need. I feel just as helpless as your husband.'

Melita patted her hand. 'Then maybe you both could do with some time out together. You know what a good team you make. Please, Glow – give it a crack for me. See what a visit can achieve.' Melita stood up, her thin frame wobbling a little from stress, and stopped to steady her posture. 'I won't hold you up any longer, but please think about coming, even for just a couple of days. At this point, I would try anything to have my husband back. You're my only hope, and you must know we love having you.'

Caitlin stood as well, putting her arms around Melita in a hug. She realised how much she did need time with her dearest friends. Maybe it would snap her out of the fog that left her drained and feeling the life was being sucked out of her. Pulling from the embrace, she felt it necessary not to give false hope. 'Please keep in mind, Melita, that I've sworn allegiance to the Cosmic Riders. My leave time will have to be passed by not only Axon but our commander, Rory. I can't make any promises, but since you're unable to bring Jett to me, I'll do everything possible to find a way to visit him.'

'That's all I ask.' Melita's eyes showed a spark of hope.

'You shouldn't have had to. Axon has some explaining to do.'

Melita smiled, and more tears rolled down her cheeks. 'I should have known you'd still view us the same way. It's our obligation towards the running of the underworld that can sometimes make things a bit muddled. Quite often it affects trust in others. Friendships can diminish if we allow it. Jett had almost convinced me you'd given us away as it's been many moon cycles since you rang. I came today to see for myself, and am so glad to find you still care as you have always done. I'm sorry for allowing this to fester.'

'I feel terrible to think you were both worried. This changes everything. You are family to me, not just friends, and I'll set this right if I can. But as I said, Melita, I'm in bad condition too.'

'I trust in the friendship you two have. It's magical. Please bring Jett back to me, Glow.'

'With luck, you can expect a visit in the next day or two.'

'Glow, I'm leaving for the winter and staying at Mother's. It breaks my heart to watch him every day. When he feels better, I know he will come for me.' She hugged Caitlin once more. 'I will never doubt you again,' she said and left a confused Caitlin to work out what to do next.

Caitlin felt a rush of guilt for letting Jett and Melita down. She remembered the time she needed only Jett. He ended up being her shining saviour. How could she not have felt him withdraw so profoundly from them all? What had happened to her ability to foresee the future?

She went inside to talk to Axon and Rory. They had been just as surprised as she was when Melita turned up. Both would have guessed why the Queen had come to see her and most likely had planned their response. Caitlin wondered how they would stop her going, and was sure they'd have conjured up something to make her feel guilty about leaving. *Whether they liked it or not, I intend to visit Jett.*

Rory was waiting. He was her boss and best friend, yet while he observed her now, his usually gentle hazel eyes were frosty. He hated her leaving his side. She knew by his messy, sandy hair and the way his legs sprawled out in front of him that he was ticked off but trying to act calmly. Even the freckles around his nose seemed darker against his handsome face as it paled with uneasy tension.

Axon could hide his feelings better, and his dark curls fell softly against his forehead as he got up to greet her. 'Hi, sweetheart.' He put his arm around her.

By the look on his face, she could tell her husband already knew the problem. She felt his gaze on her while she pulled up a chair. Once seated, Caitlin discussed Melita's visit with them, including what had been asked of her.

'My mind seems just as foggy and disorientated as Jett's,' she said, as she tried to explain her unwellness. She figured this approach might allow her at least a couple of days' break to rest up. 'Maybe what I need is some time out as Melita suggested. I can't think straight, and time is running out for all of us if I don't clear my mind, get my head together and come up with something soon.'

Axon searched her face, with eyebrows furrowed. 'You told me never to let you go again. Please don't ask me to break my promise to you.' His dark eyes danced with golden lights as he spoke, but not in a good way.

Caitlin had expected cunning but hadn't thought he'd throw the words uttered on their wedding night back at her. 'Axon, if there were another way... please, don't be like this. I'm no good to you the way I've been working lately and no good to Rory and his team on this mission. If you allow me time to visit Pluto, I can do two things at once; see Jett and maybe mend the rift you have created by ignoring his requests, and also have a couple of days' break. You are forgetting, Jett is my friend and is devastated I haven't been to see him after so many requests. You must allow me to go and set this right.' Caitlin's face was tight with worry. Axon had... *no*... written in his eyes, and if that was his answer, it burned something bright inside her. Someone was going to get hurt here today, as suddenly her heart ached with the strong desire to go to Pluto. It pulled at the very fibre of her being.

Rory's chair was shoved back as he stood up, irritated. 'We need you here, Cait. I'm your friend too, and if you leave me at this stage of the negotiations it will devastate me... us! I'm telling you now, I will climb the walls without the calming influence you have on us all.' He threw his hands up in frustration. 'You don't know how hard it is when you're not here, Cait. Last time it was two blatzing years! Damn Jett and his frigging problems.'

'Rory, can't we talk about this a bit more civilly?' Caitlin asked.

'I hate to agree with him, Cait, but he's right,' Axon put in. 'Your loyalty must be to us first, or Earth is a goner. May I add, you are also a team member of the Cosmic Riders and that role takes priority over spoilt gods who *cry wolf* to get attention. Jett can wait! After your work is done here, you can have as much time as you need with him.

Today, it's Rory and I that need you.'

Caitlin studied them. She couldn't be in two places at once but had a growing need to follow her gut instinct. If it meant suffering the consequences later at the hands of these two, then so be it. They couldn't understand the real issue. Not only had they kept the truth from her, but she was drained of energy, and even this argument was exhausting her. These two men, with all their love for her, couldn't see she was in trouble physically and mentally. *I am not the warrior they once knew!*

She fisted her hands, her eyes dark as night when she looked up. 'We both know I can't go without you agreeing, Rory, so if it takes resigning as a Cosmic Rider, then that's what I'll do... then, the only permission needed will be my husband's.' Caitlin could see her words were a slap in the face to Rory. It was a low blow and she knew even to suggest this course of action might cause irreparable damage to their bond, and to the friendship with her team. It flashed in her thoughts... was Jett that important to her? But the words had been said and she couldn't ... no wouldn't ... take them back.

Rory went pale and flopped back in his chair, not quite believing what she just threatened. 'You have to be frigging kidding me, girl!' he snapped.

Axon moved and held her by the shoulders to make her look him directly in the eyes. 'That was way below the belt, Caitlin. Even as a husband I would have a hard time agreeing with this bullshit. Are you kidding? Do you think I'd approve of you racing off with another man? Never mind the callous lack of responsibility shown towards the team!'

She pulled out of Axon's grip and glared at him. 'I do everything I'm ever told and never once complain; *never*. Rory says *jump*, and I say *how high*. And you, Axon, my bossy boss.' She stabbed her finger at him. 'You tell me where you need me and I'm there. Never mind that some days I would like a bit of me time for once! I'm tired, and I'm not thinking straight. Just maybe ... if you stopped being selfish for a moment, you might see Jett could be the key to all this. He is linked to me. Is he feeling like this because of me? Well, I hope not.

Because it would have been sorted out a long time ago if you had kept me in the loop. You have all lied to me. Who are you people? Do you care about me at all or just my abilities?' She flung her arms in the air in frustration. She was so angry she couldn't find the words to express how she felt.

Axon stood with a placating look.

Caitlin had not shown that side of her temper very often, and he thought this was one of her tantrums.

He doesn't think I'll go through with my threat.

She realised he'd blame the surprise visit from Melita for her 'irrational' behaviour.

Instead of fighting with her, Axon stared at his wife and kept quiet while he waited for her to calm down.

She glared at him. 'Even now, you're not taking me seriously.'

His eyes sparkled with menace. His wife sure knew how to push his buttons. 'So tell me, Cait, are you also willing to give up the man you have promised to spend the rest of your life with to go to someone else?' Axon spat the words out before thinking.

Caitlin put her hands on her hips, furious. Her red curls bounced around her shoulders, and her green eyes flashed. 'Now you are being ridiculous. What I am telling you is that for all the good I'm doing here, on this mission, I might as well be back at home, lazing around all day. And, as for that comment, Axon, if you have such little faith in me around other men then we have an even bigger problem. That proves to me what a useless job I've been doing, not only as a workmate but as a wife. You could have prevented this by letting me know what was happening to Jett. A couple of days would have been enough in the early stages, but now it's got this bad, who knows how long it will take! All that hard work I've put into the Dwarf Planets, and it didn't occur to you this would upset me? Those Dwarf Planets are just as important to me as this one. Your thinking is just as bad as the rest of the Planets; if you're not big, and perfectly round, you don't frigging-well matter.' Her face was red, and she was close to tears. 'And need I remind you if he turns back into Hades and wants me, he may just try the kidnapping thing again. Next time I might not be so easy to find. He does run the god-damned underworld. Shit Axon.'

Axon made a grab for her. Caitlin shook out of his grasp, backing away. 'You're not the man I married. Leave me alone you … you bastard. The man I married would never have let one of our best mates suffer for the sake of stubbornness, and what looks to me like spiteful jealousy.'

She stormed from the room and into one of her team members. Nathen took one look at her and wrapped his arms around her as she sobbed, telling him she had just resigned. As always Nate was charming to her. Once he heard her side of the story, it was enough. 'You want me to punch them both in the nose for you, Cait?' He made her stop crying and handed her a hanky from his pocket. 'My boy Zeke and I will take you to Jett. Be blowed with what they say. We know you need a break. If they can't see it, they're crazy. But no one is resigning, Cait. No more talking like that … please. You're breaking my heart.'

Just as he finished speaking, Rory flung the door open, banging it loudly against the wall and getting their attention. Not expecting to find his second in command with Caitlin, he stopped and straightened, showing his authority. 'That will be all, Nathen,' he dismissed him.

'As for you, Cait, I don't know what the hell that was all about, but your resignation is not accepted. Look, if you needed a break that badly, you should have talked to me in private. Axon need not have been involved. Now you two are at loggerheads, he is going to be one big pain to work with while you're gone if you don't make amends with him before you leave.'

He looked up at Nathen. 'Thought you were dismissed?'

'Well, I've just told Cait that Zeke and I will take her.' Nate stood up to him, annoyed they had upset Cait.

'Nathen! Stand down. Axon will take his own wife to wherever she needs to go. He needs no help from subordinates.'

'I'll be okay Nate.' Caitlin looked up at his windswept blond fringe that partly covered his loyal pale grey eyes. A soulful stare told her he would support her no matter how much trouble he got into.

'Sure?' He stood firm until he knew she was telling him the truth.

She nodded. 'You're a good friend Nate. Keep my horse happy for me while I'm gone.'

He wiped the tears from her cheek. 'Only if you promise there will be no more of these.'

'Promise,' she replied as he let her go.

With a nod in Rory's direction, he strode off back down the corridor.

Rory waited for Caitlin to look back at him. 'Axon sends his apologies and said if you are ready, he will take you to Pluto now. He wants you to know you can take as much time as you need.'

CHAPTER TWO

Axon, the Boss or the Husband

As Axon waited for Caitlin to come back, he paced and felt like throwing up. *How did all this just spiral out of control?* Very rarely had he seen his wife so livid. *She thinks I didn't tell her about Jett because I was jealous. Why did I make such a stupid comment?* He and Rory knew what was coming when Melita visited. Both guessed Caitlin's reaction but thought they could win her over by using their status to muscle her into staying. *It did not go as planned.* They had totally backed her into a corner, and with nowhere else to go, she turned on them. *What in the hell, did we expect?*

What was worse was Axon knew Caitlin was right. For the first couple of years on the job, she'd run herself ragged helping Jett in between their demands of her. For the last two years, Caitlin had given Axon her all; not once did she consider herself. Most nights his wife fell to sleep on the top covers and fully dressed if he wasn't there to change her. Yet next morning she'd get up with the sweetest of grins and soldier on. She had asked him before the wedding if she could give up the battle for a few years so they could start a family. He was the one who hadn't wanted to lose her skills, kept pushing for more, knowing her potential and needing every ounce of her expertise.

He leant against the wall, his hands in his pockets. As a boss, he admired and respected everything she did. When he married Caitlin, it was because he loved and trusted her. Yet today, he suddenly felt jealous because she was choosing *him! If I lose her, it will be entirely my fault.*

Axon kicked off the wall in frustration and paced again. He remembered when they had married he promised he would show her the world. Not once, as a boss, had he even given them a weekend away to enjoy one another. Axon worked so many hours that life with her so far passed him by. It was so easy to think they had all the time in the world for each other. *But what if it's too late? What if all the time in the world ended now, today?* She had very few sweet memories of their time together to even want to be with him. Not like the memories she shared with Jett. He paused and looked out the window. He hated knowing she was off to visit Pluto. There, Jett would spend every minute with her... Time Axon never seemed to find, because his job was too demanding, or was it? He put it first before everything else, even before her. *I've been such a fool. If she gives me one more chance, I'll change.* He made a silent promise that from now on he would treat her the way she should be taken care of. Not like an employee or possession, but as his wife. *God, don't let it be too late.*

Caitlin came in with Rory, flushed from crying. If she let him touch her, Axon would give her a hug and take her somewhere to cheer her up. But he knew it wasn't his company his wife craved. It was Jett she would sooner be with... *and I don't blame her.*

'She's ready to go now, Axon,' Rory politely said and left the room.

'I know you don't want to talk to me, Caitlin and I don't blame you. But before I take you to Pluto, please know it breaks my heart to think I've hurt you like this. I've been a terrible husband, and if given forgiveness, I promise when you come home to me, I'll be the man you married, a proper husband and never again act like a dominating controlling, arrogant prick.'

She stayed silent, barely holding on to her nerves by a thread. In a crumbled emotional state, she had no energy to discuss the issue any further.

He spoke again. 'I don't need an answer, but please think about coming home to me.' He moved over to her, close enough to transport them both to another world. If she had wanted contact, she'd have walked over and held his hand as always. For the moment he'd give her space.

The room faded from their sight, replaced by the outside entrance of Jett's castle. The guards held steady as Axon and Caitlin shimmered into view, their guns aimed, cocked and ready to fire on the intruders. The warning alarms were the same on all planets, and would have picked them up moments before arriving unannounced. This being the reason for the welcoming party.

'Oh, it's you, Axon,' Jett's Royal Commanding Officer called out from the top of the stairs. 'We didn't have you down for a visit today.'

'My wife is here on orders from Queen Persephone,' Axon shouted to him over the racket of guns being raised and the bullets being readied in the chambers.

'Come!' The commander beckoned them to join him. 'Her Majesty has gone on an extended holiday with her mother. However, did share with me she was visiting someone very special to her. I should have guessed it would be Caitlin. Let me dismiss my men, and I will take you into the den and announce you. I'm sure the King will be thrilled to see you both as he always looks forward to your visits.

Caitlin was bewildered. She had never been greeted with guns before, and it mystified her why his security was so extreme. There must have been fifty or more rifles still pointed towards them as they were ushered through the enormous hall entrance and left to wait inside the great walls.

The first thing she noticed was Jett had switched off the power. After he had domed the entire castle and grounds, the temperature had warmed the cold grey interior, giving it a bright and luxurious gleam. Today it was dim, dark and cold; a definite sign her Jett was once again trapped inside the monster, Hades.

Axon spoke quietly to her. 'You look surprised to see Jett's military, Cait. He has one of the largest armed forces in the heavens. Our latest data shows he has increased them recently. We assume it's his new status as King that has called for so many.'

'The King and his Kingdom are well protected then?' She eyed him.

'Yes. Hades is a powerful deity. He has always been careful to protect what is his by putting fear into others that dare call him an enemy. So, our concern is why the need for these extra forces. Maybe you could find out for us while you're here?'

'I have come to help, not spy. Can't you step out of work mode for even a few minutes while you transport me here? That's the trouble, husband of mine, you never knock off.'

'Sorry Cait, an old habit. I promise to stop it if you just come home with me after a quick visit. There's something not right here today, and I'd prefer you not to stay any longer than necessary.' He looked around, worried. The castle had an unfriendly presence, and it was making him nervous to leave her.

'Don't concern yourself with me, or what is going on here. Go back to work. I'm okay to visit with Jett, alone.'

* * * *

Once the Commander returned, they followed him into the den in silence. He opened the door and in a big voice announced them. 'Your Majesty, the Lord of the Planets, Axon Stanton, and the Goddess of Peace, Caitlin Stanton, are here to have an audience with you. Axon – Caitlin.' He nodded, bowed to the King and left quickly, closing the door behind him.

Hades was in his chair, staring into the fireplace, transfixed by the red-hot embers that blew slightly with the wind that travelled down the chimney. He looked in their direction. His skin tone was grey with anguish, and his deathlike stare had Axon shiver.

Hades bellowed at Axon, 'Why did you bring her here? Take her home! Now! I do not want or need... her! In fact, I do not want any of you here... ever again! Now, get the hell out of here!

The words thundered in his ears. Axon felt the strength of hatred and anger directed towards them. As Hades, Jett was a scary piece of work. This gave him an uneasy feeling about leaving Cait. Hades held the chair, his knuckles white. Gone was the friendship Cait had fought so hard to build. And gone was Jett. Hades was disturbingly irate, and Axon felt he was out of control. His first instinct was to run with his wife and offer her the world not to have to go through this again. She had confided what Hades was like when he first kidnapped her and now seeing it first hand, he understood the reason she had given him so much time. To turn this monster into Jett, his little charmer must have used every ounce of her energy and magic. Axon recalled how seethingly angry towards the god he became when she chose to stay with Jett for so long. It hurt she never seemed to miss him, or the Riders. His mouth dropped, and his gaze went to his wife. As if given the key, the penny dropped. *Hades was her job.* For a second time, he was her focus until she felt calm in him. The peace goddess, and to all who knew her up here, she was Glow Girl, a name Hades himself had given her. *I should have seen it sooner, this is not my Cait.* He was certain it was the Goddess Glow Girl who now stood beside him. The spirit in her had once again taken over, and he knew at that moment, he would not get his Caitlin back until peace in the universe was felt by her. He wondered what it would take this time to bring Hades back from hell's doors. *What have I done? Not only to my beautiful wife but to Jett, who once called me friend?* All those times he stubbornly refused Jett access to her, he'd been jealous of what they had. She was part of his team, *his Rider, his wife* and not for Jett's beck and call. *Now they both hate me and rightfully so!*

Cait walked over to Hades and dropped to her knees in front of him. When she placed her hand over his, only a jaw muscle quivered. Axon stood ready to transport her if he used his magic on her. *Surely, he'll do her no harm.* The clenched knuckles were from a man in a lot of pain, and even though listening, Hades never spoke, just looked ahead and ignored her. With a stretch of her neck, she changed her approach, and Axon guessed she was talking to him telepathically. Still, he stayed motionless. Not giving up, Caitlin reached out and ran her hand over his wrinkled brow, as if trying to smooth away his pain. This action caused Hades to grip the arm of the chair tighter, and the sound of wooden fibres started to snap with the increased pressure to ignore the feel of her soft hands. Her delicate hands at any other time would calm the evilest of men. *Has she lost her touch?*

'Caitlin,' Axon said softly, 'do you want me to stay? He isn't responding, and I worry for you.'

She shook her head not even looking at him. 'Go... please,' she murmured.

Jett turned and glared at him with distaste. 'Take her, I don't want her here, I just told you I don't want anyone here! Just – leave – me – alone!' His voice had risen to a roar.

The angry vibration of his temper didn't deter Caitlin. She looked up at Axon defiantly. 'I'm staying whether he wants me here or not. Melita invited me here for a visit, and he – has no say in it.' She got up and walked to the door. 'I'm going to my room. I'm exhausted and need a break. You know where I am if you need me. I am perfectly safe here.'

Her usually bright sparkling green eyes were flat. The happy glow she often radiated was dull, and she looked gaunt. Axon wondered how long she'd been feeling like this. They'd been so busy, and now, viewing her in the light of the open fire, he saw what hadn't been apparent until now. *Cait is frail. And she would sooner stay with this tyrant rather than me.* It said a lot about how he had disrespected her. Realising he hadn't given her any quality time for so long made him uneasy; was it too late? *What a treasure I've held, yet so carelessly let slip through my fingers.*

Defeated, he said goodbye to them both before he blew her a kiss. 'Forgive me,' he whispered as she faded from his sight. The sadness he saw would haunt him always if he couldn't find a way to make it up to her.

Chapter Three

Moonjuice Spice

After Axon had left, Caitlin sighed. Her mind was numb and had nothing left to give to him, or to this man in front of her, that once called her a friend. He had reverted to Hades as Melita had said. He sounded so angry... so very upset with her. Why she had insisted on staying was a mystery. But even as Axon begged, she couldn't leave. Yet now, she wondered what had held her here. Sad and at a loss as what to do next, she went over to Jett, kissed him on the cheek and touched his cold, hard hand. If his knuckles went any whiter, they would break. He had hold of the armchair so tightly it was a marvel with his powers how the chair arm didn't shatter. But then, up here, who knew what furniture was made of? Darn strong stuff was her conclusion. Unable to get a response, she left the room, mindful of closing the door to keep him warm. Upstairs, the room she always stayed in was cold, dark and uninviting. If only she knew where the climate control was she would turn it on. Not willing to ask while he was so bad-tempered, she climbed under the bed covers, leaving the fancy thick quilt on to help warm her up. It was there she stayed for many hours. Cold and shivering, fatigue kept her on the edge of sleep and eventually, her mind lay dormant of worry, allowing her to slip into the first real sleep in some time.

Many hours later, thirst stirred Caitlin. Wrapped in the thick blanket from the bed, she slipped her boots back on and went downstairs to the kitchen. Here, she found coffee brewing. When her call for assistance went unanswered, she pulled out two mugs and poured coffees into them. She picked them up but put them back down when a bottle of coffee-Starliqueur, caught her eye. 'Just what I need,' she said. The splash was a bit more in each than planned, but the strong aroma smelt divine and, after sipping hers, she decided to add a dash more, filling both mugs to the brim. It warmed her instantly. Feeling a little better, she carried them into the den.

'Oops!' She giggled, spilling a dribble on the floor as she struggled to close the door behind her. When she'd arrived, it was mid-morning. The best she could tell by the quiet in the castle now, it must have been around midnight.

Had he moved? Caitlin stared at Jett who still sat in front of the fire where she had left him. He gazed blindly into embers that had almost gone out.

'Here, this will loosen your tongue,' she said, holding the mug to his hand. 'Take it, or I'll drop the hot coffee in your lap.'

His hand moved and took what she offered.

Usually, Jett would have looked up at her with dark, mysterious eyes lightened with an amused twinkle, but alas, there was not a flicker of acknowledgement.

'My humour is wasted on a sulking god. I will wait for my King to return.' She made herself comfortable on the couch, wrapped up like a mummy in the folds of a big blanket. They silently sat sipping their coffee. When hers was gone, she went over to the bar and selected a bottle of Moonjuice. She filled two goblets, and after successfully swapping the mug for the decorative cup in Jett's hand, she studied him. 'Are you ready to talk yet?'

His eyes stared directly ahead as he ignored all attempts of friendly banter.

She shrugged upon not seeing an expression in his creamy complexion. 'Maybe one of these on top of what I just gave you will loosen your tongue, my friend.'

She planned to go back to bed after that drink if he continued to ignore her, but he surprised her and emptied his goblet.

'Good.' She drank hers down to join him in another and kept their cups replenished until the two bottles she had found, were empty.

It had been awhile since visiting Pluto and drinking the gods' especially brewed elixir went straight to her head. With a sudden burst of energy, she threw the blanket aside. 'This place is too quiet. It's like a frigging morgue. Oh, that's right, it is one!' She giggled, lightheaded. 'It's the Land of the Living Dead.' She cracked up laughing. In front of the NAVsound centre, she tapped at her chin. 'Let me see what deadbeats like to boogie to.' Again, she gave a silly laugh, finding her words amusing. With a stagger, she picked out a CD and once the music began, cranked up the sound and sang out loud. Her body moved to the rhythm, but she soon found herself stiff and tight. *What's wrong with me?* The drink gave her a false sense of fun, but it was the first time in a long while that she had enjoyed anything, so she continued singing and eventually was so unsteady on her feet she fell into Jett's lap. She gazed up at him. 'It has been far too long my friend, and I've missed all that is familiar here. I've missed the historic but elegant furniture, lovingly cared for and kept looking immaculate. Not forgetting the massive, painted portraits encased in antique frames that decorate every wall, the warm rug beneath our feet and last, but especially — you.'

He didn't return any warmth, but it did not deter her. 'I don't care if you hate me forever. I will never stop caring for you, Jett.' She gave him a few light kisses on his forehead and cheeks, just mucking about.

Although meant as a friendly gesture it took Jett by surprise; he had not expected her to feel such affection towards him. *This traitor dumped me. Never once came back to visit.* His trust in their friendship had broken down, and it had left a sour taste. He hated her for not caring about him. Yet, while he reminded himself of this and stood firmly resisting her charm, his heart did a little flip as a sudden warm spark of hope seeped inside it. *She still cares?* His eyes glanced unwillingly to her. The shock of what he saw confused him and was enough to snap him out of his own worries and fears for his future.

His gaze darted back to her. *This woman looks nothing like my old friend.*

Her skin was pale, the delicate thinness exposed impurities and fine veins beneath. Dark black rings circled dull emerald eyes that had lost all signs of health or lust for life. Her natural lush, silky red hair was matted and drab. It was such a shock it was as if an electric charge entered his mind and body. It felt as if he had just had a voltaic jump-start that took him back to her, back to where he had once been happy. *What am I doing?* Never again did he want to lose what friendship they had, and he swore in those minutes that followed, that Axon would never stand between them again. No matter how much he respected her husband, Glow Girl lit up his world. It woke him up to the fact that, yes, his other problems were real and needed handling, but he felt like this because he missed her. Darkness could never consume him while she was in his life.

Jett felt his internal strength to balance good and evil start to return, and after blinking a couple of times, he shook his head. Just to move his eyelids hurt at this stage, but he was determined to pull out of his depression. Glow needed him, and Jett hoped it wasn't too late. He should have realised there was more behind the reason she hadn't visited him. *I should have ignored Axon as I've always done... just gone to her?* But he had befriended Axon, become confused on where his loyalty should be and tried to do the right thing by him as Glow's husband. He'd given Axon the same courtesy he would expect if in that position.

'I can't stay awake.' Her voice so soft he barely heard her.

The time for self-analysing was cut short as Glow Girl's lids suddenly dropped and her body slumped like a dead weight into his arms. *Usually, she can drink as much as me.* He doubted the alcohol had this effect on her. *What's happened to cause this exhaustion? Why didn't she use her magic within to control her state of mind?* Mulling over these questions drained him and, not able to think up any reasonable answers, he decided rest was all she needed. *Axon must be working her too hard.* In a mind blur from the mental state he had been in, Jett debated if he should leave her here on the couch or get her up to bed. He hadn't been upstairs for many months, and couldn't bear to walk past her room. He had missed her, was mad at her, but tonight, having her here had dampened his anger. As weak as she was, her presence still had a way of calming him. But he too was poorly. He'd become run down with the frustration and worry over his duties, not only as King but as a God to the Underworld. *Have I the energy to transport her upstairs?* He wobbled as he stood until he felt how lightweight she had become. *I can do this.* With his mind on her room he wished himself there and was pleased when the room they stood in faded. 'At least one of us has some power left,' he said to his sleeping friend.

Once in her room, he looked down into the prettiest face he had ever seen. 'Unwell as you are, Glow, you still look beautiful to me.' It was then he noticed her drenched lashes lying on wet cheeks. Before she fainted, she had shed tears. He didn't know she'd been crying. She was laughing when she fell on him. These were tears for him and he melted at the visible emotion evoked to bring him around. 'This showy singing and dancing was for me?' He smiled down at her sweetness. His future he felt he now held in his hands and he shivered with bliss. They had been friends. Best friends. He placed Glow Girl on the bed and covered her, but it didn't matter how he tucked in the blankets or how much bedding he piled on, she continued to shiver uncontrollably.

Over by the fire, Jett prodded the logs he put flame to until they crackled and burst into a blazing fire. On a chair away from so much heat he sat to wait, but still, she trembled. Finally, he threw his hands into the air. 'Okay already, I give up.' He had struggled to stay away from her but it was no use and with a sigh, he lay down beside her. As soon as he did that, she rolled immediately towards his warmth. While she hugged him, he wished to fight this comforting feeling and not allow his heart to care as much for her this time. What if Axon took her away again once she was well? He struggled with the thought and was in two minds. One side of him wanted to forgive her for staying away. The other side of him wanted to keep being mad at her, wanted to get up, go back downstairs and stay angry. Instead, he hugged her and as the shaking eased, he too slept … and slept.

CHAPTER FOUR

The Rescuer is Rescued

Caitlin didn't know how long she slept, but when she woke she was incredibly cosy and warm. *Jett's still here!* Or was it Hades? Caitlin wiggled around to face him, pleased he had forgiven her enough to stay and keep her from freezing. This was something Hades would not do, but Jett would. His eyes, when they opened to look at her, were still very dark, but in them, she saw a glimmer of her friend. He needed time to forgive her, but this was a start and Caitlin would take whatever she could get. If she lost his friendship, it would devastate her. When she arrived, her magic had been depleted and she was unsure how to bring him out of the darkness he had slipped into. Being together again like this proved to her that their friendship was more than magic; it was real. The thrill of this knowledge gave her a sudden lifting of her own mood. He, however, looked exhausted.

'Are you mad at me?' she asked.

'You know I didn't want you here. I was so ticked off at you for not caring about me. But something about the magic of us just being together has, for now, dragged me back from hell's doors.'

He went quiet, and she felt a *but* coming on…

'But know this, Glow, I'm fine there, in hell, so if you don't want me around anymore, I would prefer you to get up now and leave. And this time, never ever come back. Is that understood…? You're killing me here, Glow; it's been two blatzing years!'

He was still a little Hades, but she didn't care. Her days had run into months and months to years. Her heart sank, and she blinked away tears that stung her eyes. 'I swear I want what we had before. Honestly, I don't know where the time went.'

He saw and heard trustworthiness loud and clear while her eyes held back tears and the quiver in her voice showed it saddened her too. 'I know where... with that pathetic bunch you ride with. And that no-good husband that stole you from me.' It was a shock to see her eyes go blank as he mentioned them. He saw Caitlin blinked twice before speaking. She had lost focus and he wondered what caused it.

'But in my defence, it only seems like yesterday I was with you. This is the second time in two days I have been told this. Are you sure it's two years?'

His brows furrowed together. 'Yes! And if you do still want our friendship, this must change. That husband of yours must take off those chains from around you and let you live a little, see your friends and be man enough to apologise to me. He might have been a mate of mine once, but he has a lot of work to do to get back in my good graces again. Glow, you're my best friend, and I knew after that display last night, I'm still yours. So, no one has the right to keep us apart.'

'I'm so furious at him right now,' Caitlin confided. Her lip quivered. 'Did he really prevent us from seeing one another?'

'He did, many times. And I can see by your reaction that if he doesn't change he'll lose us both.'

She gave him a slight lip curl as she tried to hold back tears. 'I just want to be here with you for a while. I can't think straight anymore. Don't send me away.'

'I'm not going to do that. Are you crazy as well, woman? I want you to stay for as long as you like. But I swear, this time I won't be Mr Nice Guy. If Axon stops me seeing you in the future, he and I will have a problem. You'd better get ready to pick a side.'

'I'm not sure we are even in love anymore. We never see one another and I barely remember our wedding day. I feel so terrible feeling like this at times, but I don't seem to recall any holidays or fun to draw from… nothing memorable that inspires me to try and keep us together.'

She began to cry, and all Jett could do was hold her. *What happened? They were so much in love.*

When she calmed down, he told her he would speak to Axon later about his mistreatment of her. Jett touched her nose affectionately. 'Your husband needn't think he'll be getting you back until I see that he truly loves you.' He shook his head at the thought. At times he really did feel like a protective father towards her. Hell, he was old enough to be her great-grandfather and then some. He pulled a sudarium from his pocket and once again felt his age. Many used tissues now, but he still liked to use a sudarium, and it had to be ironed correctly. He patted dry her tears. 'How about we order breakfast and go rug-up by the fire in the den and eat. Have a couch day together. Catch up on old times.'

'Sounds perfect.'

* * * *

While they waited for breakfast, they kept the conversation light and less stressful. Caitlin rested her head on his shoulder, and he put an arm around her. Feeling how frail her frame had become, he hugged her with both arms. 'There's nothing to you without that big blanket around you, Glow. What's been going on?'

'Hang on, aren't I here to help you? Are you asking if the rescuer needs rescuing?' She dug her fingers into his ribs. 'What about you, skinny?'

'I think we both need rescuing.' He sat back with just an arm around her. 'The universe has linked us, Glow. That's why I couldn't give you up and why I've decided I'm not going to.'

'Neither can I stop seeing you. Yesterday I was so cross! Axon and Rory refused my request to visit, so I resigned.'

'Yesterday! Seriously! That was the first time you heard I needed your help?'

'Axon had mentioned once that you were having some problems, but that you had it under control. I knew nothing of your true situation until Melita came to see me yesterday. Jett, she was so worried about you.'

'Melita visited, did she? I told her not to, and she promised me. I didn't want you here. Doesn't that woman listen to anything I say?'

Caitlin gave a faint grin. 'She's your woman and knows exactly what you need, even when you don't.'

'I guess so. And now you're here, I must admit I'm glad in this instance my wife dared to ignore me. But back to you, Glow; have you really resigned?' He dropped his shoulder and his head slanted with an inquisitive stare.

'Yes, but Axon and Rory are giving me time to rethink it.' She threw her hands up. 'I don't get it, and they say I'm stubborn. They know I'm not the powerhouse I used to be, and yet they refuse to replace me.'

'I can't believe that.' Jett eyed her.

'I'm seriously no good as a Rider anymore. Geez, my horse has more magic than me and may I add, has done for quite some time. Rory is so, so Grrr...,' she said and put her hands up to her cheeks in a frustrated gesture.

He pulled her hands away and held them. 'What's Axon doing about it? He must see what's going on.' He spoke in a gentle and caring tone.

'Our relationship has been strained. We barely speak anymore. Let's just say Axon's not the man I married.' She paused. Sadness filled her eyes as she turned to face him. 'I think he sees me as a Rider first, wife second. This is causing a rift. You see, as a Rider, it's my job to come up with solutions but nothing I think of works. Then he blames himself for my confusion and backs away to give me time to think. But I've lost my magic, Jett. I can't see a clear picture of how to fix anything, never mind work out how to repair my marriage.'

He hugged her again when tears rolled down her cheeks. She had mentioned marriage problems upstairs, but he hadn't realised it was this bad.

She sniffled into the hanky he gave her earlier. 'As I told Melita yesterday, I didn't know how to help you because I can't help myself.'

'What did she say to that?' It surprised him she was still Glow, honest as the first day he met her, not keeping anything from him. It was one of her qualities he adored. It made him feel special that she chose him to confide in no matter how confidential the information. She trusted him with her heart.

'Melita wasn't taking no for an answer and suggested it was together we would find our answers.'

'She said that?'

Caitlin nodded, 'in her polite way.' She shifted and placed a cushion behind her back. 'Melita told me that to give us time to sort it out, she was going to her mother's place and would stay with her for the winter. Said you'd go pick her up when you're feeling better. She's a good woman, your Melita.'

He smiled. 'I love her with all my heart, Glow, but would never have expected such loyalty and support after treating her so poorly. Yes, she sure is one fine woman that I married.'

A knock on the door, followed by servants bustling in with trays, put an end to their conversation. The aroma was mouth-watering. Caitlin's stomach rumbled and it left her to ponder how long it had been since she last ate. With the combination of a crisp cold morning, the crackling of the fire and good company, she felt hungry. They moved to the table set for two in the corner of the room and sipped fresh squeezed orange juice while percolated coffee was poured. To her delight, piping hot fluffy omelettes topped with crispy bacon were placed before her. 'Mmm … Earth food, I will enjoy this,' she said to the servant girl, who smiled brightly.

'It is an honour to cook for the Goddess of Peace.' The young server curtsied low, and her dark lashes lay gently on flushed cheeks.

Jett waved her and the others away. 'I'm afraid you have become quite the celebrity around here. Your work as a Rider and peacekeeper has become legendary. The chef and his assistants trained hard for this day. I have had nothing but Earth food for many months now as they experimented and waited for your arrival. You see they, like Melita, they didn't give up hope either.'

'Wow, I'm thrilled. Well, not that you have had to suffer my food choices, but that they bothered to impress me makes me feel somewhat important. And yet I am just me... and quite ordinary without my powers.'

'Glow, you could never be ordinary. You are tired and need a break, that's all... Ordinary!' He shook his head. 'Never!'

'You're good for me, Jett. Here with you. All this,' she waved her hand around the room. 'It's so familiar and comforting. Maybe if we find energy from this meal, we could do something together, like old times.'

'I'd like that... but nothing too strenuous because you look exhausted, Glow.'

'Maybe that's it?' She felt a jolt of hope. 'We just need some fun in our lives.' She lifted the filled fork; the aroma was divine. 'And something has to loosen that tongue of yours. She wiggled the fork of food at him before putting it in her mouth.

He smiled. 'I think we both need to talk, but I'm not ready to discuss what's been going on until you look better. I second your motion, let's go and have a few laughs and see how we feel after.'

She shrugged. 'Laughing hasn't been a strong point for either of us lately, so a mere concerted effort to make ourselves feel happier would be a start.'

Jett finished eating first and sat back watching her intently. 'Okay, Glow Girl—if you could go anywhere in the universe, where would it be?'

'What... now? Right this minute?' She was thrilled he chose sooner than later. Her energy only spiked after eating and she had shovelled in enough to help kick start it.

He nodded. 'It can only be for a few hours as I can't leave Pluto for too long.' His posture slumped slightly.

Caitlin saw the responsibility of what he was going through weighed heavily on his shoulders.

'So...' He moved his hand to gesture he was waiting.

She took a sip of coffee. 'Well, there is a place on Earth that comes to mind. It's in Thailand, the tropical Island of Koh Samui. I saw this venue advertised and thought of you. I dreamed of a time we could visit it together.'

Jett took his NAVscan from his pocket and clicked his fingers, suddenly impatient to get moving. 'Coordinates or address, whatever?'

'We're doing this now—cool!' Her voice was high pitched. Before he could change his mind, she rattled off the address.

He found the location but it was an empty block. 'You must have mixed up the number.' He changed a couple of numbers around and re-entered the address again. 'Is this it?' He held it up for her to see a basic building, unsure why she would choose somewhere so populated. Also confused she made a mistake. She was usually so articulate with details, even small ones.

'That's it.' She watched him placed the device back in his pocket.

'I want that plate empty, or we go nowhere,' he insisted.

'She nodded and took an even bigger fork full of egg so they could leave soon.

'No rush Cait, I don't want you to throw it back up.' He smiled at her rush.

While he waited for her, he was pleased that even though not seeing him for a while, she had still thought about going somewhere with him. 'Is it cold or hot in Thailand this time of year?'

'It's hot in that country now, but you could say a little chilly indoors.' She took off her thick jacket to reveal a light beige shirt and earth-toned scarf. 'So that makes me ready.'

'A skating rink?'

'Maybe—maybe not.' She shoved the last forkful in her mouth.

He was at her side before she finished swallowing it and eager to leave, held his hand out to help her up. 'Let's go, shall we?'

She swallowed hard and grinned. Was glad of his old-fashioned attentiveness. She had eaten far too much and leant into his warm frame, slightly dizzy. 'You are always so lovely and warm.' She said it to hide her fragile state, and make it seem her need to be close was for reasons other than her feeling poorly. He would never take her if he knew.

No sooner had the castle walls vanished from sight than the

landscape changed, and they reappeared on Koh Samui Island in an alleyway adjacent to the front of the venue.

'Ah—Seven Themed Ice Bar, I should have guessed.' He put out his elbow, and she wrapped her arm through the crook as she used to do. Satisfied she was eager to do this with him, he chatted with her as they walked. 'I can't believe people on this planet find ice so amusing.'

'Told you ice is a treat here. I only hope this is as good as advertised.'

Inside, there were three distinctive areas, the Garden Bar, the air-conditioned Main Bar and the Ice Bar that ran at temperatures well below zero degrees Celsius. Before entering the Ice Bar, they were given fur lined hooded capes and thermal gloves. As they walked into the separate rooms, they stopped to admire the many ice sculptures throughout; Caitlin especially liked the elephant and a tuk-tuk. 'Look, the bar is entirely made of ice,' she commented while they waited to be served.

Jett shook his head. 'Madness, but I love it. Now, what to drink. We have a choice of cocktails or vodka.'

'Mmm.' Caitlin squinted while reading out the many flavours of vodka. 'How about we try one of each?'

Jett called over to the barman, 'One of each of them, buddy.' He pulled out his wallet and gave him some bills. 'Keep them coming until that runs out.'

'Yes, what he said.' Caitlin sat up on a stool and watched them being made. She was fascinated by the pretty colours that started lining up in front of them.

'Ready Glow?' Jett sat beside her.

She nodded and gulped down the first shot and licked her lips. 'That's what I needed.'

'Me too!' Jett matched her, and with each shot, they balanced their empties to build a wall of shot glasses.

As fast as they drank the liquid shot of warmth, the bartender lined more up. By the time they were ready to go, the different coloured lighting, which gave a strong attractiveness to each room, had blurred. The only face Caitlin could see was Jett's as he helped her from the bar. He took her back into the private alley where onlookers could not see them vanish. From there, he transported them back to Pluto.

Once inside the castle, Caitlin got head spins and had to run to the bathroom. She was so ill she couldn't get her head out of the toilet. Jett, who barely had any reaction to Earth's liquor, came to the rescue. He got her into the shower, although he had to stand in there with her as she kept collapsing against him. Eventually, she stopped dry retching, and it was then he lifted her out.

When Caitlin woke some hours later, she was dry, dressed in a nightshirt and in bed. Jett was nowhere to be seen, but he'd left a change of clothes to warm in front of the fire for her. Once dressed and feeling much better, she went in search of him. Downstairs she could hear talking.

Zeus, for goodness sake, please quit nagging me,' Caitlin heard Jett say and realised it was his brother who had arrived.

Jett referred to him as Calyx for her own ears, so it was unusual to hear him called by his Godly title. She had got to know Calyx very well, yet she saw in his eyes that they knew each other on a different level. It left a question mark in her mind. It was as if they had been romantic once, and yet she knew this to be untrue. One day she would ask him what that look was all about... But the thought never stayed in her mind long enough for her to speak to him about it. Why it came to mind now, she didn't know. As quickly as it came, it was gone, replaced by the sound of Jett and Calyx arguing. It was strange for Jett not to confide in Calyx. He always did. *But today, Jett was keeping her a secret and Calyx was giving him a hard time.*

'Save the blatzing bull-crap for someone else, brother! So, what you expect me to believe is, you just woke up this morning and for no reason, broke out of that depressive state you were in, just like that?' He snapped his fingers. 'In fact, you're looking happier than I've seen you in some time.' Calyx was cross and getting boisterous. 'You've been unapproachable for months, even with me, your own flesh and blood.'

Apparently, Jett did not want Calyx to know about her visit. Silently, Caitlin turned and went back up the stairs. In the room, by the window, the two-seater looked inviting. Taking a throw rug and book from the nightstand, Caitlin curled up comfortably and waited. Her balance was off and head dizzy. *I have a hangover?* She couldn't believe this was from the alcohol. *Surely it's just stress,* she reassured her subconscious. As an immortal, Caitlin didn't usually get a hangover. Maybe she had a headache occasionally, but it was never the way humans feel after a binge. *What is wrong with me?* Contemplating this took her mind off why Jett didn't want Calyx to know she was there. She knew he was possessive of her at times, but for him not to tell Calyx was strange. Unless of course, Jett didn't want his brother to know his private business? She'd been sure he shared everything with Calyx—but maybe not. Her head hurt from overthinking. After all, she couldn't work out what was wrong with her, so no way had she a hope of understanding the relationship between two gods.

Her thoughts were interrupted when the door squeaked open.

'Cait are you awake?' Calyx called out.

She wondered what deviousness won him the argument. 'Sure, come in!' Caitlin tried to sound her usual self.

'Ah good, you're up and about.' He walked over to the window where she lay lazily on the lounge.

'What a lovely surprise.' She pulled herself up, but couldn't hide the tired grunt. 'Sit with me while I put my boots on.' She patted the seat next to her.

'Take your time.' He did as she asked, quite happy to stay and wait.

'It's been far too long, Calyx. I see you got your own way down there.'

'You heard us?'

She nodded.

'He still thinks I was born yesterday. Sneaky sod.' Calyx was seemingly good-hearted about it now he had won. 'I figured it had to be something or someone exceptional to get him off his buttocks. And as we both know, my brother has never liked sharing you, so that was my first clue it was possibly you. He only came clean because I was getting ready to search the rooms anyway.'

'He didn't give me up easily by the sounds of it.' She finished lacing both boots and gave a slight grin.

'No!' His eyes took her in. 'But enough of my sneaky brother, he will get his due penance. Let's talk about you, Cait. Honestly, I nearly didn't recognise you. You're so thin! Jett said you're fine but you'll have a hard time convincing me. You're not fine, are you?'

'I'm just weary. Yesterday with Jett, I had a bit much vodka and I am paying the price.' She saw he wasn't buying this reason.

'I'm sorry Cait, but it's got to be more than spirits. It couldn't have made you this thin overnight. Anyway, since when has alcohol made you so weary? I can hear it in your voice; you sound exhausted.' When she didn't answer, he saw her dazed look and searched the room. 'Maybe you just need some fresh air and something to eat.'

'That sounds perfect.'

He stood and put out a hand to help her up. 'Let's get out of this room and get you by the roaring fire in the den. Jett stayed down there to organise dinner. He said you've slept all day and will be starving.'

'You're kidding! I slept all day?' She took the hand he offered and got to her feet. She was a little unsteady but hoped he hadn't noticed.

Calyx smiled. 'Yes, sleepyhead.' And as she turned to the light he saw how transparent her skin looked, her cheekbones prominent. He wondered what had brought this powerful goddess to such ill health. He had fought her once and knew whatever it was, it was stronger than him. *Surely, she would know what evil ran through her?* He would not rest until the beast had been exorcised from her body and killed.

'You know you can share anything with my brother or me. After all, Axon did appoint us as your guardians while he isn't around. Don't be shy with us Cait, please.'

'I'm just a bit overworked, that's all. This break is what I need, and it will do me wonders. Truly Calyx, I'm all right.'

'I'm sorry if this upsets you Cait but all right is not good enough, and you know I don't mince words. Axon is a fool. I knew he wouldn't be able to separate his marriage from his work. Bet you barely see him because he keeps you so busy? I'm right, aren't I?' His eyes squinted in anger. His temper as Zeus rarely surfaced, but this was too much. He felt out of control but reeled it in. He didn't want to frighten her but had to get it off his chest. She had to know Axon's refusal to let them see her had not only hurt his brother but him too, deeply. He'd been on the verge of confronting her infuriating husband and refusing to leave until he got to see her. Axon had to know he couldn't keep her from them forever. She was the Goddess of Peace and belonged to the universe. She was not just for him.

He faced her. 'Axon promised us he would give you time off to visit, and he hasn't. Cait, you have no idea how many times we have invited you and Axon on family outings or holidays. He always had an excuse not to attend.' She surprised him with a questioning look. 'Axon never told you, did he?'

'No!' She shook her head with the shame of Axon's behaviour. *Is he really that jealous?*

'We have missed you. Don't let Axon, take away what you've worked so hard to win.' He looked directly into her eyes. 'That would be the hearts of all of us here... especially mine and Jett's.'

'Don't you think I've missed you guys too? I couldn't understand why you never visited me! Now I know they kept you away, I'm even more cross.'

His blue eyes showed genuine concern. 'Enough! I will not allow my issues with your husband to upset this visit further. I should have known you'd have sorted this out if you'd known. But good lord, I never thought he'd keep you in the dark like this.'

'Jett mentioned something about it yesterday, but it didn't hit home until now how badly Axon has been behaving.'

'You're not well, and things are hard to comprehend when one is feeling poorly. You leave this for me to sort out with your husband. Neither you or Jett is in any condition to worry about anything but getting your lives back on track.' He took both her hands gently in his, his features softened at having her near again. 'Is that okay with you, Cait?'

She sighed. 'I'd love that. I know you'll handle it diplomatically. The thought of going another round with Axon exhausts me.'

'You're here now, so please allow my brother and me the chance to make you welcome. We want you to enjoy every minute with us, so when you leave, you'll fret to come back.' He laughed in the mock-evil way which always made her smile. He had missed it so much—*hang on—oh dear—where has her gorgeous smile gone*. It was replaced by a confused look. *Cait my love, what has that bastard done to you?* His heart ached to make her better. He wanted to pick her up and use his magic to mend what ailed her, but not knowing what it was, he had to contain the need to fix this quickly. He could use the wrong spell and make her worse. Also, he acknowledged Axon to be one of the most powerful immortals alive. With skills learned while working beside the Guardian Angel, Zoren, for so long, surely if there were a way to get her well, he would have used it already.

Caitlin suddenly got what Calyx meant. He was being funny for her sake. 'You always manage to amuse me.' She slanted her head to the side as the rest of his words resonated. 'You also have my permission to spoil me.'

He shook his golden locks and grinned, having decided to put the Axon issue aside while Cait visited. 'Come on, let's eat. I'm starved. How about you?'

'Sounds good.'

He saw she tried this time to smile, and although weak, it was what he needed. Happy about her response at last, he let her go so they could leave the room but he hadn't taken two steps when she wobbled on her feet. He stopped and reclaimed her hand.

Caitlin lifted her head. He seemed taller… or was she just feeling short from being out of sorts? Only reaching his chest she bent her head back to admire a tanned, faultless complexion. His blond wavy hair had grown, and those deep-set blue eyes that burned into hers told her she was in good hands, the best.

'Oopsy!' she lost her balance again and knocked lightly into him.

He laughed and picked her up in his arms. 'Steady there, lady, you really are struggling aren't you?'

'Most likely the atmosphere.' She tried to stop his worried look beneath that sweet smile.

With her head on his shoulder, she rested on him as they left the room. He held her gently as he had done so many times before. Unlike Jett, when they had worked together, Calyx was always holding her hand or carrying her somewhere. He was like a big cuddly harmless teddy bear, and she had come to care much for him. She had learned so many stories about Zeus, but they left out his best quality; his loyalty to those he held in those hands. Particularly now, they were very welcome and drew from his strength. It made her feel better. His muscles flexed, and dark blue eyes glowed brighter than the sky on a dark night. Caitlin sensed that, as her guardian, he was on a mission, and it was all about her. Caught up in his tenderness, she stretched her hand up and held his cheek momentarily, her eyes drawn suddenly to his lips. In a daze, she stared at them. 'If I didn't know better I would swear I'd kissed these same lips before.'

'You have. Don't you remember?'

The lips she couldn't take her eyes off turned from soft to firm as he frowned. 'Don't I remember what?' She looked into his eyes, confused.

'You really don't remember!' His voice rose in surprise.

'Calyx! Stop mucking around. You said, don't you remember— remember what?' She shook and wiggled to get out of his arms. He was genuinely ticked off, and all she did was mention his mouth. It moved in some words she couldn't hear. It was freaking her out.

'I knew it! They did something to you to make you forget. That's why you've never once spoken about our trip together. I bet that's why you... well, for a long time, looked at me like a stranger. I thought you were paying me out for kissing you. Then one day you just started to trust me again. I had earned your respect, and you were so wonderful to be with again. But I was wrong, yet again! You didn't know me at all, did you? Grrr—that blatzing husband of yours!' he called out in frustration gritting his teeth with anger.

'Stop this! What are you saying? This is crazy talk. I can see your mouth move but only get a word here and there. Calm down and talk calmly. Tell me again... What did we do? What time away together?'

'That's why you're having trouble. If those cowboys have made you destroy an essential part of your memory, and if they never replaced it, then we have a bigger problem going on here. That experience would not have harmed you; it would have made you grow and learn. Why have they spoilt it for you? I don't understand.'

'Calyx, you're really not making sense.'

She turned and headed downstairs, hoping Jett could explain it better. When they arrived in the den, Jett stood with arms folded leaning beside the fireplace. By the look Calyx gave him and Caitlin's confused state, he'd figured out what was going on. His telepathic link to his Glow Girl gave him all the information he needed to know what was playing out between the two of them.

Calyx had taken her arm and led her to sit on the couch. Once she was comfortable, he placed a rug over her legs. She shivered, not with cold, but with confusion.

Calyx turned to Jett. 'Those idiots have deleted the memory of our trip away. Blatzing fools! Who knows what else has been removed. They've stopped her growth! And that magic you told me she's lost, well, I will put money on it, Cait is like this because of their idiocy!'

'Calm down Calyx, you're scaring her.' Jett knelt to talk to Caitlin. 'Glow, sweetheart, before you were married, what is the last thing you remember about Calyx?'

She thought carefully, but the details were blurry. 'Umm... The day you took me to Delphinus Island we saw Calyx with another woman, and that's all I remember. I told Woody the same thing when I woke up from his session the day before my wedding. Axon was there.' She shrugged. 'But I'm not sure for how long. What's going on? You two are seriously acting weird, and you're scaring the pants off me.'

'Sorry Glow, but we haven't finished.' Jett frowned. 'I want you to think carefully—have you ever been told you have a gift that will turn back the clock of time, so to speak? Make something that has happened disappear from your memory?'

'Yes. That I do recall. It was when we were training with the Cloud Riders. Cassie said she thought I possessed the power to erase my memory of an event, but it could only be used once.' She squinted and rubbed her head. It hurt as she evoked the memory. 'Listen here guys, if I've used it, Woody and Axon must have given a totally sound reason, or I would never have agreed to it.'

Jett was white when he turned to Calyx. 'I bet they thought it would destroy her innocence and render her powerless later in time.'

Calyx groaned. 'Well, it's worked the frigging opposite way now, hasn't it? I wish Axon had the guts to discuss it with us first. We could have warned him of the outcome, which we both know is a shocker. How many times have we tried to use magic such as this and made things worse?'

'Calyx!' Caitlin's voice was raised. 'What did you do to me? What in the hell could you have possibly done to make me want the memory of you gone forever?' She ran her hand through her hair.

He tried again to explain. 'Cait believe me... '

His mouth moved, but she heard nothing. She rubbed her ears in confusion and then shook her head.

Calyx turned to his brother. 'Did she hear any of that?'

He shook his head. 'Nope, not a word.'

She threw her hands in the air. 'I'm not sure what game you're playing here, but this is ridiculous. You would never hurt me, Calyx, I know. But even so, I don't understand.' She stood and faced him. 'I know you can show me the past; you have that power. Show me now!' She had her arms folded.

'I can't show you that particular moment.'

'Why?'

'Because it was you who removed it from your memory. Just like now, even if I try to explain it, all you would hear is Blah! Blah! Blah! My words make no sense. I'm sorry, but only you can bring it back.'

Caitlin swung around to face Jett with a disturbingly blank expression. 'Then *you* have to tell me what he did.'

Jett was beside himself with concern for her at this moment, and to mask his emotions, he kept a neutral expression. No matter what he had done so far, she had not improved. In fact, she'd drifted further from reality. It was going to take the power of more than one god to fix her condition. He needed help with her this time. He wished he hadn't allowed his duties to get to him as it had weakened his own magic. Yet, seeing her now, not even in his fittest form could he do this alone. Maybe together, he and his brother could reverse the spell.

Caitlin moved her hand in front of Jett's eyes, waiting for an answer that would make sense of what had gone on. 'Hello, a little help here.'

Jett sat her down on the couch and settled beside her. 'I know you want me to tell you what you need to know but it will be the same coming from me. My words would be jumbled to your ears. I'm as sure as Calyx. Terminating that memory is why you can't hear us and why your health suffers.' He spoke softly so as not to rattle her too much. 'However, I think your subconscious is trying to find it. This is the reason you came back here and worked so hard to pull me out of my depression. Those kisses really snapped me out of it. I wasn't expecting so much friendliness from you after so long.'

She nodded, deep in thought. 'I guess so.'

'She what!' Calyx whipped his head around and glared at his brother.

'Hang on!' Jett put a hand up and matched his moodiness. 'It wasn't like that. They weren't on my lips.'

'Just as well—brother.' Calyx sounded flat, still smarting she could remember kisses she gave to Jett but not those to him. 'Maybe I should kiss her again and see if that works.'

Jett eyed his brother. 'You know that won't work. And luckily she didn't hear you say you'd kiss her or this time you might be wearing a well-earned slap.'

'Don't you let her kiss you anymore either? Grrr... It makes me boil with that image. She's my girl. Keep your blatzing mitts and your face away from her from now on or else.'

Jett couldn't help but grin at his sibling's protectiveness. 'Brother, she belongs to Axon. Not us. I know it's been tough for you not having what you want for once in your life, but that's the price you paid for being underhanded. She chose Axon. You have to respect that.'

'Well, that was before I found out he doesn't deserve her.' Calyx turned to the hearth and leant on it, watching the flames while pulling his temper in check. He could see Caitlin's eyes were wide, trying to soak in what was being said, but knew she understood none of their bickerings as it was all about the kiss she had eliminated from her memory—and heart.

Jett turned back to Caitlin, unsure how much she was now hearing. Her eyes had glazed over in thought. He wanted to help her and needed to pull her mind back into the conversation. He held her shoulders, facing her to him. 'Glow, honey, stay with me! The immortal subconscious is an amazing mystery. Yours is trying to fill the empty space. The missing memory is causing a malfunction. It's as if you're trying to fly with clipped wings. I should have known there was something more serious going on and trusted in our friendship.'

Caitlin moved a lock of dark hair that had flopped forward on his forehead. 'And I should have felt you were in trouble.'

Her caring melted him, but moments later she was lost to him again. Her eyes went blank and he couldn't hear a thought, which made it worse. Seeing his brother had calmed down, Jett got up and moved back over to the hearth to talk to him. 'We should have realised straight away something was wrong with Glow when she didn't turn up the first time as promised.'

'I know, my thoughts exactly. We should have gone to see why instead of saying to hell with Axon, he can have her all to himself. What seriously irks me is how he got so blindsided. Yes, her mind had evolved into a powerful goddess, but her health and well-being in the physical form still needed close attention, more so for someone so fragile. He is a fool not to know even divine beings can become ill. Hell, why does he think we are taken such good care of by those around us.' Calyx kept his tone low but the seriousness of this situation, Jett heard loud and clear.

To hear his brother so upset, Jett confided in him. 'Seeing how sick she looked really snapped me out of my doldrums. It frightened the hell out of me, literally. I forgot all about my own problems. I wanted to start using magic on her but didn't know what was wrong,' Jett confided quietly, although they didn't need to whisper. He sensed Glow's mind was still. There were no thoughts, just glazed eyes that stared at nothing.

'I thought the same upstairs. And as you did, I held back from meddling as it may have done more harm than good.' His forehead dripped with worry and he wiped the sweat beads from his brow. Calyx wished to stay and help, but his commitments were infinite. *Maybe I can squeeze an hour in here and there.* 'It astounds me how someone so important to the universe is handled with such disregard. Her team and Axon must have been unbelievably busy not to notice, and if not, they just don't deserve her. If I am to stay and help in any small way I can, my demand must be met. She stays here until this is fixed, no ifs buts or maybes. Do you hear me, brother?'

'Loud and clear and I agree.' Jett crossed his arms, showing how stubbornly he too felt about it.

Calyx continued, 'And now I want to talk about you, and I want the truth, brother. I'm aware you are both linked somehow. You can read her every thought, but can you also feel her physically? I only ask because I wonder now if Glow's condition has affected your health. Could this be the reason you've ailed for all these months?'

'Maybe, but I feel better today, and yet I'm still connected to her.'

Calyx lifted his eyebrow. 'Are you — can you hear her now?'

'She isn't thinking.' Jett spun around to look at her.

'Or is she? Is it possible the link is weakened as her condition worsens?'

Jett searched the flatness of her eyes. *Could I be losing that part of you too, Glow?*

Calyx saw the way his brother viewed her. He looked worried sick. He put a hand on his shoulder to get him to listen. 'To reverse this, she'll need to be a lot healthier than she is now… And sorry to break it to you brother, but so will you.'

'I know, and I will do it for her.' Jett nodded. 'But now you know what's wrong, can you spare more than a moment here and there to help our Glow Girl?'

'You ask a lot. It won't be easy caring for her 24/7 as we both still have our duties. It will take time and patience to get her back to the healthy state she was in the last time we saw her.' It pained him not to be able to give this his all. 'I hate it I'm so busy. This will need more time than I can give. But as I said before, I am willing to help when I can.'

'I'm not sure I can do this alone, but if I have to, I will. I'm not giving up on Glow.'

Calyx put an arm around Jett and squeezed him. With a sigh, he let him go. 'Okay, my stubborn sibling.' He slumped his shoulders. 'You are my brother and have become my best friend. She has my heart. I don't care how much time this takes, nothing is more important than the two of you.' He pulled at his chin, thinking. 'I'm sure I can rearrange my timetable. It won't hurt the Congress of the Heavens to work around my schedule for a change. While she sleeps, we can take it in turns to go and check on matters of importance.' He smiled. 'I guess you can count on me too.'

'Thanks. I suddenly feel stronger knowing you'll by my side. We can do this, can't we? Let's get our girl back on her feet. I miss her terribly.' Jett shook the hand Calyx extended in agreement, and they both looked happier.

Calyx placed his other hand on his brother's. 'And when we get this done, they will have to go through both of us before ever taking our friend from us again.' He let Jett's hand go and shook Jett in a playful grip. 'I have missed you. Welcome back.'

Jett stood motionless as Calyx went over and sat on the arm of the sofa. He was overwhelmed that his brother who held such status in the universe had committed to helping him. He sat down and relaxed in his armchair to rest. He too needed to heal, and for his Glow, he was starting that right now. His first step was to stop feeling negative. *Jealousy is negative.* He smiled. *This was a tough one.*

'Cait, I'm sorry you find that I am the culprit in this.' Calyx tried to find words she might hear. 'You started to trust me again, and

I feel terrible you have to revisit my error of judgment. I hope you won't hate me when your memory comes back because although well deserved, it will cause me terrible pain.'

Cait ran her fingers over Calyx's wrinkled brow as he frowned. 'I knew you were a bad arse when I met you, but you've changed. Zeus no longer visits me, it's Calyx that sits before me now. Whatever it was, it has to be both our faults.'

'You always manage to take a situation and make the guilty party feel better.' He gave her a sly grin. 'But can I say, when you find out what it is, you can hit, kick and hang me from the heavens upside down by a chain. Even then I will still say it was worth every minute of the punishment.'

She tilted her head, so her hair fell gently on his leg. 'So now I understand why Axon was a supporter to dissolve you from my mind. '

Even unwell, he loved her more than words could say.

The door opened. 'Dinner is ready, Your Majesties.' The servant bowed towards Jett and then Calyx. Next, he bowed to Caitlin. 'Goddess.' He opened the door wide for them. The big fire in the dining room had been lit too.

'It's lovely in here.' Caitlin thanked the maid that seated her. She felt better suddenly. The mystical castle had its own power over her as she felt its warmth and welcoming vibration. This was one reason she loved visiting. There was something so healing about this planet and Jett's home. Suddenly tingles of strong magic ran through her as her two companions were seated. She could only imagine it came from Calyx who sat opposite her and Jett, who, although seated in his usual place at the head of the table, was closest to her.

Jett reached over and put his hand over hers. 'You're so sweet, Glow, but I really wish you'd made Calyx sweat a bit more. He's not that innocent I'll have you know. You forgave him way too easily.' Jett patted her hand in the old-fashioned way she adored. He then picked up her glass and poured her water.

'I should have made you sweat for not coming to visit me for all that time. You're not totally innocent in all this either.' She smiled as she stirred him.

'Hang on, how did this become about me? It's that husband of yours you should be giving a hard time. He was the one who kept us apart.'

'Oh, and you haven't shown jealousy like he has?' Her eyebrow raised while teasing him.

'When? Give an example!' Calyx was amused and preferred this change of topic which put his brother in the spotlight..

'Glow!' Jett put his finger to her lips and hushed her.

She started to giggle, and it shocked even her. She was her old self, having fun like before. The guys were wrong. She was fine and was set to show them. In high spirits, she blurted out a story to Calyx who listened on with amusement.

'Is that right little brother? Your intent was to steal my girl?'

'She wasn't yours then or now. She's still mine.' Jett winked at her.

'Mine!' said Calyx

'Mine!' Jett smirked.

She jumped in, and waved at something behind them. 'Oh... Hi, Melita and Zuri.'

Both men spun around with guilty looks only to see no one there. She had tricked them both and was pleased when they threw their heads back, laughing heartily at her cunning.

'You... you'll keep young lady.' Calyx chuckled as he poured a drink out of the craft. 'Moonjuice, brother?'

Jett held his goblet out. 'Please.'

'Bad married men!' She sat back and grinned. 'Now what were you saying?' She enjoyed watching them squirm.

Jett slapped his brother's back. 'Guess we can be ourselves tonight. Glow's got her mojo back and in fine form.'

Caitlin's expression was full of mischief. 'No holding back either, I've missed you guys and intend on making up for lost time.'

'Keep that up, and by tomorrow we'll be dropping you off at home,' said Calyx.

'Keep that up, and I'll be dropping you off home. Won't we Jett?'

She turned to Jett.

'Keep that up the pair of you, and I'll drop you both off after dinner.' Jett said, looking serious.

'No, you won't—would you really?' Caitlin's eyes were wide, thinking she might have pushed it too far.

Both men laughed, secretly hoping they had got it wrong and she had suddenly been healed, just from being around the magic of Pluto, and them. She was following the conversation just fine.

'What did she always use to say to us when she got us good, Calyx?'

Calyx punched the air as she would...'Gotcha.' He laughed again after taking her off.

She leant over the table and high-fived him. 'Finally, you're getting a sense of humour.'

He sat back, mock-offended. 'Mean Girl.'

'Grumpy old fart,' she said, making Jett laugh and smiled at him. 'What are you laughing at? You hear dead people.' She chuckled.

It had started. Dinner was noisy, insulting and although Calyx and Jett did their utmost to give it back, they couldn't outwit their redheaded guest.

During the meal, Caitlin turned her attention to Calyx. Her mind was in full swing as she came up with all sorts of amusing scenarios of what Calyx might have done that was so bad. None of them was anywhere near what did happen, but nevertheless, both men found them funny and very entertaining.

'I know!' She held her hand up like a school girl. 'Last one I promise,' she added, and spat out the final one. 'Calyx fought Axon for me.' It was Calyx that laughed this time. 'Ha! I would have kicked his arse, and you would be mine, beautiful one.' He wiped his mouth with the serviette, quite confident that it would be so.

'So that wasn't it?' She blinked. It was a hard blink, and after one more it was as if she ran out of steam. She shut down. Her eyes glazed over and her face was expressionless. Until now neither could get a word in edgeways, both enjoying every minute of the Glow they both knew and loved. Before this, she had eaten her first helping and loaded her plate up with more, had been the life of their small dinner party. They waited quietly to see if she could pull herself out of the haze, but she didn't recover.

They turned to each other.

'What was said that shut her down?' Jett's brows were pulled tight into a frown.

Calyx shrugged. 'Your guess is as good as mine... Maybe the mention of Axon.'

'She's listless, and I can't hear a thought coming from her.' Jett waved a hand in front of her, but there was no reaction.

'Well, while she's still eating, let's stay here until she's finished. There's nothing of her and that, right there, is what she needs.'

They studied her as she pulled off strands of chicken. Each piece was held up and given her silent approval before it was slipped into her mouth and chewed upon.

'Let's just chat for a minute and see if that chicken she has taken to is what she needs. It may be what's fuelled her tonight. If I'd have known she was this run down, I would have taken it easy on her. But she loves to stir, and I can't help but give it back,' Jett admitted.

'I agree it was like old times. I too got lost in the moment. Blatz! I can be such an idiot. We took it too far,' Calyx worried. 'If she was fragile like this when she first arrived and had seemingly no real magic left, how did she pull you out of that hell you were locked in? You were a mess when I visited last, and not even my powers could pull you from that dark place where you'd gone.'

Jett bit his lip. 'I love Glow, it's that simple. I'm not in love, as I am with Melita, but I love her as if she was my own child. If she hurts I hurt. If she laughs it brightens my world. I never want to be without the many sides of her personality. They can rock my world, or in a flash, she can crumble it around me with the mere quiver of her lip. She's amazing. So, when she fell on me, and her goddess fragrance had gone, I knew there was a big problem. I was shocked and looked at her for the first time since she arrived, and the sight of her almost brought me to tears. Where had my girl gone?' His eyes watered as he recalled her lifeless features. 'I thought she was dying and was devastated.' He wiped his eyes. 'Of all the things that have gone wrong for me, just knowing she is out there somewhere, my Glow Girl, was enough for me. I only need close my eyes, and I could see her clearly and swear it was her thoughts I sometimes heard. But not to have her at all, would kill me.'

'Then we are both in trouble if we cannot bring her back.' Calyx shook his head and leant on the table. 'This is going to be one tough task we're about to embark on, but one thing we do have in our favour is, she did come to us. The goddess side of her must believe we can help.'

'You think the goddess is dying.' Jett's eyes were wide.

'Yes.'

'And that is the mortal element of her physic side sitting here trying to survive. It's waiting for us to do something.' Jett turned back to watch her.

'Yes.' Calyx nodded.

CHAPTER FIVE

Shared Life Force

I t was next morning before Caitlin shook out of the silent place she went to after dinner. She remembered having fun but it was blank after that. Had she fainted? Her eyes fluttered open. She was in the den, and the fire still burnt brightly. Jett or Calyx must have brought her here to keep warm. *So sweet of them.*

'She's awake,' Jett hovered over her.

'Hi,' she said and wondered what she did to deserve such loyalty. Her eyes swept the room upon hearing other voices. It was Calyx talking to someone familiar, but she wasn't sure who it was. Hearing the name Axon, she pricked her ears up and sat upright. By the desk, she saw Calyx and Axon, both with arms folded and having words of some sort. Their conversation stopped when they heard she had woken.

'Ah, you're in the land of living again.' Calyx grinned when he saw she looked rested and better than when he carried her in last night.

She rubbed her eyes. 'What time is it?'

'Good morning honey,' Axon said. He stepped towards her and with an artful sweep of his hands, lifted his wife and sat with her on his lap. He looked more than pleased when she cuddled into him.

'I wasn't expecting you.' She eyed him.

'I only just arrived. Couldn't stay away, hon. I feel rotten for behaving so badly. Haven't slept and had to come tell you how sorry

I am. Please don't hate me.' His eyes were red from lack of sleep, and his face pale with worry. 'I swear whatever it takes whatever you want, I'll do it, just forgive me and come home.'

He waited for her to speak but she just stared at him.

'What's going on?' He glared at Jett.

Jett leant forward. 'I think she's gone again, Calyx.'

Both men stood over her.

Calyx agreed. 'She's unwell and getting worse.'

Axon lifted her chin and searched her face. 'She was okay when I dropped her off.'

'No, she wasn't, Axon.' Jett frowned. 'Apart from the gauntness, she has been listless and only acts semi-normal when she drinks or eats food. Unfortunately, the alcohol makes her ill, and so she is banned from drinking spirits otherwise you would be holding her over a toilet bowl at the moment.'

'No! She never suffers after-effects from alcohol.' Axon gave him a suspicious stare.

'How long has it been since you shared a glass?' Jett raised his eyebrow.

'Us two, not for a while but the guys drink after most missions to wind down.'

'Have none of you noticed any difference in Cait, like how easily confused she gets by some conversation and that her memories of many events have faded.'

Calyx cut in, 'and let's not forget the major change, she has no blatzing powers.'

'Okay, what have you guys got going on here? Is this... *get Axon* for keeping you guys apart? A game to make me feel bad? Well, it won't work. You're reading far too much into this. Cait's tired and needs a break, that's all. And of course she still has her powers. I was watching her on the last mission. She was riding Shargan and they managed to extinguish a rogue meteor without the team's help. Maybe she is not as strong as she used to be, but it's there and she gets the job done,' Axon defended her.

'Shargan still carries the magic she taught him. It's all him,' Jett said.

'That's unheard of in any of the horses, even Cassie's,' Axon scoffed.

Calyx gestured towards her with a hand movement. 'Haven't you noticed she's lost her glow, that her eyes are dull? That her goddess power of scent has gone?'

Axon dropped his head to look at her again. 'Oh honey, you really do look poorly.' He ran his fingers gently through her hair. 'I'm such a fool.' He looked up at Calyx. 'How did I miss it? She looked fine the other day.'

'She was angry, right? Temper could have given her that spark that deceived you. But what I want to know is how long has it been since you spent time with her. I mean really looked at her and loved her.'

Axon moved her on his lap, too embarrassed to answer.

'You never cuddle me like this anymore,' she said suddenly. Her lips pouted.

'Well, that has to change.' He felt flushed and cross he had neglected her, and annoyed that they knew it too. He couldn't look them in the eye but tried to explain himself. 'It's no excuse but it's been crazy out there. The team has worked from dusk to dawn every night. During the day I'm at the Alpha base with my boss, Zoren. We put in eighteen to twenty hours most days, seven days a week. It's the only way to win whatever war is going on out there. Cait and I have had no time to ourselves since ... well... since the wedding.' He took a breath and collected his thoughts. Was he under interrogation? It felt like it and yet because it was about Cait he was flustered where normally he would keep his cool. He looked up at them. 'And now we have this issue on Earth. So truthfully, we've barely seen each other. I admit we sleep at separate times and good lord I feel guilty enough knowing I have become a terrible husband. But I can't lose her. You must help. Tell me what to do to fix this.'

Jett shook his head. 'I'm sorry to be the bearer of more bad news, but this is something you did to her as well, Axon. Unfortunately, your magic cannot fix this. Neither can mine, but together with my brother, maybe we can reverse what is destroying her. But we will need your permission to keep her here and let us try.'

'Or?'

'Or this... what you see right here... will get worse.'

'And what do you mean I was the cause of this? Oh, I get it...' He shot them a cranky look. 'This is just more payback for keeping her from you. You've given her something and this has been concocted to take her from me!' Axon's complexion was crimson with anger.

'No Axon.' Jett's voice was calm. 'Your wife lost an important experience. Do you remember which one? The one where I bet you said you would replace it after the wedding. But you never got around to it... did you?'

Calyx huffed exasperatedly. 'I can't believe you, Axon. You removed me!'

'You bet I did. You tried to destroy her innocence,' Axon spat at him.

Jett put his hand up. 'Calyx, let me do the talking, you're too upset.'

'Damned right I am. Look at your wife, really take a good look what you've done.' He fumed at Axon. 'What you did has caused this! What I did was leave her with a gift. Woody and you should have left her with it. Not made her forget. She thought it was you, idiot. She had no idea it was me. I fixed it for you! Grrr,' he growled. 'You should have let me have her if you were going to be so pigheaded and not treat her right. I was, am... still in love with her and hate the arrogant use of magic and what your neglect has done to Cait. I am the King of Gods, the Master of Magic... you should have talked to me before doing something like this...'

'Calyx, enough!' Jett stopped him with his tone. 'What's done is done!' He turned to Axon. 'Look, let's calm down. This blame game is not going to help. Excuse my brother, he hasn't slept. While I have cared for your wife, he has searched the archives of the heavenly council for a spell, anything to set this right.' Jett plopped down in the chair opposite them and for a split second, with his guard down, Axon could see how truly upset he was about this. It wasn't about any of them. This was about her, his wife. He was speechless; grasping this was no gag.

Jett leant forward. 'Calyx is right, if you had come to us, we could have told you the problems we've encountered using a power such as she used. It has never been reversed as far as we know, because the immortal that used the magic hasn't got it anymore, and have no memory of it to retrieve the spell.'

Axon stared directly at Calyx. 'Now it's my turn to get personal, so let me talk. This is half your fault too, Calyx. I will not take all the blame here. You forced my hand and should have told me the truth about what you did. All I could think of is how was she to fight for good with a heart that you, yes you!' He pointed the finger at him — 'tarnished!'

Calyx breathed out slowly before answering. 'I know. I know...' He trailed off, his own guilt in this evident. 'Yes, I played a hand in this too. Jett figured that's the reason you had Cait delete my time with her. I just wish you'd discussed it with us first.'

'And I wish you'd been more honest with me.' Axon threw back. 'You said you kissed her but made out it was nothing. That's not how Cait remembered it. You tried to steal her from me!'

Jett cut in, 'Enough! This is not helping. You two have to get over your egos and work together.' Jett eyed Calyx. 'Let me explain it. You two snapping at each other is only going to upset Glow.'

Calyx threw his hands up and sat down, his temper under check for her, not Axon.

Jett faced Axon. 'Glow went from being a powerful immortal to goddess status. She was elevated by a supreme heavenly power as a reward for her hard work. As such, her experiences are essential to her growth as an immortal and a goddess. Her powers evolved, and she needed to as well. To remove those moments upsets a balance that's not understood. We believe evil is drawn in when this spell is activated. Both the evil and memories must be removed together. Glow would not have known to do this. I'm afraid in this case, evil stayed, and your wife is slipping from us. Cait needs to get those memories back. They will destroy the evil killing her mind. It's that, or she'll gradually get worse.'

Calyx sat forward to speak. He said what Jett couldn't bring himself to say. 'And if she does turn evil and somehow works out how to tap back into her power…' He shook his head. 'No amount of gods' magic will save us. She will become the most dangerous weapon in the universe.'

Axon felt sick. His complexion turned a shade of grey as he tried to control his concern. 'I did this… to my beautiful wife?'

'We did this!' Calyx felt a rush of despair at having to tell him. He knew how Axon felt. 'Feel free to throw up. I did, twice.'

'She's not in good health, mate.' Jett stood up and stretched, not feeling well himself. 'I have spent the last few hours thinking what we would do if Calyx came back empty handed. Firstly, she'll need to get herself physically and mentally well. That means lots of healing power injected into her life form. She will need magic to help her sleep, planned meals and someone around to ensure she eats it and make sure she feels happy in her environment.'

'Her team and I will do that.' Axon saw a glimmer of hope that he and the team could fix this.

'No disrespect, Axon, but she is happy here and we think we can take better care of her than her team. You have already told us how busy you are. And with one Rider down, it'll be double the workload for you.' Jett flinched away from the hurt in Axon's face. 'May I remind you, my power is stronger than yours and if we have any hope at all of saving Glow, she will need heaps of it.' Jett had no intentions of letting her go and having Axon stuff it up a second time.

Calyx agreed and did his best to keep the emotion out of his voice. 'Axon, let us help you. You know she believes this is a healing planet. In her mind, this is the best place for her. Why do you think she fought you to come here? This is where we believe she needs to be.'

Caitlin suddenly sat up straight and turned to Axon. He could clearly see it was the goddess who had taken over and decided to weigh in on the conversation.

'Calyx is right. This is where my inner self-calls me to be. If any place can heal me, it is here on Pluto.' She saw her husband's eyes water. 'Please don't be sad. You are not to blame either. I did this to myself. I can't imagine anyone making me do something against my will. So whatever Calyx did, we did it, and I'm so sorry you were hurt in this process. Maybe this is the reason our marriage has never been all roses. You had a lot to forgive me for, I'm assuming. I don't like myself much either since finding out I did something bad enough that all traces of that memory had to be erased.'

As soon as she had finished speaking she collapsed back against the cushions, still listening or maybe not. Axon tried to keep her attention by talking directly to her. 'Honey, you can be as kind as you want, but I did force you. Calyx is right. I made false promises. I told you I would replace all those memories Calyx gave you, with better ones... and I didn't as I was always too busy. Damn this job. If it's a choice I must make, then I choose you. I'll tell Zoren he can find someone else. I can't live without you and your love. Give me a chance to help you. Come with me now. I can and will replace it all. Please trust me. I will do this!'

'It's too late,' Jett said quietly. 'The only solution is magical now. As we have found, she is having a tough time holding on to even what we speak of now. Her senses are all but gone; she didn't even know she was eating chicken last night. We talk in front of her now because she is only grasping part of the conversation and I wonder now how she even heard my wife's plea to come here. I think the goddess in her is helping, or should I say, helped her, to get here and is letting us know this is where Glow should stay for now.'

Calyx went over to them and put a friendly hand on Axon. 'She still only loves you mate, that I promise. We just want to help her, not steal her from you. When she's better, she'll be just as in love with you as before. Trust us to do what you employed us to do, protect the goddess, Glow Girl, as we of the high council, trusted and accepted you as the Lord of the Planets. Don't even talk of resigning. We won't allow you to give up the peacekeeping empire you've built and the respect you've earned thus far. We have faith in you, and it's time you showed us the same courtesy. Let us do what we're good at and when the time is right, she'll beg us to bring her to you.'

Axon calmed down and was now watching her face. 'She's so expressionless. What is she thinking, Jett?'

'She feels confused and sick for hurting you but doesn't know how to repair it. She's listening to what we're all saying, but none of its making much sense.' Jett stood over her.

Axon smiled and cheered up for her. 'You're not hurting me, honey, I'll be fine. These two men are your rightful guardians so if I can't trust them, who can I trust? I want you to have a holiday here with Jett and Calyx and don't worry about anything but having a good time.' He smiled again. 'Would you mind me calling in from time to time to see my favourite girl?'

She liked his new mood, and the knot in her stomach released. 'I'd like that.'

He looked up at Jett. 'Keep me in the loop?'

Jett nodded. 'Will do, thanks, Axon. You're doing the right thing.'

Axon looked helpless. 'I've got a lot of humble pie to eat. I've been hard on the three of you because of my ego.'

Calyx patted him on the back. 'We all have times when our personal feelings rule. It's normal and nice to see you are one of us.' He stood up and stretched. 'But hear me now Axon, we make no promises. This is going to be a tough road and it will only work if she trusts us. Let's hope she keeps remembering she can.'

'It breaks my heart I have played a part in this and understand the gravity of what you are trying to tell me. The goddess side of Caitlin is dying isn't she?'

'Yes,' Calyx bit his lip and looked away to collect his emotions.

'And this is the real reason why you are so reluctant to let me take her.' He allowed his thoughts to be heard. 'Because only a deity has the power to bring back one of their own if it is at all possible.'

They nodded.

'I get it now, and as much as I hate the thought of leaving her when she is so unwell, it looks like I have no choice.' He breathed out heavily and stared at them. 'If anyone can do this you two can and as thanks, whichever way this goes, I'll make sure she has time for you both from now on.'

'I'll hold you to that Axon.' Calyx shook his hand. 'I never want us this distant again. You or her... understood?'

'Understood,' Axon agreed wholeheartedly. 'However, friend or foe, if you fail, you know as well as I do her time will be limited. Therefore, you have my permission to give your way a go. But if it isn't working by the end of the moon cycle, I take Cait home and the Riders and I will take care of my wife and enjoy what time we have left with her, is that understood.'

'Fair enough,' Jett uncrossed his arms. Pleased they had reached a reasonable outcome.'

Axon's features softened. 'I apologise for everything Jett. I let my jealous and possessive nature take over. This here has been a real wake-up call. Bring back our Caitlin and I promise things will change.'

While still supporting Caitlin in his arms, Axon stood. He kissed her and getting a slight response, smiled. 'I'm only a NAVcall away if you want me, sweetheart. Get well and come back to me.' He grinned and feeling she was steady, moved back a couple of steps to give enough room to transport back to the office without her. She looked drained. His last glance of her frail image as it faded from sight stabbed at his heart. He had never felt so helpless, and once out of sight and alone, he crumbled in a heap behind his desk. Emotional and terrified she might die, he prayed they were enough.

With Axon gone, Caitlin collapsed. Jett caught her and put her back on the couch near him. 'I feel as if I'm going to be sick again.' Her weary eyes squinted as she tried to focus.

'Come here.' Jett put his arms out and she got up using his hands to steady herself and sat with him on his big chair. Even hugging into his body and being by the fire she shivered. Eventually, the comforting hug and the heat radiating from the fire warmed her and eased the sick feeling. She wrapped her arms around his neck and buried her head in the softness of his shoulder. Here she felt the full benefits of his godly charm. He must have heard her ponder it was him who was making her feel better. She felt thankful when his arms went back around her. His powerful grip throbbed with magic that helped heal her confused state. She wasn't sure how many hours it had been, but her stomach rumbled as she woke.

'Oh... I think that was me.' She sat up and smiled. 'I think that confirms I'm hungry.'

Both men took a minute to recover. This was the first time Caitlin had spoken in hours. 'What did you do to her?' Calyx eyed his brother.

'Just the usual... and a touch of healing.' Jett cringed under Calyx's gaze. He knew his brother didn't believe him but wasn't game to tell him he had tried something different. Calyx would be cross if he knew he had given her a little of himself, his own life force. When they first met, he asked her if she would swap to the dark side with him. She had refused. Today with her he walked the line, not good, not evil, so he shared some of that with her. It was only enough to get her to eat and have a few laughs and, he hoped, to ease her state of mind. He would not let her die or become evil. Not now, it wasn't what she would want. Nor did he wish it on her. He had seen both sides. She was the one who showed him what he was missing, and he loved her for the happiness it brought him. Without her it faded. He wanted it back and knew only the goddess, Glow Girl, could turn his darkness to light. With a happy heart, he was able to live the good life with his Melita, something he so desired.

Calyx looked uncertain. He was no fool and guessed his brother had given her more than healing. However, he was pleased she had gained spirit, so he let it slide. She scooted towards the door and glanced back when she got there. 'I can't hear the servants, so if you two want something other than a cheese sandwich you might want to come and help.' She closed the doors behind her, and ran off towards the kitchen.

Caitlin barely reached the galley door when she was lifted and placed on the bench.

'Where did that burst of energy come from?' Jett chuckled.

'You filled me with something more than healing. It kick-started something.' She grinned.

Calyx growled at him, 'Let's just keep her happy naturally.' He grabbed a pan from the cupboard, scowling.

'Brothers!' Caitlin smiled. 'Do you ever agree on anything?'

They both looked at her and grinned. 'Yes, you.'

Caitlin laughed for the first time, and this reaction encouraged them to continue.

CHAPTER SIX

Goddess Dedication

O ver the coming weeks, whatever made her laugh the most, they did more often, like fighting with the gallery equipment while preparing the meal.

Caitlin became encased in her own little bubble. She had no thought of the world around her. If she tried to think of anything outside the castle, direct her thoughts towards the past, her head would ache, and she would collapse. Therefore, she spent her days enjoying the company of those she didn't need to think about; Jett and Calyx. They never left her side. Morning or night they were there, and she looked forward to waking up to the madness each day. She never tired of the fun the two of them had, especially at mealtime. There were moments it surprised her they managed to have food to put on the plates.

It was some weeks before any proper thoughts entered her mind, and when one did, she blinked, pulling a face. They had been discussing what to do and she felt sure they had better things to do besides babysitting her. The idea of being up high came to mind. 'How about we go to the cabin and you guys can spend the day skiing? You must need a break from me big time.'

Calyx smiled at her. 'You must be feeling better. This is the first time you've mentioned you'd like to go anywhere.'

'It just came to mind. I think it will relax me too. I've had many a good time in the cabin.' She shook her long red hair and unconsciously wrapped it up in a bun, pinning it.

'Another first.' Jett glanced at Calyx and back at her. 'Glow never ties her hair up.' He saw her eyes glaze back over, a look they were now very familiar with, zoned out on them, not hearing Jett. She'd said what needed to be said and as with her other requests, her energy after that was saved. Jett was unsure why. He found nothing magical about the cabin... except... She had him wondering. Why hadn't he thought about the phenomenon she uncovered during her stay there? He started to think it wasn't such a bad idea after all. 'I think we'd better take her where she needs to be. If it's the cabin, then it's my bet our goddess is ready to claim her life back.'

Calyx had a look of hope. 'You think so!'

'Yes.' Jett smiled.

'Then get ready to give this all you've got! We'll only get one go at it.' Calyx rolled his shoulders to loosen up.

'Given something else to focus on and having to eat well to get Glow better has helped me too. My magic's at full capacity, let's go get our girl back.'

'Agreed.' Calyx turned his head sideways, one way and the other. His neck cracked, making him smile. 'Ready.'

'Yep, ready.'

* * * *

'After a night of being ruined and made to feel like their much-loved princess, Caitlin woke to the darkness of the ski lodge cabin. The fire that kept them warm was only embers flickering. It was near daybreak, so she got up off the couch that had been her bed and padded over the men on the floor. It felt like forever since she watched the dawn lights on Pluto. She wanted company to enjoy this with her and hoped the men didn't mind an early morning wake-up call. She sat on a stool by the window and when the time was right, she threw cushions at them. They lay on loose pillows, and both clumsily thrashed about to break free of them when they saw she was up.

Calyx got to her first and slung an arm around her. 'What are we looking at?'

Jett put on the kettle and stood the other side of her. He knew he had time and made two coffees, handing one to Calyx. To Caitlin, he gave herbal tea; a perfect brew he pre-concocted to jump-start her memories. Holding his own strong blend he dragged another stool over and sat the other side of her. He shook with excitement. It all led to this one moment. He could never remember a time he and his brother had ever been this dedicated or worked this hard to save anyone. He was surprised they never fought anymore and how having a common interest had brought them so close. He found it comforting to have Calyx around. Without realising it, they had become mates.

He turned his head to look at Caitlin. There was something different about her this morning. He felt a confidence in her that had not been there since she came to visit. Hoped the magic she sought after from Pluto, and them, was enough? He smiled at her; she was glorious in this light and he knew he would never give up trying to help her if this didn't work.

'Just watch,' she repeated. She kept her focus straight ahead.

'Can't see a thing.' Calyx shook the sleep from him as he stretched and yawned.

'Now!' Caitlin pointed. 'Isn't it amazing?' As she said it the faint light of dawn had reached the surface, just enough to make the snow glisten. Through the darkness, it looked as if crushed glass had been scattered over the white snow, the gleam of it sending up laser lights of green, brown and red into the sky.

'Isn't that the prettiest sight you've ever seen?' She turned to Jett. 'Have you shown this to your Melita yet?'

Jett shook his head. 'I'll have to, now that you've shown Calyx. He'll use this to get me to do things I don't want to do. You should have heard the list of bull-twang he was going to blab if I didn't tell him my secret that you had come to visit.'

Calyx gave a throaty laugh. 'A man's got to do, what he has to do.' He reached around to clip Jett across the ears. 'Worked didn't it?'

Jett moved his head quickly to miss the slap to the head. 'Missed!'

Calyx continued, 'Anyway, you're just running scared. You know if Melita sees this she'll get all romantic and nag for kids again.'

'Kids!' Caitlin had a vague memory. 'Didn't I tell you once I saw kids jumping on you and you loved them?'

'The only kids I'd ever have near me would be if I was an uncle and they would be your little rug rats. Yours and Axon's.' He poked at her.

She leant into him, wrapping an arm around his waist. 'You're such a scaredy cat.'

He laughed and tickled her. 'You're the frightened kitten!'

'Why me?' She turned her head to the side confused.

'You're better now, and it's time to face up to those demons and reconnect with those missing memories.' I thought you were doing something here, but I guess not. You were just enjoying the light show, weren't you? I think you're the scaredy cat.' He stirred her back.

She wiggled out of his grip, laughed and got up. As she ran in through the open door that led to the spa room, she tossed her robe and slippers aside. This left her half-naked in knickers and bra. 'How do you know I got nothing out of it?' Caitlin ran into the spa. They heard a splash as she jumped in.

Her body relaxed the minute it hit the warm water. Electricity seemed to shoot from her. Both men now understood she had used the planet phenomenon to charge this next step they would help her through.

Caitlin was instinctively aware this was her one and only chance to get well too. After this, she would have used all the magic kept for this moment, and no more would she exist as a goddess, although Caitlin hoped her friends by her side gave her enough to carry on after. Even if only as a powerless human wife to Axon.

Jett slapped Calyx on the shoulder. 'I can hear her. She's ready and is thinking water will amplify the magic between us. Are you ready for this?'

'I stand the chance of being hated after she remembers. You know that, right.'

They stood at the edge of the spa watching Caitlin float on her back, with barely a movement.

'Have faith she comes back to us as she was, and my advice is, wear the slap if she gives you one.'

Calyx smirked evilly. 'She might just get her second kiss from me if she does. You know I like it rough too.'

'Like hell, you will! Not on my watch!' Jett saw his smirk turn to a frown. 'It's okay, just kidding Calyx. I know you'd never hurt her. We're both suckers for our lovable, sassy girl. Now let's finish this and fingers crossed you come out unscathed.'

'Right beside you brother.'

Jett pushed him aside to get to her first, knocking Calyx off balance, so he fell into the water, clothes and all.

Drenched, he shook his head, and water sprayed everywhere. Jett had tossed his shirt aside and already stood beside her, with one hand on her forehead the other under her, so she stayed afloat.

Calyx, screwed up his face, lips pinched as he took possession of the other side of her. 'My side,' he mouthed at Jett, who frowned. 'You don't share very well do you, brother?' He pushed Jett's head back with the palm of his hand. 'Hate you, but we do this together, ding-a-ling!'

Caitlin had put herself in a comatose state and was floating calmly. She couldn't hear the chatter. It was more of a mumble but the hands that held her were familiar. Both men had their own touch and it was easy to tell who was who. Her body felt invigorated as power flowed internally, and the magic boost was evenly distributed from both directions. Calyx placed his other hand on her shoulder and it was Jett's palm that lightly pressed against her forehead.

Time passed and, almost ready to give up trying to remember, Caitlin experienced a gold flash of light that illuminated from her very soul. The heat from it burst forth and flooded her entire body before it entered her mind. Her first image that came to mind was his lips that pressed against hers with lustful force. The erotic passion of powerful emotions surged and with it was the desire to dominate her. But suddenly this shifted and the evil in the man kissing her dulled and dissipated. His genuine heart now unveiled melted Caitlin as his raw passion and adoration showed her a heartfelt timeless love that he was now prepared to give. The sensation of this deep eternal commitment had Caitlin dreamily surrender, and at that moment, she was a woman in love with this adorable man she now remembered kissing. The memory of feeling safe and happy in his arms flooded back as did the memory of her willingness to give herself to him forevermore. The unspoken emotion unlocked a part of her she kept only for that special someone. Mesmerised with this good-looking man, and feeling that love returned, she allowed him to experience the full force of her kiss. This was a moment that, unbeknown to Caitlin, would bind them together for eternity. His fate was in her hands, and hers in his.

Suddenly an explosion of memories licked delightfully within her as their time long forgotten, began to surface. One particular tender moment caused her to let out a loud sob when reliving the heartache she saw in his eyes as he realised he had to pull away, a gallant testament of his love. Tears flowed as she cried for the hopelessness of the situation. It was Calyx's love that swept her off her feet. It was him who took her to all those wonderful places on Earth. In doing so, this allowed her to see so many joys that the Earth had to offer, which gave her an even stronger need to protect it. She remembered the hours he devoted to her learning experience, the soothing voice that chatted happily, and the loving arms that held her while they sat admiring the views. She remembered longing to stay in them. It was him who had, for a brief moment, heated and ignited her inner flame.

Her eyes opened, happy to still be in those same loving arms, but grimaced when she saw his sorrowful, anxious stare. *He didn't know. How could he? We never got a chance to discuss it.*

She lifted her hand up and traced his frown. 'I loved you too. They are beautiful memories and should have been treasured.' She whispered.

'Then you have not remembered it all and you must so you can get well completely. Even if you hate me after, your health is more important. Caitlin, I was vicious, wished you dead and when you lived, I came up with a new plan to seduce you and turn you evil.' He said what he had wanted to tell her for such long time. He was a monster and didn't blame her if she never spoke to him again. 'I wore you down Caitlin, and found the key to unlock your goddess passion.'

She shook her head, 'No Calyx, you did not find my weakness. It was me who turned the key and let you in. At that moment, I felt your kiss change from cunning to pure passion. What you didn't know is that it was the same for me, but even so, it was wrong of me to kiss you back in that same way. A goddess gives her true self to only one man. My love should never have strayed and yet it did. There was something strong between us that you must have felt too.'

'My dearest Cait, I know it was only a kiss, but I didn't just love you, I fell hopelessly in love with you that night. I've had to learn to deal with it because you are Axon's wife now. But there is one thing I cannot deal with, in fact, neither of us can. We are lost without you in our lives. You must never do this to Jett, or to me, again. We need you as we need to breathe.' His eyes showed her he still loved her deeply.

'Unless you haven't noticed,' she said, smiling, 'I need you and Jett just as much.'

'Do you?' He grinned.

'Yes. This proves to me I have to be allowed to spread my wings a little. Take some time to spend it with those I have made friends with up here. I still would have got sick after what I did, but you guys would have seen it earlier and maybe sorted it out before it got that bad. As for Jett's problems, again, we could have sorted it out before it sent him running to hell for a fix.' She smiled and winked. 'You do get what I mean?'

He nodded. 'I can take it. You're right. I did retreat to where it was easier. But as Calyx said, without you, we went to pieces. We're a right ol' trio. How did we become so in need of each other?'

Caitlin pulled herself from the water and sat on the step, arms wrapped around her knees. 'Not sure, but it's true.'

'For me, you felt like family.' Jett smiled.

'It's like that for me, too.' She agreed.

'Well, that's not true for me. I thought you were the hottest chick I'd ever seen. Never once did I look at you like family.' Calyx nudged her. 'Sorry, but you want the truth.'

She lifted her hand and pushed him. 'Dirty old man! You're thousands of years older than me.'

His lip dropped, which made her smile.

'Seriously though, I feel I owe you both a big apology.'

'Why you, Cait?' Calyx blinked in surprise.

'I loved you both at different times, more than I should have. Now I'm married, and it's easy to identify the difference between love, and being in love! These emotions are both beautiful, but both so different. In one, you give your mind, body and soul. In the other, you give your caring heart in friendship. I understand what we three have now. It's a deep, strong bond of friendship very few people find. So I really want to apologise for leading you both on, especially you, Calyx, and I hope my childish and uneducated ways do not cause either of you any further grief. So from now on, I guarantee I will not act promiscuously towards either of you again.'

Calyx moved over to the seated side of the heated spa and sitting, lay back against the headrest. He looked exhausted. She was just about to say more when she saw Jett copy him and also lay back on his headrest.

'She's back.' Jett finally spoke and breathed out slowly.

'Yep,' Calyx agreed with a broad smile.

'What! So that's it? Where's my apology?'

They grinned at one another, shook their heads, closed their eyes, relaxed and didn't say a word. They felt Caitlin's power strum through them. Her magic was back, and so was she. They peeked through their lashes to see what she was doing.

Caitlin was about to throw a temper tantrum, and they nudged each other at the sight. Her eyes glowed bright emerald and her red hair shone glossy and soft around perfect features. She was more beautiful than they had ever seen her and they both felt proud of what they had accomplished.

'You rotten pair of male egotists! If you think I'm going to take all the blame…' Caitlin huffed and attacked them with a scurry of splashes. Both men laughed but didn't move. 'I'll fix your arrogance.' She waded through the water and at the side, lifted out easily. Once dressed she turned and seeing they still had not moved she went to the refrigerator and took from it, two jugs full of ice water.

Both men grinned at each other, turned up the jets and closed their eyes again to rest. That had been a real drain and neither had any intentions of moving just yet. Not until they were startled with ice cold water that was suddenly dumped on their heads.

That was the last straw for the two of them. Caitlin was chased, tackled, tickled, thrown back in the spa and harassed until she gave in and took all the blame. She also had to agree never to blame her friends, them, for anything they did in the future to her. And lastly, they made her confess that everything was all her fault because she was just so damned adorable.

After much fun with her new magic, she finally got the better of them. She froze them both to the spot and there they stayed until they promised her a wonderful time of her choosing.

'All right then! We have to give in or continue to stand here like dills,' Calyx finally agreed. 'Where do you want to go?'

'Well…' She smiled with a devious little sparkle in her eyes. 'I've just spent a very long time in a spa with two of the hottest gods in the universe. Therefore, what I want is a night with a man I desire… my man.' She chuckled and elaborated when Calyx gestured for it to be him. 'How about we have a night with our partners, you know, loving… dinner, dancing… loving…'

'So, what if lover boy doesn't let you come back to help my brother? And won't share you because you're so sexy again?' Calyx was suddenly annoyed. 'We didn't help you to get well only to have that friend stealer hubby of yours, happy. Axon is still not totally out of my bad books, yet.'

'Oh, he'll share, but will you.' She ran her hand down Calyx's muscular arm.

'He'd better,' Jett growled, not liking her touching Calyx. 'And

Axon had better as well, or else.'

'Ah, feisty one!' She leaned on Jett. 'You will share, won't you?' She took the spell off him and his arms hugged her. 'I can share because I know you're really mine.' He stirred Calyx who was still frozen.

Calyx growled as he tried to break free of her spell. It was so loud it thundered. 'Okay, I'll bloody well share. But no more games...' His voice lowered. 'Please Cait. Let me go!'

His tenderness made her weaken and he found himself able to move. As quick as a flash he scooped her up and snatched her from his brother. 'Mine!' he yelled back at Jett from the couch where he had transported her to.

Jett walked in, putting on a tee-shirt, and ignoring his brother. 'So, Glow, where do you want us to take you?' Jett gave her a caring smile. He trusted her loyalty to him and not even Calyx could shake his belief in how much she cared for him.

He is so worthy of my friendship. She glowed with happiness while watching Jett. 'Um...' She turned her head at an angle, thinking, and chewed her lip. 'Well, the first time I met you guys was one of the most treasured memories I have.'

'That island is perfect.' Calyx sounded keen. 'It's the most secure place I know. Good choice!' He high-fived her.

'I agree, and think it's time we all put our relationships back on track.' Jett stared at his brother. He was in trouble with Melita, but Calyx had to stop loving Caitlin the way he did and fall back in love with his wife. This was perfect for them all.

'That's if they want to join us—I mean—I haven't been the best wife of late,' Caitlin said.

'Don't let him off that easily Cait.' Calyx felt a pang of annoyance.

'She let you off that easily, so why not him.' Jett wiggled a finger towards him.

'Fair enough.' Calyx had to agree.

Delighted, Caitlin clapped her hands. 'So now we have spoken of the where I'd like to propose the length of time we stay. One night is a sleepover, two nights is a weekend of absolute bliss. Are you both on board for two lustful nights on a tropical Island with the person of your dreams?'

'There is no way Melita will knock back an overnight stay in a warm climate. Even mad she would join me.' He chewed his lip. 'However, one night might be all I can give with the chaos that surrounds me. What about you, brother?'

Calyx squirmed uneasily. 'It was insisted Zuri and I attend a function tomorrow that I can't get out of but until then, I am all yours. I'm sure Zuri will love to come too if she knows Cait will be there.'

'At this stage, I will take whatever I can get. A sleepover it is then.' She was thrilled they'd go and was sure once there, she'd be able to talk them into an extra night. 'I'm so ready for some fun in the sun, followed by some hot damned sex on the beach.'

'Cait!' Calyx laughed. 'Have we put some of our bad-boy magic in you?'

Jett put his head back and roared laughing. 'Hope it stays a while. I don't want the fun to stop just because the boss is around.'

'Oh shytzer, forgot about sourpuss. Well, ain't this going to be a hoot? He'll kick our derrieres if she's too much of a bad girl.' Calyx rubbed his hands together liking this idea.

'Good, hope she gives him hell.' Jett folded his arms. 'We just got frozen for not behaving... freeze him too, sweetie—please!

Caitlin tapped her chin, thinking, and grinned.

'Love my girl!' Calyx put his arm around her knowing she was at least thinking about it.

Chapter Seven

Dolphin Island
(Delphinus)

Showered and getting ready in her room, Caitlin's mind was still on Calyx and Jett. She smiled, thinking about the deal to come to Delphinus Island. She was made to apologise again and promise never to use her powers on them, ever, even if they were to turn evil and cause havoc in the universe. Of course, she crossed her fingers when making that promise.

Ready and waiting for Calyx, Jett took both Caitlin's hands. He had to talk to her before they left. He feared that once she was in her man's arms, Axon might convince her to go home with him, leaving Jett without the necessary help to protect his Kingdom. 'Glow I really need you here, but Axon needs you too. I'm not sure how you're going to work in two places at once. I must ask, have you thought this through? I can see it going down an entirely different path, and not in my favour. Instead of going there, how about we spend the afternoon talking and who knows, the solution may surface, and instead of me needing you for days, it might only take hours.' He let her hands go and restlessly stuck his in his pockets.

'Jett, don't you see, this is for you as much as it is for me. Yes, you made me well, but you're still running on half steam. I know how much power I zapped from you to get better. This is why you're worried now.' She ran a hand gently down his arm.

Jett's hands in his pockets were rounded and folded into fists. 'Please help me, Glow.'

'This is why I have requested we spend time with our partners. If we're not refreshed, content and happy with those we love, and we continue to worry about how we left things, how can we give full support to each other? No, this is going to happen, and you are going to enjoy it regardless.' She placed her hand gently on his arm again. 'Trust me, Jett. You knew what I needed and helped me, and now it's my turn.' She lightened the mood and curtsied. 'Allow me to help you, my king, whom I admire and love.'

He lifted her chin and stared at her before his head went to one side. 'Jett to you.' He smiled and let her go. 'Okay, you win. But you better be this good at manipulating Axon and the ones causing my headaches.'

'I'm sure when I find out what is bothering you, I might run for the hills, but for now, allow me to care for you. Let me get you back to the man you were too.'

He shrugged and smiled, 'guess I have been a bit of a pain. I'm a proud man, it's not easy to ask for help.'

'You don't need too, I will.' Caitlin turned to Calyx who'd joined them but stayed quiet. 'What about you, Calyx? Can you give us some more of your time after this rendezvous to help with the mess drowning us both? Earth is as much a headache to me, as Jett's issues are to him. Maybe between the three of us, we can nut out a great plan to fix both much quicker. What are your thoughts?'

'It concerns me you are committing to my brother before you have all the facts. When it comes to his issues, you can be sure they are epic, and it's more than just the Dwarf Planet owners causing him grief. He needs to tell you everything before this goes any further. As for you Cait, you can say no to Jett's issues, and regardless, we will still help you with Earth.'

'Jett's not well, and until he is, I'm happy to wait. These issues have been drowning him for quite some time, so a day or so won't make an ounce of difference. However, it will make a big difference to Jett. It will give him back the inner peace he needs to tackle whatever it is, head on. But rest assured, I will be supporting Jett no matter what the difficulty.'

Calyx put his hand up and shook his head. 'You are one stubborn, beautiful goddess, you know that right?' He ran a hand through his hair and looked back at her. 'Caitlin—' He started to lecture her and stopped. 'Okay, when he does open up to you, and after if you do decide to get involved, I guess you can count me in too.'

She turned and gave a happy little clap. 'I knew you wouldn't let us down, either of us.' Her eyes drifted back to Jett. 'I don't care what it is, I want to help. But you must help me too. My worries can't be solved without difficulty either. So the plan is, sort out the relationship with our estranged partners, have sex... a lot, then reconvene back here, refreshed, stress-free and ready to work miracles.'

'I feel fine, really. We can talk now if you want,' Jett tried one last time to change her mind.

Caitlin put her soft finger to his mouth. 'Shush, it's my turn now. Let me give you back what I took. You've been walking on the edge of death and destruction for long enough, Jett. Come over to my side and walk a little with me in the light. Let love and goodness heal the fragments of you that set you aside from the dead souls you oversee.' Her smile dazzled him.

He knew she was using her new-found magic on him at this moment and yet he didn't care. He believed in her fully and would walk in her happiness forever if he could. Even for a while sounded to good to pass up, and he smiled. 'You're right. A few drinks with the family and a cosy night with Melita does sound good.' Jett turned to Calyx. 'Surprised you've committed to come on board if Glow does. Are you sure you're okay with this?'

'We are Cait's guardians, and I'm almost sure Zoren will not appreciate his secret weapon going it alone against some of the meanest, most uneducated, sons of bitches that rule those troublemaking Iced Planets of yours. And it will take more than you two greenhorns to get them to accept you as king.'

'Seriously!' Caitlin remarked with a smile. 'There are worse than you two?'

'That's real supportive.' Jett smiled and mouthed, *'bitch!'*

CHAPTER EIGHT

Holiday

Delphinus had fast become Caitlin's favourite holiday destination. It was on Dolphin Island where she first met Jett and his family. That was the reason she chose to come here.

She hoped it wasn't too late for her and Axon, and believed if anything could save their relationship it would be the magic they once found here, together. Silently, she wished for it to be Jett and Melita's saviour too.

In her holiday hut, Caitlin sat on the bed. She looked forward to seeing Axon, but was nervous at the same time. She had been annoyed at his secrecy, and it had made her bad-tempered. For this reason, she was prepared to take some of the blame regarding her abrupt departure from Earth, but he did have it coming. He had neglected her as a husband, and as a boss, he should have trusted her enough to confide in her. The only reason she wanted this reunion was to help her decide their future together. It was her destiny to keep peace in the universe. She couldn't fulfil it tied to his side. He had to give her some freedom, or she might have to deal with what was coming, alone.

Now Caitlin had her powers back and more, her goddess side was being hailed once again, and there was no way to ignore this sharp tug from the universe's force. Axon had to understand she was a goddess and, like it or not, she had a purpose. He'd married her knowing this, so his insecurities of losing her and jealousy towards Jett and Calyx had to stop.

Caitlin stood in front of the mirror and smeared gloss on her lips before she ran a brush through her copper-toned hair. It was more vibrant than ever, and her emerald eyes sparkled with health. Her friends had done well getting her back to peak health, *'and then some,'* she muttered. Her memory had fully returned and was very much intact, as were her senses. She was more than ready to go back to work, but first, she had to settle where her home was to be. Would it be with her dependable friend Rory and his team, or with Axon, the man she had long ago given her heart? Maybe it was not too late to rekindle the love she once had with Axon. If it were no longer there, her path would never be happy, but it would be easier.

Her mind drifted. It had been some weeks since she had spent more than a few moments with her husband as he had been so busy.

If Caitlin added this to the time they had spent apart while she was on Earth, it had been a good twelve months since they had even slept together. Yet her candle did still burn for him and him alone.

When Caitlin finally plucked up the courage, she walked down the beach to the restaurant where they had all planned to meet for drinks and a meal.

Jett and Calyx were nowhere in sight. They must be still getting ready. She was almost positive they were sitting back having a cigar first, enjoying the peace without her. *Rotton sods...* She smiled. Familiar with the sound, she heard his laugh first before rounding a tree and spotting Axon, leaning against a pillar. He stood chatting with Poseidon and wife, Amphitrite. Talking work with Axon, the God of Neptune stood commanding and godly, yet as soon as he saw her, she knew Poseidon would be Razor again, and almost family to her as he treated her so kindly. She was thrilled Razor and Angel could make it on such short notice.

After big welcoming hugs all round, Caitlin chose to stand next to Axon and put a shaky hand on his. He smiled down at her and pulled her into him while he continued his conversation with their friends. As his warm body pressed close, she stopped shaking and relaxed against him. The scent of his aftershave made her head swim. *Yes!* She was thrilled her senses had returned and she knew this was where she wanted to be… *with the man of my dreams.* She hoped he still felt the same. Axon's presence was overpowering, sending chills up and down her spine. Magical vibrations from his powers ran through her body. But even though she was feeling him again, she was at odds and would have preferred to go somewhere alone to talk. But she had arranged this get together so for the moment, their marital problems had to wait. Razor held the door for them and with a bright smile, she followed Axon inside the restaurant.

At the table, Jett and Calyx had already ordered drinks for everyone. When a cocktail was handed to Caitlin, she refused it, not wishing to disguise the sexy vibe coming from her husband. Caitlin hadn't felt this way for a very long time. *How could either of us feel the connection gifted to soul mate immortals, when my power had shut down?* Now united and healthy, the sexual tension each time they touched was incredible and made wanting him more urgent than ever. But that had to wait. With the rest of the family there and given she had missed them, her energy, for now, she would direct towards social interactions with much-loved friends.

It was well into the afternoon when Calyx suggested they all go their separate ways to enjoy the rest of the day with partners. Some went bush-walking, and others hired buggies. She knew where she was heading, and hoped Axon felt the same. 'We promise we'll meet you back here for dinner,' she called to Jett who looked unsure but did have a good amount of trust in his eyes that pleased her.

Walking back to the cabin hand in hand with Axon, Caitlin wanted to yank his hand and jog but somehow contained her pent-up rash behaviour. She was stunned how aroused they both were by the time they got to their cabin. Inside the room, they battled to close the door, their arms fought to pull from around each other, their lips lost in sweetness, hands busy touching, feeling, caressing and pulling clothing out the way.

Her magic was stronger than ever, and Axon could feel the strum of lust throbbing through him. He had absolutely no control over how she was making him feel. Axon was a man who nearly lost the love of his life, and although he wished to show her she was the only woman in the world, with this much power projected towards him, he didn't know how long he'd last. Not wasting a minute and leaving nothing to chance, he eagerly ripped at his clothes to get naked. Buttons flew across the polished wood floors, and his pants landed on the fan that spun them around. He cared not as he picked up and carried his wife to the bed, and it was here he was able to show her the strength of love that still existed. The sound of his wife panting and the sound of her loving his every thrust made him feel the happiest of men.

* * * *

Caitlin and Axon got up feeling in high spirits. They put on bathers and jogged down to the beach and splashed into the sea. The cold, clean, salty water cleansed their skin leaving goosebumps because it was so fresh. Caitlin flicked water towards Axon, and as he wiped the salty splash from his eyes, she jumped away quickly, enticing a game.

After they had got out, they strolled arm in arm along the sandy shore. The waves lapped at their feet as they walked, chatting comfortably for the first time in many months. Here in this beautiful setting, relaxed and contented with their new-found relationship, Axon shared his heartache over her time spent with Calyx. He confessed how hard it hit him. 'Even though Calyx used magic to get his way with you, I found it so difficult to forgive.'

'I was so innocent, Axon. You were the first man I ever kissed. He was the second, but it was you I came back to, and you I wished to marry. I chose you.'

He found it so therapeutic even to be able to speak to Caitlin about the incident. With her memories back, they were able to work through old hurts from the past years on both sides and heal the wounds. Axon admitted the turning point with his jealousy was this current visit to Pluto. She had just spent more time with Calyx, yet still chose him; this alone silenced many of his fears. Feeling better, he even invited her to talk about her last few weeks with Jett and Calyx.

For the first time ever, he was seeing her as the powerful woman she had become. He hoped she felt comfortable enough with him now to share what was coming up next for her. Her magic was a lot stronger and he wondered why. He had to know where he stood in her future.

'Really, you're okay to talk about everything now?'

'Actually, I'm interested,' he said and smiled.

Caitlin told him about their effort to get her well. She was thrilled to tell him what wonderful friends she had made since living in the heavens.

'Sounds like the pair of them worked hard.' Axon sat with her on the sand.

'They sure did, and to tell you the truth, I was gobsmacked Calyx could cook so well. I mean, he is a King and does play on that everywhere we go. He rarely lifts a finger.' She giggled. 'But to his credit he did well, they both did. Each meal more entertaining than the last, and I swear they put on a comedy show each day just to entice me to eat.' She smiled at the memories.

The examples she gave left Axon astounded two gods would try so hard to get their friend well. Fascinated he kept quiet, enjoying this moment alone with his wife.

'Then eventually, as my health improved, they had me playing board games and cards geared to stimulate my mind. They wanted to keep me thinking. Then yesterday I woke up with a plan, dragged them up to the cabin and it was there they brought me back from the land of mortal life.'

'Mortal; seriously? It did almost come to that!'

She turned on the sand and crossing her legs, faced him. 'Yes, I could feel immortality slipping away. Without them both I would have become human.'

He nodded and in that moment his guard dropped showing his own fear of this happening.

'I figure with how unwell I was, I'd have been lucky to live fifteen or maybe twenty more years, and that would have been without any memory of my past. I would have had to start learning all over again. I can't cook or clean, so I'm not sure what good I would have been to anyone.' She shrugged, 'I can't imagine the burden I'd be on you if they hadn't been able to fix me.'

'I would have cared for you. Never think I only want you because of your powers. They're just a part of you and are not what kept me from your bed at night. It was my ridiculous jealousy, and I am so sorry I hurt you like that.' He held her hands and kissed them. 'I promise that Axon has gone forever. I sent his jealous, sorry arse packing.'

'He'd better be gone, or my guardians will not let you off so easily next time. You have no idea what I went through to visit with you. You have a big bridge to build and lots of humble pie to eat.'

'They're here because they trust you, Cait, I can feel that, but they will soon see I'm true to my word. This stops here and now. I trust you as they do, and no stupid antics will ever have me mistrust my wife again. The goddess...' He smiled. 'That's another story, but Cait, the woman I'm in love with and adore... never again, will any man or any preoccupation stand between us.'

'I'm glad to hear that because you've ruined me for any other man. If Zeus, the god of all gods, couldn't steal me away, no one can.' She giggled, and he laughed heartily with her.

'I know that now, and it makes me feel like strutting around like a goddamned peacock because I'm so happy.' He punched the air and hugged her. 'But they are real friends to you Cait. I see everything so much clearer now, and I give credit where it's due. They stuck by you and did as they promised... gave you back to me healthy and happy. I'm such a fool for not seeing what you mean to them. The relationship between the three of you is unique. I knew, before our wedding day, how special you are to the universe and that I would have to stand aside occasionally and let you do things that ordinary immortals would never dream of doing. Let's face it, you're the Goddess of Peace and with that comes great responsibilities.' He took both her hands and kissed them. 'And because of the job you do, I'll always understand and not judge you ever again. I love you and know I could never live without you. Come home, Caitlin.' His eyes were soft and loving.

'Axon, it's complicated.'

'You're not coming back with me, are you?' He sounded dejected.

'Well, I can spend each night if you don't mind dropping me off and picking me up.'

His eyes lit up. 'For real?'

'You said I could have as long as I needed. For the time being, I must hold you to that. I owe Jett and Calyx big time for getting me well. But not only that, the messages I'm receiving from my heavenly guide are not good. I believe, not only Jett but many planets will be in deep trouble if I don't intervene soon. There's a shift coming of power that is dark and dangerous, and it has to be stopped. Jett must stay the King. I've even pulled Calyx in to help, and fortunately, he has agreed.'

'Then it's big.'

Caitlin nodded. 'But there is hope now for Earth too. Both will, in turn, help me figure out Earth's dilemma.'

Axon was worried, but he was not about to stand in her way and hurt her again. 'I know you're telling me in your own sweet way you want to work alone, without the team. And Rory understands a lot better than me at times.' Axon grinned. 'I must trust in his and your relationship more. It's a bond only you two share; he will never replace you. He's a stubborn shit and says your place is beside him, and always will be. He will never replace you no matter what Zoren or I say. He frowns on our concern for you and ticks me off because he's so sure you'll come back once you accomplish whatever mission you're on. He's happy to wait until you're ready to join them again and the confident sod says you will.'

'Rory's right, I will always come back to him. He is family, but you are home to me and this time when I do come back, I want a baby, Axon. I want us to have a real family after this is done, as you promised me on my wedding night.'

He grinned. 'Mmm keep you barefoot and pregnant in the kitchen. I think we should start right now.' He stood and scooped her up in his arms. 'I can't believe any of this. You're well, I'm here with you and not only have you forgiven your crazy fool husband, but

I'll have you back in my arms again tomorrow night. Pinch me, I'm dreaming.' He spun her around and carried her back to the cabin. 'So if I have to say goodbye in the morning, I want to enjoy every minute of you until then.'

'We have a dinner date with some gods,' she said, and chuckled.

He looked at the sun. 'Not for another two hours.' He ran up the steps and laid her on the bed. The warmth of his body and tingle of magic he projected as he pressed his hardness into her left her weak, and she groaned, melting into his lips as they met hers.

* * * *

When they arrived at the bar to the restaurant, Axon was in such a good mood he even joked with the barman. *This is going to be one hell of a night,* she decided.

Calyx and Jett greeted her.

'My powers are coming back big time. I want to dance and party all night. Shytzer, maybe even blow something up if I'm allowed.'

Jett chuckled. 'We've been feeling you since you left us, Glow.'

She giggled. 'Well if I have to take you both on my journey tonight because you overloaded me with too much of your magic, then you better buckle up, boys because it's going to be one wild ride.'

Calyx kissed the top of her head, leaning close, so his words kept private. 'Then show us what you're made of Cait. We're with you all the way.'

Axon had ordered star shooters all around with Moonjuice chasers so by the time the rest of the family joined them, they had the party started and it was in full swing.

'I can see this is going to be one of those nights.' Razor stood next to Caitlin with his arm around her. 'You're doing this, aren't you happy one.'

She chuckled. 'Me!'

'Yes, you! That power that's thumping through me isn't coming from anyone else... well, I'm up for it. Let your hair down Glow Girl, I haven't had a night like this in a very long time.' He tossed down two Starshooters. 'I'm going to need a lot more than this.' He called to the waiter, 'Bring me the bottle.' His eyes danced.

* * * *

It was close to sunrise when the restaurant closed. The party of three brothers and their wives followed Axon and Caitlin down to sit in the sand on the beach. Caitlin had one more surprise to show them before they went to bed. 'You have to lie back and look up,' she instructed.

'Come on Cait, I hate the sand,' Calyx complained. 'I want to take my sweetie to bed.' He kissed his wife.

'Just do it, brother.' Jett tackled him to the ground.

All lay with their wives looking up at the sky, and Caitlin closed her eyes. She imagined hundreds of small rockets full of fireworks and shot them up into the sky above them. Opening her eyes, she watched them and forced them higher into the night at different levels. She set them off and the night sky erupted with spectacular colours, shooting up and lighting up the darkness above.

'Beautiful, honey,' Axon said as the whizzing colours exploded into smaller lights and lit up for a second and third time. Every rocket was more colourful than the next, each one projecting a sound that floated a melody through the stillness.

When it finished, they cheered. Calyx turned and smiled. 'It's been some night Cait. We're all very pleased your powers are back, but I need some sleep. You'll be right now.' He grinned.

'Sure,' she yawned. Her eyes were already closed.

Axon scooped her up. 'I'm taking my wife to bed. It's been fun, guys, but I have to leave after breakfast in the morning, so I need some shut eye too.'

Jett helped Melita up. 'See you around 10.30 for a late breakfast, Axon. I'm sure Zoren won't be expecting you in too early.'

'I'll get Rory to cover for me,' he grinned.

* * * *

They stayed and had brunch together. Immediately after, Razor and his wife Angel left. Having other commitments, their wives, Melita and Zuri reluctantly said their goodbyes to their husbands soon after. Calyx and Jett looked refreshed, having needed and enjoyed the time with their women more than they'd thought. But needed to hear where Caitlin was at, so both hung back to take a moment with her alone. Seeing Axon was still on the NAVcom to Zoren, they suggested a walk along the sandy water's edge and were pleased when Caitlin agreed. Arm in arm they walked and chatted. It wasn't until they were on the way back that they approached the subject of the next step with them.

'Did you ask Axon if you can help me?' Jett asked.

'Yes, I spoke to Axon yesterday. He'll drop me off on his way to work each day and pick me up after he knocks off. We'll have all day together for as long as it takes.'

Jett picked her up in a big bear hug and spun around with her laughing. 'You're kidding. Really!'

'But!' She put her hand up.

He stopped and put her down. 'What is the *but*?

'Not until tomorrow. I want Intel on Earth. I need to know where Rory and the team are up to with negotiations before I can discuss it with you both.'

'You're kidding. Axon's okay with us working together again.' Calyx had an eyebrow raised.

'Well, he did say to come home when I was ready. I'm not ready.'

Jett hugged her. 'You're the best, Glow. But you did have us worried when you didn't mention anything until I asked just now. We thought we were going to have to beg Axon.'

'Payback for being spa bullies and making me take all the blame for everything, forever.' She chuckled and became serious. 'You can do without me for one more day, yes?'

'Sure. We figured you'd need to grab some Intel about Earth's mission to bring back to us, so that's fine.'

Calyx slapped Jett's back. 'And we have places to be today.'

She put her hands on her hips. 'Without me?'

Calyx ruffled her hair. 'Nothing to do with Pluto, beautiful. The

Heavenly Council has summoned us.'

Jett slung an arm around her as he walked her to Axon who was still on the NAVcom. 'Go and enjoy your last day of rest. For tomorrow we begin... and Glow, believe me, it's not going to be a walk in the park.'

'Mine's not either, so ditto.' She smiled.

CHAPTER NINE

Dwarf Planet Pluto

As promised, on the way to the Alpha Site, the very next day, Axon transported Caitlin to Pluto. He had taken on, Calyx and Jett, as Caitlin's guardians a few years back due to their unlimited powers to track and find her if she got into any trouble. Until now he had not needed them, as Rory had kept Cait by his side refusing to use their help. But today it was time to call on them for a mission as guardians for the first time... his mission, and knew they weren't going to like what he had to say.

Once inside the castle on Pluto, the commander directed them to the dining room, where Calyx and Jett sat waiting for Caitlin. Both smiled and enjoyed the fuss she made of them. Axon shook their hands and surprised them by sitting down with them. 'We need to talk.'

Caitlin shrugged at their questioning looks at her. She'd had no idea he was staying to talk but assumed there were areas of concern that he alone held jurisdiction over.

Axon nodded to the waiter who poured coffee from the elegant silver percolator and handed it to him. He took it without looking up, focusing instead on the two men that sat opposite. 'Not sure what you've got going on Jett, but the way I see it, you have lasted this long without help, and I'm sure it will keep for a little longer. However, my issues won't. So, if you intend to hijack my best Rider and you three really do intend to work together to sort out both Home Worlds,

I insist you make Earth a priority.'

Calyx leant forward. 'Before you continue, Axon, keep in mind that my brother's business affairs were put on hold while he helped Cait recover. Therefore, it's imperative we also start working on his issues, ASAP.'

'I do understand that, but the three of you do still work for me, remember.' Axon pulled out the agreements that were nicely rolled up and tied with thin gold rope. He placed them on the table in front of them. 'I made up these copies in case you forgot what you signed. If you want Cait's help, I'm sorry to say, I come with it.' He took a sip of his coffee, and he could have heard a pin drop. 'Caitlin has been briefed on what I'm about to tell you but I thought I'd wait until I have you three together before giving full disclosure. First, some history.'

They approved with a nod.

'I'm sure you've met Chandra, who is the Queen of the dark side of Earth's Moon.'

Jett shifted in his seat. 'Yes, we know the evil witch Chandra, what of her?'

'Evil through and through,' Calyx added.

'Well, Chandra is not the only criminal involved in the chaos on Earth, but I believe she was the instigator.' He leant back and spoke quietly. 'Many years back, Chandra visited Earth. No one is sure why, but she wandered in the woods near a castle built into the hills. Some say it was to spy on a man who had attracted her, others say the evil queen had it in for him and was looking for a way to destroy him. We will never know. What we do know is that while she was in the woods, she met and befriended Zylon, the God of Woods and Forests. Chandra changed for the better and allowed her sister, Rhiannon's, light of the moon to shine brightly every cycle at his request. This encouraged the animals to come out from beneath the ground. During these hours, she and her immortal lover Zylon enjoyed many hours hunting in the woods he loved so much.'

Jett scoffed, and said, 'For Chandra, it would have been more about the thrill of killing than caring for Zylon. She hates anything living, and knows nothing of love.'

'True. Therefore we cannot fix what the goddess has put into place. The turn of events that follow she does nothing to help, and in fact, she laughs about it.'

Jett raised an eyebrow. 'Let me guess; another woman?' he questioned.

Axon agreed. 'You got it. Far below the Earth's crust, in her own magical kingdom lives Quinesha, Goddess of the Waterfalls. One day while hunting alone, Zylon stumbled across Quinesha and couldn't take his eyes off her. He thought she was the most beautiful goddess he had ever seen. They became good friends, and in time the two women met and became friends too. Chandra never saw Quinesha as a threat, as she believed she was the most beautiful woman in the universe and that Zylon loved her best. She liked having the competition which proved this.

'As time went on, both women competed for Zylon's love. Quinesha supplied sufficient water that ran below the ground, so Zylon could water the woodlands, and Chandra provided the glow of the moon that allowed growth during the night, giving the nocturnal creatures a chance to see their prey and feed.' Axon pushed his empty cup aside.

'Through Chandra's persistence, Zylon slept with her, but he wanted it kept secret from Quinesha. The affair meant nothing and he looked upon it as a fill-in until he could win over the goddess he actually started to have real feelings for. As for Chandra, she never believed for a minute he could be serious about anyone other than her, so she played his devilish game, thinking it fun to sneak around. From that moment on, she came down to Earth on the night of each new moon once she had plunged the world into darkness. Chandra convinced him that under the dark blanket he could be certain the Waterfall Goddess would never see them, and thus never find out. So, the rendezvous continued behind Quinesha's back.'

'That sounds like Chandra,' Jett huffed, 'sorry, not a fan of hers at all.'

Axon nodded and continued. 'Zylon's affair with Chandra

suited him because she never forced him to make a commitment to her. Therefore, he could keep in both goddesses' good graces, thus keeping the life he enjoyed.'

'So what was the problem? Chandra and Zylon were adults. I can't see why Quinesha would destroy the world just because she found out her two best friends were having sex. That's ridiculous,' Calyx said. 'My brother has much more serious issues going on than petty jealousy. '

'Let me finish.' Axon put his hand up. 'One day when Zylon and a couple of his mates were out hunting, they came across Quinesha swimming in a waterfall not far from his home. Up until now, Zylon had never seen Quinesha naked, and she took his breath away. He was stunned by how much he wanted her and not just for sex as he did Chandra. The fact she bedazzled him with her wet golden hair, cream complexion, and bright blue eyes was just a bonus. He had finally fallen in love.'

Axon stopped while Caitlin got up and poured a glass of ice water. When she sat back down, he continued.

'Zylon's two hunting buddies tried to follow her down the river, and the noise they made in a rush to keep up with her gave the maiden a fright. Scared, she called out for help. Zylon answered her plea, not realising his friends were the culprits. He turned them into deer, so he could hunt them later, and show them how it felt.

'Smitten, Zylon wooed Quinesha, eventually winning her over. She had always wanted his devotion, and it was perfect. In a few weeks, he had made her fall as deeply in love with him as he now was with her. He forgot all about his rendezvous with Chandra.'

'The evening of the new moon came, and as Chandra promised, she used the darkness to hide her arrival and came down to reclaim her lover. He still felt for Chandra and like a fool gave in to his desires and made love to her. Quinesha just happened to choose that night to visit him and caught them. The goddesses fought, and when Zylon stepped in to stop the squabble between them, Quinesha felt he was taking Chandra's side and ran from him, ignoring his plea to stay.' Axon paused to take a gulp of coffee.

'And now Quinesha won't forgive Zylon.' Calyx was impatient to get this story over and done with so he could move on to his brother's issues. It sounded so trivial to him so far. He waved his arm amused. 'So enlighten us, what could a mere Goddess of the Waterfall do to cause such a fuss, seriously?'

'Well, the next part had to be kept secret, because you and your family went to war with half the goddamned planets.' Axon bit back. 'It is only through Caitlin's plea you will not take advantage of Earth's weakened state that I'm willing to share the following details.'

'Can't argue about that!' Calyx looked pompous then smiled. 'But for Cait, you have our word not to take gain from this situation… proceed.'

He waved a regal hand for Axon to continue. Caitlin had to hold back a giggle. He was such a god sometimes.

Axon's gaze darted to Cait. He hoped she was right that Calyx, as well as Jett, had changed enough to now trust. He turned back to Calyx. 'Since then, Quinesha has refused to send water to the woodlands and forests to hurt Zylon. The world foliage is dying, and we've been unsuccessful in our efforts to negotiate with Quinesha.'

Caitlin took over when Axon gave her the nod. 'Obviously, Quinesha is heartbroken and won't see reason. I've worked tirelessly on Zylon while both Rory and Axon tried to befriend Quinesha. That didn't work so we swapped, but none of us can get the pair to reconcile or to work it out.'

Axon smiled. 'I didn't know Cait at the time had no powers, yet my girl still managed to have Zylon wrapped around her little finger. However, without the Waterfall Maiden agreeing, nothing has changed. Earth is dying.'

Caitlin frowned. 'I felt for Zylon. He's beside himself, watching everything die around him. His indiscretion has not only destroyed all he has ever treasured, but he has also lost the only woman he has ever loved.'

Axon put his hand over hers. 'You did a fantastic job with him Cait. The guy is now agreeable to whatever we suggest. Since your last contact with Quinesha, we offered to replace Zylon, and he agreed, but this made no difference to her. Whether he stays in the role or goes, she is determined to destroy everything he holds dear, so he can feel real pain too.'

'Relieve her of her position.' Calyx stated what he thought was obvious.

Axon shook his head. 'Quinesha has cast a spell, and it's preventing us from eliminating her. As Earth dies, she becomes stronger and we have not yet been able to penetrate the magic she has used.'

'What about Chandra?' Calyx started to sound aggravated.

'Chandra will not speak to any of us. She is said to be furious that Zylon made a play for someone so dull when he had her. We talked to her twin sister Rhiannon, and she is unable to help either. Chandra has fought her for many aeons. Her plan has always been to destroy the light in all living souls and turn them evil, and Rhiannon believes Chandra has orchestrated this turn of events.'

Before they started to speak about matters of importance, Jett dismissed the staff, so Axon got up and poured a second cup of coffee.

Calyx joined him for a more private discussion. 'I know Zylon. He is a foolish, selfish deity who will never change.' He wanted to try and fix this issue quickly and get back to his brother's difficulties. 'How about I go down there and turn him into the weasel he is? He has never cared for anyone but himself. We thought throwing him into the woods would keep him out of our way. Now he's still causing us grief. This was Zylon's last chance. You may be trying to negotiate with him Axon, but I, as the King of Gods, need to call an emergency meeting and remove him immediately for punishment.'

Axon squinted as he tried to keep his cool. 'As a sworn peacemaker and under my control, you will do no such thing. He is a vital part of getting this sorted. You remove him, and Quinesha will get even angrier that he is not being punished by her. I'm sorry to do this to you, Calyx, but I have no choice but to hold you to your sworn duty to me. You are just going to have to work this out as a team because I want this insanity to stop, but it has to be the old-fashioned way, by negotiation, and before all life on Earth is dead!' He placed his cup down in the saucer louder than he expected. He was really ticked off that Calyx was attempting to use his authority. He turned and spoke to the three of them. 'I have to leave now, and I'm sure I don't have to threaten you with what comes next if you men do not stay loyal to our code.'

He walked over to Caitlin and knelt beside her. 'I'll collect you tonight, honey.' He kissed her lips sweetly, wishing it was him she spent the day with and him that would make her smile, not them. He had missed her so much, but dwelling on it did neither of them any good. Standing, he nodded to Calyx and Jett. 'Keep her safe.' He smiled at Caitlin, said, 'miss you already,' winked and faded from her as he transported to the Alpha Site to meet with Zoren.

Caitlin slumped back against the seat and sighed. 'Sorry guys, if I'd known he was going to be in such a bossy mood I would have got you to pick me up. He's been so strung out about Earth. He was up all hours chatting to Zoren. His boss is pushing hard to get it wrapped up.'

Calyx sat down beside her. 'Axon's really strung out. Bloody... snap my head off... the sod. Good mind to...' He turned to see the look on Caitlin's face and paused. He could never walk away from her. He was just annoyed and sounding off. He had to sort out his feelings towards Axon or every day he dropped her off it would be more of the same. 'Actually, I have an idea how to mend the rift between us.' He turned to Jett. 'Tonight, when Axon comes to get Cait, what if we welcome him with a drink and encourage a boys' night with him?'

'Well, if we have to see him every day he'd better be the old Axon, or he and I will be taking it outside.' Jett breathed out heavily.

'Umm... so pray tell, what is it that I'll be doing while this is going on? Hello! Boobs mean girl!'

'Don't even think about not joining us, Cait. You're our girl, and he's going to have to get used to seeing you with us. I'll put a tee-shirt on you if I have to, but we do this together.' Calyx got up and poured a star shooter. 'Want one, Jett?'

Jett shook his head. 'We can drink later.'

'I suppose so. Just wasn't expecting to be spoken to like one of

Axon's team members.' He sat heavily in the chair. 'Your turn. I'll zip it so you two can talk.'

Jett leant forward with his hands clasped tightly. *How to put this?* If Glow was anyone else she would run screaming to safety, yet he knew her better. She was made of tougher stuff than he had ever come across.

'Come on Jett, you're up,' Calyx prompted him.

Jett chewed on his lip. 'Glow... I admit this first issue might come as a surprise because I've never spoken about the underworld. I certainly haven't taken you there, because I didn't want you scared by the hideous creature that guards the entrance. Actually, he's not hideous to me; he is my pet, and his name is Cerberus.'

'I've read about this guardian of yours. He is a three-headed dog that prevents souls escaping from the underworld.' Her expression dropped. 'Oh, has something happened to him?' He heard the kindness in her tone.

Calyx sat forward. 'Cerberus—what's wrong, is he ill?'

Calyx had the same concerned tone, and Jett realised these two were not just anyone, they were his best friends, and he could tell them anything. Somebody else might have scoffed upon hearing it was a dog that had put him into such disarray. He decided to tell them everything.

'He is alive and well, but not working as he should.'

'Maybe he just needs a good pat and some hugs,' Caitlin suggested. 'They say dogs don't work for money like us, they work for food or love. I guess you feed him well, so it must be the other.'

Jett shook his head. 'Nice idea, and although I admire the simplicity of your thoughts greatly, it's not going to be so easy with Cerberus.' Jett caught Caitlin's frown, and explained. 'He's no ordinary dog, Glow, he is a giant of a dog, called by most a three-headed monster. No one can get near enough to pat him for fear of his serpent mane and a reptile tail that can spike, bite and poison you instantly. His saliva is pure acid, and the barking from his three throats fills even the blessed dead with fear. His sole purpose is to prevent anyone leaving the underworld of the dead. And there lies my problem.' He stood and leant on the ledge, looking into the fireplace. 'Not that I want to frighten you Glow, but affection is not the answer.'

'What is he doing?' She softened her voice.

'Cerberus has missed my presence in the underworld. With my new position as King of the Dwarf Planets, I can't be there every day as before. You have no idea how much I rely on Cerberus and the trouble my absence is causing. He has not only gone off his food but has been letting souls escape. I've been able to retrieve them, but because of it, I've been unable to resume my duties as a King of the Dwarf Planets. Then there is Thanatos.' He shook his head and went quiet.

'Thanatos?'

'You may have read about him Glow.' He turned to her. 'He is the God of Death. Thanatos lives in the underworld and has been helping out, but is annoyed having to cover for Cerberus. The Congress of the Heavens has come down hard on Thanatos, so he has dobbed in Cerberus. Up in arms, they have given me an ultimatum, go back to the underworld full time and give up the planets and my title as king, or sort out my pet.'

'Have you given them an answer yet?' Caitlin blinked. 'Why have they not discussed this with Axon? He has jurisdiction over all your Home Worlds, and I'm sure if he knew he would have sent me here sooner. In fact, the whole team would have been here to support you, Jett. You resign as king at this stage, and it will cause discord throughout the universe. Fights for the position would cause a war. That is not an option. I can't believe they gave such an alternative before looking at all aspects.'

Calyx could see this had upset her and wished her to understand why these matters weren't shared. 'We are not always privy to the backstabbing, and the deals that are done behind closed doors... just like your Earth politicians, Cait. But I assure you, the Congress know what is best. My brother has possibly taken on more than he can handle.'

'Oh phooey!' she snapped. 'Stop taking the easy road, Calyx. Jett loves his new position and has earned it. Isn't that right, Jett?' She swung around and stared at him.

Jett breathed out, was glad she was here while he told his brother. He was greatly influenced by Calyx, but Glow always gave him the confidence to ride the waves and not give in so easily. He had to say something but what? His silence annoyed Glow. The first sign of this was her hair. It started to shine bright red as her temper kicked in. She spun around to Calyx.

'See what you've done! Now he wants to give up!' She threw her hands in the air and sat down, crossing her legs and arms in frustration.

Jett had never heard anyone handle Calyx as Glow did and almost smiled at his gutsy little friend. 'Actually, I had almost given up and am close to my wit's end. If I don't go down there every day, Cerberus sulks and refuses to guard the souls. I've done all I can to reason with him, and so has my wife. Melita has gone down there many times to visit him in my place, but he doesn't relate to her the same way. You see Cerberus, although part monster is also part animal, and this can make it hard for anyone else but me, who he trusts, to communicate or reason with him.'

'I'm so sorry, Jett. I wish I'd known about this sooner.' Caitlin reached over and patted Jett's firmly closed hands.

His shoulders slumped. 'Sad to say that is only one of my problems.'

'Oh?'

'The other is Vador.'

'Is he another underworld pet?'

'I wish, but no, Vador owns Sedna, Quaoar and Orcus, three Ice Planets currently being considered as Dwarf Planets. Vador has made his home on Sedna, and two of his best mates rule Quaoar and Orcus. To cut a long story short, Vador was on board with the change from Ice Planets to Dwarf Planet until I was proclaimed king. He feels this position should not be held by the ruler of the underworld. Vador has made it public that he's after my head and the crown. All my correspondences are met with death threats and he refuses to listen to anything I have to say or offer. And unfortunately, I can't just transport there because his protector will not allow me to enter without permission.'

'Protector!' Calyx scoffed.

'All three of Vador's Ice Planets are guarded by dark destroyers.'

Caitlin frowned. 'Rory has never mentioned them.'

'These creatures are only found living on Ice Planets, our frozen sector of the universe.' Jett waved his hand above them and an image of the mythical creatures formed in the air from the dark smoke. 'You might as well know about them as you are bound to run into them while helping me.' He looked up at the creatures he had formed. 'Being dark by name, they are dark by nature and are attracted to spheres furthermost from the sun. This is why Rory has never told you about them. He may never have dealt with them yet.' He rubbed his brow. He'd never used his magic in front of Glow and trusted she would keep his powers secret as he did hers. He wanted her to see he was so much more than a friend called, Jett. He was a god, and like her goddess side, he was also powerful. He wished her to understand this was not going to be an easy, quick fix, or he would have handled it himself.

Caitlin blinked at the image, pleased Jett finally trusted her enough to show off one of his magical gifts. Until now, he had hidden so much from her. 'You are one surprise package, my friend. Please... continue,' she said while studying the creature.

With a couple of flicks with his fingers, he gave the images more detail. 'As you can see, the ones on the left are hideous winged Furies. They dress in black robes, have blood dripping from their eyes and can turn anyone they choose to madness and eventually death. The ones in the centre are winged screeching Harpies. These are flying monsters that rip you to bits, making everything they touch filthy. Their smell is so ghastly that if they don't kill you, the smell makes you nauseous for the rest of your life. The one on your right is probably the most repulsive of all creatures, the Gorgon. This is the creature that guards Vador's planet, Sedna. This female is hideous. Instead of hair, she has an ugly mane of snakes that covers her entire head. When on the hunt, her head stays the same, but her entire body transforms into a snake-like creature with massive arms and huge claws that easily kill when in battle. The Gorgon is so hideous and cold of heart it turns all those who dare look directly into its hypnotic eyes to stone.'

'Surely, we can transport there and use our muscle to speak to him,' said Calyx.

'Even if we get past the creature, we can't get a lock on where he lives. We are almost certain he has a hidden fortress deep underground for us not to be able to find him. We can't get eyes on his Ice Planet because the NAVblocker they must be using, blurs all the imagery that feeds back to us.'

'What about heat or movement sensors.' Calyx crossed his arms listening.

'Same, the display is black, we get nothing.

'He must be one clever techno super-wiz.'

'Recently I gave the okay for another team of men, the best I had this time, to go in and source his home base, but unfortunately, it turned out badly for those that went. The beastly Gorgon found, captured and turned the covert teams to stone.' He fidgeted and chewed his lip before speaking again. 'So you can see why I wanted to give up. I was losing men, good men and the rest of the time I was chasing souls who kept escaping. And not good ones either, the worst kind of criminals found the glitch and are taking advantage of it and escaping out in droves. Even now I'm not sure what you can do about any of this, Glow, but I wanted to see if that simple logic of yours would help me sort this mess out.'

Calyx put his hand over and grabbed his arm. 'You are my brother and my best friend and from now on I want you to come to me, but be honest. You asked me when you first had issues if I could spare you some time and I said I was too busy. Thought like me, you were just missing Glow. As for your royal status, never for a minute think I am not proud of you, because I am and even if Cait can't, I will help in any way I can.'

'I appreciate that Calyx. For so long I retreated, thinking I was on my own and got myself into a real state. I see now I should have gone to you both and explained what was really going on instead of sending mixed messages and when no one responded, withdraw from you all.'

Calyx gave him a supportive nod. 'We are here now and hearing you loud and clear. As for that NAV3 ruler, Vador, he will have an audience with you, or I will bring him down myself.'

Caitlin stifled a chuckle. 'A stone body would at least keep you out of trouble.'

Both stared at Caitlin, and Jett recoiled. 'Glow this isn't a joking matter. Your reaction is childish.'

Calyx turned to her annoyed, 'This is serious Cait, and if you can't be in tune with the gravity of the situation then maybe we shouldn't be discussing it with you.'

She stood up with hands on hips. 'Okay Mr personality plus, if that's how you feel I'll leave you to it. Shytzer! You and Axon could sure use a dose of loosening up pills. Since this morning I've had Axon acting all pigheaded, and now you both carry on like you're the only ones with the weight of your Home World on your shoulders. I can't think straight with so much male testosterone going on. I mean, that poor dog has spent forever down there with only one friend. Now that friend is missing for days, weeks. I hear no compassion; all I hear is that he is ruining your life. Blah Blah Blah! Well, I think the dog has worked hard all these centuries and deserves at least one entitled melt-down.

She flipped her hair back over her shoulder. 'As for that suitor for the crown, who hides behind hideous creatures of darkness, him, I will deal with when the time comes.' Cait breathed out and turned her attention to Jett. 'I would not be standing here offered my time if I didn't think you, Jett, capable of this magnitude of a task.' She glanced at them both. 'I think you're both just grumpy because Axon growled at you this morning and ordered you about. So, when you feel like discussing this without all the goddamned emotional bull, come and get me. I'm going outside to enjoy at least some of my morning and take a swim in your heated pool.' She flounced off and swung the double doors open, not bothering to close them after her.

Outside Caitlin removed her clothes, and as always, a swimsuit appeared on her body. Pleased her magic was working just fine, she looked forward to beginning her day with these men, sorting through the disputes at hand...but not until they brightened up. No way would there be an action plan given by her until these pigheaded men got a grip on their macho attitudes. In the headspace they were in, they would never have the magic she felt they needed as a team. They would have to summon up a potent mix from a powerful three, to not only help Jett, but to sort out Axon's problem too. She imagined them inside working it out alone and smiled, knew they needed her and she couldn't wait to start work on it, but not yet. When they did come out, she needed them to be walking in the light with her. *Or those bad boys can march straight back inside again.*

Caitlin dived in. The water was lovely and warm from the heating Jett had installed. She did a few laps before lying back and resting on the step. Her gaze wandered up towards the roof of the dome covering his castle and its surroundings. The joy of designing and choosing the perfect colours for the ceiling flooded back. She remembered all the planning and then the colour charts they went through to have the dome painted to give the effect of blue sky with white fluffy clouds. The lighting had to be correctly positioned too, making it look like sun rays bursting through the cleverly formed 3D placed clouds. Her mind drifted to the day spent on Dolphin Island. The memory of blue sky, humid weather and the loveliness of their surroundings while spending it with their partners still lingered.

Caitlin assumed Jett and Calyx hadn't forgiven her, or they would have come out by now, but she was enjoying this time to relax and had no intentions of giving in either. She closed her eyes. Her thoughts drifted to the underworld... what was it like? The image of Jett's dog with the three heads had her fascinated. The first thought that came to mind was which head to pat on meeting Cerberus. If you had a bone for him, to which mouth would you offer the treat? And if you didn't pick the alpha head first, would it bite you for getting it so wrong? She chuckled silently at her own stupid thoughts, visualising the fun Jett must have with him. If he only took down one ball, when he tossed it to them, would the other two heads snarl, snap, and get cross at the one that did catch it? *Stop it!* She gave another chuckle. It suddenly crossed her mind that Jett may be listening. She stopped her thoughts in case he found her insensitive again for finding Cerberus amusingly fun to think about. *I want to see him.*

Laughter came from inside. She opened her eyes. It sounded as if they were happy. She heard footsteps coming towards the door that led to the patio. She watched intently, hopeful she was off the hook and forgiven. If they were the ones giving in, it showed her they did respect her and would work well together. There would be lots to forgive one another for in the future.

Jett looked happier, but he said, 'No, you're not off the hook. You must stop thinking. Otherwise Calyx wants to know what is going on and why I keep smiling, which causes us to lose track of our thoughts. Unlike you, miss-lay-around-in-the-pool... we are trying to have a serious conversation in there.'

'Well, I want to go visit Cerberus,' she whined.

'Cerberus is not a priority, remember. Axon will want a proposal presented tonight on how we three are going to tackle the Earth issues at hand as a team. Calyx and I have to work on this first.'

'But aren't I part of your team? Should I not help?'

'How about you hop out and we can discuss it.' Calyx held out a towel to her. 'I know the way you think, and I shouldn't try to intimidate you or force you to change. I'm just not used to having you in the business side of the relationship.'

'Nor am I used to working with you.'

'I guess I can be a bully and that behaviour, I promise to stop. You have my attention. I don't want to argue with you any longer,' Calyx assured her.

'You're not so scary. I mean I don't even use magic on you anymore. But I can tell you now,' she smiled. 'It was a different story when we first met. You were one massive drain on my magic and a huge big handful.' She poked him. 'Just promise me you will try and relax. Jett, I get; he is freaking out. But I'm relying on you to keep him calm until this quest is over. Look, I'm sure all you both need is a nice outing.'

'With our partners again?' Calyx winked. 'I think I'm going to enjoy working with you.'

Caitlin chuckled. 'Not this time, Romeo. We're on a mission, and today we should check out Jett's puppy and Earth's goddess... and I want you to behave.' She eyed Calyx before turning to Jett. 'What do you think, Jett? Feel like getting out of here for a while and introducing me to Cerberus? Then we can go and see what we are up against on Earth. Let's face it, we can't even begin to structure our time if neither of us has had a peek at the other's problems.'

Jett screwed up his lips. 'Are you positive you're up to my side of things? I mean, less than an hour ago you seemed... well, angry. Cerberus will pick up on that emotion straight away. Maybe we should leave him until tomorrow.'

'You mistake feisty for angry. You see, when I work I draw on the light to find answers, and your darkness was blocking me at every turn. The humour was me trying to ignore the pain in your voice and counteract the negativity of those visual creatures you showed me. They filled the room with thick, murky black ink. So to refrain from giving you the wrong impression and annoying you in future, I promise to stay quiet until the mood changes or we leave. It is then I should be able to come up with something sensible you can use.'

Jett put his arm around her. 'You don't need to refrain from anything. You were right. We did get annoyed at Axon, and it did change our mood. In future, we are the ones who will refrain from smothering you with our darkness and let your light shine a little more. You were also correct about me being freaked out, and I shouldn't be. I have the strongest god and goddess working alongside me. Forgive us, Glow.'

'Forgiven!' She smiled. 'So... can we go now?'

* * * *

An hour later they were ready. Caitlin dressed in a simple but elegant sundress and sandals. Both men wore three-quarter pants with summer shirts and loafers. They had dressed as Caitlin suggested as it was hot on her part of Earth this time of year. First stop was to see Jett's dog Cerberus, so she put on a thick bearskin coat and boots to wear while in the cold cave.

CHAPTER TEN

The Canine Cerberus

'Cait, what are you doing now?' Calyx called out, impatient to get going.

'Hang on, one minute.' She ran into the galley pantry to look for something she could offer the dog as a treat. On the bottom shelf, she found individually wrapped honey cakes. She shoved these in her pocket, not willing to share what she was doing in case they thought her crazy. 'Ready!' She skidded to a halt between the men.

Jett transported the three of them to just inside the entrance to the realm of the dead, referred to as the underworld. He put his arm around Caitlin as they walked into the tunnel to the cave. 'Cerberus is unpredictable,' he coached her. 'So if you feel nervous or scared as everyone does when they see him, think *out*, and I'll transport you from here immediately.' He was concerned, yet excited. Having Caitlin meet his pet was a big deal to him. The worry was for Caitlin, as it might not go as well as she anticipated. He thought her a little delusional when hearing her think honey cakes would win Cerberus over. He smiled, amused, yet he hoped it worked and he silently wished her luck that her gentle way could work on that degree of evil. *It did with me!*

In the depth of the cave, it was dark until Jett waved his hand in the air. Flames lit up along each side of the corridor. Deep-throated growls came from the darkness ahead. It was eerie and uncomfortable on Caitlin's ears. Jett had warned the dog's bark was frightening so she ignored its noise and proceeded. She intended to meet Cerberus, and no number of wild ear-piercing howls would prevent it. Once they were in the mouth of the room, it lit up with flamed lanterns placed around the walls. A monstrous shape that almost touched the ceiling cowered in the corner, snapping and growling. Jett spoke a command with authority to calm the noise and, recognising his master, Cerberus came out from the shadows to welcome Jett. He stood tall as the heads moved to look from Calyx to Caitlin.

'Cerberus! You know Calyx. Now settle,' Jett said in a firm voice.

Caitlin noted the change of Jett's tone. It was the god, Hades that spoke to his pet. Her heart pumped at the enormity of this beast that stood before them. The dog had three heads as she had been told, but she hadn't known how abnormally large they were compared to its body. On seeing someone new, the snakes on his mane stood up and hissed. The reptilian tail sprang above the dog's middle head and paused, both snakes and tail ready to strike her. She didn't dare move while it was in a battle stance.

'Cerberus, have some manners. This is my friend I've been telling you about, Glow Girl... Glow this is Cerberus, guardian of the underworld.'

The dog body didn't flinch. The massive claws stretched and protruded from its paws. Caitlin wasn't making a great first impression. She realised Cerberus blamed her for his master's change in routine and looked ready to pounce and kill. And yet, there was something in its eyes when looking at its master, Hades that made the creature less terrifying. Caitlin smiled and breathed in deeply.

Jett and Calyx felt Caitlin's power as she decided to take control. Never had they felt it so strongly. Both fought the initial impact of magic and glad when she directed it entirely at Cerberus and not them.

Jett and Calyx relaxed when released. It was only then they realised she drew power from them to strengthen hers.

'She grows stronger every day,' Calyx whispered.

'And smarter.' Jett read her mind. 'We need to support her in times like this. Glow has seen something and has called on the power of the universe to help her understand Cerberus. She's seen what I'm unable to.' Jett smiled at his friend. The goddess had this, but he would stay close in case he was needed.

They watched as her goddess fragrance, now strengthened by the power of the three of them, had Cerberus dropped down on his belly. The serpent's mane flopped each side of his body and his tail that had been above ready to strike her regardless of Hades' strong influence, slumped flat behind him.

'Did I imagine it, or does he look friendly?' Calyx whispered to Jett who nodded in agreement.

'Now, that's better.' Caitlin stepped towards Cerberus. When there was no movement, one hand went up to the heads of the dog. 'Now stay!' The voice she used had much authority. She had almost imitated Hades and had it down pat. Her other hand slowly reached into her pocket.

Cerberus moved a fraction and once again she commanded the creature. 'I said, stay!' Slowly she removed three pieces of honey cake, and, bringing her other hand down, she began unwrapping the first one. A slight movement had her call out in a short, sharp tone, 'Ah!' And once again Cerberus stopped fidgeting. The first cake uncovered went on her now gloved hand. Caitlin had remembered Jett say the dog's saliva was acid. Her magic allowed her to call up the gloves she wore as a Rider. The foreign material made it safe enough to complete her next task.

Holding her hand between them, she banked on the alpha head taking the first cake. A pecking order had to be maintained if she was ever to communicate efficiently. The middle head was Alpha, and it gently removed the cake from the palm of her hand. The right took the next unwrapped cake and then the left. All three waited patiently, and it confirmed to her that Cerberus was a very intelligent and well-trained beast. Hades had done a marvellous job with him. The three heads looked so different that it was as if they were from three different animals.

The last dog was so excited some drool escaped as he took his piece and she pulled her hand back quickly, so the acid missed her arm. She said, 'Careful there doggy, you don't want to hurt me now, do you?' She waited until the last head finished eating and when it lay flat like the other two now did, she patted the Alpha head. 'You're the toughest and biggest, the ruler no doubt.' She spoke quietly. 'You embody the present. The name Cerberus suits you, fella.' She scratched his nose.

She patted the head on the left. 'So, you embody the past. Therefore you should have your own name. You look to have conquered much in your time. I might call you Tymur. You like that?' She scratched his nose after she got a goofy smile and moved to the next.

Last was the head on the right. 'You embody the future. You need a name that means long life because that is what I wish for you. I will call you Juro.' His head swung to look at the other two and dropped suddenly when Caitlin stepped back from him. 'Juro, I know you're excited, but you have to remember your size compared to mine.' She scratched his nose and standing straight she looked at them all. 'So, you have your names, but I'll shorten them so I can call them out quicker.' She tickled each on the nose as she said their new names, 'Ty, Cerb and Juro,' and then stood back to give them room. They panted happily. 'See, you feel better already, don't you? How can you all be friends and keep each other company if you all have the same names?'

She moved back, taking Calyx and Jett with her. They had still not left her side. She turned back to the dogs. 'Now, stand up and show me how you play. She lifted her hands up above her head enticing them to stand up. 'Now play!' she ordered them.

The dog's heads just looked at each other. Caitlin encouraged a playful manner.

'Ty, give Juro a kiss.' He just looked at her, turning his head a little confused.

She turned and licked Jett on the cheek. Jett wasn't expecting it and wiped his cheek and chuckled.

Ty bent his head under Cerb and gave Juro a lick. Juro shook his big head and licked Cerb who then licked Ty back. They went silly and rolled around the floor playing and nibbling at one another's ears and licking faces. They had never been taught to play with each other. They were so rough that Jett snatched her out the way a couple of times when they got too close in the tussle.

She pulled away from him and picked up a stick from the ground. As it flung into the air, she called out for Cerb, who flew up in the air after it and grabbed it with his large mouth. He made it look like a small twig between his massive jaws. It made her laugh. Her happiness had him toss it in the air, and she yelled out for Juro, who snatched it up but broke it. Picking up another, she called for Ty and as this one was a branch, they fought over it, ripping it to shreds. Jett had to keep moving her. When she was sure they got what she meant by playing, she clapped her hands and called out, 'drop!'

The dog's body collapsed on its stomach, and the heads followed, puffing and excited. They wanted more. Ty couldn't settle, and head-butted Cerb. 'Ty, behave,' she giggled at him. 'You're the naughty one, aren't you?'

'Cerb you're the boss, and you must make him behave. He's holding all your past and will want to play all the time to forget.'

She patted Juro. 'You are the future and can change it if you want to. Make it happier, so your brothers don't feel so sad. Can you do that, boy?' She scratched his nose.

She stood back. 'Do you want me to come back tomorrow to show you some more games?'

They jumped back on their feet, panting. Caitlin chuckled. 'See you in the morning and don't forget your new names because I'll be testing you when we come back.'

She turned to walk out, but Cerberus wanted to follow.

Jett growled a command, and it stopped and sat still. At the mouth of the cave, he helped her remove the thick fur coat and threw it onto a hook. 'Guess where you're taking us, you won't need this.

Caitlin smiled and shook her head while kicking off the boots. Feeling inside one of the pockets in the oversized fur coat, she retrieved her sandals and slipped them on. 'I will need these, though.'

Jett stood smiling. 'Now, explain, how did you do that? You

were amazing in there. When you told us to calm down, and we'd see how simple it was, I didn't have faith in you fixing anything that fast. Well, I stand corrected. You're damned good, girl!'

'Good, she's extraordinary.' Calyx put his arm around her and gave Caitlin a gentle squeeze. Letting her go he held her cold hands together in his to warm them. 'Okay, it's way too cold for you to stand here chatting, where to next?'

Caitlin unfolded a piece of paper she held and passed it to Calyx. 'These are the coordinates Rory wanted me to show you first.'

Calyx pulled a NAVscan from his pocket, punched in the first set of coordinates and tapped the window to enlarge the details. 'Got it.' He put an arm around Caitlin and Jett to transport them there.

Jett winked, and said, 'thanks, Glow.'

'Don't thank me yet. Let's just wait until we see if it works. Just in case it doesn't, remind me to call into a pet market while we're on Earth?'

'Sure,' Jett said, noting her mind was hiding the purchase she wished to make.

'Ready!' Calyx shook his head wondering what she was up to now. *No pet store in the universe had a toy big enough for Cerberus to play with.* His amusement quickly sobered upon seeing Caitlin's face drop.

'Earth will shock you, so be forewarned.' For moral support, she held them tight.

CHAPTER ELEVEN

The Water Maiden

Moments later Caitlin, Calyx and Jett appeared on Earth, standing on a high mountaintop. The devastation of their surroundings had them drift into reality as they soaked in the smell of death. The three of them linked arms and stood to stare out at the barren land. All that was left were withered stems, the remains of trees and shrubs, which stuck out from dusty dry dirt. There was not a living plant or tree for as far as the eye could see. There were no sounds of birds singing, bees humming nor was there rustling in the bush from animals that scurried to find food and water. Sun-bleached carcases and bones protruded from the windswept sand, left from animals that died of starvation and thirst.

'There's nothing left but death and silence.' Tears ran down Caitlin's cheeks. 'It's worse.'

'Is the entire world like this, or are some countries still thriving?' After taking a neatly ironed and folded sudarium from his top pocket, Jett mopped up her tears.

She nodded. 'Rory gave me a couple more locations to look at, but I envisage they are no different. It's only cities and towns living adjacent to the ocean are doing okay. They are using a new technique which turns sea water into fresh, clean, drinking water only it came too late for those inland. The countryside is gone. Those that could make it to the coast have overpopulated the cities and towns. Demand is not being met and water is liquid gold to those living. Crime is the bigger issue. The military has taken over and although they have introduced a curfew, the looting and break-ins are still out of control. We believe this is only a temporary fix and is not working in many areas. The governments must know, as we do, that with the lack of oxygen, food, water and the way the world is heating up, it's only a matter of time before these cities die too.'

Calyx wiped his forehead. 'It's heating up all right. It must be fifty degrees Celsius here.'

Without warning, the earth under them began to shake. 'This is happening all over the world. Without the trees and their roots that keep the ground stable, landslides are taking out entire villages. Axon helped relocate the families who would leave. He even took the surrounding wildlife so they could live as normally as possible.'

'Where did he take them?' Jett's eyes swept the nothingness.

'He moved them to his Home World, Ara. That's why he's so exhausted and why we barely get to see each other. The stubborn ones that were unwilling to leave were moved on by the military and taken to the coastal areas. They're forced to live in camps set up by the governments. The families, who couldn't handle losing everything, hide. At night you see them in parks and alleyways. Those caught after dark now are herded into camps where at least they can keep them safe.' Tears trickled down her cheeks again. 'We did our best to help, but it was crazy down here. Just to call a town meeting took days to organise. In some outback towns with farmers, it took weeks to gather them together, so Axon could transport them away from the hot spots. The problem is, Axon's Home World villages are now overrun and to make matters worse the Earthlings refuse to work because they want to come back here, but to what?' She shrugged. 'They won't listen to reason. They cause trouble by fighting and stealing and treat Axon's villagers like slaves. Not having the powers to fix this yet breaks my heart.'

'Cait you should have come to me, to us sooner. We had no idea.' Calyx hugged her as she sobbed.

'Come on Glow, you have your power back, and us.' Jett handed her the sudarium again. 'Show us what we need to see and then take us to the culprit. Do what you need to, and let's make this right. Get those selfish people back here as soon as we can. My brother can wipe their memories of Axon's world. Let the fools figure it out alone for being so ungrateful.'

'I can't believe how unappreciative they are.' She sucked in a breath and shook off the sadness, feeling better after Jett's encouraging words. She turned to Calyx, and said, 'let's move to the next coordinates. This spot here is not only depressing, but the earth under us feels unstable.'

Changing location did nothing except make them realise this was one mammoth task ahead. Each landing was significantly worse than the last. The drought had caused massive issues worldwide. With no water to put them out, fires still burned in some areas, ravaging the land, leaving it black and steaming with smoke.

'I get it now, Caitlin. I don't need to see any more.' Calyx shook his golden locks; his bright blue eyes were dark and hidden behind a mask of uneasiness. 'I understand now why Axon was so insensitive this morning. I'm serious, Cait, I want to help and will work day and night beside you to assist in any way I can. If this is what your husband's been dealing with, it's a no-brainer why he and Rory tried to keep you tied to them. I would be freaked out too.'

'Me too,' Jett agreed. 'Axon and I were, and still are, dealing with things out of our control. We both looked to you, Glow, to fix them. And here you were, powerless to help either of us. You must believe me; none of the other planet rulers knew it was this bad down here. Axon has kept so tight-lipped about his work. I guess he felt the rest of us had enough on our plates with our own Home World issues. I'm glad you've both let us back into your life. I'm with Calyx on this, let's fix Earth first, as this must stop. Earth is important to the universe, and we cannot let it die. '

'That is true, but you've already put your own issues on hold for far too long. I am healed, and we can do both,' Caitlin reasoned.

'Maybe, but with all this death and heartache it flickers your light. I see it now, in your eyes. This is strong magic doing this and made stronger because it's mixed with so much hatred. Even our godly powers couldn't fix what is happening here, not alone, anyway.'

Caitlin reached out, and each took one of her hands. 'Only together working side by side can this be sorted if it's at all possible.'

'Together,' Calyx agreed.

'Together,' Jett repeated. His worry lines and sincerity turned into a cheeky grin, 'And after I will have you both to myself to help save my title.'

'That's the plan brother; so let's get this done,' Calyx chimed in.

Jett grinned and punched knuckles with him.

'With that said, my plans have already begun, and as much as I appreciate your loyalty to work on Earth first, with you both by my side, I can function proficiently on both our issues, no matter what, "flickers my light".' She used inverted commas in a gesture while saying it, and grinned.

'Well here's hoping lover boy sticks to his agreement. Guaranteed if it takes a bit longer than he expects we will surely be back in the doghouse,' Calyx said.

'No, not me!' Jett shook his head. 'Put you back in the dog house. I did nothing wrong. We were friends until you kissed Glow. Axon put me at arm's length only because I was your brother.'

Calyx put his arm around him. 'I kidnapped her for a few days. You kept her on Pluto and away from him for many months. Don't act the innocent one here. Axon put us both at arm's length, but now he's let us back in, let's not stuff it up by arguing whose fault it was. We need all the energy we have to help Cait save this planet. I would like to be back in his good books.' He dropped his arm from Jett.

The corner of Jett's mouth twisted into a smile as he eyed Calyx. 'I guess I have to agree. But in our defence, it was in the days when nothing was more fun than causing terror and discord. That was until Glow, here, made us see our wicked ways.'

She teased, 'you're both still a pair of bad-arses… but loveable.'

Calyx threw his head back and laughed. 'You mean we don't fool you for a minute.'

'Nope, but you are beautiful to me and have my heart.'

It was Zeus who addressed her. 'You have my heart, and it does sing to be with you, Cait, but don't let it mislead you. My soul holds the memories of my past that cannot be changed. Wicked to the core is my makeup. Love for you keeps it at bay. But let anything happen to you, or let Axon try to hide you from us again, and I swear, evil will come out to play.'

'Hear, hear!' Hades faced him.

He was back too. Caitlin knew it was the surroundings triggering off the dark side in them. She touched both on the arm in a light grip.

Hades disappeared first. 'So let's not take any chances of that happening. It's time we got back in his good graces and have him trust us with Glow, permanently. Let's go visit this Goddess of the Waterfall and see if we can offload some of our wickedness to fix this.'

'Agreed,' Calyx said.

Caitlin released them. 'I agree too, only there are rules if you want to be with me while I work. All past is forgotten, and all that matters is right now.'

Jett smiled. 'So none of us is married, etc.—etc.'

'So, if I kiss you on said mission and you are single, it is okay, and Axon will not mind.' Calyx gave her a nudge.

'There will be no kissing anymore.' Then she tilted her head and screwed up her lips expressing a thought. 'That is of course unless the job requires us to act like boyfriend and girlfriend. Then it is pretend kissing, not real.'

Both men laughed at her changing her mind from no kissing to maybe some kissing. 'Admit you love us too,' Calyx stirred.

'She loves us too, brother, and now it's time we made a move.' Jett tried to change the topic, but Calyx wasn't ready.

'You must see, she's done it again. Made us both look forward to what lies ahead. Maybe a kiss...' Calyx let his voice trail off. Then he grinned when he saw her unamused stance. 'Come on Cait. Just stirring, I'll shut up, I promise. Now, where is this maiden I have to woo to get you off my mind?' He chuckled and pretended to lock his mouth up.

'Better.' She stayed stern to calm Calyx. He may as well get it all said now because for what she had in mind, there would be kissing.

'If you've both finished having your fun; the Waterfall Maiden, Quinesha, lives in her magical realm below us.'

Calyx wasted no more time and transported them to the Maiden's home. The vision as they appeared was the opposite of what they saw on the surface. The birds flew overhead, the plant life grew lush, plentiful and the precious atmosphere burst ripe with energy and life.

'Over there.' Caitlin pointed to the waterfall.

Quinesha frolicked in the water. Spotting them, she waved. 'Hi Cait,' she called out. She swam like a delicate swan and, reaching them, walked out of the water, instantly dried as she moved. Her golden-glossy hair hung way past her waist, big uncertain eyes shone from the healthy tanned skin and the skimpy bikini of nature's vines only just covered her feminine attributes.

'She is delightfully beautiful,' Calyx whispered and smiled brightly at her when she came close. He was immediately taken by the maiden and stepped towards her, offering his hand. 'Hope you don't mind this intrusion, but my brother and I are from off-world and asked if we could meet one of Earth's goddesses. My name is Calyx, and this is Jett. Caitlin told us she personally knew Earth's Waterfall Maiden, but she didn't say how beautiful you were.'

She giggled sweetly, and her head hung shy and slightly to the side. 'So lovely to meet you and your brother.' She shook their hands and turned to her friend. 'Cait, what a surprise. Rory said you were elsewhere and couldn't come to visit me. He didn't tell me you were back. I've missed you. There is so much I wanted to confide in you.' Her voice was melodious and angelic.

Caitlin leant towards her, and they hugged for a short few seconds. When Caitlin stood straight and spoke, her sexy tone surprised the men. It didn't sound like their innocent Glow Girl at all. 'I was off-world having a break with a new beau. I missed you as well, but the only way I could get here was to be transported. Well, my beau isn't a ruler so when his brother turned up this morning I was thrilled. You see, he is the ruler of a little Ice Planet on the edge of the solar system; so small it hasn't even been named yet.'

Quinesha put a hand to her mouth and chuckled. Caitlin did the same and reached out and held her other hand. 'I know, fancy being an unknown.' They both laughed again. Feeling the thunderous undertones of his vibes, Caitlin didn't continue, so as not to tick Calyx off too much. She knew her next move would have him really irritated. This would keep him cross enough not to care what she did. *Gods can be so sensitive.* Happy with how it was going she continued, 'So I hope you don't mind me bringing them both.'

'Which one is your beau?' Quinesha's eyes lit up.

'This one.' Caitlin pulled Jett in and gave him a hug and Quinesha a wink. 'They are both very handsome, don't you think?'

Quinesha nodded as she eyed off Calyx, yet kept quiet and expressionless, so Caitlin continued, unsure of her thoughts.

'I was thinking… if you're not too busy, we could get Calyx to transport us somewhere for a drink.' She waved her hand towards Calyx and Jett. 'Those two can go play pool and amuse themselves and allow us time to catch up and have a chat. I'm sure you can't wait to find out what else I've been up to while holidaying off-world?' She sounded so sexy and worldly even the men were sucked into her enticement and wanted to hear what she had been up to. They'd had no idea Caitlin could make up stories of a colourful life. But they did now. 'What do you think?'

Quinesha bounced on tippy toes over to Caitlin and wrapped delicate arms around her in a genuinely friendly manner. 'That is exactly what I need, my friend. I enjoyed it so much when we did this last time. I feel I've been stuck here forever. I'd love to come.' The goddess sang with happiness. 'Come. You three can sit and talk while I change.' She held onto Caitlin, guiding her through the thick brush to her home. 'Won't be long!' She left them to enjoy the very much alive fairy garden while she went to change.

Her home was a cave dug into the side of a mound of dirt. They sat in furniture carved from the same trees that surrounded them. The mouth of the cave was covered in soft vines with pretty purple and pink flowers. As she walked through, the vines opened for the lovely maiden and then closed behind her. *Who could believe she could cause so much devastation and destruction in her wake.*

When she came out, instead of heading off, Calyx asked if she could walk them through her picturesque garden.

'Sure!' She was happy to oblige, proud to show off her underground paradise.

Caitlin knew it was Calyx's way of getting to know her better, which would make it easier to magically manipulate her. With luck, he'd overpower her and find what magic spell was used so he could reverse it. They looked comfortable together as they walked in front of Jett and Caitlin. If Quinesha didn't have hold of his arm, Calyx held her hand. If she looked back, Jett played the loving partner well. He had Caitlin laughing as he spoke in an alluring manner and, she stared into his eyes as if he was the only man alive.

Quinesha observed Caitlin carefully, so she had a lot of acting to do. Suddenly Quinesha began to glow brightly.

Calyx stared back at Caitlin. Quinesha was about to work out what he was doing if he didn't stop. She was too powerful. Caitlin saw it and nodded in response.

She used telepathy to alert Jett. *She doesn't realise it yet, but the glowing is her inner senses trying to block the power Calyx projects. She's too strong here in her own environment. Let's get this party on the road to see if a few drinks can soften her and help Calyx gain the upper hand.*

Jett winked in response.

Caitlin left him and went up beside Quinesha. 'Are you ready to come and have some girl time? I think the men have stolen enough of our day.'

'Oh Caitlin, I'm so sorry! I was enjoying having company so much the time has slipped by me.' She turned to Calyx. 'Hope I haven't bored you.'

'Not at all, I have hung on your every word. You are enchanting.' He kissed the hand he held before letting it go.

'Oh!' She blinked, apparently surprised. 'You are such a gentleman.'

Calyx gave Quinesha the warmest smile and moved over to stand with Jett. He whispered. 'No go brother,' and turned back to

Caitlin and said loudly, 'where to, Cait?'

While Quinesha tended to some flower maintenance she just couldn't ignore. Caitlin moved over to the men and acted overly excited about the day ahead to encourage the goddess to get a wiggle on. The day was slipping away and they needed as much time as they could get with Quinesha, to figure her out. 'How about we head to the mainland where there is a pub I'm sure we will all enjoy. It overlooks the Pacific Ocean. Downstairs is cosy, there is always a band and the food is delicious. Oh, and for you guys, they have pool tables with competitions running around this time every day.'

Calyx eyed her with an angry glint in his eyes. 'Watching you two made me want to kick my brother's arse so it may as well be at a game of pool instead,' he murmured so only they could hear.

She pinched her lips in a smile. 'It could be you next, so stop being such a spoilsport.'

Calyx gave her a stunning smile before turning back to Quinesha. 'Are you ready, beautiful?' He sounded so caring. All jealous tones were gone. Caitlin had to stifle a chuckle.

'Sure am.' Quinesha grinned.

* * * *

They appeared at the side of the pub where there was no one in sight to make their sudden arrival a spectacle.

'That was clever of you, Calyx. How did you know where to land so not to get caught?' Quinesha asked.

'I have an app on my NAVcom. I looked at it while I spoke to Cait. There were heat images front, back and in the car park, but nothing this side. I would like to take credit but it's just smart technology.'

'Well, I think you are brilliant to think of it.' She twisted strands of hair into a curl and smiled up adoringly.

At the front entrance, Jett opened the door to the Pint and Pickle pub. Both women clutched an arm as they navigated their way down the steep stairs in high heels. It was dark for only moments until curious eyes adjusted. A band was on stage playing a rock and roll number. The fast-paced music had a few patrons on the small dance floor doing a jive. The pub was busy but not overly packed, so they found a booth empty and sat together. There was a disco ball in the middle of the room flickering and sending lights around them. It enticed Quinesha, who had never been there before, to jig to the tune and smile happily. Caitlin pointed to the far side of the room where many of the men played pool and darts. 'It looks like a competition,' Caitlin commented as she listened to what was being said over the PA system.

Jett and Calyx couldn't get over there fast enough.

Jett whispered to Caitlin, 'If you need me, you know how to get my attention.'

Telepathy, she thought, and he nodded and left.

Caitlin had been without powers for so long, she felt wired and needed this more for her than Quinesha. Since Calyx and Jett had helped her regain lost powers, her perception was stronger than ever. She smiled inwardly. She felt good and was ready to take on this goddess opposite her, head on. *As a peacekeeper, of course*, her inner voice said as it kept her in check.

'So how have you been?' Caitlin started off the conversation when the musicians stopped for a break.

Quinesha reached over and clasped her hand. 'I have been miserable until today. You make me feel happy just being with you, Cait. I wanted to tell you so much but don't want to spoil the mood by rehashing old ground. Instead, will you drink with me and allow me to enjoy this moment? I want to dance, play pool and find new love.' The band had stopped playing, but she was so into the moment she swayed to the soft music that played in the background. Caitlin was chuffed at the apparent rapport they had. Quinesha looked at her as a real friend. But friend or not, she had to bring this goddess down. She knew from her experience with Calyx that goddesses are weakest when tired. Calyx would know this and be waiting for the girl time to finish so he could take her on to the dance floor. If she didn't need to talk, it was time to party. With luck, by this evening, Calyx would have the edge over their destructive goddess. *This is perfect.*

'Cait!' Quinesha snapped her fingers in front of her eyes. 'Lost you, sweetie... you okay? I was asking what we should get to drink. I only drink the natural spring waters from my world unless you visit and bring that yummy Moonjuice.'

Caitlin grinned. 'I doubt it will ever be available here on Earth.' She snatched up Quinesha's hand and dragged her to her feet. 'Let's go and ask the bartender what the locals drink.'

A few cocktails later, Quinesha dragged Calyx on to the dance floor. He was winning his game of pool, but there was no prize bigger than winning over this Waterfall Maiden. He bowed out of a game for the first time ever, took Quinesha onto the floor and danced up a storm to a rock and roll melody. Afterwards, they sat at the bar playing drinking games together. Caitlin could see Quinesha was smitten and had earmarked Calyx as her new love interest. Unfortunately for her, she wouldn't find love with Calyx as unbeknownst to the goddess, he was married. Leaving Calyx to what he was good at, wooing women, Caitlin and Jett ducked out to go to the pet shop across the road.

She spotted the store and pointed. 'See, I'm not leading us on a goose chase. I saw this store when we arrived. This same franchise advertises on TV. They apparently have rubber treat holders that will be perfect for your pet.'

His eyes darkened and smile dissolved. 'All that's going on in there and you seriously prefer to be out here, buying a toy for Cerberus? And what happened to my party girl?'

'She's still here. But work first.' Caitlin pulled at his hand for him to follow.

'That's what I mean... my little girl is growing up. I'm astounded you are choosing work over having fun at the pub.' He placed an arm around her and kissed her forehead. 'Love you Glow. You know that don't you?'

'Love you too.' She pulled his hat down over his eyes and ran off on him. Both busted through the shop door with Caitlin squealing joyously, as he grabbed her from behind.

'That playful side has not entirely gone. I still know how to make you laugh.' He spoke quietly before freeing her from his grip. 'You get what you need while I wait outside. I want to concentrate and hear how Calyx is doing.'

'You're using telepathy again?'

'Just for now, while trying to work out Quinesha, although the girl doesn't think much.'

'Her innocence maybe?' Caitlin shrugged, unsure.

He nodded. 'She is hard to read, so I'm following the conversation through Calyx instead. Will fill you in when you're done.'

She put her hand out. 'I need your credit card if you're not staying.'

'I knew I was brought along for more than my good looks.' He pulled out a wad of money and gave her a few bills.

'I just want a toy, not the entire shop.' She held the hundred dollar bills up and chuckled.

He smiled and wandered off to allow her to buy whatever it was she needed. Give Earth toys to his pet and… well, he couldn't wait to have a laugh at her expense. It was about time she did something hilarious. *I have so missed my Glow.*

* * * *

When they got back to the pub, Calyx and Quinesha were on the dance floor doing a slow rumba. Caitlin was in such a high over getting what she needed at the pet store, that she took Jett's hand and said, 'Want to show them how it's actually danced?' She glowed.

It was the first time Jett had seen her glow like she used to. Caitlin was back; really back. He wondered what the final trigger was that made the last of her powers kick in, but was too thrilled to give it much thought. Right now, Jett danced with the most beautiful woman in the world, his saviour and best friend. He leant Caitlin back in his arms, her green eyes glistening like jewels. Fair, flawless skin and hair as shiny as polished copper mesmerised him. He did the right thing saving her. She was all he needed in this happy universe into which she had brought him kicking and screaming. Having her in his arms, made everything right. He would fight to keep his status as she kept fighting to be with him. Never again would he let her down. A good king had to have a queen by his side and someone in the kingdom to trust completely.

He trusted Cait like no other, and Melita, his soul mate, was a queen like no other. He spun Caitlin out, her dance style hypnotically languid and perfect. *Yes, I am one lucky man.* Today he was going to change. He'd get serious and make both women proud of him again.

* * * *

It was late afternoon when Quinesha had enough and asked to go home. She'd had too much to drink, so Calyx transported them while holding Quinesha in his arms. Back in her flourishing water realm, Calyx laid her on the bed of flowers she pointed to, and tenderly kissed her lips before standing up to leave.

'No, don't go.' She dropped her lip as a child would and put out her hand to him.

Calyx smiled, 'allow me a moment to take my friends to where ever they wish to go. I'll be back shortly.' He patted her hand affectionately and transported Jett and Caitlin to the surface. Once there he pulled Jett aside to explain.

Caitlin heard them murmur, the sound muffled by another earth tremor not far from them. Part of Jett's raised voice was heard over it. He said something like… keep it in your pants, right before Calyx transported away.

After he had gone, Caitlin puckered her brow. 'Is he staying?'

'Only so he can keep working on her. He said he'll catch up with us for breakfast. And I think you heard the rest as your thoughts came through loud, so I relayed it to him but from me.' He grinned.

'Good. We don't want the goddess causing any more damage because she now has the hots for another god, and him being married, it will be one more she'll lose.'

'Yes, we both get that. But Calyx is right. We need to wear her down. Make her tired. He knows what to do.'

Caitlin breathed in deeply. 'So I take it I'm getting ignored because I chose you as my boyfriend.'

He nodded and grinned. 'Yes, and is ignoring you for just that reason. It's why he said he won't come say goodbye as he is upset that you hung off me all day and sexy danced with me. He said if you ever want him to speak to you again, you owe him a dance and a kiss.'

'But we didn't kiss.' She flushed crimson.

'He misses you, that's all, Glow. Just his way of saying it. Let's blow him off and get out of here. He'll do us proud, you'll see.' He put his arm around her and within seconds they reappeared inside the castle on Pluto.

'Might take a shower and wash off the smoke and booze if that's okay.' Caitlin started to head up the stairs.

'I'll be in the den. Axon will be here soon, so I'll keep him company,' Jett called after her.

'Thanks. Won't be long.' She waved.

* * * *

When she arrived downstairs, Axon and Jett sat in the armchairs having a drink. She gave him a quick kiss hello before settling down on the couch nearest the fire. 'Rough day at the office?' She smiled at Axon.

'Not too great.' He took a sip from the goblet he held.

Caitlin had already figured that out. For such a long time now he had a permanent storm cloud over his head, and she hoped that she, Calyx and Jett were the ones to shift it for him.

When he felt her intently watching him the corners of his mouth lifted in a smile, not bright and bubbly but still a smile. 'I would sooner hear about your day. I can tell you all about mine when we get home.' He turned his body to face her, interested. 'Jett tells me you were very impressive the way you handled Cerberus and Quinesha. You accomplished much, and just in a day. More than pleased to have you back working at full capacity again, Cait.'

'Couldn't have done it without Jett and Calyx.' She covered her mouth and whispered to him. 'Needed a boost and Shargan wasn't here.'

'I think he can hear you,' Axon said, and smiled.

'She only took a little, the rest was all her.' Jett eyed her proudly.

'So tell me, have you gone all gushy on me and going to demand a puppy now?' Axon teased.

She chuckled. 'Only if you can duplicate Cerberus. He's one magnificent beast of a dog, can't wait to see him and his buddies tomorrow.'

Axon looked from Jett back to Caitlin. 'His buddies?'

Jett laughed. 'I was just about to tell you.'

'Better rewind and start from the beginning.' Axon sat back to listen.

Caitlin's eyes shone as she told Axon about the names she had given the three heads. 'You see, I figured if they stopped thinking of themselves as one and became friends, they wouldn't miss Jett so much. So tomorrow I have a training toy to keep them amused while I drag Jett back to Earth.' She sounded pleased with her purchase, but was careful not to think what it was to keep Jett guessing. She didn't want to spoil the surprise for him.

Jett hoped he didn't uncover her secret. He looked forward to a laugh when Cerberus gulped it down in one bit or the acid drool melted the rubbery toy on contact. 'I'm sure whatever it is, Tymur, Cerberus and Juro will love it.'

'Are they honestly the names you picked? Out of all the legendary names?' Axon laughed and stirred her. 'For goodness sake, if we ever have kids please let me choose the names.' He chuckled which made her lean over and slap his arm.

'Rotten sod.' She laughed with him. 'They happen to mean something significant.'

'What... left and right head?'

This time, Axon even made Jett laugh.

'Oh, you two will keep. Think Axon's funny, don't you Jett.'

They laughed louder. Next thing they found themselves in the pool outside, apparel and all.

'Why the hell did you do that?' Axon bellowed at Caitlin.

'Cerberus and his mates did it... I swear. He heard you laughing about his friends' names.' She giggled. 'Come on, you have to admit it is funny, though, right. He was playing.'

'Did you know he was telepathic, Jett?' Axon asked while he pulled himself out the water.

'Nope... well not until today. Glow was giving them names and said Juro was future. I assume you meant he can see the future, Glow.'

'Sure can. Juro must have told, Cerb and Ty, and I guarantee they were ready for that conversation. So I suppose it's kind of my fault for teaching the pups to play.' She turned to Axon. 'Somehow they tapped into the overabundance of magic Jett and Calyx left in me when they healed me. I felt them draw on it. But in my defence, it wasn't mine to keep and I let them use it. Don't forget, this is their turf too, and they have always been able to see what goes on within Pluto. It's not just the underworld. Why do you think they liked me and listened to me when I visited them? It's because they know I make Jett happy. They liked that new side of him. His misery devastated them. I'm just teaching them they can have that same happiness together. They don't need to rely on anyone else to make them feel great. They can do it for each other. Well, that is the plan.'

Next thing the three of them were in the underworld, in the cave. The dogs were rolling around making the strangest sound and stood up when they felt company.

'It was them! They're laughing.' Jett shook his head. 'Blatzing Shytzers! They thought that was hilarious.'

He turned to a stunned Axon and Caitlin. 'I'll take us back now. I just wanted to prove a point. I thought Cerberus would be asleep and sulking. I'll be blowed!' He grinned.

Cerberus's stance was suddenly stiff and menacing upon seeing someone new. Caitlin and Axon were transported out before Jett's pet got a chance to pounce or even bark.

'What the hell!' Axon shook his head as the castle walls came into focus.

'Sorry Axon, just wanted to prove Glow wrong. Didn't believe they were that intelligent or magical. But I stand corrected, it was them, the sneaky pranksters. And having a great old time together at our expense. Did you hear them laughing at us being dumped in the water? They'll keep.'

'Seriously Cait, that's what you were doing today, treating that monster like a cute puppy and teaching it magical tricks?' Axon's eyes were wide in disbelief.

'Well, they have always had magic. That's how they stop souls leaving the underworld. But like all puppies, this is all new to them. We just have to teach them to be good pups. But don't you think they're adorable?' She beamed.

'You have no fear, Cait.' Axon wiped down with the towel Jett tossed at him. 'If something that evil-looking has you go *aw... isn't that cute...* then don't go picking out any pets for us either. Forget the bloody names. That's the ugliest...'

She put her hand over his mouth. 'Want to end up in the pool again? I think I've just a tad more of that magic Cerberus used before left over.'

Axon cracked up laughing. 'Cait, you're a bad girl. You wait until I get you home. Be blowed if you're using it all up here. We're heading off, Jett. I'll drop Cait off on my way to work. Sorry, mate, but this is too much fun to pass up.'

Jett could hear the echo of Axon's laugh as he transported Caitlin home.

Jett shook his head as he looked at his wet clothes. 'Well, she could have used some of it on me to dry me off before she left.' He grinned and felt extremely happy. It had been a good day. For now, his pet was in a good mood, and his girl would be back in the morning. He used his magic to change his own clothes and walked inside.

His butler met him at the door. 'Your Majesty.' He inclined his head. 'Dinner will be ready in fifteen minutes. Your nephew has just arrived and is waiting in the dining room with a drink. I was just about to come out and ask if your other guests would be staying.' His gaze roamed around the pool.

'They have left, and I'm ready to join Orion now... if you can let him know.'

Jett ducked into the den to retrieve an exceptional vintage Moonjuice. While there he spotted a box of his favourite Nova cigars that had been on order. Both went hand in hand and, pleased with the special surprise delivery, he snatched them up to help celebrate this perfect moment.

As he walked into the dining room, he held up the wine and cigars. 'Nothing but the best vintage, and smoothest tobacco for my favourite nephew.' He looked forward to this fresh start he had been given. Once he poured the glasses, he held his up. 'Let's toast to tomorrow and many more to come.'

'Hear! Hear, Uncle.' Orion reached out to touch his glass.

'And many more of these nights with you,' Jett added.

Orion eyed him and smiled. 'Glow's back?'

'Sure is.' He winked.

'Can I see her?'

'Soon nephew, soon.' He moved over and put his arm around Orion. 'I regret not being here for your last few visits. I have missed our chats and I apologise.' He sat next to him at the head of the table. 'Now tell me, nephew, what's been happening since we last spoke? Leave nothing out.'

Chapter Twelve

Love Will Find a Way

Caitlin woke to the feeling of being lifted. Axon had her in his arms. She groaned and smiled as she wrapped her arms around him. He lowered her into a sweet smelling rose scented bath before giving her a kiss on soft lips that tasted of honey. He got up from the edge of the tub and grinned. 'Would love to join you but we slept in.'

'Really?' She glanced around. The sun shone brightly through the bathroom window. 'Have I got time for this? I can have a quick shower and be ready in a jiffy.'

'Soak, my sweet. I rang Zoren and said I'd be late; told him I have a meeting.' His lips curled on one side, and he winked.

She read him like a book. 'You lied?'

'Well, kind of. We're having breakfast at Jett's, so that's sort of a meeting wouldn't you say?' He smiled. 'I've just organised juice and coffee. It's on the way up here. Therefore, I will leave you to have your bath alone while I take...' he looked down... 'A cold shower.' He tossed off his robe and stood there, butt naked.

Her smile turned into a big grin. 'Oh, my... Don't go wasting that, lover.' She put her hand out to him.

'Don't, Cait. I swear this is left from last night and if you encourage my boy here, you'll not be getting to Jett's. And if I make him mad again, it will be me who's visiting the underworld... permanently.'

Caitlin chuckled. 'Guess you're right. He was pretty ticked off.

But you have redeemed yourself.'

'Think so?' He stepped into the shower.

'Yes.' She immersed her head under the water, dreamily remembering their perfect night together.

When she got out, Axon was reading news from his NAVcom and drinking coffee. 'Want one poured?' He watched her towel dry herself. She looked different today, radiant, and he couldn't take his eyes off her. Rather than blow-wave her hair, she twirled in a circle, and her hair dried and looked like she had spent the day in a salon. Clothes formed on her. A loose cream, embroidered top sat scalloped over a tight leather skirt. The bra was red to match the leather skirt, and on her, the sexy look was stunning. Rubies decorated cream stilettos and the same jewels dripped from long earrings and wrapped around her wrists and on one ankle.

'Amazing!' He blinked. 'You can do that without your horse now. You've come a long way developing your magic, Cait. Doubt even Cassie from the Cloud Riders is capable of that transformation.'

'Can't expect me to work in close collaboration with gods and goddesses and not pick something up.' She checked her image in the mirror, moved a few strands of hair and added a flower. She turned back to Axon. 'We've decided to revisit the goddess on Earth today. I plan to make her jealous. What do you think?' She spun around for him to make a comment.

'If that's your plan, you nailed it for sure. I'm envious of those who get to take you there.' He glanced at the clock. 'Time to leave, but do you want a coffee to go?'

'I'd prefer to have one with breakfast. I'm starving.'

He stood, smiling. 'And I'm suddenly ravenous.'

She moved and stood next to him. He put an arm around her, and quickly his other hand scooped her up, and she lay in his arms. 'But not for food.'

She squealed and kicked lightheartedly to be put down. 'Don't you dare! You had your chance earlier.' She chuckled.

'But you weren't dressed like this.' Axon laughed and transported her to Pluto. This time, he was able to land them inside the castle without the alarms going off. 'You're mine tonight sexy lady,' he whispered seductively before putting her down.

Suddenly the door swung open, and Jett came rushing out. 'I heard Glow scream and thought she was in trouble.'

'She nearly was in trouble wearing that outfit,' Axon teased her.

Jett glanced at Caitlin and back to Axon. 'Um, yep. It looks as if we're in for one entertaining day. Want to join us?'

'Love to, but my day is full. However, I do have time for a quick bite if you guys are eating. Then I'd best be on my way.'

'Follow me then. Breakfast is about to be served.'

When Jett turned and led the way, Axon winked at Caitlin and slapped her lightly on the backside. 'Save some of that energy for tonight, sweet one.'

'Ouch, you'll keep.' She chuckled and ran off from him. She caught up to Jett, put her arm through his, and turned her head slightly to give Axon a cheeky smile.

As Axon pulled her chair out to seat her, he leant close to her ear. 'You are very naughty. Remind me later that you need a spank.' He ran his hand lightly down her back. It gave her tingles, and he felt her shiver. 'You're mine and don't you forget it.' He sat next to her, pleased. The response was what he needed to wipe away any jealous thoughts. Only now was he happy to get on with his day. Caitlin working with Jett and Calyx was just what they needed. All her time before this was spent with the Cosmic Riders on Earth. They very rarely saw each other and just knowing she was home each night had him walking on sunshine. Feeling the love she had for him left him contented and extremely happy.

Calyx shimmered into focus and headed straight to Caitlin. 'Morning beautiful.' He kissed her cheek. Moving next to Axon, he shook his hand. 'Hi, competition,' he said, and grinned.

Axon turned and punched his arm. 'Hi—thorn in my arse.'

Both laughed.

'Good morning brother.' He ruffled Jett's hair and sat the other side of the table opposite Caitlin.

Axon stared at Calyx while breakfast was placed in front of

them. 'Well, how did it go last night? Cait tells me you stayed behind to try and find a countermeasure to combat Quinesha's magic.'

Calyx screwed up one side of his face. 'You know what ticks me off more than anything… that I am a god and yet didn't get any further with the goddess than your team. That spell is strengthened by more than the heartache of getting dumped. After just twenty-four hours I was so over it, I wanted to turn her into one of those flowers she loves so much.'

Axon laughed heartily which in turn caused a chain reaction. Calyx and Jett laughed too. Caitlin was pleased she didn't need to use magic anymore to smooth the way back to mateship for these men. They had just got over it by using humour. *They're so different to us women…* She was astounded.

* * * *

After Axon had left, Caitlin listened to the men discussing Earth, but her mind was elsewhere. Quinesha reminded her of a time long ago.

Of me!

The instant the thought hit, she put her hands up in the air and interrupted their conversation. 'She's never had a man.' The words popped out of Caitlin's mouth. 'I bet that's why Zylon slept with Chandra. He knew!' A lightbulb moment went off in her mind. She could imagine Zylon watching her, almost feel what he must have felt. She continued the relay as her mind drifted further into the idea of what might have happened next. 'He didn't want to frighten or hurt her the first time they made love...' She rubbed her forehead. 'No—surely not, it's too simple. Don't tell me the answer was in front of me all this time, and only now I get it! Oh dear, that was so me! I should have guessed months ago.' Caitlin's frustration to only now realise showed in her high-pitched revelation to the men.

They sat silently following, waiting for the rest. As yet, it made little sense.

'How stupid could I be? Why didn't Zylon confide in me—was it because I was female? Didn't he think I'd understand? This could have been sorted out months ago.' She got up and paced in agitation then stopped and stared at them. 'Shytzer, we can't break her walls down, because there are none. This isn't hatred. We aren't dealing with a woman who knows hatred. We are dealing with hurt, the purest form, and from an incredibly innocent child-like mind!'

'Hang on, back up. What do you mean it was you?' Calyx sat up straight, listening to Caitlin's sudden revelation that although odd, sounded feasible.

'When I first started going out with Axon, Rory didn't know I was still a virgin. When I told him, Rory freaked out knowing Axon was to be my first, so he blabbed to him. I was so embarrassed and didn't understand what the big deal was, and I felt he overreacted. It was only afterwards that I got how excited a man, especially a mighty immortal male, gets and how, for the first time, they need to curb that... a lot!' She chuckled, her face bright red at having to reveal to them such an intimate moment.

With eyes wide and a knowing stare, Calyx and Jett glanced at one another and back at Caitlin.

'See!' She pointed and snapped her fingers lightly. 'You know I'm on to something here, don't you?'

Jett tapped at his chin. 'You could have something there, Glow. But how do we make Quinesha see he went the wrong way about solving his concerns? He should have manned up and discussed it with her.'

Calyx leant forward. 'I agree. He should have if that is what happened. But this is Zylon we're talking about. If I remember correctly he was never caring towards women.' He turned to Cait. 'Still, what you say holds merit. He is somewhat a beast of a man and that's why he was put in charge of the forest.' He considered what was being said here. 'And yet in saying that, if you're right, then I have mistaken Quinesha's innocence as teasing. If she really has never been kissed, it explains a lot. Her kisses were a very basic peck on the lips and trust me, no tongue. She may have looked like a woman, but I felt I was caring for a child most of the day. If she is thinking like one, no wonder none of us has got through to her.

Children can be so spiteful and stubborn, yet sweet and adorable at the same time.' He shook his head, alarmed as he now supposed this to be true. 'That's why I was having so much trouble controlling her!' He slapped his forehead. 'If she hasn't yet become a woman, then you're right, we are dealing with the most dangerous of all... an innocent female immortal holding unlimited goddess powers. We do need to change our tactics.'

Caitlin sat with her hands clamped in front of her. 'I'll contact Axon and see if Rory is available to go and speak to Zylon, firstly to find out if we're right. If we are, I'd like one of them to bring Zylon to rendezvous with us later today.'

Jett hoped she wasn't rushing it. 'Will you have Quinesha ready to talk to him by then? Of what Axon has said she won't see Zylon... absolutely refuses to.'

Caitlin sat back down and nodded. 'I'll have her ready, but I'm not going to like what I have to do. I do have a plan, but I can't tell you yet. I need to keep your reactions as surprised as hers. Quinesha's response will show me how much she still loves Zylon.'

'But she hates him, and that's the reason why the spiteful vendetta continues!' Calyx looked confused.

'I believe this is Quinesha's way of showing him every day how she feels. She's holding his attention the only way she knows how. But even using her goddess power and destroying his world for attention doesn't bring him to her door. I just need to be sure and I don't know why I couldn't see it before. Her stubbornness will not allow her to admit to any of us how much he hurt her. Instead, she acts all tough and cold about what her venom is doing to the world. Nothing matters but him. She will destroy all until he falls to his knees in front of her, begging for forgiveness. She wants him to feel the embarrassment and hurt she has been made to feel.'

'What makes you think that, Cait?' Calyx said.

'I felt that way when Axon did the same to me. We had only kissed, but like her, I knew he was the one. But oh, how I wanted to punish him for choosing another over me on one particular night! I swear, had it not been for the Riders keeping me busy with training,

I would have thrown a supernova at his world, I was so furious. Instead, I kept it in it and ended up unwell for some time. Quinesha could end up the same if this problem is not aired and dealt with.' Caitlin took in a deep breath. 'It isn't going to be easy, but this ends today!'

'You should explain your plan to us. We won't ruin it. We want this fixed too.' Calyx shifted, uncomfortable he wasn't being told the *how*.

'Put it this way, she is going to be as mad as hell when I'm done, and when I am, don't follow us. Best give us girl time.'

'I really want to know how you will set her off, but the more I hear about Axon and how he treated you, the more I'd like to wring his two-timing neck.' Calyx's lips were pressed tight.

'Ca—lyx, remember our agreement. What we say and do at work stays at work.' She grinned. 'I only tell you this to make you understand why I believe my theory is correct. As we have found by erasing an experience, they are put in my way to teach me about life. Each unique in their own way and they help me to become a better peacekeeper.

'I get it, but I don't have to like it.' Calyx shifted restlessly.

Caitlin gave him one of her caring looks and smiled. Seeing it cheered him up she continued. 'As for my plan, it must look natural, not staged, so no, I'm not telling you, yet.' She slipped her arm through his to show she was ready to go.

* * * *

On the way to Earth, Jett stopped in to see Cerberus.

'I'm so excited to see them,' said Caitlin. 'They're going to be stoked with their new toys.'

'Cait, I hate to break it to you, but Tymur, Cerberus and Juro are going to destroy those Earth-made toys in seconds.' Jett was amused at how keen she was but warned her anyway. 'You have no idea what you're dealing with here. If it's small enough to fit in your pocket, Cerberus alone will swallow whatever it is, whole.'

'Maybe, but let me try. By doing this, I hope to bring out some of their puppy instincts to help ease their sadness when you're not with them. It won't affect the brutal nature, just add balance to create a more conscientious protector. But your concerns are duly noted.'

Jett threw his hands in the air. 'I give up! Lead on, evil-whisperer.'

Calyx walked beside her, his arm slung over her shoulders. 'My brother is such a buzz kill.'

Jett caught up and walked the other side of her. 'Crawler.' He eyed Calyx.

'Girlfriend stealer.' Calyx lifted his hand off Caitlin's shoulder and flicked his ear.

Jett was just about to retaliate when Caitlin spoke, sounding very goddessy.

'We're here; now stop it you two. It's time to set an example. We don't want to teach your pet how to argue like brothers, do we?' She raised her eyebrow at them.

They both smiled.

'Guess not,' said Calyx.

'Hell no!' Jett agreed.

Walking through the cave, they could hear growls that rumbled from deep inside the darkness. Caitlin figured it would be unusual for the dog to hear three sets of feet walking on the stone surface. It was quite loud, as they trudged along. Jett called out a command, and as the flames lit up the room, his pet had heeded his advice. It cowered in the corner of the huge cave, but the beast side of the dog was still uncertain. The serpent mane stood up on end, snapping at the air, smelling the intruders. Jett had a grin on his face as he returned the favour from the day before and leant over to Caitlin, and licked her on the cheek. 'See? A friend.' He laughed.

'Eww! Caitlin whispered and wished to rub her wet cheek, but didn't want them to think it yucky. Instead, instincts had her lash out and playfully slap Jett on his cheek.

Jett's pet got excited, and the heads started to lick one another. It surprised her friends further when the dog rolled onto its side, careful so as not to squash the serpents. Its front and back paws on lanky legs reached up to the heads at a fast rate as they tried to slap one another's faces. It growled, enjoying this new game they had just learned.

Caitlin, Jett, and Calyx burst into hysterics as the dog performed acrobatic moves to slap one another's heads with the four paws.

'Please stop!' Caitlin called out and clapped her hands. 'You're killing us. That looks so funny.' She calmed herself and stood closer to the huge protector of souls, leaving Calyx and Jett to wipe the tears from their eyes. They hung off one another in fits as the last couple of hits were finished off by Cerberus. He was not letting either of his brothers get away with slapping him last.

'Well, I doubt Glow meant to teach them that, but how funny did it look?' Jett said as he moved to the left of Caitlin to protect her, although he doubted she needed any. The dogs loved her. He could see that. The serpents not so much… but they couldn't attack without his pet allowing it.

'Do it again.' Calyx chuckled, egging them both on. 'Go on, Jett. Lick her!'

Caitlin giggled. 'Calyx, stop that! We'll never get the day started.' From the pocket of her oversized coat, she pulled the brown paper bag.

The rustling sound attracted the three heads. With a thud, the dog's body dropped to the ground. On its belly, the dog-heads panted as they waited. Unwittingly, the serpent tail swished back and forth with the dog's excited anticipation.

Using her magic, gloves appeared on Caitlin's hands, keeping her safe from the acid drool. To teach them self-control, Caitlin took her time taking off the wrappers of the honey cakes. The tension in the air was electric as the patience of the dog tethered on getting up and snatching what surely was theirs. But Cerberus, who had the strongest mind, controlled them and made the other two wait until it was offered.

Caitlin's satisfied smile had them look goofily at her. She chuckled. 'Okay then, Cerb, come!' She held out her hand to Cerberus.

The big dog crept on its belly toward her and Cerberus took the first cake very gingerly. She patted him, and said, 'Good boy, Cerb.'

'Ty, don't be shy.' She held out the treat to Tymur.

Tymur took the cake and got his pat.

Juro put his head up and panted, knowing it was his turn. He took the cake. 'Good boy Juro. Now!' She flicked her fingers in a gesture for them to move back. This they did quickly to give her room. Interested, they watched her every move as one hand slipped into her pocket, and a three-knotted fluffy-ended rope was pulled into view. The body of the beast stood with three sets of ears up, and noses sniffed. It was poised and ready for a command.

'This is to play tug of war with, but if you pull too hard you will break it, so you must be gentle… Watch.' Caitlin gave one end to Jett and one to Calyx to hold in their teeth. She bit on the third end and pulled quick and hard against it. Both men laughed when the ends slipped from their mouths, making Caitlin the winner.

'You cheated; you didn't say ready,' said Calyx.

'I won.' She did a happy dance for the dogs' sake and threw it up in the air, yelling out, 'Cerb... catch.'

He flew up and snatched it from the air in his mouth. Ty and Juro made a grab for the other ends and missed.

'Remember, not too hard,' she warned.

This time Ty and Juro made a grab for it and caught an end each. After a slight tug, they found they enjoyed the tugging against each other's mouths. Amazingly enough, it didn't snap, nor did their acid drool dissolve the human-made rope.

'Okay Cait, spill. Where did you get that made? You didn't buy that from a pet store. I was expecting it to last all of a few seconds.' Jett was stunned.

'Just a little magic learned along the way to strengthen Earth items for galactic travel. It's the same magic that we use on the gloves we wear during missions.' She held her gloved hand up. 'Just wasn't sure how strong it was, so warned them in case they were too rough.'

Juro and Ty playfully took an end in their mouths and tugged at Cerberus. The three begun to growl at each other, in a way that showed their enjoyment. At times one or the other dropped an end and had to fight to retrieve it.

Caitlin was happy it was a toy they liked and stopped the game. They could play it later. She clapped her hands. 'Drop!' Her command had the dog drop to its stomach, and the rope toy was tossed aside.

Caitlin sat on the floor in front of them and crossed her legs. Out of pockets, she took out three Tuff toys and stuffed them with doggy treats.

'See boys...' She grunted, stuffing the final treat in the small opening of the Tuff toy using pressure to pack them nice and tight. She continued, 'the trick is to roll and bounce this shape until the treat drops out.' She looked up at them as a teacher would look at her students, and added, 'but no cheating and breaking the casing. If you do, I will know. You see, you will get your own design, so I'll know who was naughty by the one that's busted.'

Caitlin ran one along the floor and bounced it to show them how to get the food out. She made sure to replace the small biscuits and chewy hide that dropped out before handing them out.

Once they had received their Tuff toy food dispenser, they ran to the back of the cave. When she heard them banging their toy and chewing, she stood, brushed off the dust from her clothes and smiled. 'All done... time to go.' She turned and began walking out through the corridor of the cave.

'Aren't you going to say goodbye?' Calyx asked. 'Won't they sulk or something?'

Caitlin stopped. 'That's what all this is about. I'm teaching them not to miss human contact, but to rely on one another instead. If I said goodbye, they might fret that we are leaving. I'm guessing by the time they've finished their treat they will most likely sleep a few hours. On waking they should remember the fun they had and look for the toys or at one another for more of what they had before falling asleep. At feeding time is when Jett will need to return and make a fuss of them. They'll look forward to those visits but once their bellies are full and he is gone again, it will be one another they look to for entertainment, fingers crossed.'

'That makes sense.' Calyx got it.

When reaching the mouth of the cave, Caitlin removed her fur jacket and boots before she turned to Jett. 'Are you okay to take over from here? Just make sure after you do feed them that their toys are filled with treats too. After, you should be able to transport out without worry, knowing you left them happy. That's of course if those toys do survive their big sharp teeth.' She looked upwards towards the roof. 'The top of the cave is a long way up, mmm...' She tapped her lip. 'What about finding a way to hang from the roof a couple of ropes with knots at different levels so they can jump up and swing from them? Also, you could purchase some caterpillar-tipper truck tyres we use in the mines on Earth. They should be strong enough for these guys to chew on and throw around the cave and entertain one another.'

'Great idea. You can use that same magic on the new items that you used to protect those Earth toys. That'll help prevent their acid drool from wrecking them too quickly. I'll get on it. Just not sure the cave roof is strong enough to hold him—them.'

'Use magic!' She grinned. 'Anyway, a couple more ideas if you get time.'

'I'll make time.' He nodded to Calyx. 'Can you help?'

'Sure, I'll try and find a spell to make it work, but if Cait's not here to calm those snakes, you better stick him on a lead. The last bite from that thing annoyed me for weeks.'

'Awww, softie,' Caitlin teased and leant into him.

Jett grinned at her. 'So spend ten minutes, feed and fuss, give them their treats and leave.'

'Well it works for dogs on Earth when their owners go to do their daily chores or jobs, so why not for you? So far I haven't heard them howl like they did last time we left. If any souls escape, we come up with a new plan because you are going to stay king and that is final!' She straightened with confidence.

'Let's hope this does work, and then we can tick one problem off our list,' Calyx said. 'Next.'

'Earth!' Caitlin and Jett said together.

Calyx screwed up his lips. 'Thought you might say that.' He wasn't too pleased with the next stop, as this one was on him mostly and he didn't look forward to spending the day pandering to the needs of a spoilt goddess again.

'It's okay.' Caitlin chuckled at the look on his face. 'I'm breaking you and Quinesha up today.'

'Oh... well, in that case, I can't wait.'

Chapter Thirteen

Just a Kiss

When they arrived on Earth, Quinesha waited for them and waved from her garden patio. 'I'm over here!' Her beauty enhanced by the backdrop of delicate roses in bloom behind her, and seated on a chair of twined floral vines, she was a stunning vision in sheer-lilac, the loose-fitting sundress opened at the side, showing tanned slender legs.

'Zylon would kick himself if he saw her today.' Jett spoke quietly. 'She's one stunning young lady.'

'Amazing how happiness can change an appearance.' Cait thought about how Jett's features changed when happy. This was a new look for Quinesha. 'Maybe we are getting through. Looking at her today, my plan might just work after all.' Caitlin put her arm through Jett's as they walked along. 'For this to work, you two will have to do what I say. No strange questioning glares or getting jealous. I have to get her seriously mad at me, so I'll have to play a tart today.'

Calyx rubbed his hands together. 'Can't wait to get this show on the road then; maybe I get my second kiss.'

'Over my dead body, Calyx, you keep your goddamned lip to yourself.' Jett glared at him.

'Come on, guys, this is serious stuff. If I can't crack her today, this hell-raising goddess might never relent.'

Calyx pulled his eyebrows tight. His lips pinched. 'As soon as Quinesha breaks, she's history as a goddess of any kind of water, this

I swear.'

'Let's just do our job and leave her punishment up to Axon. Our priority next is your brother.'

'Yes Cait, but if Axon can't see her teenage attitude is dangerous and that she is out of control, then I will step in.'

She spoke quietly. 'Trust in us as peacekeepers, Calyx. She's not a bad person, but she will have to live with the consequences and the devastation she has caused once it's over.' They neared Quinesha and had to be careful not to be overheard. Caitlin patted Jett's arm. 'It's time for us to become a loving couple.' Caitlin leant in close to Jett's body, being flirtatious.

'Why can't I play the boyfriend today?' Calyx whispered so the goddess couldn't hear.

'Bad luck, brother. It isn't always a blessing to have the better looks. Quinesha picked you. She went all swoony as soon as she saw you, so lucky me.'

'Stop it you two. You're both good-looking,' Caitlin hissed. 'Jett will have his time with her too.'

'When?' Jett stared at her.

'Soon… This must go down making me look like a two-timing wench, exactly how she sees Chandra. So please, be ready when I start to make my play.'

'I get a turn. That's going to piss you off, having to share,' Calyx gloated.

Caitlin dug him in the ribs with her elbow. 'Stop it. This is not a competition. It's business,' she snapped in a whisper tone.

Calyx slapped Jett across the head.

'What!' Jett whispered.

'Have to hit someone. This sucks. I have to pander to Quinesha.'

Suddenly Quinesha was on her feet and moved quickly towards them. With a big smile, she hugged Caitlin, then Jett. With Calyx, she kissed his lips and looked deep and affectionately into his eyes.

She's toast. Caitlin squeezed Jett's hand. *I'll have to kiss you to get this started. Sorry if it makes you feel uncomfortable,* Caitlin thought so he knew what was coming. Jett's mouth curled up in a secret smile to her. She muffled a laugh at the evil within it. *You are such a bad, bad man.* Her thought made him turn his head, so the goddess didn't see his smile widen.

They had sat and chatted for a while before Caitlin got up and sat on Jett's lap. She leant in to kiss him, only he unexpectedly leant Caitlin back in his arms and kissed her, actually kissed her.

Hello, that was meant to be a pretending peck.

He leant close to her ear. 'If my brother is getting a kiss, I'm getting one in too. He will play dirty, trust me.'

You two are so competitive. Try to behave. She smiled at his devilish grin.

Quinesha giggled at them.

Calyx frowned. 'Break it up, you two. How about we go for a swim where you can both cool off.'

'Sounds good.' Caitlin went to stand but struggled to get up. Jett held her to him. When Quinesha turned and walked off to the water's edge with Calyx, Caitlin slapped Jett's hand, put her finger up and scolded his behaviour. He let her go and stood smiling. 'Beautiful little pipsqueak. Bully a god, will you?'

She slapped his arm. 'You're impossible.'

He chuckled. 'Okay, I'll play nice now… well, until he kisses you then look out. He may just end up a popsicle that melts in the water, the girlfriend stealer.'

This time Caitlin laughed. 'You're so full of it, Jett. As if. Now stop it, or I'll tell Melita you were flirting with me.'

He quickened his pace to get beside her. 'I promise. But you have to promise to keep work at work.'

'And I will. But no melting your brother.' She smiled as he agreed but grumbled the rest of the way to the water. Suddenly his eyes widened as he stared at Caitlin, listening to her thoughts.

Jett, can you amuse Quinesha for a bit? It's time to put my plan into action. Be charming, please. I'm all out of ideas. This is a last-ditch effort and must work.

Jett breathed out heavily, blinked in recognition and walked ahead. She knew she could rely on him. He had her back and didn't need to say a word.

Calyx swam off the instant Jett dived in between them. He was notably getting some exercise and swam towards the other side of the bank, pretending he was doing some laps. Jett had won Quinesha over, and she seemed happy to stay and chat with him. Once Caitlin heard her laughing with Jett it was her cue to join Calyx. She swam towards him. He had cleverly guessed what came next and had stopped by the waterfall but still in sight of Quinesha. He smiled as Caitlin slowed and changed to a provocative sidestroke while she moved around him. Her eyes burned into him as she wrapped her arms around him. He responded without any prompting and kissed her so lovingly it made her heart leap. She pulled away and smiled. 'Boy, you sure know how to kiss a girl. But this is just playacting... right!'

'Shush, no ruining the only moment I'll most likely ever have. This is me helping to make her jealous, and I want you to know you can trust me with any task.' He grinned. His face glowed, and his blue eyes lit up like precious jewels as he laid her back in the water and floated her, gently kissing her fingers, arm and back to her mouth again.

He was an angel, and if Caitlin wasn't taken she could easily fall for his charms. But this was business and their time ended swiftly as Quinesha huffed and waded quickly from the water.

Caitlin smiled. Her plan was moving along fast and ended the kiss. 'Your work is done, Casanova. That was deliciously dreamy,' she said, and giggled. 'But my Axon still has my heart.'

Calyx helped her upright with an evil snicker. 'You can't blame a man for trying.'

'Hey, nice try too.' With the cheekiest grin she dived into the depths of the water and swam back to shore. She eyed Jett as she pulled herself up and out of the water using the floral bank as leverage. 'Wish me luck.'

'Luck Glow, she's really ticked off,' *and me too*. He winked, not letting her see his jealous streak, turned and headed over to join Calyx. *Bastard kissing my girl like that!*

CAITLIN II

Caitlin found Quinesha sitting on a swing in her garden. She would have been trying to contain her anger by drawing strength from her plants and flowers.

'If it is me who upset you, I'm terribly sorry.' Caitlin sat beside her as she swung slowly on the other swing. 'You seemed happy with Jett, so I thought we would swap for the day. I mean, you two haven't slept together, so he and I didn't believe you were that into him.'

Quinesha never spoke for a minute as she thought about what Caitlin said. When she did, her voice trembled with contempt.

'You knew I was with Calyx yesterday. He knew I liked him. I can't believe he kissed you. He didn't even care I was there and could see you both.'

'He does care about you. But when you didn't make a move on him, and I did, he figured you just didn't want him in that way. You know, he thought you only liked him as a friend. I mean he stayed the night, and you just slept, from what he tells me.'

'He should have known. I kissed his lips.'

'Yes, I did see you kiss him. It was a friendly peck on the lips, not passionate as if you're hot for him.'

She started to cry. 'I don't know how to pash. I've never kissed anyone before. This is the second man I've lost because I haven't understood what to do.' She broke into a sob and Caitlin went to her and gave her a hug.

'So, you and Zylon never kissed... or made love? Did he know you'd never had a man before?'

'Yes, the night before I found him with that witch. I confided in him that I had been saving myself for Mr Right. However, it came out all wrong. I realised after he left that he assumed that someone I waited for, wasn't him. Without so much as another word he left. I knew it was what I told him so that night I went to his home. I intended to throw myself at him and say it was him I wanted. He was my Mr Right. That's when I caught him in bed with another woman. I was such a fool.'

Caitlin was so pleased Quinesha had finally cracked. It was the first time she had mentioned what really happened. She was open and ready to discuss it logically. Caitlin sat back on the swing next to her.

'I want to tell you a story about me that might help you put this into perspective. You see, I too had never been really kissed until I met the man I wanted to spend my life with. But the problem was that he was many immortal years older and much more powerful in opposite ways. You could say I had the power of the mind, and he had the power of strength.'

'That's the same as Zylon and me. But I'm not following what this has to do with him choosing another woman to sleep with.'

'To take a young immortal, these ancient men have to adjust their powers magically, and may not always get it right if they're too excited. If they don't get it right, they will frighten their young love from their bed, in most cases, forever.'

'So, he chose someone else because he was too scared to try. That is such a cop-out.'

'I believe he chose someone else, as my first did, to calm down. He meant to come to you less hyped-up and thinking straight. He'd then be able to adjust where needed and make your experience perfect.'

'Glow Girl, that's a hard pill to swallow, even for someone as green as me.'

'Okay, let me put it to you like this. If you were to take on a human lover and he truly excited you, would you have sex with him while in that state?'

'Oh no, I could never even think of sleeping with a mortal. I have learned that this is very bad. They may die from—' Quinesha went quiet.

'You get what I'm saying now, don't you? In your case, it's slightly different because the maiden has powers to make this reunion sing. Only in the event of a virgin, those powers are dormant. It's the sacred stimulation from an immortal partner that helps us to unlock these powers, but only if we wish to satisfy and please that mate. As you get more experienced, you can sleep with your god on his level.

But why did your parents not tell you this?' Caitlin asked.

'My mother died in childbirth and my father slept with a human and so was banished. I was left here alone.'

'I'm so sorry, Quinesha. I know how hard it is growing up without a family. I only met my dad four years ago. He's a good man and he was trying to do the right thing by staying away from me, but nothing excuses that time lost. My friends are my family, and I love to choose who is and isn't.'

'The animals are my family.' She smiled. 'Still, I have always dreamed of having my own one day, and I thought I'd found the perfect man.' Sadness edged her lips that trembled.

'You need to talk to Zylon. What if he felt the same about you, but went about it all wrong, and slept with another woman to settle his passion before he came back to you? I would say if he were really hot for you, he wouldn't have understood how else to calm himself.' Caitlin knew she was thinking out loud but what she said gave comfort to Quinesha. Her sniffling stopped as the goddess listened intently.

'What is it like?' she asked.

Caitlin smiled. 'With the man of your dreams it is the most perfect of experiences.'

'It was just my luck to fall for a man who can't control his libido. He totally ruined everything.'

'Do you believe in second chances?'

Quinesha shrugged.

'I'll take that as a maybe.' Caitlin smiled. 'Look, the day is too beautiful to waste. Let's go somewhere and forget all this. And now I know you really like Calyx, I will zap any girl who even looks at him sideways. But just remember, if you really want a man to be faithful to you, you need to claim him. But only claim him if his kiss melts your body and soul, okay. Everything else is just a kiss.'

'Like you and Calyx. I can tell you don't care about him that much or you wouldn't dream of giving him back.'

'See how quickly you get it. And yes, his kiss was just a kiss.'

'Mmm… for me too. Maybe I'll keep looking; after all, I did

attract Calyx. And even though he is a hussy and not my type, I'd like it if we could all stay friends. I've really enjoyed hanging with you guys.

'Me too.' Caitlin got off the swing and put her hand out. 'Then come on, friend. Let's go find someone who will rock your world.'

Quinesha stood up giggling and took her hand. 'I'd like that.' She hugged Caitlin. 'Thanks for helping me understand men problems. I guess women aren't the only ones that get confused.' She sounded more like a grown woman suddenly.

They both came up with men jokes on the way back to collect Jett and Calyx. Quinesha had a great sense of humour that Caitlin had only now uncovered. She was enjoying this moment with her. She could see how she had lost her way and hoped this set her on a new path; one that wasn't destructive.

The men turned with a smile when they heard the girls approach in good spirits. They had expected to be waiting a while and had made themselves comfortable under a purple jacaranda tree.

'They sure look hot lying half-naked on the blanket of those purple petals,' Quinesha gushed.

'They are that, but let's find you someone not only hot but sizzling hot.' Caitlin smiled and patted Quinesha's hand that held her with a gripping need to have a friend beside her. 'Hot isn't good enough for my girlfriend.'

Quinesha stopped and threw her arms around Caitlin. 'You're like the sister I never had. I'm so glad I met you. Thanks for liking me too.'

The men were on their feet and moved towards them. 'What are all the happy hugs for?' Jett said.

'Just girl stuff.' Quinesha winked at Caitlin.

Caitlin wondered where this side of her character had been hiding. It was as if Quinesha had grown up before their eyes. Caitlin watched the goddess continue to speak and although aware from her own experiences that knowledge taken in by any life learning lessons can give immediate growth, this was a huge turnaround. Caitlin saw now why others would shake their heads as her journey continued.

Each download of knowledge gave her a greater understanding of the universe and all it had to offer. Maybe Quinesha was at last drawing from her kin, the supreme beings of the heavens. Her childlike nature had been shed and was developing. Caitlin could only hope so.

Jett stood up. 'We were just discussing having a bit to eat and wondered if you ladies would like to join us? My shout.' Jett smiled.

'Sounds fantastic,' Caitlin agreed. 'But can we make it somewhere extra special? I owe Quinesha some fun for upsetting her before.'

'Yes, you do!' Quinesha's slipped her arm through Caitlin's in a friendly way. Her confidence showed she was much better.

'I think we should do an overnighter. Stay at a resort for the night. Have some real fun,' Caitlin suggested.

Quinesha clapped her hands. 'Wow that sure is something I have always wished I could do. I hear tourists talking about their adventures as they sit around a campfire at night, and it sounds fabulous.' Her eyes had lit up, and her skin glowed in a gold tone as she started thinking about what she would pack. 'I'll need a hairbrush some lipstick and...' Her eyes took Caitlin in. 'But what about you, Caitlin, you came in bathers and a sundress. Did you want to borrow something of mine?'

Caitlin chuckled and spun around. Her image disappeared in a glow of light before coming back into focus.

'Seriously... You look as if you just stepped out of a beauty salon. Your dress is gorgeous.' Quinesha felt the sheer cream fabric embroidered with gold thread that overlaid a slim-fitting cocktail dress. 'How did you do that?'

'I have magic, but it's limited to this trick.' She smiled. 'Maybe one day you can show me how you keep this place so beautiful and lush and I'll share how I do this.'

'Can you do that to me, save me changing?' Quinesha was more than impressed.

Caitlin wanted to give her something to show her trust but was not prepared to give too much. She didn't want to be seen as a threat. 'Love to, but this is it.' She held her hands up and shrugged. 'All I got.'

'Then Calyx, can you walk with me to collect a small overnight bag?' Quinesha smiled at him.

Calyx's expression was of pure relief as he left with her. Caitlin knew he was most likely eating humble pie about now, but she didn't need to worry about him. She knew his background and apologising for his indiscretions was something he would find all too familiar.

Jett nudged her. 'Forget about him. I want to know whose kiss you liked the best.'

Caitlin grinned. 'Stop it. It was work-related, and no one gets a score.'

'I know you liked me the best,' he said confidently.

Caitlin searched his face wondering how he knew that and forgot for a minute he could read her mind.

He smiled. 'Because just now you didn't deny it. You were wondering how I knew.'

'That's not fair; you tricked me.' She laughed.

'I'm evil too, remember. It's what I do. But more than that I felt you melt in my arms and I never used magic on you, as he had to.' He waved his hand and stood dressed in a cream short sleeved shirt with gold trim. His shorts were pleated at the front and pocket on the side. On his feet, he wore sandals of the highest quality leather. 'You're my girl, not his.'

Caitlin shook her head. He had dressed to match her. 'Axon will not be pleased to see us matching if he is the one who brings Zylon to us.'

'I aim to annoy my brother. I promise the colour will change once I tick him off.'

At that very moment Calyx and Quinesha joined them. Calyx took one look at them both together and his smile faded. 'You're blatzing kidding me,' was all he got out.

Jett had already begun transporting the four of them, and when arriving at their destination, Caitlin did notice he had changed. He wore a grey shirt tucked into black pants, more in the dark tones she was used to seeing him in. *Will they ever stop competing?* She thought not.

CHAPTER FOURTEEN

Love will find a way

They rematerialized on Turtle Island Resort far from prying eyes. It was a location Jett and his family had purchased and made safe many years ago. It had become a favourite spot for the rulers of the Home Worlds above, now making it possible for universal travellers to enjoy the hot summer months on Earth. However, apart from them, Zoren had put a sanction on outer universe travellers while Earth was in crisis. So while business was low, the rooms were let out to the wealthy inhabitants of Earth to keep it operating.

It was a short walk to the resort and on entering, Caitlin and Quinesha held each other, letting out squeals of excitement with the luxurious setting. 'This is beautiful, Glow.' Quinesha's eyes soaked in the pool that wrapped around the grounds. 'It has waterfalls and look...' she pointed to a bar in the middle of the water. 'It comes complete with seats.'

Caitlin grinned. 'It's a bar all right. Let's go order a cocktail while the men book us in.'

'Is that right!' Calyx was still a bit ticked off with Jett. 'I think my brother can organise the rooms. It seems he didn't give me time to change before we left.' Calyx was still in his swimming shorts. 'Catch you later, brother.' Calyx gave a royal wave and grinned. He turned back to Caitlin and Quinesha who had already removed their dresses and were in bikinis, ready to dive in. He was suddenly charming.

'Oh, and brother, take those discarded outfits and have them put into their rooms.'

Jett didn't show any emotion, but he smirked as he picked up the clothes. He did stir Calyx, and his behaviour showed him it had worked. Knowing that alone had him whistle a little tune as he walked off.

Jett finally joined them, and with both women paying the men equal attention, the mood changed, and things became a lot more fun. The men started pushing each other off the stools, ducking one another and later, dirty tricks using magic came into play, but Calyx was careful to hide their trickery from any humans looking on. Drinks disappeared out of hands just as they touched lips, straws grew and poked them up the nose, stools turned into sharks and chased them away and eventually, they turned on the girls. Caitlin hadn't laughed so much in a long time. If she wasn't laughing at the men she laughed at Quinesha, whose laughter, once started, sounded like a seal. She was hilarious, but all the fun stopped when Quinesha spotted Axon and Zylon.

'What's he doing here? And Glow, isn't that your boss?' She pointed to Zylon and Axon who sat by the outdoor bar having a chat. 'This is my chance, Glow. Let's join them and sort this out once and for all.'

Caitlin had instilled confidence in Quinesha today, yet she had a feeling it was the work of Calyx that gave the goddess that extra bit of gumption to suggest the reunion.

Caitlin gathered up her hair and tied it into a bun as she spoke. 'Well I can't be rude, I guess. Better come with you and say hi to my boss. That's if you're sure you're ready to face Zylon?'

'I'm very sure. I'm owed an explanation for being led on, as Calyx has taught me. No more am I going to play the victim.'

Calyx put his hand up to her. 'That a girl!' She high-fived him. 'Go give him what you did me... but not so sweetly. Get the whip out.'

'What does that mean?' Her brows squeezed together.

'Don't worry, I'll teach you that later. Just go say your piece and feel better.'

'I will.' She looked determined and started to wade towards them but came to a stop, spinning around to facing them when she realised she wasn't being followed. 'Well, aren't you coming?' She eyed them.

'Didn't know I was invited. Wouldn't miss it, we're right behind you,' Calyx said.

'What did you say to her, Calyx?' Caitlin had a questioning grin.

'That's between her and me. I doubt that the new and improved Quinesha will put up with any nonsense from us men from now on.'

'Fair enough.' Caitlin shrugged and nudged him. 'You sure have proved your worth.'

'Good job!' Jett followed them.

'I'm not finished yet. Watch me make the boyfriend jealous.'

Just before they reached the table Calyx picked up Quinesha. She squealed with laughter as he ran with her towards Zylon and Axon. Placing her on one of the chairs, he noted the jealous eyes of Zylon as they burned into him. Zylon knew him, and of his reputation, and therefore, Calyx enjoyed this torment all the more after the mess the God of Forests had caused on Earth. After shaking Axon and Zylon's hand, he made himself comfortable in the chair next to Quinesha, putting an arm around her just to annoy him a little more. Calyx spoke to Axon. 'We spotted you, and thought we better come see if there was anything you wanted of Glow Girl before we really get our party in full swing.'

'She's on break and free to enjoy her time off.' Axon acted official to show this was a coincidence.

'Thanks, Boss.' Caitlin and Jett had arrived in time to hear what was said.

This was tricky. Everyone knew why they were there except for Quinesha and Zylon.

When Zylon stood to greet Caitlin, she smiled, pleased he had come. 'Wasn't expecting to see you today.' She hugged him and spoke quietly to him. 'Here's your chance to take Quinesha aside and sort this out.' She stepped back and introduced the final party. 'Jett, this is Zylon and my boss, Axon.' The men shook hands. *Phew, this is getting complicated.*

She sat down next to Calyx, leaving the rest up to destiny.

Jett grabbed a chair from the table next to them and sat between her and Zylon. Upon hearing Caitlin's thought, he nodded to her, agreed he too could see the hurt in Zylon's eyes to see Quinesha with another man. It confirmed to Caitlin how much in love Zylon was with her also. She had been right to bring this couple together. It would not just end the world famine, but reunite a spark of love that was sabotaged by the vengeful Goddess of the Moon, Queen Chandra.

The waiter placed glasses in front of them, and while filling them with water, Zylon leant across and spoke to Quinesha. 'Would you like to talk?'

She nodded, and they both got up and headed for the stools at the bar. As they walked their hands touched and he grabbed for it, stopped, held it to his lips and kissed it. Words were not spoken, but a rainbow appeared above them. Human eyes would never capture the bright glow that followed them to the seats where they now sat. Not for a moment did Zylon let her hand go, and when they started smiling, Caitlin breathed out deeply. It had worked, but would it be enough for Quinesha to remove the curse she had put on the world?

'Where did they go?' Axon stopped talking at one stage and looked around.

Jett grinned. 'I've been eavesdropping. Quinesha invited him to her room so they could speak in private. They're kissing so we could be here awhile.' He tuned out. 'Time to give my telepathy powers a rest.'

* * * *

It was the wee hours of the morning when Zylon and Quinesha finally did surface. Axon, Jett, Calyx and Caitlin had enjoyed a late dinner and were playing cards. They were unable to sleep until they knew the spell had been removed and the rivers ran free again.

'Glow, can we talk in private?' Quinesha sounded older.

'Sure!' Caitlin walked away from the others with her.

When they were far enough away from prying ears, she stopped and turned to talk. The glints in her eyes were now windows of the intelligent woman she had become.

Quinesha stood tall and confident. 'I see through those games you played, you know. I did as soon as I saw Axon look at you. I realise it's the same way Zylon looks at me. I knew at that moment he loved me as much as your Axon no doubt loves you. I had got to thinking before we came down to see you, how those games you played to open my eyes up must have been difficult for you. You're in love with Axon. To kiss Jett and Calyx must have been very uncomfortable. I know that because I couldn't kiss Calyx, while in love with someone else. Yet kissing Zylon before felt just right, perfect in fact.' Her eyes lit up as she gave it a thought and smiled.

'Guess my acting wasn't that good after all,' Caitlin admitted.

'I will never forget the sacrifice you made. Or how hard you worked to make me see what was truly meant for me could not be taken. I was so childish and my tantrum almost lost the man of my dreams. To have a goddess of your stature be my confidante for so long, has made me want to grow up and be you. I fully understand the way this was handled, and I appreciate the patience shown to me. These last two days especially, really shook me up. It opened my eyes, and because of this I have been deemed worthy and fed much information from the universe to help make me a better goddess. I'm now one, I hope you will not only like, but one day be proud to call a friend.'

'Quinesha, goddesses are given powerful magic. It is how we use that magic which defines us. If we use it for good, we stay genuinely caring and loving goddesses. If using this honourable magic to harm others, it draws power from the dark side, and any goddess caught knowingly doing this is banished as a sorceress.'

'What happens to them?' Quinesha suddenly went pale.

'The highest title ever held as an evil witch is that of a Queen. And this is the reason why Chandra was relegated from Goddess of the Dark Side of the Moon to Queen Chandra. With this in mind, it's only you who can decide what path you walk. Up until now, I have protected you from the Congress of the Heavens, but now you know who we are, I can no longer defend you. That time has run out. Here and now you need to show me if my loyalty to you was misplaced.'

'My answer needs no words. I don't want to be bitter any longer. And I know now I don't need to be like you, Glow. Zylon loves me just the way I was before all this madness. I want to be that woman again. I'm in love, and I want to bear children to that man and raise them in a healthy environment. And as you have pointed out numerous times, this dry, arid and broken land out there is no place for kids anymore. I want for them what I never had, so I start today, right this moment. I am going to have to work at it, but I want to become a true and worthy goddess. My first job is to fix all I have wronged. I'll make this a safe and fruitful life for not only my future children but for all children.'

She closed her eyes, her hands went straight up high in the air and with a certain grace, Caitlin hadn't seen in her before, Quinesha chanted in a language unfamiliar to her. The goddess was doing as Caitlin had hoped, reversing the spell on the lands. The ground shook. The sound of water bursting through the lower levels, deep within the Earth's surface, rushed beneath them. It was a testament that Quinesha was choosing to walk in the light and keep her status as a goddess. She might not be the Goddess of the Waterfall, but she must be something to keep her and Zylon close. Definitely, she needed a position where her powers couldn't be so destructive. She'd have to spend many centuries proving her worth.

Caitlin smiled. Earth didn't have a Goddess of Vegetation. That, she thought, would be perfect. Quinesha would never destroy that which she loved so much. To Quinesha, a garden was a precious sanctuary. This Caitlin would put to Axon and the Congress of the Heavens at Quinesha's hearing. Her recommendation to be a mentor should get this new title passed quickly.

Chapter Fifteen

Masquerade Ball

C aitlin had tears in her eyes later in the day when Axon took her back to view the locations that had been destroyed. Already nature's seeds from the earth had begun to sprout. 'In a few weeks, we can start bringing back the Earthlings that you gave sanctuary. This will be beautiful by then.' Caitlin felt overwhelmed.

Axon held her close. 'They will need housing, so it might be best to transport the temporary housing we had built for them as well. The communities are overrun and won't be easy to shift, so we'll need Calyx and Jett to lend a hand.'

'I know they will. This was quite a shock for them. Calyx has already mentioned he can wipe any memories to do with off-world living and the magic that got them there.'

'Mmm.' Axon rubbed his chin between his finger and thumb as he gave it some thought. 'Maybe we can move them while they sleep. They will think it's all been a dream. Not sure about the memory-wiping thing after what happened to you, my sweet.'

Caitlin turned to him. 'Having a mind and soul that is both immortal and goddess was my problem. The human brain is much easier to manipulate. Calyx wouldn't have suggested it if he had doubts. This race, the gods wish to keep alive.'

Axon pointed to the river so full of running fresh water that it almost overflowed the banks. 'I will organise with Aqua, for the river to be filled with fish from, Aquarius. The ruler Aurus from, Taurus, has already offered to fill their pens with cows for milking. He will also throw in a couple of prize bulls for breeding. Many other constellations and planets have also offered to lend a hand.' He wiped Caitlin's tears that suddenly ran down her cheeks.

'That is so warming to hear.' She gave a sob from the kindness of others.

'They do it because of you, Cait. Peace is spreading across the universe. In some areas, it's slow going and some places it does not exist, but they haven't met Glow Girl yet.' He grinned.

'Even with all this help, Earth will take time to recover.' Caitlin shook her head, wiped her wet stained face and looked up at him. 'My heart breaks for not being able to prevent this before it got out of control and I so wish it could have been fixed while with the Riders. I really let them down. Will Rory ever forgive me for walking out?'

'You know Rory. He looks at you like family. He will be over the moon, as I am, that you are you again. It's wonderful to see you in your element. It took me some time to see I love that about you. And yes, I know jealousy got in the way. But my promise is that I will always keep your work separate from our private life. You work with hardened criminals at times and your dedication to showing them the right path to travel should never come between us and never will again.'

'I appreciate that, Axon. This job has me so focused at times reality disappears. I am at peace with it now and glad you are too. Honestly, it's nice to come home to family and friends who love me for real and don't need my magic to make that happen.'

'I love to hear you say that Cait, but don't underestimate the friendships you are making outside the home. It may be your inner goddess that sets you off on these missions, but when you're with them, it's you who wins them over. Look at Calyx and Jett. They are amazing friends to you... to us both... although I'm still not sure why they did forgive me.'

'They forgave you because they see you as their equal. You're up high on a pedestal in their eyes, and you have deserved your place amongst these gods. The three of you may not always see eye to eye about me, but you are fair and just. These qualities they admire.'

'And once again, this foresight is credit to you, Cait. They carry your light. It's as if you leave a little piece of you wherever you go. I saw it today in Quinesha and Zylon. You have worked hard on both. In the case of Zylon, it was without your magic. Yet, even so, that look Jett gets in his eyes when he looks at you is that same look they had when saying goodbye to you. Being a part of this is amazing. I feel privileged it's me who gets to take you home.'

Axon always made her feel so loved, and she hated having to spoil this moment. 'Unfortunately, with you, I feel I'm always the bearer of bad news.'

'There is more to come?' Axon's eyes widened.

'I can share one thing; there is something terribly unsettling in the universe. But please remember, if it does require my time, I am only going to ever be in love with one man, and that is you.'

'I know sweetheart and those feelings are mutual. I've been one first-class fool in the past, but never again will I question your love for me.' He kissed her long and romantically. Suddenly his mind was taken over by her scent, her delicious tasting mouth and the feel of the most incredible body he had ever felt. It moulded so perfectly into his, he grew large and hard. He wanted to take her right there on the mountain top but knew it was her fragrance that suddenly turned up high, which had changed his usually calm persona. To take this further would have him in a frenzy. To ever hurt her would break his heart. He had to get her back. The goddess had begun to work within Caitlin, and this was always the first sign. He had to allow her to do her job as the Goddess of Peace. He kept mindful the warning from his boss, Zoren. 'If you marry her, Axon, you will have to stand aside when she is called upon. She belongs to the universe now.' Somehow, he found the strength to pull away from her and in a flash, he had transported them both back to their room.

'Where are we?' She was disorientated for a few seconds.

'We're back in our room, honey. We have to get ready for dinner with Calyx and Jett.' Axon watched her nod and head for the shower.

It had started. She was despondent and questioned nothing. Her mind was on what was ahead and what she must do to accomplish her next task. When she came out, she was dressed in a tight black cocktail dress. The thick belt made it quite short. Her hair was up. Delicate curly strands rested sexily on her shoulder. She looked amazing but this show, unfortunately, was not for him. He sighed and kissed her forehead. 'You look beautiful, Cait. I guess we may as well go then. We're due to meet up with Calyx, Jett and their wives in a few minutes.' He would never like this side of her work, but he loved her too deeply to give her up. In his world, he was also called upon, and many times she had been the one who waited patiently for him. This was his turn to be tolerant, and he had to step aside to let her work. He wondered if Caitlin heard him, although she did give him a mesmerising smile when he opened the door for her. *Her beauty radiated health and he wished he was the evil she was set to encounter.* But he knew he would be a pushover, give in within seconds, and bow at her feet. This thought at least made him smile. He took her hand, and they walked down to the restaurant that overlooked the sea.

* * * *

As Caitlin walked with Axon, she couldn't help feeling dark eyes burn into her. There were three men at the bar that stopped talking and watched her intently. She wasn't used to this attention on Earth and it surprised her. They had almost reached their friends when she stopped and pulled Axon close to her. 'Do you know those three by the bar? Not sure, but have a feeling they are not from this world.'

Axon looked dumbfounded at her talking to him. Yet, as smooth as they come, he slung an arm around her and kissed the top of her head. At the same time, he took a peek at them and bent close to her ear. 'Never seen them before, but they sure are picking up your goddess aroma. To notice it from that distance they are from off-world. Definitely immortal and have that hard-core ruler air around them. Not just one, but the three of them can't take their eyes off you.'

'I've attracted them for a reason. I best go find out why?'

'Cait honey, let's wait until we join up with the guys. There's something not right about them and my danger radar is up. I'm not saying no, just think it best if we know who we are dealing with, and it wouldn't hurt asking Calyx and Jett if they know them. It will give you an edge.'

'Don't look so worried, Jett and Calyx make those three over there look like boys.' She grinned. 'Seriously, I'll be okay.'

Axon dropped his arm from her. 'Then if you're sure I'll back off and let you do what you do best. Be gone my lovely and attract every goddamned man in the universe, you sexy wench.' He pulled her in for a hug. 'And when you're ready for a real man, come and find me.' His smile was charming.

'I'll be sure to find you when the night is done. But for the moment it's been a long time since I had a girls' night. Hope you men remember how to party on your own.' She chuckled. 'I'm taking the girls to help me catch three fish.' She ran off from him. Throwing her arms around Melita and Zuri, she whispered to them. 'How about us gals go and have some time out from the guys.'

'Girl time sounds wonderfully wicked. What did you have in mind?' Zuri licked her lips sexily and made them laugh.

'Do the boys know?' Melita whispered.

'Axon's telling them now.' Cait grinned. 'Listen.'

'Looks like our women are blowing us off. Feel like a drink?' Axon spoke to Jett and Calyx.

'Bye guys!' Zuri chuckled and enjoyed the idea.

Melita ran to Jett and gave him a peck on the lips. 'Sorry.' She smiled sweetly.

'Go have a good time, sweet pea,' he said, and shook his head at Caitlin. 'You better look after my wife.'

Melita ran back to Caitlin and Zuri, looking happy. Slipping her arms through both girls, she smiled. 'Where to?'

Zuri turned to face them. 'There's a masquerade party going on inside with music and free cocktails for the ladies. I say we get a mask from reception and go join the festivities.'

'Couldn't be more perfect,' said Caitlin.

As figured. The three men Caitlin noticed earlier followed them into the reception, and they too waited for masks. To get a better look at them, she stood back from the desk, leaving Melita and Zuri to go through the box and pick out three reasonable-looking masks.

The men chatted in low voices, just occasionally loud enough to hear. What stood out to her was how different they were from each other. She thought maybe they came from worlds apart. One had a shaved head and tattoos running up his neck, the tall one kept fidgeting from one leg to the other, apparently not comfortable with the chosen venue. With his crooked nose, scars and sturdy build, she thought he looked like a boxer, and a dance would not be his choice of fun. The third one with the dark skin, hair and black piercing eyes acted very proper. He stood quite regal. She would have thought him royalty, but that made no sense with him being here unguarded. He didn't seem to fit in with the two he was with, yet was comfortable in their presence as they joked around. The boxer was getting teased about not being able to keep a beat. She could only just hear him say that it was his turn to choose an activity next. If they didn't quit it, he'd be making them sit through the opera. The other two cracked up laughing.

'We love the opera, twit.' The one with the tattoos pinched his mate's arm.

'You'll keep, you little pest!' the one she thought looked like Rocky said in good humour as the receptionist moved over to them.

'Here are the masks you ordered, Mr Howler.' She passed them to the regal one of the three.

Caitlin was surprised to find the men who'd stared at her outside, had pre-booked in for the Masquerade Ball. She shrugged, for they sounded as if they looked forward to the dancing as she did. Always on the job, she hoped she got an opportunity to speak to them. She was keen to learn what they were doing here when Zoren had forbidden all off-World travel to Earth while it was under threat.

She watched Mr Howler hand a mask each to his friends. Still joking around with each other, they headed towards the door that would lead them to the party.

As Mr Howler, which she doubted was his real surname, walked past Caitlin, he gave her a smile. 'Can I ask you for a dance later?'

She grinned. 'Sure, but I have two left feet. Better make sure you're wearing steel caps.'

He bowed his head slightly and looked up with a glint of amusement at her words. 'Look forward to the bruises then.' He walked off with the other two in tow. Both nodded politely at Caitlin as they passed her.

* * * *

'This is a fantastic idea, Caitlin.' Melita leant back in the lounge where they sat together.

They had danced with so many men, yet many still looked keenly at the three women who had stopped to take a break.

'Wow, so much eye candy. You know I can't remember how long it's been since us three enjoyed time alone. It's been too long.' Zuri sipped on a cocktail and shifted the umbrella out of the way to lift the strawberry from the edge to eat. 'Yep, looking at the menfolk in these parts sure makes you see why Cait picked this venue to have some fun. It's been a good night.' They touched glasses.

'Hear, Hear, to that!' Melita agreed.

Caitlin found Zuri so entertaining. She had one of the hottest hotties in the universe but always managed to turn the conversation around to men. Caitlin guessed it was from all those indiscretions she had to deal with when Calyx was Zeus. He was a different person now, and in time Caitlin hoped she would trust him and not keep looking for that other someone 'in case' she was tossed aside again. Caitlin's thoughts shifted to Mr Howler as he danced past with a young woman dressed in designer clothes. He sure could pick them, giving her cause to wonder why he persisted with her. He had come up several times to claim Caitlin for a dance but was never quick enough. Interested, yet not knowing why, she watched him dance the rumba. He sure knew his steps, and his moves were flawless. *A man who can dance like that couldn't be all bad.* Not quite sure why she watched him so intently Caitlin looked away and starting up a conversation with Melita.

The music changed tempo, and on hearing a man's voice close to her she looked up at him. 'You promised me some bruises. Reckon this tango might just work for you.' Mr Howler stood very straight and tall with his hand out.

'They're your feet, why not!' She placed her drink on the table and stood. She had no sooner walked to the floor with the dark-eyed mystery man than his friends were at the table asking Melita and Zuri to dance. Caitlin heard them accept and smiled to think they could enjoy a dance they both loved. Proficient in all dance genres the girls made it easy for anyone they partnered with. She, however, had never been a fan and only knew enough about the tango to get by. If her intuition hadn't been screaming at her to get to know these three, she would have rejected him and fobbed him off to one of her friends. Moving close to him, she noticed her dance partner had got hot and had unbuttoned the top area of his shirt. Dark skin, black chest hair and ripped muscles flexing made it difficult to concentrate. While her head was turned to the side, she followed his moves easily. It was when facing him and being so short, that she had trouble with Mr Howler showing so much chest. Embarrassed for not knowing where else to look at times had her stumble once or twice. *Gee, I'm married. Cover up.* She chuckled to herself, wondering just how strong her goddess aroma must be. *Sure wants me to notice him. I get it... now pack it away.* She giggled again, only out loud this time.

'What's so funny, beautiful?' He smiled radiantly.

She had been sprung and had to scramble for a reason. 'Oh, just wondering how long you can handle my torture. Your feet must be battered and bruised by now.'

'You are but a delicate butterfly in my arms... not at all torture. Your laughter is what leaves the mark. It is mesmeric and has me floating, my lady.'

Caitlin grinned up at him. *Yep, the goddess scent was set to maximum.* She glanced around the room. Females never picked it up and neither did mortal men. But Mr Howler and his two friends danced near to her. Why that was, she still tried to work out.

'That is very kind of you to say.' She reacted to his flattery by fluttering her lashes, and bowed her head slightly, feeling this would appeal to his old worldly vibe, yet why she cared she didn't know. She was glad her mask hid her more than confused expression. He seemed lovely and danced wonderfully, yet she was pulling him close with a need to be with him too. What a strange night it had become. There was so much magic in the room it was hard for her to break from him. It dawned on her it was coming from him. He was almost as powerful as Calyx. She had to break from him. This was not good. In his arms, she was practically helpless.

The music stopped, and so did the magic. She realised it was the energetic dance that made his power so extreme. At least, she hoped that was the reason. Otherwise, he would be a force she would struggle to beat. Now released, Caitlin once again had the upper hand and breathed in and out to relax. At the same time, the three men walked their dance partners back to where they found them. It was a polite nod after thanking them before they made a quick exit through the door together. They had noticed something not quite right, and Caitlin knew they had gone to discuss it— *her.*

'Wow, what was all that about? You sure have attracted some outer space bad boys.' Melita sat back with a drink, sipping it while waiting for an answer.

Zuri watched the men leave. 'That guy you danced with is one powerful sorcerer. Not sure what Home World he comes from, but my guess he rules over more than one.'

'You're right and sorry to involve you, I had no clue his boys would ask you two for a dance while I was gone. I noticed them earlier but the one I was worried about looked harmless dancing with other women so started to wonder if I was wrong about him. The only way to be sure was to dance with him. It did expose him but in doing so, I have blown my cover. My goddess scent was up high and it has made him guess I'm immortal too. I suppose he's gone off to discuss who I am with his friends.' Caitlin shook her head. 'It was the dance. It provokes the man to strut around and be domineering. I can tell you one thing, he is very powerful and if I'm right he doesn't use it for good. Worst is, I think he just worked out who I am and will be cranky he fell for my charms.'

'But he didn't show it.' Melita looked towards the door, but none of the three had re-entered.

'I felt it at the very end. He worked it out the same time as me.'

'I don't like this, Glow. We should go find our men and stay close to them for the rest of the evening.'

'You should go,' Caitlin agreed. 'But I have to stay and see this through. There is always a reason for everything, and the reason for this will present itself.'

Both ladies stood up. 'We know you're working and can take care of yourself, Glow, but this is way out of our duties and we'll have to leave. Our husbands would be furious if we stayed where there is a danger. I suggest you come with us but know you won't, will you?' Zuri had a pleading tone.

Caitlin shook her head. 'Sorry, but I swear I'll be okay and join you shortly. Please don't worry. This is what I do.'

'I know.' Zuri patted her hand. 'But if we don't go now, we'll be in more trouble than you could ever get into.'

They hugged her and with a spring in their step they left quickly.

Now alone, Caitlin put her head back against the seat and closed her eyes. What could these men have to do with the future? Yes, they were breaking the law, and she may just have to serve them a slap and a warning, but she knew there was something more going on here. The why, she was not yet getting told. They had set off her goddess side, and generally, this meant something so much more sinister was brewing. Her thoughts went to Mr Howler. He drew power from the dark side but didn't strike her as evil in himself. Neither did his friends. They were charming and polite from what she saw when they danced with Melita and Zuri. Maybe they were just here on holidays having fun, and being so wound up over Quinesha, had her react strangely to these off-world travellers. Really, they were no different to most rulers she had met. They were all a little dark, although not as dark as Hades and Zeus were. *Until they became friends.*

She smiled and decided the lure was just left-over energy and anxiety from her last mission, which ended only that morning. Her mind was sorted and breathing out calmly, she stood up. She was ready to join her own party and leave well enough alone.

'Where are you going?' Mr Howler's voice came from behind the couch.

Caitlin had just removed her mask, so she had no choice but to reveal herself. She turned and grinned politely. The three men had also removed their masks, allowing her to see them too. This, she admired.

'I was heading out to join my friends and find my husband.'

'They left?' He raised his brows.

'I stayed to finish my drink and listen to the last song in the bracket. I rarely get a chance to have a night out. Unlike my friends, my work consumes me, so I tend to drag every bit of excitement from the evening.' She smiled. 'They aren't far away, just at the bar on the far side of the pool.'

'Would you mind if we walked with you, to see you there safely?'

'I'm sure it's safe enough for a woman to walk around these secured grounds, but if you are heading that way I wouldn't mind the company.'

'You have us as bodyguards anyway, as we think we know who you are, and it would be our pleasure to look out for you down here.' Mr Howler raised his eyebrow, daring her to deny it.

Caitlin smiled. 'Then you are one up on me as I have never met you before, but I do know you are breaking curfew by being here when not permitted. Aren't you worried one of my friends will rat you out?'

'What curfew? We haven't received notification or NAV caution. Not that we'd take notice of it anyway.' He grinned.

'Ah, rebels of the universe.' She was amused with such outright honesty. She had called him out for doing wrong and liked the fact that he took it well. 'In that case, please share with me your aliases you use while off-world. That way if I do decide to ask you to join our party, no one will know you to dob you in.' She put her hand out and introduced herself. 'They call me Glow Girl.'

'Ah yes! I thought so. But the rumour never said you were

married.'

It surprised her that being married didn't deter him from wishing to be in her company. Instead, he looked pleased he had not only guessed her identity but found out what others didn't know yet.

'You listen to gossip?' She grinned.

Mr Howler tilted his head and eyed her. 'When it amuses me. For instance, I was greatly pleased to learn about a certain redhead who broke the heart of Zeus. You are she, I am positive, but I assume this was before you were wed.'

Caitlin chuckled. 'Yes, I met Zeus before I was married. But don't go repeating this story about me breaking his heart. It is far from the truth.'

'That is debatable. You are very beautiful, and I like to think he finally got what was coming.' He looked at his two friends and, getting a nod of approval to introduce them, he turned back to her. 'I go by the name of Jovis while travelling. We call this big goof Rocky, because of his crooked nose and scars. And this one...' he rubbed his friend's bald head, is Artisan. Yes, because of all his artwork.'

It was then she shook their hands. Each one looked at the hand she placed in theirs with interest. Jovis turned it over and studied her carefully. 'I don't mean to offend you, but you have skin as soft as a baby. How is that so? Do you live in cotton gloves?'

She pulled her hand from his. 'No—and no! It doesn't offend me but is a story too long to tell.'

'I will look forward to you entrusting me with both stories if we ever meet again. It interests me how you stole the King of Gods' heart and smashed it beyond repair, with only the hands of an angel.'

'I look forward to boring you to death then.' She laughed and made the three of them chuckle. *Good, they had a sense of humour.* Jovis was extremely attentive, and she found his kindness towards her awesomely sweet. 'You are very flattering. I wonder then why you have no women with you. Or have you a *hall pass* from marriage?'

'Ah yes! That movie was hilarious. These Earthlings have quite a sense of humour. But alas, none of us has found a suitable mate yet.' He looked at the ring on her hand. 'Have you been married long?'

'A little over four years but unfortunately working gives us little time together.' Her eyes rested on the ring before looking up. 'However, this evening there is no work; not for me, anyway. So we are staying here to celebrate with friends. Well, that's after my husband wraps up his last meeting. This is the reason we women decided to go dancing. Now work is out the way for him too, it's time to join the party I came with, and enjoy the rest of the night.'

'And the other women you were with, I assume they are not close friends.' He paused as she looked confused. 'I don't mean to imply this, but if they were real friends, they would never go and leave you alone. It's not wise to be amongst masked faces that could possibly take advantage of a lady on her lonesome.'

'Oh no!' She got serious. 'They are two of my dearest friends. They went back to break up the meeting so when I arrive, they are ready to have some fun with me. You see, that celebration I spoke of is because of the success I had with my latest mission. You should stay for a drink after you walk me to them. Meet my husband and friends, and maybe even enjoy a few laughs to repay the gallant offer of protection.'

'We only need to see you safe, madam.' He bowed and held a bent arm out for her to take. She did, and as thanks for trusting him, he patted her hand. 'We are at your service until we reach your husband, fair lady.' He grinned with a glow to his dark skin. 'And after all those rumours about you, I am taken back with how beautiful and sweet you are. I was expecting...' He paused.

'You expected a mean old bag with tough leathery skin that is many centuries older.' She looked up at him with a smile. 'Don't believe everything you hear. Rumours are mostly exaggerated. I am just a woman who enjoys her life with a small circle of good friends. I don't get out much so if you see me overdoing it tonight you'll have to forgive me. This is the first time I've been out with my husband in a couple of years.' She chatted as they walked past the reception and out the automatic doors. As they strolled, they spoke of the lovely night sky and shared their amazement at the clear atmosphere on Earth and how lucky this planet was.

'Most of us are so used to breathing in gas, ice, and dust from asteroids, we take pleasure in the clear nights here,' Jovis said, baiting her with dark brown eyes, daring the inquisitive side of her he had yet to see to ask where he lived.

Caitlin ignored the temptation to find out more, confident he had dropped a hint deliberately and he would be gone in a second if she became too nosey. For this reason, she kept the conversation on lighter topics, enjoying the banter and dynamics between these extraordinary men. Although charming, they gave no further hints as to who they were or where they were from.

Back in the company of Axon and her friends, she introduced them. 'These are my guardian angels, Calyx and his brother Jett, and these are their wives Zuri and Melita.' They all shook hands. She put her arm through Axon's, and added, 'and this is my husband, Mr Wolf.'

'Just Wolf will do.' Axon shook Jovis, Artisan and Rocky's hands and greeted them with a warm smile.

Guessing Jovis was the boss, Axon offered him a stubby of beer. 'Drink?' When Jovis accepted Axon whispered in Caitlin's ear. 'And so it begins.'

CHAPTER SIXTEEN

Viewing the Damage

Caitlin and Axon slept through the wake-up call next morning. Well, that was what they were going to tell their friends. After finally pulling from each other's arms, they showered and dressed in casual clothes.

'Do you think anyone will be at the restaurant?' Caitlin brushed her hair and twisted it up into a bun.

'Maybe Jett and Melita; they were still partying when we came to bed.'

'They got on well with Jovis and his boys, didn't they?' Caitlin smiled.

'Sure kept us entertained. Those cocktails you ladies were drinking must have had some kick. You girls were one big handful last night. You had, Jett and Calyx laugh so hard I thought they were going bust a rib.'

At the restaurant, Caitlin saw a couple of her friends and squeezed Axon's hand. 'They stayed to say goodbye. Love those guys.' She couldn't wait to get inside. Her pace quickened.

Jett stood up and firstly shook Axon's hand before he bent and kissed Caitlin's cheek. 'Good morning sleepyhead.'

Melita hugged them both while chatting. 'Calyx and Zuri were unable to stay as they both had prior engagements.'

'Sorry, we're late.' Axon seated Caitlin then himself. 'That was one hell of a good night. You guys wake up all right this morning?'

'I had a great time, but we have only just arrived as well.' Melita eased Caitlin's worried look.

'Really... I don't feel so bad then.' Caitlin smiled at Melita. 'I had a great night too... at least what I remember.' Caitlin picked up the glass of water in front of her and drank heartily. 'I'm parched in fact; how many of those cocktails did we order?'

'Too many.' Jett peered over the menu at her.

She sipped her water.

Melita handed her a menu. 'Jett said you'd be here soon, so we waited to order. What do you feel like?'

'Think water will do.' She turned her nose up at the food at the next table and handed the menu to Axon. 'Tell me I wasn't loud and obnoxious and frightened those poor men away.'

Jett leant forward. 'You were on fire last night Glow, whatever it was you were doing, it worked. You had Jovis wrapped around your little finger. He didn't have a clue why he was so drawn to you and was quite spellbound by night's end.'

Caitlin sank back into her seat slightly drained. 'I'm not always aware of why, but that boost given from the heavens to have a good night sure has me wrecked today.'

Axon rested his hand over hers, 'better find that second wind because I doubt it's over yet, honey, your goddess scent has just kicked in again.'

Jett agreed with Axon. 'Yep, just picked it up. Jovis must still be here.'

Suddenly, Caitlin felt a boost of energy feeling that spark return and sat up straight.

'I want some of what you just had.' Axon noted the sparkle was back in her eyes and her skin glowed healthily.

'Maybe the redhead is coming out to play because you're picking on me and telling me I smell.'

Jett and Axon were back under her goddess powers again too, and snapped out of the hazy-lazy feeling from the hangover they both sported. Earth liquor was not something either was used to drinking.

'Pick on you? We haven't even begun.' Jett put the menu down, suddenly bright and alert.

Axon ruffled the top of her head. 'You, my darling wife, are so in for it. Flirt!'

'You should talk! Who stood talking to a blonde most the night?' She pushed at him.

'Well if my wife would behave once in a while I wouldn't have to entertain the woman whose eyes happen to be on your man toy, Jovis.'

She slapped his arm. 'Hard job you got! We could swap places, but you would look silly in a cocktail dress and heels.'

'Honey, I was born to wear lipstick and heels.' He puckered up, making them laugh.

That got Jett going. 'Calyx and I were so pissed at being ignored, we dropped a fart and blamed you. Should have seen Jovis's look... classic.'

'Bastards.' Caitlin giggled with Melita who leant over the table and slapped her husband for being mean, making him and Axon laugh louder.

It was then Axon spotted Jovis and Rocky. They had walked in, and the laughter attracted their attention. Axon gestured for them to come and join them.

'How's the head?' Jovis smiled at Caitlin.

'Fine now — and you?'

'I had very few drinks so I'm feeling okay. Was too busy keeping a certain someone out of trouble,' Jovis said.

'Really... who was that?' She received a smirk as he shook his head.

'So what's on your agenda for today, troublemaker?' Jovis teased.

'Coffee and something light before we head off— unless someone has a better plan. Work is the last place I want to be today,' she glanced at her friends seeing if they felt the same.

Axon reached for her hand. 'We can stay one more day if you're enjoying it here.'

'Wow, that would be great,' she turned to Melita. 'Do you want to stay? Maybe fill in a few hours this morning at the resort spa. It's been ages since we hung out, just the two of us.'

Melita leaned towards her, 'me, knock back a massage, facial and a chance to get my nails done, love too!' She turned to Jett, excited. 'If it's okay by you, dearest?'

'I guess so, how can I say no to that gorgeous smile.' He touched her face. 'I guess I can amuse myself for a few hours.'

He spoke to Axon, 'what about a game of golf while we wait?'

Axon shrugged, 'been a long time, sure, you can count me in.'

'What about you two.' Jett raised his eyebrow at Jovis. 'Got anything better to do?'

'Not until the boat leaves at two o'clock.'

'You're leaving then?' Jett secretly hoped they would so the four of them could have a quiet night together.

He smiled watching Caitlin inquisitive stare. 'When we can spare the time to come here, we always include a sleepover on Otto Island. You should come; they have some great entertainment on the beach and the sports activities can't be beaten.' He noticed they seemed interested and continued. 'If you have nothing else planned, and are possibly considering outdoor activities, it's worth the trip.'

'Tell me more; it must be awesome fun to beat what we have here.' Jett sipped on a coffee unconvinced.

He sat on the chair adjacent to talk. 'Just so long as you don't get caught up in the welcoming ceremony and drink their Kava it's a fun place.'

'Kava, never heard of it. Sounds intriguing,' Melita put her elbows on the table and leant in to listen.

'More than one and you'll hallucinate for the rest of the night. It works differently on immortals.'

Jett punched knuckles with Axon. 'Our kind of fun Axon,' Jett grinned. 'But unless we want a repeat of last night, there had better be other entertainment for Glow, other than sitting around drinking Kava.'

Jovis glanced at Caitlin and looked amused as he spoke to Jett. 'I agree. And yes, there are many activities on the island, and at night the beach is alive with massive fires where the locals dance in their ceremonial costumes. After the new moon ritual, it's followed by a hangi.'

'A what?' Caitlin screwed her face up.

'A traditional meal of roast meats and fresh vegetables tightly wrapped in banana leaves and placed on hot coals and left to cook underground. Takes a few hours but when they dig it up the cooking process infused with the earthy flavour is mouth-watering. Seriously, it's really quite delicious.' He added after seeing Caitlin's scowl.

'Eww, dirty food,' she shuddered.

'Ah finally, a chink in your perfection; you're a fussy eater.'

'Fussy!' Jett laughed out loud. 'You have no idea how hard it is to find food this little one will eat. Tell him, Wolf.' He nudged Axon, making sure he used his alias.

Axon joined in. 'She would sooner starve than eat anything other than what she classes as normal.'

'She cooks her own meals then. I'm guessing bacon and eggs are on her menu so she must be very handy to have around at breakfast time.' Jovis made comment.

'Hell no, she is banned from the kitchen, seriously, if you ever catch her anywhere near one and we are not around, save yourself. Cook something for her or shout takeaway.'

Caitlin screwed up her nose at Axon. 'Dobber,' she chuckled with them.

Jovis smiled without comment. She intrigued him more than any woman he had ever met. A female that couldn't cook, what then was her talent that had all the men around, adore her… *even me*? He glanced at the others before resting his eyes back on Caitlin. After revealing he knew Glow Girl, he wondered if she had told them. If so they didn't seem worried either way so he extended the invite so he could have a chance to know her a little more. 'We were surprised to be able to hire a boat complete with the captain. It's the busiest time of year and normally we are not so lucky. Also, reception tells us they have plenty of cabins available on the Island. So feel free to join us.'

Caitlin eyed him. It was apparent he had no idea what was

happening here on Earth. With so many humans living off world, it was not a shock to hear the resort had few guests.

Melita put her arm around Caitlin. 'We'd love to tag along if you have room on the boat. It sounds wonderful.'

'What she said,' Caitlin stood to pull Melita to her feet. 'But until then, we girls have other plans. See you guys at the Jetty.' She kissed Axon on the cheek.

Melita leant over and did the same to Jett before getting dragged out.

'Bye boys,' Melita waved back as they ran up the beach together.

* * * *

Walking towards the boat, Caitlin saw Artisan had joined the party. He was shirtless and leant back on one of the lounges chatting to Jovis and Rocky. His skin was covered in tattoos, and it was plain to see why they called him Artisan with all that art on his skin.

Caitlin's magic had gone ballistic when she thought island clothes. She had a white embroidered sundress over a fluorescent lime green bikini and on her feet were floral flip-flops. Her braided hair was finished off with small white flowers. The manicure she just had disappeared. French nail polish was replaced by fluorescent lime green varnish with a white floral pattern. It didn't matter how many times she tried to change it, the image of the island Jovis described put her back in the same outfit.

In the end, Melita gave up and let her be. 'You look sweet.' She smiled.

'I wanted a grown-up look, not sweet!' Caitlin grumbled and followed her to the jetty.

Axon and Jett leant against the boat waiting to help them aboard. Axon picked Caitlin up in his arms. 'Don't you look adorable?' He smiled as he lifted her into the boat.

'Stupid Rider magic kept making me all girlie,' she whispered.

'Well it is working fine if you ask me, I might just race you off for a few hours.' He spoke low enough so only she could hear.

She chuckled and leant close to his ear. 'You're so full of it, husband mine. You are just as intrigued as me to see where this adventure is taking us and why.'

This was Caitlin's first ever boat trip. She moved to the front of the vessel when it started up to get the full impact of the wind and spray of water as they sped along. The captain steered from far above in the fly-bridge, so here on her own, she was able to be herself. This meant keeping the secret of her inner glow when enjoying such natural elements.

Axon had encouraged her to experience the sea air, and although he wished he could have kept her company, he stayed put to keep her new friends occupied, allowing her time alone.

When they pulled up at Otto Island, Caitlin joined the others. The precious elements had left their mark. 'Now I get why they call you Glow Girl. From all that fresh air, you have a light sheen around you.' Jovis tilted his head down to look closer at her face. 'You must have thoroughly enjoyed that boat ride,' he said as they climbed out of the boat. 'Wish I could have joined you but your husband, well let's just say he sure can talk.'

'Can he? I've never noticed.' Caitlin grinned up at him. 'Actually, that was my very first time on a boat, and that was him letting me enjoy it.'

'You're having me on, that was honestly your first time?' he said. 'True!'

'You told me you didn't get out much but never to have had a boat ride...' His words trailed off... a goddess, so unworldly. He found it hard to swallow, yet there was an innocence about her that made him believe it to be true.

The captain interrupted them by bellowing from the deck. 'Head towards the palms. The welcoming party will show you to your rooms.'

Caitlin turned and gave the captain thumbs up before leaving Jovis with Jett and Axon, who had just caught up to them.

Jett grinned at Jovis's thoughtful stare she didn't want to hang with them. 'She goes where it's fun, and stays where she's loved. She'll be back once they bore her.'

Caitlin had latched on to Melita's arm and, ignoring the captain, they ran off together, giggling like schoolgirls, towards the ceremony held on the beach.

Jovis turned to Axon. 'Is she always this excitable?'

'Pretty much.'

'Well it's not my place to say, but I am a regular here and your wife has headed for the Kava drinking ceremonial area. My suggestion is, if you don't want her hallucinating the rest of the day, best you join her and take her somewhere less destructive.' He grinned politely.

Axon and Jett glanced at one another and back at Jovis. 'Holly crap... forgot about that!' Axon had no sooner finished his sentence than he was off after her. Jett jogged by his side.

Jovis waited for his mates to catch up before joining them. They arrived just in the nick of time. Caitlin had got into a sculling competition and was just about to throw back drink number three. She was having such fun that Axon and Jett stood back, letting her have one more. Surely it wouldn't hurt in her healthy state? Jovis took no chances. He wanted to have fun with her, not have to look after the crazed immortal she'd become. He pushed through the crowd and snatched her from the circle. Holding her in his arms, he made a quick dash and plummeted them both into the ocean. 'Trust me, with that stuff in you, my lady, your entire day will be ruined.'

She was still laughing when he lifted her out of the water and put her on her feet in the sand. 'You frightened the life out of me. Hope you know I can hold my liquor.'

'Not that stuff. So think of something else to do besides going back there and drinking.'

'Good idea.' Axon stood shading his eyes. He wasn't happy Jovis was acting so protectively of his wife, but was pleased that if she was to work for these rulers down the track, Jovis, at least, would treat her well.

Caitlin looked up and pointed frantically. 'I want to do that.' She ran to Axon.

Axon turned to see what had caught her eyes. 'Seriously! After drinking that rubbish?' He shook his head.

'I promise not to throw up. Come soar with me!' she tugged at Axon's hand.

'I can take her,' Jovis offered when joining them. 'I have participated in hang-gliding here many times.'

Axon shrugged. He knew Caitlin needed a chance to gel with Jovis for some unknown reason and decided to wait it out and see why. While she worked her magic on Jovis and his boys, it would give him a chance to catch up on his own affairs. At least staying close he could keep an eye on things at the same time. 'I'm sure Cait won't mind who takes her just so long as they are ready to take her now. As for me, I have to organise a room and after ditching these bags, I have a couple of calls to make before I'm free.' He smiled at Cait, who on hearing she had an escort, had already turned to leave. 'Have fun, honey!' He called out as she ran towards the chairlift. He did get an *okay, you too*, but the ocean drowned out anything else she called out.

'She doesn't like to wait, I see.' Jovis left quickly to catch up.

'What's going on, where's Cait going?' Melita asked.

'Hang gliding with Jovis,' Axon held back a smile at Cait's squeal of delight as Jovis caught up with her. 'He knows what he's doing, but sure don't envy him. Hope he has earmuffs.'

'Hope he wears her out for us,' Jett was amused.

'Can we go too?' Melita looked enthused.

'Maybe later, sweetie, the boat trip turned my stomach. Let's go and check in, and after a drink, I promise to take you.'

Rocky tipped his hat politely at Melita. 'If you want, you can come with us. I'm just waiting for Artisan to stop gasbagging to a local. That ride up there is the only reason we come here.'

'Really, you'll take me? That would be super cool.'

'If your husband doesn't mind.' Rocky eyed Jett.

'Sure, go enjoy yourself, love,' he said, and smiled.

Melita gave him a quick peck on the cheek.

That sorted, Rocky clicked his fingers at his mate to get his attention, and they headed up the beach. Closer to them now, Artisan waved and called to Jovis and Caitlin, 'Hold the chairlift. We're coming too.' The three of them jogged up the beach, puffing as they squeezed into the bench seat opposite, seconds before the lift moved off.

From a distance, Jett and Axon waved.

'You're not worried about Melita.' Axon turned to him.

'Have you felt Glow's powers? They wouldn't dare cross her and hurt her friend. Plus, I'd have to kill them, and Glow knows that. Then she'd be none the wiser who they were.' He smirked.

'It looks like we've both been dumped then, so how about a drink and cigar at the bar?' Axon suggested.

'A rest before Hurricane Glow Girl gets back sounds good,' Jett joked. As Axon had, Jett had also made the excuses not to go, to give Caitlin bonding time with these men. They didn't know who they were, but the energy surrounding them while with Glow proved this was big, and they both knew it.

Chapter Seventeen

Promise to Visit

At the top of the hill, colourful hang-gliders were soaring off the steep cliff.

Caitlin squealed as the ground under her disappeared as the one she and Jovis were in dropped over the cliff. Her scream was loud while the nose of the flying object plummeted towards the ground.

'It's okay, I promise we won't crash.' Jovis spoke confidently even though the grass below was coming up quickly.

In an air pocket, they finally lifted. Higher and higher the glider flew until the view was fantastic. The silence was eerie, more so than when Caitlin's ride flew her through space. Up there she could rely on the horse's magic, but here they had no motor and no magic, only gravity and the elements, which made it one scary ride. The thrill had Caitlin shuddering.

'Are you okay?' Jovis felt the shiver of her frame against him. Their weightless bodies sailed past mountains, giving his new friend spectacular views of the island.

The adrenalin rush had her heart beating fast. 'I'm excited, that's all. It's so beautiful. The view out to sea is to die for.' Caitlin wished she could share how pleasurable wow moments like this, on the different planets were the reasons why, as a Rider, she swore to protect them. 'It's so surreal I don't want us to land.'

'Can't prevent that but we can have another go if you want.'

'Really! Yahoo!' she yelled out in a big loud voice.

Upon landing, Caitlin wrapped her arms around Jovis. 'That was so cool.' She let him go to struggle out of the harness.

Jovis had not expected the heartfelt hug. It earned his friendship and he wanted to share a little more of himself with her. Once they were free, Jovis put his arm around her and transported them back to the top of the cliff. Skillfully, he landed them behind a clump of bushes out of sight.

Caitlin's eyes were wide, and her mouth opened in surprise. 'You're not just immortal, you're a ruler of a Home World?'

He nodded.

'Oh dear, I wasn't expecting that. Just promise me not to spoil this day by giving me details,' she said, worried.

'Agree. No details sound perfect.' Jovis was sincere. 'I just wanted you to know, so it's not a shock if we do cross paths up there. I'd hate for our next get-together to be ruined because I never told you.'

Caitlin grinned. 'I'd never get cross with you now you're a friend.'

'I won't hold you to that. I'm not a nice person when I'm on home turf.'

'The man Jovis, whom I have come to know, will always have my friendship. The other you, if he plays up, I will deal with when the time comes. But I'm not sure you are near bad enough to get a visit from me.' She poked him and grinned.

Her grin was cheeky and made him smile. 'Well don't say I didn't warn you. Here, there is no pressure, and so I am simply Jovis. This place always puts me in a good frame of mind, and you have put me in an incredibly cheerful mood.' His eyes lit up. 'So, let's give hang gliding another go and this time, can I have some fun?'

'Hell yes! Didn't realise you were taking it easy for my sake. Feel free to make me squeal like a little girl.' She chuckled when he roared laughing.

After the third go, Jovis shook his head. 'No… no… and hell no,' he said, before she could nag again. 'My ears cannot take one more scream.'

'Well... What about snorkelling.'

'That, I'd be happy to do. Only wouldn't you prefer to go and find your husband and drag him into the dark blue depths with you?'

'Yes, but trust me, if we go back now you will see him working and talking on the NAVcom, and unless we can find a doctor to amputate the earpiece, you can be sure he'll be like that until dusk.'

'He will join us for dinner?' Jovis asked.

She shrugged. 'Maybe he'll meet us on the beach later, but for dinner, he might have other plans once he knocks off.'

'It makes me inquisitive to know what would possibly keep him from someone so delightful.' He touched her nose gently and smiled.

'He works long hours like most men. I bet you do too.' She smiled. 'So go find your friends and enjoy the rest of your day. I have wasted far too much of your leisure time already and must apologise. The diving instructors will show me what to do.'

Jovis watched her glance around for where she needed to be. Her eyes were saddened, and she looked genuinely worried she was a bother. He realised she must have taken his reluctance to go one more time on the glider as a sign he had enough of her. That was far from the truth. He was the one who felt bad he'd taken her from the man who called himself Wolf. But if she was going to leave him and go it alone, *stuff that!* He had no intentions of that happening. His eyebrows pulled in tight, eyes opened wide. 'How did you conclude you have wasted my time? I believe you think far too much.' He took her hand and started pulling her up the beach towards the shack where they would be hiring the snorkelling gear.

She almost ran to keep up.

'I'll go it alone...' He mimicked her. 'Over my dead body an instructor will replace me!' His prattle made her laugh.

'Only a suggestion.' She giggled at his grumpy playful mood.

* * * *

Walking into the water's edge, Caitlin looked behind her, and could feel Axon's gaze on her. She waved to him and grabbed Jovis's arm. 'See, I told you. He's on the NAVcom.'

Jovis squinted against the light. 'Fair enough. So long as I don't go home with a black eye from stealing you away, I am more than happy to be your escort for the day.'

'Then escort away.' She pulled down her mask and put the breathing apparatus in her mouth. Jovis threw his head back and laughed as she lifted her flipper feet and started to run into the water. He thought she looked ridiculously funny. Yet he knew that was her plan to get him back in the mood and it had worked. Still laughing at her clumsy antics, he chased her.

In the water, Jovis kept her near. When large marine life came too close, he would pull her from them and put himself in harm's way. There were a surprising number of sharks, but most didn't seem to worry about them. It was mainly the tiger sharks that he protected her from. A sharp slap on their snouts and they would swim off. Down among the seaweed, on the ocean floor, he finally relaxed. It was here she had the most fun and patted small colourful inhabitants living in the coral reefs. A couple of hours later, feeling waterlogged, she gave in and followed Jovis back to shore. It was then a tiger shark came out from nowhere. Jovis had spun around but too late to help. Caitlin smiled at him and with a gentle motion held up her hand. The power generated from her magic created a transparent wall between her and the shark. The vicious creature had picked up speed to catch its prey when it hit with force against her shield. There was no sound. The shark was knocked unconscious for a few seconds as it floated towards the bottom of the ocean. *Whoosh.* Its strong tail began to work, and it took off quickly and soon was out of sight.

They surfaced, and Caitlin removed her breathing apparatus. 'That'll teach that girl-eating shark to sneak up on me.'

When Jovis removed his mask, he had the same look on his face as she had when finding out he was a ruler of a Home World up in the universe somewhere. 'What was that? You've acted like a fragile flower since I met you. I thought you…'

'Were a weak female that needed protecting.' She grinned. 'I can do some things. So Jovis that was me... being me. Just in case we cross paths up there and you get mad that I didn't share my skill with you.'

She turned his words back on him.

'Touché.' He grinned. 'Just remind me not to come at you too quickly. That shark is going to have one hell of a headache for the rest of the day.' He held her hand and helped steady her over the rocks, and out the water.

* * * *

Up in her room, Caitlin showered. When dressing, she imagined the festivities she was heading to on the beach and allowed the magic of the island night to cover her. On her lower midriff, a handprinted sarong of tropical hibiscus, palm leaves and frangipani appeared. Along with it was a matching bra. It seemed a little revealing, but she was getting used to this style of dress now. She smiled, thinking of the look Axon would give when seeing her. She reached up and adjusted the frangipani in her hair and then bent, twisting the ones around her ankles until they were how she liked them. *I sure hope this sexy look is for my husband for a change.* She blew her image a kiss. She and Jovis had shared a secret, and because of this, she was sure Jovis was content now he knew her better. She was confident she would have time with her man as Jovis was sure to be looking forward to time with just his mates after babysitting her all day.

The island was delightful this time of the evening, but as she strolled along the beach, she noticed Axon busy, deep in conversation with Jett. No doubt he was finding out what was really going on with the Ice Planets. Jett would tell her when he was ready. For the moment, a tropical sunset called her. She sat on the sand, mesmerised as the colours not only lit up the sky but reflected in the water below.

The moment was short. Music had her turn cross-legged to watch the entertainment that had begun right near her. She was glad they had time for this short stay.

Jovis came and sat beside her. 'Penny for your thoughts.' He said it quietly. 'I don't want to spoil your solitude, but wondered why you're alone?'

Her face lit up. 'Axon will join me soon. I have plenty to enjoy while I wait.' She smiled. 'I'm so glad we met, and Axon allowed this extra day. I'm having such a lovely time.'

'I thought you'd be up there enjoying this moment with him.' He glanced up towards her husband.

'I don't like interrupting him when he is so deep in a conversation. I could see he was discussing business with Jett, so I came down here to enjoy the island magic. Rest assured, he will find me when he's done.'

'If I were your man I would want you by my side twenty-four seven.'

Caitlin chuckled. 'If you knew me, I doubt that. Jett is my best friend and even though he looks forward to my visits, he is so happy to say goodbye, so he can kick back and have a rest.'

He laughed. 'Sure he does. You can clearly see how jealous he's been with me taking up your time. No doubt he generally spends it with you while your husband works. And anyway, you haven't mentioned what Wolf's important job is?'

'That's secret off-world stuff. If I tell you I'd have to kill you,' Caitlin joked. He looked letdown at not being trusted, so she smiled. 'It's important we keep who we are from spoiling this time we have together. It's been a blast, and when you do find out who is who, I hope it doesn't destroy the way you feel about us when next we meet. I mean, can you honestly say you have thought about your own responsibilities, up there, over the past couple of days? I sure haven't.'

'Well, no... Hell no! This has been a blast for us too.'

'Then I rest my case. What we do up there is tough, but when we are together like this, to me you'll always be just Jovis, my new friend.'

'If that is so, can I make a request?'

She nodded, 'sure.'

'Will you come and visit me, you know, up there? I'd like for us to become allies without all these secrets. So, if I promise to be Jovis, will you call in on us as you, not as a Rider? I mean to visit with the three of us... Artisan and Rocky as well. They think you are one fun, top-notch chick. Their words,' he smiled.

She searched his face. He seemed genuine. 'I have a demanding job, Jovis. Unless you were to cause me grief, there would be no excuse to visit. But we can holiday like this again one day. I mean for a couple of days maybe, but not for quite some time. I do have a lot on at the moment.'

He nudged her. 'Then I will have to cause lots of grief, so you must visit often.' His features were full of mischief.

'I'm confident you would try, Jovis, my friend. And if you did, I would have to discipline you, but then be on my way to the naughtier planets.'

'I can be a real monster I'll have you know.' He was persistent.

Caitlin watched the dancers get faster and quicker, in crazy wild dancing.

He whispered in her ear, 'that's how crazy happy I'd be if you said yes.'

'Maybe, although it will be up to Jett. My horse is injured, and Jett is my transport for a while until mine is available again.' She hoped this was a lead for Jett to grow his empire, and thought it best to include him. She also doubted Axon would ever let her go to uncharted worlds unguarded and alone.

'Oh?' He turned to her.

'Long story. Maybe trust you enough to tell you next time we meet. For now, all I can say is it's two for one.'

'So it's a yes.' He sounded thrilled.

She nodded. 'Yes.'

'Excellent.' He grinned.

'Two of us,' she reminded him.

'Okay, okay. The chaperone can come.' He was delighted she had caved.

Both were cast in a shadow and looked up.

Jett, Melita, and Axon stood over them.

'Hope I'm not interrupting, but I'm here to steal my wife back,' said Axon.

Caitlin put her arm up, and with a gentle tug, he had lifted her to a standing position. Jovis stood dusting sand from his pants. 'Kept her company while you were busy, that's all.' He turned to see his mates were ready to join him. 'Ah, and my friends have just arrived and are waiting, so I'll be on my way.' He waved to Rocky and Artisan who waited for him at the top of the stairs adjacent to the restaurant. He shook Axon's hand and as he shook Jett's, he slipped him a business card and whispered something to him. Jovis then kissed Caitlin and Melita on the cheeks before he turned from them and trudged up the sand.

He was unable to stop smiling now he knew Caitlin would visit. He had longed for the warm comfort of a happy soul for such a long time. Caitlin was someone who Jovis believed could possibly turn his dark world into a bearable living space. If she came, would he let her go? He didn't think so, not ever.

'Jovis wants me to visit his Home World,' Caitlin said as she watched him walk away. The visit must have been the final arrangement required because immediately after committing, her goddess side and the drain on her magic dissipated.

'Judging by his good mood, you said yes.' Axon eyed her.

'Plus a chaperone.' She grinned at Jett. 'But you heard me right.'

He nodded. 'Thanks, Caitlin. I know you could have taken your horse. That was very well played.'

Axon turned to Jett. 'Now that's organised, they should be able to manage the night without us. I'd like some alone time with Caitlin and bet you would like a break with Melita. I'll drop Caitlin off in the morning around nine-ish before I head into work.' He grinned and winked at him.

'Don't be late.' Jett gave him a Hades untrusting look, which made them laugh. 'We have a lot to discuss.'

'I will have her there as promised.' Axon gave him a Cub Scout salute which meant nothing but a stirring gesture.

Jett shook his head and took Melita's hand. 'I have something special planned for my Melita tonight, so I was hoping my guardian duties would be at an end.' He kissed Melita's hand. 'Come, my beautiful wife, our evening has only just begun.'

Melita gushed, 'Oh, you are my shining Knight, my sweet

husband.' She hugged Caitlin. 'Love you, girlfriend. You're my shining day.'

Caitlin smiled. 'And you, my dearest friends, complete my yin and yang. See you tomorrow Jett,' she called, watching Jett and Melita jog up towards the buggy rentals.

Axon scooped Caitlin up into his arms when noticing the goddess in her was gone. 'You're my everything, and I'm not sharing you for one more second.' He strutted up the beach towards their room. 'Mine!' he said to a giggly happy Caitlin.

He looked back along the beach before he shut the door. He caught sight of Jovis and his buddies clinking beer bottles and laughing together. Caitlin had done a good job with the one they had called Jovis. The dark, malicious glare had gone, and although the laugh he could hear was pure evil, it had a happy air about it. He closed the door. That out there was not over, but Caitlin had done all she could for the moment.

He dived onto the bed where he had left her. The giggles as he kissed her neck gave him shivers. She was one sexy woman, and he was in his element knowing she was all his again. This was his moment, she was his woman and he couldn't wait to get her naked. How his heart ached to have her to himself, forever!

Chapter Eighteen

Friend or Foe

It was early when Axon woke Caitlin. 'We have to be on our way, honey,' he said, laying little kisses on her shoulder.

Caitlin rolled to face him. 'Thanks for the extra relaxing day off. Hope you don't get into trouble with your boss for hanging out with us. I know we didn't get a lot of time together, but what we did have, was perfect.' She rolled over to get out of bed.

He pulled her back to him, his lips warm and delicious. 'I doubt Zoren would expect me to be early. After all, we did just wrap up one massive big headache for him. Earth is habitable again. He will be celebrating too.'

'Maybe Zoren will let you come in late, but Calyx and Jett will be waiting, and are not so patient. I have a feeling Jett's other worry is bigger than the puppy dog who guards his underworld.' Caitlin wiggled out of his grip.

Not giving up easily, Axon followed her into the bathroom. 'Jett has waited this long, I'm sure a couple more hours wouldn't upset him. Anyway, I am his boss and can override him.' *Mine!* He stepped into the shower with her and ran his hand lightly down her back, lingering warm lips and breath on her neck. The hair on her nape tingled, and goosebumps over her skin sent lustful chills deep within her. Weakened by his desire, she leant into his nakedness, allowing skilful fingers to find their way between her relaxed legs. He triggered a need she couldn't ignore. With closed eyes, she arched her back with pleasure.

'You are so mine, beautiful.' He turned her and kissed the soft, warm lips she offered. He groaned with pleasurable lust as he too became lost in the fire that was so easily ignited with the only woman he would ever love. *My Goddess!*

* * * *

Two hours later, Axon meekly dropped Caitlin off at Jett's and left her to explain why she was so late. Jett smiled, but Calyx looked irritated.

'If he can't get you here at the time discussed then maybe we should be picking you up. I'm a busy man and have more important duties to attend to rather than standing around all morning waiting while Axon has his way with you.'

'What makes you think that's what held us up?' Caitlin's face reddened.

'Look at you, you're literally glowing. And as for Axon, he had, *she's mine…* written all over his bloody face.'

'Calyx, we were still on the island until a little while ago. Forgive me for having some husband time.'

'Island?' He swung around to Jett. 'Did you all stay an extra night? Why am I only hearing about this now?'

'I was trying to tell you, but you've been like a bear with a sore head since you arrived. I haven't been able to get a word in edgewise.' As Jett spoke, he seated Caitlin at the table. 'Sit.' He motioned to his brother.

'Well, I'm listening now.' Calyx slumped into the chair.

Jett sat too. 'Jovis invited us to go over to an adjacent island. The girls went gliding with the newbies while Axon and I worked. He barely saw her. Poor guy needed some time with his wife.'

Calyx put his head down and took a deep breath. When he looked up at Caitlin, Zeus was gone and soft, kind Calyx was back. 'Sorry Cait.' He looked genuinely apologetic. 'You know I get jealous when it's anyone else but us that makes you that happy. It's why I left. I wanted to turn Jovis into an ice sculpture and smash it.'

Caitlin put her hand on top of his and smiled before removing it to grab a delicious-looking muffin from the basket. While cutting it in half and lavishly smearing butter over it, she looked over at them. 'Thought you might have returned after your meeting, now I know why. But let me put your mind at ease… I swear Jovis is no threat and has gone home happy. Personally, I think he just needed a friend. I don't believe for one minute he's anyone that could cause any of us any harm. I kind of think now that my attraction to him was misplaced due to my senses being slightly confused after the Quinesha incident. I mean, I'm not feeling any evil at all now. Axon commented that towards the end, even my goddess scent was turned down to normal. He seemed to think I had him wrapped around my little finger.'

'I wanted to knock that sickly-sweet smile off his fancy pants face,' Calyx snarled. 'He was looking at you as if he wanted to snatch you from us.'

Caitlin chuckled. 'Maybe he did. He told me he wasn't a very nice man and said, quote, "I was a bright light in his ordinarily dark world," at least I think they were the words he used.'

Calyx, who had got up to pour himself a coffee from the breakfast bar, stopped, swung around and stared at her. 'Where did he say he was from?'

'Just a dark world. That was all he told me. Oh, and he is a ruler as he does that disappearing thing you can all do.' She licked her fingers nonchalantly.

'So he's a ruler…' *A ruler of what?* Calyx's mouth twisted in thought.

'Well, only rulers of stars or planets are given the power to move around like that. He isn't a ruler of a planet because I know you all. So I assume he is from Kayden's sector, the stars.'

'But you said it's dark.'

'Where is this going?' Jett frowned.

'Well, if those men were under the Cloud Riders law, they would never have visited Earth, knowing it was forbidden. No, they knew nothing of what was going on down there. I could tell when it was mentioned. I had a feeling at the time they are off the heavenly grid of communication due to their positioning in the universe.'

'What are you alluding to, brother?' Jett was starting to follow his train of thought and wasn't too pleased where it was leading.

'What I think is that our little goddess here may have found and befriended your current arch-enemy, Vador, the ruler of the Ice Planet Sedna. And I bet his friends, Rocky and Artisan, are Torin and Wes, his best mates who run his two smaller Ice Planets, Quaoar and Orcus.

'What! I very much doubt those three men we all got to know could be the ones threatening your kingdom, Jett. They just couldn't be!' Caitlin folded her arms and stared at him. 'You gave me the impression the men trying to take your crown were tyrants. Maybe even hardcore criminals. I didn't get that from them. Yes, they had an evil streak, but it was so insignificant.'

'Maybe not to you, as your power has increased considerably. But through our eyes, those men were as dark and evil as they come.' Jett faced her seriously. 'You may have had them eating out of your hand, but it was the reason I stayed. I couldn't trust a word they said. You're unbelievable how you see only their good side. Hell, I couldn't find one. Axon watched you like a hawk. For him to do that, they really were bad news.'

'I want to know everything.' Calyx sat and patted the seat next to him for her to sit with him.

Frowning in disbelief, Caitlin joined him on the leather lounge by the fire and filled him in on what happened while he was not with them. She couldn't miss noticing the apprehensive glance at his brother when she mentioned using her magic in front of Jovis to scare off the shark. She tried to defend her actions. 'He confided in me he was a ruler by used his transporting powers. He said he guessed my name was Glow Girl but that was all he really knew about me. I felt more than anything, he lacked trust and honesty. Sharing was my way of showing I trusted him.'

Jett sat the other side of her. 'You had no clue who they were, did you?'

She shook her head. 'I was drawn to Jovis, but once I agreed to his wish to see him again, the magic holding us together released me. It happened just before you and Axon came down to get me, and honestly, since then I haven't given him a second thought. At the minute, I feel relaxed after a good time had by all. So figure I must have done the right thing by saying I would socially call in on him.'

'You what!' Calyx barked. 'You promised to visit him!'

Jett pulled from his pocket the business card Jovis gave him. 'I'm to text him on this number before I leave so he can shut down the security that prevents others entering.' Jett showed him.

Calyx pulled a face. 'No way, that's out of range. It has to be Vador.'

'I know that now,' Jett agreed. 'Thanks to you, bro. I was so busy watching out for Glow and listening to make sure she was all right, I didn't have a moment spare to think about Jovis as an individual and who he could be. This is the first time I have even looked at this card.' He ran a hand through his hair. 'It's all making sense now. This gives him time to stand down his guardian, the Gorgon. He wouldn't want Glow to end up a lump of stone. Me, well if he finds out who I am, I'll become the stepping stone to reach her.'

Calyx crouched to talk face to face with Caitlin. 'This man is very dangerous. I only say this because I felt how much power you had to use to keep him calm around us. He has also seen firsthand, after stopping that shark, how powerful you can be. Being a ruler of three Ice Planets gives him additional magic. At the start, you might have had him under your power to calm him, but that hold you felt disappear was all him. He wasn't letting you go until you agreed to do as he said. I can also guarantee he has shared his transporting powers with his two buddies. Drawing from the dark side of the universe makes them even more dangerous, and any of them could possibly lock up your magic and leave you helpless to defend yourself, as you know us gods can. It's not safe for you to visit him. Jovis knows if he gets you there he can keep you captive for a lifetime if he wanted to.'

Jett agreed with a nod. 'No man is equipped to make it safely past the Gorgon that stands guard for him. So if we did go, and by some miracle, I did manage to get out alive, we wouldn't be able to come and get you as nobody, not even us as divine beings, has been able to infiltrate his defences.'

'So don't even think about asking either of us to take you, because we won't, period.' Calyx crossed his arms. 'This next mission will not include you, Cait. Now I know who we're dealing with, you can't come. Jett and I will handle it from here. Neither of us would ever, risk you becoming a captured of such a tyrant.' He turned his head towards Jett. 'We have to come up with a much better plan before we even consider going near him. I just wish I'd realised who he was at the time. I would have turned them all into dust and saved us this and further anguish.'

Jett got up. 'I'm glad you didn't know him, brother. If he rules over three Ice Worlds, he would have been powerful enough to stand his ground and fight you. How that would have ended I hate to think.' He turned to walk out the room. 'I better alert Axon. Like us, he is not going to take this news well.' He left the room to talk in private.

Calyx looked into dazed eyes as he took Jett's spot on the sofa to speak to Cait. 'I know this has come as a surprise to you Cait, but talking might help.'

Caitlin could hear him, and although she wanted the thoughts she had to form into words for him, it was not what he wanted to hear. To show him she was okay, she calmly leant back and allowed her mind to drive her towards the right direction. She already knew there was only one path, and Calyx and Jett were going to flip out once they found out.

'I'm so cross with myself for leaving you there with that evil prick.' Calyx was unsure how to cope with her being this closed off and it seemed to be getting worse. Her body was there with them, but her eyes stared at nothing.

Jett came back in the room and sat beside his brother. 'Axon said if she is despondent, talk calmly.'

Jett listened to her while they chatted about politics. It was a topic that had nothing to do with the situation yet kept him calm until he felt her stir. 'She's coming back. I hear her thinking,' he told

Calyx. 'It's working.'

Calyx glanced at Jett, nodded and spoke quietly to him. 'I should have worked it out sooner, but like everyone else, I was caught up in her goddess trance. Well, until I got jealous. That pulled me out of it for long enough to say I'd had enough and I took my leave.'

'Or did she let us go? I pulled out of it when you did. But I wouldn't go. Neither would Axon. We didn't trust Jovis or his boys.'

Calyx sighed. 'I should be able to resist Cait more by now, and I will have to fight against it next time. I put her in grave danger by loving her so much and storming off.'

Caitlin frowned.

'She's back with us again,' said Jett, reading her mind.

She blinked to see Calyx and Jett speaking so quietly she couldn't catch what they said. 'I can't believe Jovis is Vador. It all makes sense to me now. The universe brought him to me as it did with you two. If it hadn't been for that chance meeting and strong bond we formed, Jett, you know you would have killed me. Or Calyx would. If you knew who I really was when you found me upstairs in the bedroom that day, wouldn't you have killed me? But before you answer, remember how you felt about me then. We didn't have the connection we have now. Tell me the truth.'

He shrugged. 'I've thought about that many times. It worries me even now, but I didn't. And as you say, maybe you stayed alive because of that first meeting. I remember feeling I missed you. I can't explain it accurately but do know this, if Jovis doesn't know anything about female friendships or love, I can see complications. The minute he starts missing you, it will confuse him, and unable to understand that emotion he might try and push it away. The instant he does, derision and hatred for you doing this to him will surface. In this bubble of evil, he can once again function normally. His normal, not yours.'

'Then I will cross that bridge when and if it happens.' She turned her head slightly, eyeing them both. Her confidence was back in spades and radiated from her poised frame. 'You both have to stop worrying further. I am now prepared and ready for what life tosses at me next. You need to have a bit more faith in me.' She put her hand up at the protests. 'He will not be happy to know you are Zeus and Hades either. If he's as smart as I think, he's searched to find out more about me and already knows where to find me. So even if he comes for me out of spite, then at least I will get to speak to him and maybe sort out this mess for you, Jett. I have been invited and this I must now do alone.'

Calyx leant forward and took her hand. 'I can hide you. Don't do this Cait. I fear for you. He isn't me. I'm a god and can control my temper.'

'I'm sorry, Calyx, but you should know better than anyone. I hid from danger half my life and ended up in the hands of the danger anyway. This deceit could mean war, and it must be sorted. My job as a peacekeeper means I can't allow that to happen. Don't stand in my way, or he will kill, and I will not have either of you die if there is a chance I can prevent it.'

Jett jumped to his feet anxiously, and irritated. 'He invited me too. I am your chaperone, and I'm coming.'

She shook her head. 'I will not risk any king's life, ever. I'm sorry Jett, but if we have worked out who he is, he will have also worked out who you are. You will walk into your demise if you dare go anywhere near him. And now you've told Axon, he will never allow either of you to go any further than this.'

'He will have no choice. I am going,' Jett roared stubbornly.

'No! This is Cait's mission now, and you men are to stand down. She doesn't need stubborn gods making this hard for her.'

Both men spun around when Axon spoke.

Jett put his head down, knowing the oath he took prevented him going against an order Axon gave. He then lifted his head to show a grave expression. 'The universe is paying my brother and me back for all the evil we have done to her isn't it?'

Calyx frowned with a heavy heart. 'How the hell did you handle it when we did this to you, Axon?'

'As you are now,' he said quietly. 'I blamed it all on how bad I had been over the centuries and thought I was getting paid back by the universe for all my evil doings. But it's not us. Cait has a responsibility to the planets first and foremost. She's a gift from the heavens to help in our quest to bring goodwill to all. She is not just ours. She is the Goddess of Peace and will always go where needed. This is what she does. If there is a way, she will come home to us when her job is done, and that is all I can beg her to do.'

Caitlin moved to him and wrapped her arms around him.

Jett sat back down with Calyx. 'Could we have seen this and stopped her meeting him? Like when she did her goddess thing? Couldn't you have warned us, Axon, and we could have all just changed locations?'

He shook his head. 'If she hadn't met him socially, it would go a lot worse for her when they do finally cross paths. Don't you see, I have thought of the many scenarios, and wished there was a way of preventing it.' He shrugged helplessly. 'All I can do when it starts to go down is to be the man she needs. I'll stand back and give them as much time together as I am able to cope with, so she can work her magic on whoever it is. After that, it is all up to fate.'

Calyx tried to stand up, but was too shaky. 'You knew.'

Axon nodded.

'Axon, you are a better man than me. I couldn't help myself and would have killed him. You know, got rid of the ache before it started,' said Calyx.

Axon shook his head. 'Then he would be replaced with maybe someone worse. Look at her eyes. She is already on the mission; she would hardly be able to concentrate on what we are saying. We've lost her already.' He smiled and kissed her nose. 'You see, she locks her emotions up, so she doesn't fear anything. We need to just enjoy the bit of time we have with her. I don't think it's long.' He smiled at her, knowing this would make her happy. 'She was pretty much like this last time.' He tucked some curls behind her ear so he could see her face better.

'How do you cope while she's away?' Jett asked, as he rubbed his hand together with nervous energy.

Axon looked up at him. 'Rider magic.' For her sake he kept his voice composed, his gaze never leaving her face while answering them. He glanced over now as the men were clearly rattled as neither had dealt with this side of her. Usually, they were on the winning side, and he understood this would not be going down well with these dominant individuals. Karma had stepped in, but would never be cruel enough to throw it at them, especially after all they had done for her. He knew Caitlin gave special friends rewards and one was the unique gift to feel her. He secretly knew that was why her father and Orion were not pestering her to spend time with her as these two gods did. He understood Calyx had also received this gift once, but when she dissolved all memory of him, the gift went too, and by the looks of Calyx, she'd never gifted it back to him. Maybe she didn't realise, *but now I do I should give him what she had once entrusted him with.* Axon felt a sense of responsibility. It was him who talked his wife into dumping all memories of her time spent with Calyx on Earth. And as for Jett, he deserved it more than anyone. His friendship went way beyond love and friendship. He looked at her as his child.

'What do you mean, Rider magic?' Calyx was intently staring at him.

Axon eyed the gods. As they were part of the team now and showed such dedication to Earth's mission, he decided they were trustworthy enough to be told the secret held between Riders only. 'I will tell you how we cope, but this is never to go past us.'

They both nodded.

'Rory has this exceptional gift. He connects all the Riders. This enables him to communicate using telepathy and not to just the Riders, but he controls the horses as well. This can be done as a collective, or just a few.'

'Even individually?' Jett sounded fascinated.

Axon nodded.

'No wonder we couldn't pick up their chatter when fighting against us.' Calyx bit his lip, now understanding.

'The bonus for the group operating in this way is they can feel each other's emotions. This way they sense when a Rider is in trouble and the nearest to them goes to help. He connected me with them, just before she was almost killed by Orion so I could feel she was okay when on missions. While she is happy and well, the Riders and I know it and can get on with day to day issues without all the worry. But it also works the opposite, if she is hurt we all feel the pain as she does. With the explosion she was caught in, it ripped through the rest of us as well. We didn't get the bruises or damage, just the pain. While recovering here on Pluto, every time Jett moved her, we felt it, but we knew he was doing everything he could, because we also felt her happiness.

Jett stood up. 'We are a member of your team, Axon. We should be allowed to join fully and have this ability too. It is not fair we are not given the same advantage as you and the other Riders.'

Axon looked up at Jett. 'This shouldn't be taken lightly, and you need to think about it. You see, Rory will be able to command you if he feels it necessary. Although you do have a choice, you can be removed at any time. I have stayed linked or, as now, I wouldn't have guessed her new mission had begun.

The Rider's magic allows me to feel her emotions. I need to know she is all right every day, every minute of every hour. That's how I cope. As yet, Rory has not required my assistance. He is very competent. However, I must warn you that he would be able to talk to you and, even command you if it meant saving a planet. I will give you time to discuss it if you like. As for Cait and me, we haven't had breakfast yet, and she must eat to give her energy to deal with what's ahead. She won't know when her next meal might be. By the looks of you two, you haven't eaten either, so I thought I might rustle something up if it's okay to use the kitchen.'

Jett nodded. 'It's yes twice over. You can use the kitchen, and we don't need to think about the other. Please go and get Rory while we start breakfast.'

'I agree.' Calyx had his arms folded and looked anxious. 'And as for her wellbeing, my brother and I know exactly what food she needs.'

Axon grinned and hid it by hugging Caitlin. Did they know better than her own husband? *I don't think so...* but he shut his mouth.

This was not the right time to tease.

With arms around her tiny waist, he smiled. 'I'll come back soon, honey. You know Rory will want to see you before you go. He may need to advise you if he's picked up on something I haven't.' Axon kissed her forehead before he transported to Earth, and to the home of his team.

Chapter Nineteen

Our Girl

Calyx casually placed his arm around Caitlin's shoulders and led her into the kitchen. She was a bit spaced out, so he lifted her onto the bench where she usually positioned herself to chat while they cooked. Today was different. Caitlin was quiet, and he didn't know what to say. The mood was fast becoming very sombre.

'Is she okay?' Calyx stared into her eyes as Jett came into the room.

They were glazed over, and Jett was getting no thoughts from her. 'It's as though she's here, able to speak and communicate when we talk about what she wants to hear, but there is another part that has closed off from us. It's got to be what Axon was trying to tell me. She's locked off the emotional side. If we brighten up, I'm sure we'll get her talking.'

They tried to sound bright and jovial. She liked them acting the fool, so they pushed and shoved each other while getting out the utensils and ingredients they required from the pantry.

To their surprise, she spoke. 'Breakfast. What are we having? I'm starving.'

Calyx moved close and tickled her, pleased when she giggled with him. 'You're always hungry. We can never fill this tummy.' He poked gently, and she chuckled again.

Jett winked at Calyx and casually mentioned something about

Vador to gauge a reaction. Her eyes glazed over even more, and it was as if she didn't comprehend any words associated with the evil she was heading towards.

Seeing the change, they suddenly understood and once again, teasingly began to argue over who was doing what task. Jett had barely started mixing up a sweet batter when they saw Caitlin blink and smile. 'Can I have bacon with my pancakes... and syrup?'

'Sure.' Jett handed his brother a frypan. 'Calyx, you're up, bacon for the lady.'

'I get the splatter pig, I'll swap,' he griped.

'Too late buddy, you "don't like mixing," remember? Cold room now!' Jett ordered and followed him in to show him where the bacon was kept. Jett used it as an excuse to speak in private. 'She has definitely switched off from anything negative, so anything we say will sound like Blah Blah to her. We're wasting our time trying to talk her out of going.'

'Yep, I got that. This sucks.' Calyx leant into the fridge and pulled out a piece of freshly smoked bacon to cut up. 'Axon must go out of his mind when she switches off like this. There must be something we can do.'

Back in the kitchen, Jett and Calyx experimented some more before Axon returned, amazed at Caitlin's abilities to combat their own power.

They were both ridden with guilt for what they had done to her a few NAVyears back, and the thought she had to go through it again didn't sit well with them. They both knew Vador was not a god. He would have no mercy, and as far as they could see, that was the real problem.

'I remembered when I snatched her, Axon called out to me and said, *please don't hurt her.*' The pain in his voice even now, cuts through me like a knife. He had known one of us was going to take her and he would have felt as I do now, utterly helpless. What an evil man I was too, but for Glow, I would never be that person again. I would die before I ever did evil and hurt her in the future. While she's gone, I swear there will be no more falling apart and sulking. She will go through far worse.' He spoke quietly to Calyx while stirring pots on the stove, a little way from her.

Caitlin jumped off the bench and put her arms around each of them. 'Don't be sad. If anything happens, I'll be relying on you both to make me better. Don't fall apart. I need you.'

Jett turned and hugged her back. 'I promise to stay strong for you, Glow.' Yet he didn't feel it. 'Please come back to me.'

Calyx flinched. 'Come back to us.'

'Sorry brother, that sounded selfish, and I know I am when it comes to Glow, but I meant to say come back to you too.'

She nodded. 'You both worry too much. Try to think of it as a holiday for me.'

'On a depressing Ice-Planet?' Calyx cringed.

She moved from their disapproving gaze and, gripping each side of the bench, hoisted herself up.

Calyx was frozen to the spot.

Jett had to dig deep to find the words to pull his brother out of it too. 'Calyx, for Glow's sake, get it together,' Jett growled in a low voice so only he could hear.

Their thoughts drove them crazy. Jett knew by his brother's silence they were both thinking the same way. Neither of them had ever been in this situation before, helpless to protect someone who had worked her way deep into their hearts. She had become their world, like a little sister or daughter to Jett, much, much more to Calyx. But Jett knew his brother had of late tried hard to put her in the sister zone too, or he would have gone mad with wanting her while working side by side again. With his emotions still raw from reliving that kiss with her, Jett had also felt the passion between them as her memory returned. His brother could be with her now. He could have won her hand instead of Axon if he hadn't backed away. It was a gallant gesture that would leave him to live in torment always. Yet he had prevailed and had found a way to live with his decision. Jett was so proud of him and as before, would be by his side helping him through yet another loss. Neither had any clue if they would ever see her again but they would wait and hope, and keep one another from knocking back on hell's door until the day she returned. He owed her and would deliver on this silent promise.

Back over at the stove, Jett spoke quietly. 'The worst part about all this is he may be like me and be able to track her within inches of where she stands. Already he may know she's here with me, and have worked out who I am and be furious with her. Most likely, he believes she used her goddess powers to make us friends when he didn't want to be. I am the enemy.'

'I was thinking the same thing. The creep could come and take our girl at any time. Between us, we have two-thirds of the power of the universe, yet we're helpless and our powers rendered useless by a mongrel that controls three crappy Ice Planets,' Calyx huffed.

Jett's eyes opened wide. 'We could send a couple of supernovas to blast his Ice Planet into oblivion. Then he can't take her.'

Calyx shook his head. 'It's probably too late. You heard Axon. It's about to happen. Cait could get hurt if she's there.'

The brothers were out of ideas to prevent Caitlin going on this mission, and the mood was grim by the time Axon arrived with Rory. Quietly, they moved away and leant against the bench at the far end of the gallery to give Rory and Axon privacy with Caitlin.

Calyx eyed Rory. He had met him, and sort of liked him but envied him at the same time. He was the one who not only worked with her every day but by her excitement to see him, it was evident she looked up to him.

Her eyes lit up. 'Rory!' She jumped off the bench and hugged him.

After she let him go, Rory led her over to the table where he sat with her. He slid his chair in front of her and leant in to speak to her privately.

Axon sat on the opposite side of the table waiting for Rory to finish. *How does he do it?* Calyx wondered if Axon felt as he did and wished it was him that brightened her up like that. Anyone could see how close they were as Rory concentrated on looking directly into her eyes. He had her full attention and it frustrated him that Caitlin answered Rory's every question. Calyx flushed red, desperately wishing for a relationship like that with her. He knew he could never have her, but to have that... would be enough.

Jett had switched on his listening abilities, not wanting to miss a word said. He heard his brother's thoughts and put a hand on his shoulder. 'You do have that, brother. At times it enrages me just how similar you two are. She only has to comment on something, and you know exactly what she is going to say and laugh with her on so many occasions when I think... what's so funny? And vice versa.'

Calyx spun around to face him. 'You've never told me this. Wish you had, I could have said, *payback*. I mean, you get to listen to Cait's every thought. That makes me so jealous.'

'Touché,' Jett replied. 'Now shush and let me listen.'

'What's he saying?'

He talks only about the mission ahead. How the team has her back and can and will get to her if she needs them. Glow is also to call to him when healing or strength is needed and is now passing on powers, so she can do this.' They watched him hold both of her hands, sit up straight and close his eyes. Once done, he let her hands go and leant back in toward her so he could keep talking. 'He is telling her that she is also protected by the universe's light and to have faith in her own natural abilities as a peacemaker if her powers are taken.'

Calyx fidgeted. 'The guy is either a saint or crazy allowing this. With all their abilities combined, I'll bet, in fact I know, he could stop her if he wanted to. Axon said it before. If Rory orders us while under his command, we will do as he says. So he could stop this, but the bastard's not going to, is he?' Calyx was getting loud.

Jett began to worry he would be overheard if he didn't defuse the situation. 'Calyx, stop!' he hissed. 'It's what she does. I love her enough to let her do what she is good at. You have to learn to trust her, not just love her. Only then will you stop wanting to punch anyone within cooee of her.'

Calyx gave his brother a sly look. 'You're reading me too.'

Jett gave him a nod. 'You're a bit hard to tune out on, as you're right next to me, and your irritable vibe has me just as cranky. But you must control it a bit better, for Glow... hang on... They're finished.'

'What else was said?' Calyx hissed.

'Not sure. Blatz! Stop talking to me when I'm trying to eavesdrop. Only heard bits and pieces, but he knows her well. As a defence plan against Vador and his boys, I believe he has advised her properly.'

'I'll kill Jovis and his goons if they hurt her, I swear I will.' Calyx started to shake.

Jett snatched up his hand and held the closed knuckles tight within his grip. 'Calm down. He's not saying, *there will* be any trouble, but has covered all bases with her rationally, just in case the mission is compromised. I can feel her more confident now, so keep your temper in check.'

'I will when he tells her she isn't to go.'

'Brother, that's like telling you not to perform your duties as a god. What would you do if you were told to keep out of something when you know you are most likely the only god who could sort out the situation?'

I would ignore the advice. I am God of all Gods, and no one tells me, no!'

'Then look at it from Glow's perspective. She is the Goddess of Peace. She is, by right, the only one who can bring peace when it gets out of control, and she must achieve it at any cost. What do you think she would do if she were told she couldn't go?'

Calyx stood with his mouth open. Then he closed it and slightly drooped his shoulders. 'Tell us to go to hell and do it anyway. So, in that case, it would be better if she had her friends' support. It would make her stronger to know she has those that love her waiting for her when she returns. She would work a miracle to come back. That's what you are trying to get through to me isn't it?'

Jett breathed out. 'Our job is to wait. It's not something we like doing or something we're used to. But even so, somehow we must.' Jett's emotions were pretty raw too. He, like his brother, just wanted to have a drink to deaden the rollercoaster of emotions.

Axon eyed them. Now that the business side of the mission was over, and he was satisfied Rory had helped Caitlin to sort out a few issues she'd struggled with, it was time to change the mood in the room. His gut too was twisted in knots, but at least he knew how to hide his feelings. The two in the corner had the air so thick with negativity you could have cut it with a knife. 'Rory!' He cut into the personal conversation he now held with Caitlin. She was asking him how her Rider friends were.

'Just a minute, Cait, hold that thought while I see what Axon wants.'

Axon could see she held still, as if Rory had hypnotised her. He had her under his control, and there she would stay in a calm state until he spoke to her again.

Rory stood up. 'I can feel them too. I either sort this out, or I'm taking her from here. This is certainly no environment for her to be in right now.' Rory frowned and glared at Jett and Calyx.

Axon gave a nod towards them. 'They're both committed to Caitlin a hundred percent, and wish to be connected to the Riders as I am... so work your magic, boy genius. Goodness knows what they'll do if they're left here in this state.'

Neither god argued with Axon, nor did they get cross at Rory's comment. He was right, they were a mess. Calyx was on the verge of snatching Caitlin and running if Rory couldn't settle his nerves soon. He had no faith in this team and wondered if anything this Cosmic leader did would honestly help.

Axon breathed out. He was already connected, and Caitlin was keeping him calm. 'Do you still want to go ahead with this?' he said to Jett and Calyx.

They nodded. 'We'll give anything a bash at this point.' Calyx shifted from one foot to the next, nervously.

'I agree.' Jett's eyes were the size of saucers as he tried so hard to hide his broken feeling that this may be the last time he saw his Glow Girl.

'Stand up straight,' Rory ordered.

Calyx and Jett immediately straightened and were unsure how Rory was able to make them move so quickly. The room thickened with a blue fog as the military leader in command of the select group stood before them, serious and without reservation. In a silver glow,

Rory looked to them like a massive bright angel. The wings were the only thing missing from this epic man. They could hear no other sound but him. He spoke in an ancient dialect they were familiar with but thought only gods still used. After their initial briefing, they had to both agree to give themselves freely to the Rider code of secrecy. Never were they to mention this moment again or speak of what was to follow. They noted how direct he was as he continued to talk in the same dialect. He wondered if he used it so the other Riders didn't understand what was being said. 'Also, if you dare lie to me about the reasons you wish to connect with us, I will know. In the event of this happening you will be dismissed from the regiment immediately and left with no memory to tell others of us, or our magic.'

They both again readily agreed and repeated the oath Rory recited. It was then they were hit with an almighty boost of emotions. It literally sucked the air from their lungs.

'Because you're gods, it will hit you a little harder but breathe it out, it will pass in seconds.'

And it did. Once it settled, a wash of calm came over them and both puffed out a thin stream of air that let Rory know they were fine.

Jett couldn't help smiling as he eyed Calyx. His brother didn't smile, but there was a light in his eyes that wasn't there before.

'I can feel her. The others are there but she is strong and her magic... well, it sings to me,' Calyx whispered.

'Yes, she knows we are with her now and look, she hasn't moved, but is smiling,' said Jett.

'That's right, boys, she knows I have joined you with our team. She is one clever girl. Now be silent while I introduce you,' Rory said. He turned and nodded to Axon first before speaking in English. It confirmed to Jett and Calyx that the ancient tongue used was to keep secret what he said to them, and they appreciated this greatly.

'Team, meet the gods, Zeus and Hades. They are to be referred to only as Calyx and Jett. This is insisted upon by Caitlin. She will not allow you to speak if you go to use their holy names. And you know she has the power to shush you if need be.'

Calyx was humbled that she so fiercely protected their privacy as gods. Cait is one incredible woman and ally to have, he thought. An intense sensation ran through him as his mind wandered to the time he spent alone with her. The emotion he felt must have gone through the group.

Rory broke in telepathically. *The others can't hear me, Calyx so no need to feel alarmed. There was an issue with what came through from you. I anticipated it and therefore was able to block it. Jett, you may as well listen in since you're new too. Let me explain how this works. Our magic has evolved, and over time we have learned to harness the emotions within the group and use it, hence this private warning. Understand I really love Cait too, shytzer we all do, and that's a good thing. But here are the rules. If any of us love, are in love or intimate with one of the others, it's not distinguishable to the rest of the team. It just comes through as light. This light, the team can turn into powerful magic to defeat the bad guys. However, sexual thoughts towards someone off-limits are the same as a hateful vibe which works the opposite and drains our light. Calyx, if you love her, love her like a sister. The puppy dog eyes must stop while you're connected to us.*

Calyx screwed up his face, shrugged and smiled. He realised from now on he'd better contain his thoughts of Caitlin. Jett nudged him and smiled too. 'In trouble with the boss already. Great start, brother.'

Rory winked and gave a grin before he turned his attention back to the group. 'Sorry about the break. Was bringing the newbies up to speed with some rules.' He went on to tell them of Caitlin's mission and the support the Riders would give. Nothing more was said, and it cemented to the two brothers that he could be trusted. Calyx kept right away from memories and didn't have a problem with Rory after that. Until now, neither of them had really known how dynamic the Cosmic Riders were, or how very much a controlled, powerful and organised group they had become. As they listened, the strengthening of the bond between this merry band of men and women gave much comfort. The power that ran through them was like a sedative that not only calmed them but gave them a shot of exhilaration. However, once Rory mentioned it was Vador she would be working on, the nerves for her strummed through Calyx like intermittent waves of emotions. He knew exactly how they felt. It was at this moment this connection suddenly made sense. Rory straightened, and the glow around him increased, almost filling the room.

'Calm down!' His order felt as if it bellowed through Calyx, yet it was only a whisper. Instantly he was filled with a warm glow apparently felt by them all as even Axon's shoulders relaxed. It was the most glorious feeling he had ever encountered. His heartbeat slowed, no painful thought could he think and every bone in his body relaxed, making him feel calmer and serene. He knew at that moment what it must felt like to be touched by an angel. And although Rory was not one, he used a skill Calyx was aware angels used to heal the sick and make the insane sane.

Team, you already have your orders for today. I still have business here but will be back soon. Rory out! He turned to Calyx and Jett. 'Feel better?'

Jett nodded. 'Better.'

Calyx breathed out heavily. 'Much better.'

Good! Rory hadn't moved and neither could they. *Caitlin isn't privy to this. These orders are specific to you men, so listen well. Caitlin doesn't need this wimpy behaviour around her. She knows what her role is in this universe, so accept it. She chose to be here with you lot, or she would have come home for moral support. Give her reason to stay, because I swear if I don't feel her happy I will come back and take her. What you must understand is she carries these final moments with her. They give her the strength needed to complete what has to be done quickly so she can come home. And no more of this nonsense, Jett, thinking this may be the last time we see her... it's blatzing ridiculous! Our girl Glow is the only real stable light in this universe, and I will go in and rescue her if she calls me for help. But she won't.* He looked at her with a softness they all felt. *Stubborn little redhead.* He smiled.

That was what Calyx waited for, and now he could fully relax. Rory did have an edge. She could call for him. He wanted him to go now so they could finish making breakfast with her by their side, hear her laugh and feel the happiness only she could give them.

Rory cut into his thoughts. *I can hear you Calyx, and yes, my workload has me rather busy, so now you've got this I can go attend to other matters.*

'Oops, busted.' Calyx could finally speak.

Jett chuckled as he could hear Calyx's thoughts too.

With that, Rory knelt in front of Cait. 'Call me if you need me, for anything.'

She wrapped her arms around him. 'Thanks Rory. Give my love to the team. I love you guys, you know that, right?'

'Cait, as if you wouldn't.'

She hit his arm. 'Bastard.' They both laughed as he stood up. He held her chin gently between his thumb and finger. 'Come home to us or else.' He let her go.

'Or else you'll kill me,' she said. 'You're so full of it Rory. Without a doubt you'd replace me with that tart you tossed me aside for, and you know it.'

He threw his head back and laughed. 'In a heartbeat baby... in a heartbeat.'

She stood and in a fluid motion was up in his arms. He only just caught her as she was so quick. 'No you wouldn't, you liar.'

He slid her back down to her feet. 'Yes, but only you know me that well. Now behave and go hang with your new friends before my girlfriend feels you playing and I get in the bad books again.'

She let him go. 'I love you. You know that, right.'

He nodded, touched her on the nose and gestured to Axon for him to take him back to his team. They all felt his answer. He didn't need to say a word to Caitlin. She saw it in his face and smiled as he vanished from sight.

Calyx and Jett had now seen how she loved unconditionally and the banter she had with Rory was how she was with them. A flood of emotion swept over them when they realised she liked them that much too. In such a short time, they had just as good a relationship with her as Rory did and he had been in her life for a very long time. Calyx swooped in and scooped her into his arms, carrying her into the cooking area with Jett right behind him. She squealed with laughter when he threw her to Jett. He gave her a hug before sitting her on the bench. This was their girl, not Rory's, and she was about to be ruined.

Axon arrived back to a lot of brotherly love and teasing that had Caitlin in hysterics. He joined in while cooking one messed-up feast. He couldn't believe the change in them. The cloud of doom lifted once they felt Caitlin was all right. While he made the coffee and poured the juice, Axon couldn't stop smiling as he listened to his wife. Her chuckles were music to his ears and he loved the feeling he got inside when she got the giggles. During the meal, they took it in turns telling jokes, and the more Caitlin's sweet laughter rang in their ears, the more they were compelled to make her laugh even harder.

Calyx watched Axon as he kept filling her plate. She ate without thought while she was entertained, and her husband seemed to take full advantage of this moment. He'd always wondered why Axon or the team, didn't raid Pluto when his brother had Caitlin. He knew now they were powerful enough to do just that, but only now understood the reason... *it is so simple.* She had sworn an oath to protect the planets, and it was a solo mission, not a team operation. Jett ruled one of those planets, and regardless if they were friends, this was what she did. So while she was away working with the rulers, if she was happy, this was how they monitored her progress. Calyx breathed in deeply as another thought came to mind. This worked both ways, and he and his brother would also feel her sadness. He had tried to destroy her and suddenly realised how terrible that must have been for them. He bent over the stove to flip the pancakes. He blinked and froze when he heard Rory's voice in his head. It certainly surprised him. *Stay steady, Rider. Keep your mind on the now. We will all deal with tomorrow when it comes but as a team.*

He was being commanded by telepathy, so Calyx immediately changed focus and got back to helping Jett entertain Caitlin, doing as instructed without another thought.

Caitlin asked to go for a ski, so after breakfast, they went out on the slopes. Calyx knew, as he assumed the others did, that it was time to go and she wanted to be out in the open, so no one got hurt. He observed her calm persona, confident as she came out with them onto the icy mountain ready take her one-way ski down the powdery white slopes. She was proficient as a skier now and didn't need their help. She beat them down to the bottom. Her technique had improved, and it even surprised Jett who could generally out-ski her even on a bad day. She had a big bright smile, knowing she had won and lifted her hands up to wave about while doing a typical happy dance… and then she was gone, snatched from their sight. Calyx's heart sank. He felt the devastated emotions of his brother and Axon. They stopped dead, feeling riveted to the spot. The situation kept them paralysed in the snow. Caitlin, their Glow Girl, was gone … this was the worst kind of payback Calyx could ever have imagined.

Chapter Twenty

Prisoner on an Ice Planet

C aitlin felt a sensation around her and immediately stopped waving her arms around when her friends vanished from her sight. She was being transported, but she didn't recognise the arms that held her at this moment. As they came into the outer orbit of the Home World they entered, she felt the grip tighten. The person with the iron grasp waited for a code and once cleared, they landed knee deep in snow. In the dark, she could vaguely see a vault door.

As soon as they entered the airspace, Caitlin felt the thick gagging sensation of evil and hatred. Now they had landed it was worse, and she swallowed back the urge to vomit. Her teeth chattered with the bitter weather. She looked within to use magic to make her feel better and warmer, and her heart sank. He had removed her ability to access her powers. *What is going on? Who is this?*

'Where are we?' She squinted to see him, but he held her tightly against him and with the snow on her face and the dark planet, it was useless to try. His heavy breathing and rapid heartbeat added to the eeriness of one of the coldest, most dismal Ice Planets she had ever visited. Up to her knees now in snow, she couldn't run, so had to stand steady as he moved closer to the door, dragging her with him. *I think I'm in big trouble.*

'Blatzing bloody ice,' he growled as he used magic to swipe the panel and lost his footing while holding her as well. A second effort did the trick, and the door opened.

'Ouch!' Caitlin complained as he pulled her onto a platform that began to move. The thing jerked, and she almost fell off as it dropped quickly.

He cussed and held her steady as they continued to move deep down below the planet's surface.

'Where are you taking me?' She looked up, trying to get a look at this man who was totally out of control. He seethed, and she didn't need to see his face to feel it. He also had two advantages over her. He still had his powers, and it was evident he was able to see in the dark. Caitlin rubbed her arm where he had grabbed her. 'You don't have to be so rough. I'm no threat to you without my magic.'

Again, no answer.

The deeper they went, the more unsettled she became and worried about what was to come. The earthy smell brought back memories of her childhood, and although Caitlin tried to shake it, that and the fact she wouldn't be able to contact Rory way down here, had her tremble with fear. If this was Vador, he could keep her here indefinitely. *How will anyone find me this far underground?* She let out a sob, and tears streamed down her face as alarm bells went off. This was not her Jovis, and it hit home that her life was in this man's hands, and she was in terrible danger.

The elevator platform stopped with a thud, and her arm was tugged hard as Caitlin was pulled for a short distance before they stopped. She heard the clunk of a key turning in a lock before she was pushed into a room and metal on metal slammed shut behind her. Caitlin turned and grabbed at the door. With her gloved fingers wrapped around thick cold bars, she blinked the tears from her eyes. 'You're throwing me in a cell? What is my crime?' She called out, but her words fell on deaf ears. He had already disappeared through the exit towards the lift. Fortunately, when the lift left, it didn't create draught enough to blow out the candle burning in a lantern. To be in total darkness scared her more than not knowing why she had been left there, alone. 'Brrr.' She shivered. It was so cold she huddled in a corner pulling the hood fur around her face. The leather protection was not enough, so she placed her hands under each arm and huddled up in a foetal position to keep warm.

* * * *

It had been a long wait before Caitlin heard the lift startup. Her mouth quivered with the cold and she was thirsty. In the dead silence, the elevator was loud as it noisily came to a stop and footsteps thumped heavily towards her. The shadow moved quickly with a grumpy stomp. Her heart raced. Was this "iron grip" back to share what all this was about? Well if it was, Caitlin wasn't in the mood for niceties. This was cruel of him, and she was livid. A torch lit up the area where he walked but trying to make out who carried it was a waste of time. Her eyes involuntarily squeezed tight when the light shone on them. His behaviour was appalling. The door flung open, and a fur rug was thrown on top of her. It landed heavily and was the last straw. Angry at this treatment, she tossed the rug off her, and it fell in the middle of the floor.

He slammed the door, and as his big boots stomped heavily away on concrete, she heard him yell, 'Stupid bitch! Freeze then!'

Caitlin sucked back a retort; to rile him further at this point could set him off, and in his mood, the outcome would not be in her favour. *Why won't he talk to me? And he didn't have to just throw the rug at me.* If this was Vador, and she was almost positive it was, why didn't he take Jett? He was with her on the icy slope, out in the open and unprotected. *After all, that's who he has the beef with, not me.* She didn't even know this Vador but did know one thing for sure, he was not Jovis. Calyx had got that all wrong. These two were worlds apart, and Jovis would never carry on like this. *What have I done to this man to deserve this wretched treatment?* But before she could fire any questions at him, he was back on the lift and out of earshot.

A torch on her much later caught her sobbing with the cold, as even the rug she ended up pulling over her gave little warmth.

'Does cry-baby want another blanket?' The sarcasm was evident.

'Go away!' she screamed. 'I'd sooner freeze to death than accept anything from a blatzing monster like you.' The words were out before she could stop them. In her emotional state, she was becoming irrational.

He grabbed the bars on the door, shook them and growled.

This was clearly a man out of control and who wanted to harm her, most likely wished her dead, but why? Her mind in tatters, she was glad to hear his steps retreat. Hopelessly lost in an atmosphere of ice she curled back up in a ball and finally drifted off to sleep. Even in slumber, she dreamt she was lost in the snow.

Somewhere in between tears and sleep, she felt warm arms scoop her up. Pressed against the heat of his chest and carried out of the cell, Caitlin felt too bitter and shaken to open her eyes.

It wasn't until she heard a crackling fire that she realised someone kind was there to help. She let out a sob at this revelation, a sad, pitiful little cry of thanks. It was lighter now, and her eyes searched frantically for features. When he turned, she saw she was indeed in good hands. She had befriended him on her last trip to Earth.

'Artisan, why are you here with this horrible man?' she whispered. 'I thought I was coming to see a friend, but there is a ruler here that hates me. Even without powers, I can tell he does and I have no idea why. Please hide me. I promise not to be any trouble. You know me. You know I wouldn't deliberately hurt a soul.'

He didn't say anything, just laid her on a pile of cushions in front of the fire and put a pillow under her head. When she still shivered, he placed a fur pelt over her. This was a big warm woolly one that she pulled up around her face for comfort. With teeth chattering she lifted a shaky hand out to him. He nodded, understood she needed help to warm up and lay down next to her, putting his arm up over his head. Not waiting for him to get comfortable, she hugged into his body for warmth. She had been forced back in time; the memory of horrifying days and nights alone in mostly darkness had her shake with fear and wrap her arms around him tightly. She worried at first, he would push her away, but he didn't. Instead, she felt him rub her head gently and say, 'Shh…' a few times until she released her grip.

If she wasn't so upset, she might have smiled that he shushed her as a parent figure might. It worked, and once her faith in their friendship returned, she slept.

Caitlin woke alone but warmer now and lots more comfortable. The voices that woke her became louder as Artisan's plea to care for her fell on deaf ears.

'Leave Glow alone! She's only just gone off to sleep. When I checked on her, she was frozen to the core. Unless you want her dead by morning, you'll need to take better care of her. You've removed the use of her powers so how can she keep warm within? And even with powers, you know she's not like any other average immortal females, she is delicate, untouched by hatred. You know this, as it was you who told me you felt you'd been touched by an angel.'

'That was until I found out she's a treacherous little liar. That she used magic to make me believe there was innocence and sweetness to her. It was all lies, and right now, the way I feel, death is too good for that manipulating little bitch. I can't believe you're helping her after what she did to me. But you'll wake up when she hurts you too. Then you'll be knocking back on my door begging for help. But don't bother because you deserve it. Blatzing hell man, you're frigging killing me here!'

'You know you don't mean that, Vador. Stop it. There must be a perfectly sane reason. Talk to her,' Artisan pleaded.

'What, so she can tell me more lies? Hardly. Well, you've made your bed. You want her, have her, but don't dangle her anywhere near me, or I swear I'll not be responsible for what I'll do!' He stormed off.

Caitlin was aware now it was Jovis. The shock sent chills through her. What had she done that would wind him up so tightly? Artisan didn't look as if he wanted to talk, so she lay quiet and watched him as he heated water over the coals. He held up a cup to her when it was ready. 'Want one?'

'Sure, I would appreciate it.' She wiped her eyes and tried to tidy her hair.

He smiled as she sat up and glanced around the room. 'The bathroom is through that door to the left if you need to go.'

'Thanks, Artisan. I do. I've been here a long time.' Her voice was croaky with the dryness of nothing to drink, but nature was calling.

'You may need to take a candle with you if you want the door shut. I haven't put one in there yet.'

Caitlin took a candle and while in there, splashed her tearstained face. When she came out, she had taken off the big jacket and pants, leaving on only the tracksuit pants she wore underneath. She'd decided this more comfortable while lounging around the lovely warm room. She wrapped the blanket around her and took the cup he offered. The fire was a blessing, the coffee was yummy, and Artisan just looked like Artisan. This made her feel so much better. At least she was with a friend who made this more bearable.

'Artisan, can I ask something without you getting mad at me?'

He nodded.

'Why did Jovis say I lied?'

He sighed. 'Glow, how did you come to be at the same resort where we were staying?'

'Well it's kind of top secret and a long story, so can't you just answer my question?'

He eyed her. 'You just saw me stick my neck out here and go up against my boss. I think I deserve to be trusted with your secrets. I do have time; we have all night.'

'Fair enough, but only because I can see no other way of explaining why I was there.' Sitting on the floor, Caitlin crossed her legs and, holding her coffee in two hands, commenced telling him the drama of the Waterfall Goddess and how her jealous rage at catching her man with another woman had almost ruined all life on Earth. 'That is why I was surprised you were there. Zoren had put restrictions on all travel to Earth.'

'Yes, I remember you mentioned something about that, but we thought you just had too much to drink as we had no orders regarding Earth travel come through our NAVcom. But please, continue. I'm still waiting to hear why you were at the resort.' He poured another black coffee from the pot and sat listening intently.

'Well, I had been working on this debacle for almost two years.' Careful not to give him private details, she continued to tell him about how the Waterfall Goddess fell in love with the hunter and how his indiscretions caused the goddess to put a spell on the land. Caitlin told of the months she worked on it and even about her powers going down and how Jett and Calyx spent weeks getting her well. The last part of the story was the joining of the two lovers and how she needed somewhere luxurious and romantic to take them, a place unaffected by the drought. She sipped her drink and started talking again after the dryness subsided. 'You see, I read about the resort in a brochure and had planned to go there on my own honeymoon, but that hasn't happened yet. My husband's work is very demanding, but one day we might get the time.'

He watched as she stared into the fire, apparently upset this had never happened yet. He felt for her. 'Glow are you sure he's right for you? He seemed too busy to spend any time with you while we were around. You even admitted it was Calyx and Jett who nursed you back to good health. Where was he then?'

'He works hard, and so do I. We just don't get the luxury of time together like other couples are lucky enough to have.' She smiled. 'Now where was I? That's right, the resort. Well, we had booked in for one night, but only so we could use the premises. However, the lovebirds disappeared so we pulled an all-nighter, waiting to find out if the temperamental goddess would lift the curse. Once we had confirmation, we were exhausted and slept all day.'

'What made you stay another night? The night we just happened to be there.'

'Well, we had to pay for another night because we slept past check out time, so the guys said we might as well get together for dinner in celebration of the win, and that's when I met you guys. The next morning, Calyx and his wife had already left, and we were just going to have a bite to eat and leave too. Then Jovis invited us to the island, and because I had such an enjoyable time with everyone, I accepted quickly when offered an extra night away. You have to understand, it was a workday, but Axon was so chuffed I saved the planet, I could have asked for anything. One more night was my only wish at that time.'

'Why did Jett stay? It sounds as if he could have left.'

'True.' She bit her lip, not sure if she should tell all but he did say he wanted the truth. 'Jett didn't trust you lot with me. He is tuned into me, and if I had been even a little panic-stricken, he would have taken me from you all. I introduced him to you as my guardian angel, and I meant it.'

Artisan's eyes were wide but kept quiet as she continued. They had thought she was just overdoing the introductions.

'It might have only been a couple of days of fun for some, but for me, it was a time I will always treasure. So I apologise if I was a bit out of control if that is what all this is about. If I have hurt your friend because I said something stupid, or acted up, I really do apologise. I never meant to cause any harm. Jovis insinuated I lied and manipulated him. As a peacemaker, I'm forbidden to lie. I would lose my job immediately if I did that.'

Caitlin handed the empty cup back. 'That's about all there was to it from my end. Nothing sinister. I was just having a bit of R&R, and you guys made it more enjoyable. I'm so sorry you lot, or Jovis at least, ended up wanting me to suffer in a cell. I'm shocked to learn I was the only one who did have a good time, but I swear if you let me go, I promise to stay clear of you and your chosen venue from now on. Jovis doesn't have to lock me up to be rid of me. I won't ever bother him again. I'm heartbroken for causing so much discord and loathing, and for accidentally being in the wrong place at apparently the wrong time.'

'It's not that, Glow. We had a wonderful time too and even though I believe you — he will not. You see, we didn't see any evidence to support your tale that Earth was dying. Therefore Vador won't buy the story you just told me. He thinks it was a set up to get him to speak to Hades. I'm sorry, but there it is. Now all I can do is try to get some proof you were innocent, and maybe he will listen. Shytzer girl, you turned on the charm! You have broken his heart. You gave him hope that there are women out there that are worthy of love. The deception he feels has totally ruined any trust he had in females, again! Seriously, I can't promise anything. He's furious. I haven't seen him this heartless towards a woman, not ever!'

Caitlin put both hands to her face. 'I told him upfront I was married! I can't help it if he got the idea there was more to my friendship. And as for Jett, he what? Believes I did what? Coerced him into forming a friendship with Jett? All I did was dance with him, once. It was he who offered to walk me back to my party, remember.'

Artisan nodded.

'I thought the three of you liked my friends and that's why you stayed. No way am I taking the blame for that. Jovis could have walked me back and left if he didn't want to get to know other people. The reasons he stayed cannot surely be for me alone. I heard Jovis laughing and having fun with the others too.' She twisted her hands in her lap, trying not to cry. 'I swear on my Riders' oath, I had no idea who Jovis was until we got back to Pluto. Calyx worked it out when Jett and I said we stayed an extra day to hang with you guys. To blame me, hate me, is so not fair. I mean… you heard him! He said if I cross his path he will what, hurt, and maybe kill me? I can't believe he has turned on me without allowing me to defend myself.'

'It's okay… Calm down. It'll be all right.' He spoke calmly, seeing she was close to tears again. With a sigh, he leant back, looking exhausted and his eyes drooped. Seconds later, he snored softly. Caitlin figured he'd been Jovis's confidante and with her dumping her stress on him as well, they had worn him out.

Caitlin let out a nervous breath when he woke her with a quick movement. On his feet, he glanced around for his pocket NAVcom. 'How long have I slept?' He snatched it up and checked the time. 'Hell, I should have left an hour ago. I have a meeting with my … anyway, I have to go to my Home World.'

She knew right away that she didn't have his trust. Not fully.

'How can I make this better?' She lifted on her elbows to talk.

'You can't. The only way is if I can prove your story.'

'Can't you take me with you and away from him? Please. Jovis said you could have me. I promise I'll be so quiet you won't know I'm around.'

Caitlin's exhaustion showed. Artisan knelt and ran his hand

across her forehead, moving hair that covered her eyes. Even crying he thought her exquisite. But none of them had any luck with women. Many times, they had been left with empty wallets and a bleeding heart. Why he had started to trust this one he didn't know. She was like no one he had ever met before. Yet, he had, as Jovis did, just hours ago, wondered if she was another wolf in sheep's clothing. That was until he saw her again. He sighed. He wanted to believe in her. In his heart, he did feel she might be the one to turn all their lives around. Now, looking into her gentle green eyes, he believed in her more than ever. But this for him would be the last time. Suddenly, Artisan was prepared to give her his all.

'Vador is very powerful and also my boss. He said I could have you in anger. But to take you from here would infuriate him further. Trust me, I know him well. Once he calms down I'll approach him, maybe he might be in a better frame of mind after the meeting but …' He didn't finish. She realised Jovis was not the person she first thought he was and as Vador, must rule his friends like his empire, with an iron fist.

She nodded and pulled the rug up around her, getting comfortable as this could be a long wait for his return. He pulled on boots and slipped into a jacket. 'Food's in the pantry by the sink.' He pointed to the general area. 'If you run out of firewood, there's more stacked outside the door. And Glow, if Vador does come to speak to you, please don't make him angry. I don't want him to hurt you, okay.'

'Would he… really?'

He shrugged. 'Vador has been without a female for a few years now. That trip we were on was to get him laid. That plan went south the moment he laid eyes on you. So just be careful, okay? I'll wrap this meeting up, do a quick bit of research on the Earth's world events and be back before you know it. Once I have proof I'm sure he'll let me take you home.'

Caitlin was unsure about being left with a monster, but had faith Artisan would find a way to sort this out. He might have been covered in strange tattoos instead of hair, but inside him stood a man with a tender heart. She had to trust he would do as he said and knew he'd return with good news.

He smiled, and the rustle of his jacket and the sound of boots on floorboards echoed as he left the room. She wanted to remember that sound. Any other would not be *him* returning. There was nothing more she could have said or done. Artisan had left her to battle the elements and Jovis alone, but for now she was warm, and that was a far cry from how she felt the day before. This, Caitlin could handle, and she sat with her arms wrapped tightly around her legs, and rocked gently while remembering the weekend with Jovis. She wondered why she had to get to know him then, while everyone was around. Why couldn't they have met some time ago where there was no connection to Jett?

She sat like that for a very long time before she stood, stretched took a burning candle, and went to the bathroom. The shower looked inviting and she turned on the water. Alas, it was cold. Back by the fire she heated some water to a warm temperature, filled up the vanity sink, removed her clothes and had a wash.

Just as she finished, she heard someone enter the room and knew who it was before he flung open the door and found her. His gaze roamed her body, and she stiffened at his glare. Her hand reached for the towel, but he snatched it.

'Jovis don't. Please leave me while I get dressed.'

He had the towel in one hand and held her by the shoulder. 'You are ugly. I hate you and don't worry, I wouldn't bother. You show weakness when you cry. I have no use for a woman like you.' His eyes flashed angrily as he let her go, and at the same time he shoved the towel at her and slammed out of the apartment. He called out, 'Keep the fire stoked. I'm taking your boyfriend for a drink to talk some sense into him, so don't expect him back for a while.'

What he didn't realise was his own strength. The light shove, so he thought, had slammed Caitlin up hard against the wall. Her leg hit a footstool, and the wooden leg of it broke off and rolled across the floor. She bit her lip and pulled a face, deciding to hide the pain until he left. She didn't want him to return and yet glancing down, and suddenly in considerable agony, she saw blood trickling out from a cut. Not one for being a hero, she had no choice but to call out for help. *Maybe he'll laugh and walk out.* Secretly, she hoped he might find it in him to help her and stop the nonsense. 'Jovis, please help me!'

The call out only echoed in the empty pit where she was kept. 'Shytzer, shytzer, shytzer!' She patted away the blood with a hand towel and quickly slipped on her knickers, bra and tracksuit top. She left the bottoms off so she could wrap the towel around the wound. In front of the fire she found it wasn't as bad as she thought and once it stopped bleeding, she groaned as she slid the leg of the tracksuit pants back on. Warm but exhausted from ridicule, lack of food and not much sleep, her heavy eyelids closed.

Chapter Twenty-One

Deathly Shove

Jovis and Artisan arrived back on Sedna five days after kidnapping the most powerful woman in the universe. Artisan had talked Jovis into going to Earth with him, and would not rest until he had proof Glow Girl had not lied. They found the Water Maiden, and under the hand of Jovis's dark magic, Quinesha confirmed the story to be true.

Back at the resort, taking a peek at computer files, it was confirmed the party of the six had booked in for one night, and another was not organised until the next day. Taking a quick visit to the mountain range, they saw at first hand, the treeless ravaged hillsides and valleys. New shoots were appearing from dirt, and in some areas, burnt remains had started to rejuvenate. For the forests to return to what they once were would take more magic than what had been used by the Goddess of Water.

'The news in on!' Artisan called to Jovis.

Both took an interest in the media reports this time. On every station, the commentators celebrated the ending of the worst drought in history. As life began to appear in the worst affected areas, everyone had their own theories. All did agree on one thing, it was a miracle to see communities start popping up all over the world. Unharmed and healthy human beings lived in houses built from materials unavailable on Earth, including public infrastructures. It bedazzled onlookers who flocked to the areas to visit these new sites that appeared. People gathered and sang praises to their gods and others to aliens who they believed saved them. No one knew, but the speculation on one talkback channel suggested there was now proof of life on other planets and it was they who helped. This made both men chuckle.

While they were away, Jovis and Artisan found Caitlin's father, seemingly by accident. He came into the bar where they sat having a drink and introduced himself to the barman as Lord Torpez. Jovis shook his head and, speaking quietly, debated his name with Artisan. 'Torpez is a precious off-world stone.'

'He might be a lord, but certainly not Lord Torpez,' Artisan agreed.

Both knew using that gem as a name was the first of many clues that he lived off-world.

'Being a lord, he is for sure a ruler, but not of a planet, maybe a star.' Jovis watched him, intrigued.

'True, lords mostly run the star Home Worlds, not planets or ice planets.' Artisan was also drawn to this strange man who didn't stop talking. He looked as if he had been on a pub crawl and this was his last stop.

The barman poured him another whisky. 'So, what's going on here, buddy? You must be either in trouble or have many worries to be in such a state! Which one is it?'

The lord leaned over the bar towards him, but the whisper was a drunken slur. 'I haven't seen or heard from my daughter for months. Those blatzing fools in power are hiding something. They say she's off-world. Phooey!' He sat back in his seat. 'Lying shytzers,' he grumbled.

The barman scratched his head. 'Off-world? Is she a space pilot?'

Jovis quickly jumped in and came to his rescue. 'Hey buddy, remember us? Let's have a drink over in the booth and leave the poor barman to do his job.'

Lord Torpez blinked. 'Yeah, see, knew I'd find 'em. These are buddies of my daughter's. They'll know where she is.' The Lord introduced them. 'This is Conor, and this one here... well, can't remember you.' He pointed the finger at him. 'That one I do, I remember Conor's bald head and tattoos.'

They didn't know who Conor was and didn't care. This guy was trouble and so drunk they feared he might cause unnecessary panic. With humans so jumpy over the drought and trying to find out who helped, they would believe anything. They wasted no time and moved him to the quiet corner of the room.

'Which Cloud Rider are you?' slurred Torpez

'He's only new. They call him Jovial because he's always so happy.' Artisan put his arm around the drunken lord and motioned for him to sit, glad he thought he knew him. Not only did they stop him giving away secrets, but the daughter was of great interest. Knowing he was connected to the Cloud Riders made them both believe now that he was definitely a star ruler.

As they moved away, the barman shrugged and shook his head. 'Must be a full moon out there tonight.'

Comfortably seated, Lord Torpez steadied his hand from shaking as he gulped a mouthful of straight whisky and continued his ramblings. 'You know the big man wanted her dead.'

Jovis could think of no other he would be talking about but Zeus and understood Lord Torpez's hatred towards him. Jovis despised Zeus and his entire family for using their position as gods to raise the vermin god Hades, to the status of king. Jovis was a prince by family lineage and had put his hand up for the title and position, but his ancestors were snubbed by the gods. Now he knew why. They wanted one of their own in charge. On their say-so, Jovis was refused an audience by the Congress of the Heavens and didn't even get a look in. As far as he was concerned, they could all rot in hell. Meeting them and being friendly without knowing who they were was the last straw, and why he had been so mad at Glow. She had put him in a position to speak with those he hated. They didn't deserve his friendship, and it hurt that she was the instigator. He wanted to wring her neck, take his frustration out on her, but was now finding that maybe she hadn't done a thing.

'Are you listening to this?' Artisan kicked him under the table, seeing he was deep in thought.

Jovis tuned his concentration back to Lord Torpez whom he suddenly guessed was Glow Girl's father. He understood his drunken state now. His intuition would most likely be picking up vibes that all was not well with her, and if Glow was his daughter he was spot on. Lord Torpez, although in a sorry state, was still able to talk coherently enough not to use names. Luckily Jovis and Artisan were no fools and knew exactly who he spoke about. They intended to stay until he passed out if they had to, wanting to hear everything about his daughter and what she was capable of. He was still not entirely convinced she had nothing to do with the recent events that made him want to commit murder. She was to be first, then her mate, Hades.

Lord Torpez filled his glass once more with straight spirits from the bottle they took to the table. He looked miserable, yet angry. 'When she was a small child, we had to keep moving. I tried to educate her but couldn't send her to school as we moved so much. They kept finding us, and I ran out of places to hide. I befriended a couple who I trusted completely and gave them good money each month to care for her and keep her identity hidden. Well, how could I know they would put her in lockdown and hide her in a basement under the ground? Poor kid didn't see the light of day until she was in her late teens.' His eyes were full of tears. 'You know, even now, that beautiful little girl has the same soft skin she had when I left her to those criminals.' His face went all red and blotchy. 'It was never spoilt by the elements and thank the heavens, the experience never ruined her. She said it toughened her up for the life she now leads. But let me tell you, it has left its mark.'

'What do you mean?' The soft skin, her job, he knew he talked of Glow Girl.

'My daughter, even today, and with all her strength, is fearful of dark and cold places. She says she would rather die than be locked up again. It is her one and only nemesis.' He passed out on the table.

The lord's saddened face convinced Jovis he'd told the truth and he rubbed his forehead hard with worry. He turned to Artisan. 'I saw

Glow Girl as being weak because she cried, but she wasn't crying because of how cruelly I treated her, she was petrified at where I was taking her. I thought the tears and tantrum were her guilt and she was trying to appeal to my softer side.' He was suddenly aware of something else. 'Blatz, we've left her alone down there. What if she has used all the candles or firewood?' He was suddenly freaked out.

Artisan's eyes were like saucers too. 'I was just thinking the same thing.' He picked up the Lord's arm, and when he let it go, it landed with a thud on the table. 'Well, the old man's out so he can't do any more harm. If you've finally had enough and have seen how harmless she is then I agree, let's go home.'

'I'm convinced and yes…' He glared at Artisan. 'I feel like a first class jerk so zip it, okay. I don't need you to harp on about it.'

Jovis pulled out his pocket-sized NAVcom. 'It's only been—blatzing hell, we've been gone for five days.'

'What have we done? Where did the time go? If her dad is right, it might be too late.' Artisan gritted his teeth.

'Come on buddy, don't even go there. I feel sick enough already for what I've done to her. I can't believe I've hurt the only person that has ever made me want to be more. We have to go—now!' Jovis was panic-stricken and immediately transported them both back to Sedna.

* * * *

Rushing into Artisan's room, Jovis breathed in a strange odour. It was dark and silent. The fire was out, and no candles were alight. His first thought was, she'd escaped. *How could that be?* There was only one way out, and he and Artisan were the only ones with the code. Had he killed Glow Girl? *But how?* His eyes had adjusted before Artisan had time to light a candle. He could see she was still there but hadn't moved or spoken. The flame flickered light, and the sight gripped his stomach. Her cheeks were sunken, and her closed eyes were lost in black pockets.

'We killed her!' Jovis snatched the light from Artisan and held it to her gaunt unmoving features. 'What happened here? You said you left her with food and water.'

Artisan glanced across at the fireplace. 'I did. There's plenty of wood, so why didn't she use it?'

'Maybe while she was sleeping it went out. How do I know?'

Artisan shook the matches he kept above the mantel in a box. 'Maybe she couldn't find these in the dark?'

'Or as her dad said, she'd sworn never to live like this again, you know, as a prisoner... below ground.' Jovis gulped back a heartfelt sob for his treatment of her. He dropped to his knees beside her and held her cold hand.

'Check her pulse... Check her pulse!' Artisan yelled it out to try and snap his boss out of his torment.

Jovis finally took in what Artisan was saying and laid two fingers from his other hand on her neck. He glanced up at his friend. 'She's still alive,' he whispered, eyes full of unshed tears. 'Quick, get the doctor and call some staff here. I want someone to light the chip heater to run her a bath—now!' He pulled the blanket back and got a whiff of what smelled like rotting skin. 'She smells bad, Artisan. If we don't clean her up before the doc comes, he'll remove her from us for our neglect.'

'I know.' Artisan reached down to feel her forehead in case Jovis was merely freaking out. 'Blatzing shytzer, she's as cold as ice.' He knelt beside Jovis. 'You go organise everything. Let me look after Glow... She likes me. If she wakes up to you—well, she might just decide to die again, seems... She hates your guts.' He was full of anger.

'We both did this, Art, and no need to be a prick. It was you who told Glow you'd be back soon, remember. You heard her dad. She lived like an animal. She probably doesn't know how to care for herself even now. So please, will you help me and quit the smart-arse insinuations or nick off. I'll do it all myself.'

Artisan shrugged and stood up. 'Sorry boss, that was uncalled for, I'm just freaked out like you are. We good?'

'Good, now go do as I've asked.' Jovis sounded lost in pain.

Artisan checked. 'Okay, so two maids to get the room ready and one to light the chip heater and a couple in the kitchen. Will that do?'

'Two only. And bring them from the barracks. I don't want civilians. I want Peon Major and her second in charge. They are the only ones I trust.'

'And Doc Lepius?'

'Yes, he is the leading practitioner in his field and I want the best. Give him full clearance... and tell Peon Major not to make the bath hot.' He turned back to Caitlin and sighed. 'We're both invested in getting Cait well, Art. So I want you to stay, but keep Rocky out of the picture. We don't need it to turn into a circus, okay.' Jovis had kindness to his manner, something Artisan was not used to.

'I'd like that. I feel disgusted with the low life I've become where women are concerned. To find I have hurt one, never mind the fact it's Glow Girl, makes me feel utterly ashamed.' Artisan's shoulders were stooped. 'You called her Cait, is that her real name?'

'Caitlin Stanton.'

'That may be so, but she will always be Glow to me. Her light gives me goosebumps. I'll do whatever I have to in the hope we can bring her sunshine back.' He hung his head low and, shaking it in disgust, transported to Jovis's headquarters to organise the staff, and to use the universal NAVcom to contact the doctor.

Up in Jovis's luxurious room, Artisan lit the chip heater and when the water warmed up, he filled the bath. This he decided to do as he didn't trust the help to get the temperature right. While he waited, Glow filled his every thought. He felt physically sick with worry and while on the NAVcom to the doctor, almost broke down. There was so much guilt he held back... wished he could say. *We think we have killed the most valuable Goddess in the universe*? Instead of blurting it out he lied and said he didn't know how the patient became so ill. Although it wasn't entirely a lie, even now he kept growling and shaking his head knowing she was fine when he left. In turmoil, he silently cursed, deliberating the fact he should have known better than to go. He saw how her friends flocked around. As soon as she needed something they were at her beck and call. They made sure she was eating, and one of them was always placing a drink in her hand or slipping a shawl around her shoulders if they saw her shiver. He even remembered seeing Calyx put a comforting arm around her and kissing her forehead the only time she stood alone. *They spoil her rotten.* He wanted her to love him as she did them. If she was to live, his attitude towards all women would change.

The maid interrupted his thoughts. 'Fire is blazing, and the bed is made with fresh sheets and pulled back ready.'

'Jovis will want some towels heated, and as soon as the pot boils, fill the hot water bottles.'

The maid nodded and swiftly left to do as she was asked.

Artisan placed his hand in the water to see if it the right temperature. *No wonder I can never keep a female.*

There was no other way to put it, the three of them were uncaring bastards and he'd only just realised it. They befriended and brought women up to their Ice Planets and once there, left them to battle the elements and loneliness alone while they worked many hours, if not days at a time, before coming home. Even then it was just for a bit of loving. The three rulers were mate's first and almost inseparable, meeting mostly at Sedna to plan their next takeover. Jovis wanted to build his own empire. He had three, and his sights were set on another two Ice Planets.

Feeling very remorseful, he reached in and flicked the off the taps. As he did so, he heard Jovis arrive with Glow. He laid her on the bed and began removing her clothes.

'Hey, perv. There are maids to do that,' Artisan scolded him.

'I've seen her naked, idiot. You turn your back,' Jovis spat at him.

'When?'

'Before I left, I accidentally walked in while she was bathing in the bathroom... It was innocent!' Jovis gave him a stern look.

'Sure.' Artisan didn't believe him and had become edgy and annoyed again.

'Peon Major, get over here and take over. And be blatzing well careful or else.' Jovis stood back as both maids tackled the task.

'Hell, what's going on with her leg?' Jovis moved closer to look once her tracksuit was removed.

Artisan pulled Jovis into the bathroom, so they couldn't be overheard. 'Just what did happen in the bathroom? You did hurt her! You blatzing liar!' he seethed.

'No way! I never touched her.' He stared at Artisan. 'I went down there, and when I saw she was naked and looked scared, I told her not to worry, that she wasn't my type and I said I thought her ugly.'

'Are—you—serious?' Artisan blinked.

'So I blatzing lied. So what! I was mad at her, but I didn't do that to her. I had the towel in my hand and gave it back to her and left. That was it.'

'You're shitting me. You were in one of your moods and Glow had no powers. I'll tell you how it went down. You didn't pass it to Glow, you shoved it at her and damn well knocked her into the frigging wall. I can guarantee she slammed into something, and it broke. That's what has made that gash in her leg.'

'Now you're just making shit up.' Jovis transported them down to Artisan's bathroom.

'Geez, there's blood everywhere and look, the foot stool's smashed. And there's blood up here on the wall.' Artisan touched the tiles and cringed. 'She must have hit her head hard, and I bet anything she got a concussion from it and why she couldn't get up to stoke the fire.'

Back up in the bedroom, Jovis felt a lump the size of an egg on her head. He looked at his hand, but there was no blood. 'Maybe it was a small cut that healed.' He was devastated he had caused this.

Artisan saw his face and kept his anger in. He was so mad he wanted to smash something, or someone, but he stayed still, unable to move as the horror of what happened set in. He should never have left her. He blamed himself. As for Jovis, he knew by the dry retch just how vile he felt.

Jovis coughed back nauseating purging as he realised he had possibly killed Caitlin. Her infected leg, now exposed, made his stomach turn sour as he tried to come to terms with what he had done. Anyone else and he wouldn't give a damn, but this wasn't just anyone. He had befriended her, invited this woman to his home and promised to be the person she made him feel. Only he had not appreciated this hand of friendship and had thrown it away. He cursed himself for being so uptight and such a bully. *If she lives, she'll never forgive me and I don't blame her.*

'Her leg's severely infected. She has blood poisoning and probably a concussion,' Peon Major told him.

'Let's just leave that up to the doctor,' he snapped. 'Wait outside.'

'Geez, Jovis!' Artisan waited until the door was closed. He wasn't thrilled with the maid's opinion.

'Zip it or shove off home, Artisan. It's happened, and I'm sorry, okay.' The slender flawless body had changed and under the towel, only a thin frame remained. Her leg was so swollen it looked ready to burst and her arms and shoulders were bruised where he held her too tightly when taking her down to the dungeon. A moan escaped Jovis's lips before speaking. 'Glow is a goddess, of greatness. How could I have possibly known she was this fragile?' he was disgust with himself.

Artisan felt his pain and put a hand on his shoulder. Jovis clearly felt as he did, only worse. Those marks were all from him, and he hoped it taught his friend a lesson.

Jovis stood, with a sickly grim expression.

'You okay?'

Artisan saw him dry heaving as he moved quickly to the toilet outside the door. It slammed shut, and the sound of Jovis being sick was enough to set him off. He called the two maids in who had been stationed outside the door. 'Bath and dress my friend as gently as you can. One more mark on her and I am going to kill someone.' He left. He was not the only one whose stomach had turned for his part in this. *Why did I leave her? She begged me to take her.* He felt just as guilty.

When Artisan arrived back, he saw Jovis had pulled it together and had lifted Caitlin in and out of the bath. He stood leaning on the mantelpiece with his back politely turned while they dressed her. This pleased him greatly and he walked over to joined him. Together they poked at the hot coals in the fireplace to help burn the frost-covered logs. With the fire blazing, they turned to the sound of one of the maids. 'All dressed Your Highness. Can we be of any further assistance?' They had her on the bed and dressed in warm socks and a nightgown.

'Thank you, Peon Major.' He addressed the head of his female guards. Jovis rarely used sentinels as maids, and neither did he allow them in his home, but he certainly didn't want any men around Caitlin. 'Wait at the landing and welcome Doc Lepius when he arrives. He has his own code, so bring him to me immediately.' Jovis turned away, impatient to get back and attend to Caitlin. Although the room had warmed up, her feet still felt cold through the socks, so he placed a hot water bottle at her feet and pulled the covers up until the doctor arrived.

Pleased she was clean and comfortable, Jovis turned back to the second in charge he hadn't yet dismissed. 'Go and prepare some clear chicken broth.' He could see she looked confused. 'If you are clueless how to make it, swap with someone who knows. That is all, you have your orders. You're dismissed.'

Both men sat each side of Caitlin's unresponsive body, willing her to pull through. Neither knew how bad it was and nervously waited to be told.

A knock on the door made them jump.

'The doctor has arrived,' said Peon Major as she opened the door wide.

Jovis and Artisan stood at the end of the bed, giving the doctor room. They had known Doc Lepius all their lives and trusted him like family, but also knew he had little patience for abuse. If the doc thought this happened deliberately, he would remove her from their care. Eyes wide, neither spoke while he 'tut-tutted' as he cleaned the wound that was leaking infection. He used a poultice on the injury and wrapped her leg in a bandage. From the way he kept glaring at them, they figured she was in bad condition. Jovis was thankful he didn't insist on taking her to the hospital. It meant he trusted this was as they said, a terrible accident.

Doc Lepius stood up. 'You're lucky you wear the guilt, or this would be going down much differently. I need more equipment so will be back shortly.' He left but was back within minutes with more equipment and a nurse.

The two men hadn't moved, waiting to hear the prognosis. They watched as the doctor and nurse placed drips from two separate bags in her arm.

'My nurse will stay here until I say otherwise, and I want no argument. I have strong NAVbiotics and fluids going into her to help with the infection and dehydration.' He gave her an injection as he spoke. 'This is to keep her out of any pain if she does wake, and I'll be back tomorrow to check if she needs another.' He turned to them. 'This woman has had quite a shock, and I don't just mean physically. I'm not sure what has happened here, but it had better be over. I'd say it's partly the reason her system has had to shut down while it tries to recover. Dealing with a wound as well as emotional distress is not a great combination. So listen up, lads, these fluids and the NAVbiotics will help with the swelling in the brain and leg, but she will also need around the clock care, complete rest and zero stress.' He ran his gadget over her leg and the lump on the back of her head. 'Mmm... You're lucky, lads, the infection is already beginning to subside, so the patient has done well to stabilise such grave injuries. She has put herself into a deep catatonic state which has helped keep her alive, but for her to come out of it will take a miracle at this point.' He slid her sleeve up to show them even further bruising. 'Not sure where these nasty marks came from on her arms and shoulders, but I assume this type of accident will not happen again.'

The doctor frowned as they both shook their heads and their faces drained of colour. For Jovis that was unusual, as his olive skin was naturally dark.

Lepius noted this. 'You okay, Jovis? You don't appear well either. Maybe I'd better look at you next.'

He shook his head. 'I'm all right. Tend to my friend—I couldn't bear to lose her.'

'I can see that.' Doc Lepius scratched his head and looked back at the woman at whom they looked adoringly. He had treated her once before and knew exactly who she was. He also knew she was pretty darn important, and not just to them. To take her from here would not be in her best interest, but he wished he could. At least he knew where she was and that she was safe. She'd done well with these two hard heads. As he packed his bag to leave, he knew she still had a way to go with them so left well enough alone. Luckily for them, he knew the workings of Cassie and Caitlin and had seen firsthand how his two favourite goddesses tamed these brutes of the sky. These two were not the worst, but Glow Girl sure had her hands full. He smiled inwardly as he left.

'Blatzing hell! Thought he was going to take her at one stage.' Jovis pulled up a chair beside the bed and held her hand.

'Me too. I was ready to do a grab and run.' Artisan dragged a chair to the opposite side of the bed.

Both settled beside her while chatting quietly until the nurse moved them away to check her vitals. She never shared any information, but they were not blind. Her colour was no better. Nor had she moved.

As they sat back beside her, Jovis searched the features of the nurse who recorded the readings on her NAVchart. Her poker face gave nothing away. After she was done, the nurse sat back in the rocking chair in the corner, and as before, he guessed for the next half an hour, her eyes would be glued to the book she'd retrieved from her oversized handbag.

He stared at Caitlin lying in his king-size bed with all the drips still coming from her that the nurse only minutes before had checked. He spoke to Artisan in a whisper so the nurse couldn't hear. 'I gave Glow's powers back before I brought her up here to be cleaned and dressed. To be honest, I don't care if she uses them on me when she regains consciousness. But even that hasn't helped.' Jovis exhaled heavily. 'I've been thinking—I've decided to leave you here while I go and turn myself in to Axon. I'll tell him the truth and let him come and see if he can help her more. I can't sit by and do nothing. I have to face up to what I feel is my fault.'

'Then I should come too. This is our fault. I should never have left her alone for all that time. It was foolish and careless.' Artisan chewed on his nails, staring at her. She moved her lips. 'Look, Glow can hear us.'

Jovis watched her mouth move. He craned his neck and leant closer, so he could hear her words 'Please don't, please stay!'

Both humbled by her forgiveness, they swallowed back emotions that filled their eyes with gratitude.

'Shh, beautiful. Whatever you want, but no talking, you need all the energy you can muster. If it is your wish for us to stay, we will, but get well, okay.' Jovis stroked her hair.

She nodded.

They were the last words she spoke for a while, so while caring for her over the next few days, they made sure one or the other was there with her. They read to her and talked much about their past and the problems they faced as rulers. They wanted her to know that not once did they leave her alone. That would never happen again. Each night they took it in turns to sit beside the bed, and although they dozed at times, she needed only to cough, shiver or move, and they would snap awake. With care, they tended to her every whim until she looked comfortable. Both felt the magic around her at times and were amazed it was helping them too. Their pain lessened as she looked better.

It had been one crazy busy day for Jovis, so Artisan took a double shift sitting with Caitlin in case she woke. His temper riled up when the nurse kept moving him away from the bed while she worked. He was reading aloud, and the interruption got on his nerves. 'Why are you doing checks every fifteen minutes?' he snapped.

'Look at her. Something is happening. Her wound has suddenly healed, and in fact, has almost vanished. And those bruises—they have gone!' The nurse pointed.

'Shytzer, you're right.' Artisan stood and bent over her, searching her arms and legs for the bruising or the scar she should be sporting on her leg.

'Nothing has worked up until now, and suddenly, a miracle has happened.' The nurse held Glow's wrist and ran a NAVscan over it. 'Your patient's vitals are normal. I don't understand.' The nurse stood back looking relieved. 'I must contact Doc Lepius. He will be thrilled she is on the mend.' She retrieved a NAVcom from her big bag and after calling, she started to gather her belongings.

'Are you leaving?' Artisan said.

'The doctor is on his way to confirm the patient is on the mend. If my diagnosis is correct, he wants me ready to leave when he does. He feels you are capable of handling it from here.' She gave him a disapproving stare. 'But then we don't always agree, so you better prove me wrong young man.' She turned and became her usual listless self.

Chapter Twenty-Two

Delicate Rose

Jovis was off-world when he got the news that Caitlin had miraculously healed. He was in the middle of signing off on the purchase of a new Ice Planet. The ruler of the Home World had so many bad debts, he was just glad to leave with money in his pocket. Quickly, he finalised the last of the details and, after authorising the terms and conditions, Jovis made a hasty departure. After such an epic win, he would generally stay for drinks after, but not this time. He had agonised and waited days for this moment. All the bed care and prayers had paid off. Glow was going to live.

As Jovis walked up to the bed where Caitlin lay, he not only felt the change of mood in the room but had noticed a difference in everything around him lately.

'Has she woken yet?' he asked the nurse.

'No, but over the past twelve hours, she has started to look much better. I didn't put any fragrant oils in the water when I gave her a sponge bath, but Master Artisan has insisted there is a delightful perfume in the air.'

Jovis smiled, looking down at Caitlin. 'Yes, there is. I think it's the fragrance of our little goddess here. I believe the tale goes, only men who are deserving get to delight in the sweet bouquet.' It filled the room, and there was nowhere else Jovis wished to be, but with her; it was divine. He felt a twinge of shame for cursing this same sweet-smelling perfume that drew him to her that very first meeting.

He'd thought it to be a potion she'd developed to attract them. He had thought of her as an evil witch. *I sure got that wrong.*

He remembered back to the first time he saw her. *In a skimpy black dress, and her hair was tied up. A few red ringlets fell softly down her slender neck and touched her shoulders. It put a shiver through him each time they touched her flawless skin. He wanted to run after her but couldn't move. He was mesmerised by her gorgeous shapely legs and dainty feet that seemed to glide as she walked in heels that were so high he wondered how she stayed upright. He found her a picture of loveliness and couldn't take his eyes from her, and neither could any other man. Yet she seemed oblivious to the attention.*

Now her powers had begun to develop, he realised there was no perfumed potion, no gimmick to attract him personally, it was just part of her, *she is the Goddess of Peace,* and it was purely all just coincidence. Deliberating, he was astounded she chose him out of all the men there to spend time with. She'd wanted to be with him because she liked his company and he made her feel happy. What a fool he had been, the goddess lived for love, and his hatred nearly destroyed her. *I get it now.* He had learned from her other friends how she should be treated if he wished to keep her friendship. He thanked the heavenly guardians for giving her back to them and giving him, in particular, a second chance.

* * * *

It was early morning when Caitlin's giggles disturbed him. Jovis had collapsed on the side of the bed, his body still sitting in the chair. He opened his eyelids and smiled. Glow's face was directly in front of his, so close their noses pressed together. She must have thought it funny and was beaming.

'You're squashing my nose.'

'You're squashing mine.' Jovis smiled, lifting his head, and sat up quickly and rubbed at his neck that cracked from the quick movement. He looked over at Artisan who had fallen asleep as well but with his head comfortably on the headrest. He moved his neck to the other side, and it cracked again. He rubbed his nose that still felt flattened.

'It's all red, so mine must be too.' She rubbed hers and got the giggles again.

The joyful sound shot through him like a bolt of lightning. 'Holy shytzer Glow!' Jovis sat back, surprised. 'Your laughing makes me feel as if I've just swallowed a happy pill or something. It tingles, and the sensation is mind-blowing.' He leant forward and ran his hand across her forehead to move her hair from her face. 'Good to see you've finally decided to join us again. You were one sick little goddess. Welcome back, beautiful.'

'Jovis!' She sat up quickly and wrapped her arms around his neck. 'It's you! You're back.'

The surprised delight shocked him. He must have been a right mongrel.

She whispered in his ear. 'When you're Vador, you are *so* mean.' She pulled back and stared at him, her brows furrowed. 'He literally hated me.'

Jovis studied her face and took a deep breath, pleased he had not harmed her sweet spirit. 'I kicked his butt, and I swear he'll never come back while you're around. This is my oath to you if you promise to keep in touch when I take you home.'

Her smile dropped, and letting him go, she sat back on the bed with her legs crossed and viewed him. He may have been Jovis just then, but she suddenly saw the much despised, evil Vador lurking in his expression. If she left now, he would retreat within days, even hours, of her departure. He would get cross and imagine her evil again. He'd never let her step foot in his world again and that was not how this was to end. The plan was to get him together with Jett to talk over their problem.

Gulping back her disappointment, she realised this was not the time to go, and he had better get used to having her around. There was a new path she saw for Jovis, and if he stayed Vador, it would never come about. She dropped her hands and held them in her lap, tightly closed. 'You know, I take promises very seriously, and I'm sorry, but as yet, they have not been fulfilled!' She folded her arms with a stubborn expression.

One side of his face turned up in a half grin, the other was dead serious. 'Understand my side of this. I want us to be friends. As for making good on those promises, I ruined everything when I stole you away. This I intend to make right, so I am definitely taking you home. After your husband calms down and no longer wants to knock me from here to kingdom come for doing what I did, I wish to ask his permission this time for your visit. That way, I can bring you here without feeling like such a villain for stealing you away.'

She turned to Artisan who had sat up listening, wide-eyed. 'And I suppose you agree with him?'

Artisan coughed; his loyalty to both had kept him quiet until now. 'I have to agree, Glow, it's the right thing to do.' He got up and moved closer to talk. At the end of the bed, he glanced at Jovis and back at Caitlin. 'We thought we'd lost you, sweetie.' His tone was caring, and calm. 'The boss and I were devastated once we realised what our actions had caused. We made a pact that if you survived, we'd fix this mess somehow and hope your husband will give us another chance. As Jovis said, we wish for you to be a welcomed friend of ours and not just for this one visit. That means giving you a choice to come back. If you don't want to revisit us because we were such heartless bastards, then that's our fault, and we'll have to live with your decision, like it or not.'

Caitlin almost smiled. They had no idea Axon would sooner her stay and do her job, this she knew for sure. Now in perfect health, it was nice to be able to think straight again.

Jovis studied her as she sat silent. He wished there was another way, but knew what had to be done. Remorseful and miserable he waited for what was inevitable, regardless of her argument. To do anything else would be dishonourable and she would hate him for it later when she came to her senses.

Caitlin glanced at them. Unfamiliar feelings of guilt had really taken its toll on the two men, but both had passed her test of loyalty. Going a step further than expected by the offer to take her home proved how much they had changed already, and it made her happy.

'Am I allowed to enter into this debate?'

Jovis smiled. 'Yes, but keep in mind, unless we take you home, how can you fully forgive us or ever trust us? We want to show you how genuinely sorry we are by doing the right thing.' He was confused. *Did this mean she wanted to stay?* 'We left you alone here, Caitlin, while we checked out your story. We nearly killed you.'

'But in the end, you cared enough to want me to live,' she argued.

'I'm so sorry Glow, I got you all wrong.' Jovis shook his head regretfully.

'And I actually believed you to be a monster. I woke up this morning and that beastly person was gone, and my friend Jovis was back. And now you have admitted you are willing to take me home, well, this changes everything. It makes me see how genuine that offer of friendship was when we first met. It took a detour, I agree, but now it's back on track. If you'll have me and want me to stay for a while, I'd feel honoured to get to know you both and learn more about these uncharted Ice Planets you live on. That is if you could handle having me stay here a little longer.'

'But your husband, your work, they will want to know you are okay?' Jovis pleaded for her to let him do this right.

'I'm on holidays, so won't be missed by the Riders, and as for Axon, he allows me to spend my leave wherever I wish.' She shrugged. 'I had chosen Pluto, but I'm here now, and the change of location won't worry him as long as I'm happy to be here. He knows I'll come home when I'm ready.'

'After taking you without his permission, I can't imagine he would want you to stay a second longer than you had to.' Jovis was shocked at her response yet happy at the same time.

'Axon's work is classified, but I can tell you this; he is urgently needed elsewhere, and this is the reason I am free to enjoy a break on my own. He also understands that as a goddess, I cannot always be by his side. Sometimes I am needed elsewhere as he is, and I guess, for now, it might be here. You see under all the tough talk I'm hearing, your expressions show me neither of you really wants me gone.'

'So now you are taking us hostage, refusing to leave.' He had a twinkle in his eye that she liked.

'You bet I am. I want to see the universe, and getting to stay on an Ice Planet will be incredible. You have no idea how much I will enjoy learning about your lifestyle, homelands and philosophies.'

Jovis gave her one last chance, and that would be it. He wanted her to stay so badly, he figured he'd most likely steal her straight back after taking her home so was glad, in fact, fist-pumpingly thrilled, she wanted to stay. 'What about clothes? Surely you'll need to go back and at least pack a bag.'

Caitlin searched his face and saw, if she left now, goodbye Jovis and hello Vador. 'I don't need any clothes.' She shrugged and giggled with Artisan who was highly astute. 'That came out all wrong, didn't it? I mean, I travel light because now you've returned my powers, outfits magically appear.' She saw their odd glance at one another.

To prove her point, she stood up on the bed and moved her hands up and down, drawing attention to what she had on. 'I'm in a nightgown, right.... However, I want to go and have some breakfast, but now out of bed I shiver and feel cold, watch...' She actually did shudder with the coolness of the room. Before their eyes, she glowed brightly, and when it dissipated, she was in a warm embroidered polar bear tracksuit with joggers and a fluffy hat. The sides of the cap extended over her ears and came down each side, forming into a long scarf. She held up the ends of the scarf that had white bear heads on the ends. She chuckled. 'Okay, maybe sometimes the designs are a bit crazy and not what I want to wear, but it is what it is. I'm sure you get the idea.'

They wore big grins.

'Damn, girl you're a crack up.' Artisan laughed.

Jovis reached up and pulled the bonnet back a bit so he could see her better. 'Well, I don't get that man of yours if he can just wave you goodbye and do without you until you are ready to return. But if you say it will be okay by him, then welcome to Sedna.' He couldn't stop smiling.

'He saw us together, remember, and trusts you with me. He would feel I have my powers back and knows I'm happy to stay.'

Jovis cocked up a brow 'How?'

'Because by now, if I really wanted to leave here, I would have blasted my way out and after, deactivated your security in the sky. Oh, and called Rory for a lift home.'

They both thought that funny.

'You?' Jovis gave a hearty laugh. 'You wouldn't harm an ant.'

Artisan had to wipe the laughter from his eyes. 'A delicate rose blasting away two evil bastards that draw their power from the dark side. Pull the other one.' He thought her hilarious. Putting an arm around her, he gave Caitlin a hug. 'Just having fun with you, sweetie.' He let her go after he got her to smile.

She sat up straight and grinned. 'Make fun of the new girl hey. Well, I can prove it if you want.'

'Love to see it. Where do you want to go? Can't zap us with your little Taser-zinger-finger in this room, there isn't enough room for us to play here.' Artisan chuckled, loving this new game they were about to engage in.

'Artisan, don't stir her up mate,' Jovis said. 'You can see how fragile she is. No need to make her feel bad about her inabilities as well as being domestically challenged.' He too wore a sly grin, wishing to egg her on a little. It had been a while since there had been any fun in his life.

'Oh, is that right!' Caitlin slid off the bed. 'Okay, it looks to me as if you men need a lesson on just how capable I can be... Let's take this outside.' Caitlin got up and headed for the door, stopped and turned. Neither had moved. 'Um, where is outside.'

Jovis put his hand up. 'Enough. You're tough. Now let's drop it.'

'Like hell.' Artisan jumped to his feet. 'I'll take you, gotta see this. I haven't had a good laugh in months.' He snatched up the thick coat from the coat stand in the corner and laid it over his arm. 'I know you can dress yourself sweet pea. Think, minus two hundred and forty degrees Celsius.'

Jovis got to his feet. 'Well if I can't stop you two butting heads I sure want to witness it.'

As soon as they stepped from the elevator, Jovis unlocked the door with a voice command and after it opened, transported them to a spot not far from the door.

The cold was instant, but Caitlin's magic was quicker and the jacket she wore, not only lengthened but a hood and some kind of breathable veil covered her face. It still allowed her to see perfectly yet she felt no chilly wind whatsoever. She was also surprised how well this lightweight fur warmed her. She had never been in these conditions before and was amazed her magic was so cleverly advanced. The mysterious fabric was perfect for this alien Home World.

As they said, it was bitterly cold and dark outside yet once her eyes adjusted, using a touch more magic, there was a beauty to this world she was glad she was getting to see. Over time, glaciers had eroded the land, causing steep ridges in the mounds of the rocky mountain landscape. Under some of the ice, she noticed horn cavities and above, sharp-edged peaks jutted out from the top of other glaciers. In front of them were large cirques, the circular basins were filled full of slushy ice from rains they must have had earlier that day. The minerals from the soil had oozed up and sat at the top of the glaciers like red icing sugar. 'This is amazing, so beautiful.' Caitlin revelled in the glorious starry night that allowed her to see the surface of this Home World for the very first time. There was no moon, but after spending so much time on Pluto, she was sure it had to still be daytime.

'Well, we're here. What now, playful one?' Jovis grinned.

'Have you got security in the sky?' Caitlin tilted her head up.

'Not at the moment. Why?' Suspicion sparked a sidelong glance towards his buddy, Artisan.

She smiled at his wary glance. 'Don't worry, it's nothing fancy or threatening. I just don't want panic alarms going off, which might prompt unnecessary security to come here and spoil my surprise.' Caitlin knew they both suddenly flinched and recoiled from the good spirited fun she had in mind. She felt them take a step back and smiled to herself. *Call me a delicate rose.*

Caitlin closed her eyes and made up rockets, like Woody from the Cloud Riders had taught her. She packed them full of fireworks and in her mind pushed them up in the sky. The ground under them shook and unsure, both men took another few steps, backing away from her. Eyes now open; her gloves were removed before she raised both hands. The sound of a rocket ready to launch broke the silence and the ground shook more as she clapped her hand and threw them higher in the air. Two rockets magically appeared and whistled as they hurtled through the sky.

Jovis was just about to intervene and forcibly stop Caitlin when the ground stopped shaking, and it was too late. He diverted eyes from her in time to see two missiles form in the sky. His first thought was, she was destroying his Home World. This was just a game she played, sucking him in until she got the chance to get rid of him, total annihilation. It was too late now; the rockets were in mid-air. He would wait for them to come back down and then transport himself and Artisan out. She, he would leave to die as she had intended them to do on this very day. Yet a small voice; one he hadn't met before; was tugging at his heart. *She would never hurt you, she is your friend. Wait, and you will finally see for yourself. This is her displaying another of her innocent acts of playfulness...*

The rockets stopped in mid-air and opened up like a floating barge. The sky had lit up with a magnificent array of colour. It was a fireworks display, and Jovis breathed out a sigh of relief. She was the real deal and someone he could trust unequivocally. She was sincere, and she was the most gifted goddess he had ever met. Tears of joy and love for this woman burst forth as the display continued. His life was going to change. It was Caitlin who had started this chain of events, and from this day forward he knew, with her by his side, he could trust, dream and start living as a man that would make her proud.

Caitlin turned and motioned for them to join her. Both took a few steps forward and each took an outstretched hand she offered, not taking their eyes from the sky. The fireworks lit up the planet and them. The surface reflected the blues and greens, making the ice look as if they stood on a tropical Island with sea all around them. Flickers of darker tones had whales and other sea creatures roll in and out the water. The sky bellowed with loud sounds as one after the other, fireworks now shifted from the surface, and an enormous red ball of light that Jovis assumed represented his planet, Sedna, filled the sky. It looked spectacular against the massive explosions behind it as pinwheels burst out into sparkling lights that represented the surrounding Ice Planets and stars above.

When the last of it burst out and faded, Jovis and Artisan let out a yahoo and fist punched each other, before they turned and included Caitlin in a group hug.

'That was such a buzz!' Artisan let out a loud whistle after they put her down. 'Wow, I've never met anyone that can do that sort of magic. I was unsure at first but my hats off to you; I'll never question you again.'

Jovis was so gentle when he lifted her chin. 'That's where your strength is and why you're so delicate, Caitlin. A person with that much in one area is bound to suffer in another. You only have to look at Artisan here. Muscle power you wouldn't believe but brains, Blatz, nothing going on between those ears.' He got a decent old punch in the arm for saying so.

'I have a kind heart too, Glow told me.' Artisan puffed up his chest.

Caitlin responded. 'Oh and so much more. You're witty, sensitive and work hard. Any girl that gets you and lets you go is crazy.'

'What about me?' Jovis said, amused. Not having discussed this in private yet he wondered as to her perception of him.

Caitlin turned thoughtfully. 'The royalty in you makes you stubborn, bad-tempered, irritable and ruthless. You find people to be false and untrustworthy. But I have found when you do trust, it is your true self that you give. This is when the real prince appears. You become an outstanding person who would fight tooth and nail for those you call a friend.'

'How do you know I'm a prince? My title is not recognised by the Congress of the Heavens, nor have I spoken of it.'

'It is for many reasons I believe this. Your speech is refined, you walk with grace, don't suffer fools and reward those who gain your trust with greatness.' She smiled at Artisan, whom she knew had received an Ice Planet for his loyalty. 'And lastly, I can feel the hum of royalty in your powers. This hum I hear only when I am with my closest friends who are kings. Like you, I find them amazing too, Prince Vador of Sedna. That is your actual title, is it not?'

He smiled wide and bright. 'Jovis is just fine. And don't go spreading it around that I like some people... It's not good for my image.'

'Jovis it is.'

Caitlin swept her eyes across the landscape and changed the subject. It was time for these men to direct this new emotion they felt for her towards this planet. 'Is that a cave?' Her eyes strained through the glass protection of her full-face mask.

Jovis turned to where her gloved hand pointed. 'Actually, there's not just one, but a couple of caves in that direction. As a kid, I did a lot of exploring and found many. They were all the same, ice tunnels that went nowhere. I haven't given them a thought in many years. It's been a long time since they were visited... not even sure they're safe.' Jovis turned back to Caitlin. Her eyes were like saucers of enthusiasm.

Artisan was already on board and was still buzzing with the thrill of fireworks. He lifted his brow. 'We do have a Rider with us, Jovis, an explosive expert if I'm not mistaken.'

'See, Artisan gets it. If we get into trouble, you know I'm capable of blowing another tunnel. Can we go, please? Both of you have transporting powers and are strong, well, in case we meet some prehistoric galactic animal down there that loves to eat redheads with attitude.'

Jovis thought about transporting her inside, but his new voice inside his head said, *why? Why not, for once, try to enjoy the day outside.* It suddenly interested him to see if Caitlin was indeed that miracle he held hope of finding one day. *Is this special lady really able to turn one of the dreariest of places into a winter wonderland? Could she be that unique a female she was capable of taking them on an expedition worth attending?* The idea was ludicrous and yet, he had started to believe in this brazen little redhead that had already captured a small piece of his heart.

Artisan shrugged a shoulder at Jovis. 'Maybe Glow's right. This is such an ice-hole of a place to live. It couldn't be more boring if we took a walk through our freezers downstairs. But then again, what if once again she proves us wrong, and there is life in the depths of this planet?'

'Slipping and sliding within an icy cave is against my better judgment but what the hell. You're only going to keep nagging, aren't you?'

She nodded, her grin wide.

'Come on then.' Jovis flicked one hand towards the cave. He was about to take her hand when Artisan snatched it first.

'Let's go, sweetie. I'll take you.' Artisan said, and they both ran off, chuckling.

Jovis saw red. 'Blatzing little shytzer!' he mumbled as he caught up to them and slapped Artisan on the back of the head before holding her other hand. 'My girl!' Jovis snapped.

Artisan smiled at her. 'My girl.' He stuck his middle finger up at Jovis which earned him a double head slap.

Both Caitlin and Artisan laughed so hard they had to pause and lean on each other. Jovis ended up laughing at them and now in a better mood, transported them to the mouth of the cave.

Chapter Twenty-Three

Cave Trujillo

On entering the cave, the air seemed warmer, even a little steamy but Jovis knew better. There had never been warmth on this planet. *Maybe smoke from Cait's fireworks.* Yet the walls were wet, and their boots made sloshy sounds as they sank into the icy red slurry. Jovis turned to where hooks held old gas lanterns. Glad they still hung there, he reached over and took two. These he lit before he handed one to Artisan. The other he held up high, giving light to a couple of passageways. 'Which one?' he asked.

Caitlin pointed to the one where steam floated and was more visible.

Jovis scratched his head. 'This is too weird... I thought the vapour was smoke from the fireworks but can definitely feel it's steamy... And warm. Could one of your fireworks have exploded in here and caused this, Cait?'

She shrugged. 'Only one way to find out; let's go look.'

'I'm not sure we should go any further in case the core has punched through, and we are about to have an earthquake.' Artisan walked to the next offshoot where the heat came from and stood to pull at his chin, trying to decide if they should go investigating while they had Caitlin with them.

'Come on guys, we won't find out, standing here gawking. Let's do some investigating. Live a little.' Caitlin gave them a friendly nudge to take a look. 'I mean, you've got transporting powers to get us out if it's dangerous.' She used her magic to help steady her steps, and suddenly ice cleats appeared on the bottoms of her boots. She looked at the men and grinned. 'Now why didn't I think to call on my magic a little earlier?' She eyed their smirks. 'Yes, I have tried to use it when I pick up a frying pan to cook… Mean old magic only works on clothes.' She chuckled.

They both rolled their eyes and let her be as she had her balance now, and they watched intently as she scooted ahead of them.

'Like it or not, we're about to find out the mystery.' Jovis shrugged and followed.

'Can't hurt to take a peek,' Artisan said. 'I mean, trust the redhead to make us look like girls 'cause we took too long to decide.'

They both chuckled.

The deeper they went, the more amazed Caitlin became. She couldn't help touching the pink ice puffs that jutted out of the corridors from different angles. 'Looks like fairy floss,' she called back to them.

Jovis caught up. 'Most ice caves are white with shades of blue. But on Sedna, the red soil seeps into the ice and the stain is more noticeable the deeper we go. If you like these light shades of pink, wait until you see the vibrant shade of red further down this corridor. When the light hits the ice it looks like glowing rubies.' Jovis ran his fingers along the icy wall and lifted his hand to show the staining on his palm.

Taking off her glove, Caitlin did the same, and it reddened her skin as well. She had noticed the pink snow mounds outside but in here it was even more beautiful, and fascinating. 'It leaves a stain like the antiseptic made of iodine that we use on Earth. I should have rolled myself in this stuff when I was hurt; might have helped me heal a bit quicker.' She tried to rub it off her skin. When it wouldn't budge she put her gloves back on, knowing her magic would take care of it once they sat for a moment and rested. She had just used a massive amount of power showing off but smiled. *It was so worth the look on their faces.*

Jovis kicked at the soil. 'I know on Earth iodine is sourced from the ocean, but here it's plentiful. Does give these caves a rare look compared to other Home Worlds.

Artisan grabbed a handful of mud. 'If Glow is right, and this has a healing property, we should have it tested, Jovis. This ancient iodine is mixed with precious minerals. It could be the healing goo that researchers seek.' He turned the mud into a cube, wrapped it in his bandana, and slipped it into his pocket. He faced Caitlin. 'Jovis here could be sitting on a fortune.'

Jovis laughed. 'I have a fortune. But one can never have too much.'

Caitlin walked on without a word.

Jovis caught up with her. 'What!'

She stopped, turned to him and folded her arms. 'If you have so much money, why do you live as you do? No electricity, absolutely no modern comforts. I'm a little confused.'

'I live on an Ice Planet, Cait, what would you have me do?'

'There is much you can do, but are you ready to change yet? Meet with Jett and...'

'No!' He stomped off.

They walked in silence until the tunnel fanned out into a massive room. The steam made it hard to see too much at first, but with the second lamp now in the opening, they could see it came from a central location.

'No way!' Caitlin took a sniff of the air. 'You have a mineral hot tub in here, and I've been taking cold showers.'

Jovis stared at the phenomenon. 'This is no hot tub. My guess is there has been a shift in the underworld plates, and the fissure in the core has been big enough to heat up the ice and form this hot spring. If I had known, I swear, I'd have been out here all the time.'

Artisan couldn't take his eyes from it either. 'Do you think when we helped the King drilled to find the best location for the fortress all those years ago, that we could have hit something here, maybe have pushed through to the core?'

'We were just teenagers. Surely this couldn't have been here all this time. How did we miss it?' Jovis was cross he was only finding this now.

'I suppose it's because we never come out here.' Artisan shrugged. 'We hated being outside, remember, blamed out here for all our problems.'

'You can thank me for helping you find it later, but for now, let's try it out.' Caitlin knelt with her hand in the water. 'Feels like about 37°Celsius.' With her magic working fine below the surface, Caitlin's fur jacket, boots and tracksuit disappeared, leaving her in a modest red swimming costume; a one piece with a tiny skirt attached. She chuckled and dived straight in, shocking both men.

'Glow, no!' Artisan called out, too late.

Jovis was out of his clothes within seconds and in boxer shorts, dived in after her. Both surfaced, Caitlin laughing in Jovis's arms.

Artisan had just landed in the water and cursed. 'Blatzing hell, Glow. Anything could have been in here. What if there had been some nasty chemical that melted your skin off?'

Caitlin put both hands to her face and dragged her skin down screaming. 'Oh no ... I'm melting. You were right... Help!'

Jovis's eyes were like saucers. It made her smile, but there was always a reason for her actions.

'How do you think I knew it was exactly 37°Celsius?'

'You scanned the water first,' said Artisan.

She nodded. 'You have to start trusting me more.' She wiggled from Jovis's grip, and added, 'both of you.' Although her words came with a firm message, her look was sensitive and caring. 'I swear I'll never cause you pain, not ever. I am here to help, so let me. Coming here, we've uncovered something that will not only give you hours of enjoyment, but the entertaining possibilities are endless. An ice bar comes to mind. I tried to sell this to another friend of mine, but it wasn't for him. Maybe it's to your taste as you men are frequent visitors to Earth. I'm sure you've been to one.'

'We sure have. You're right, Glow. This will make for one impressive event venue. What do you think, Jovis?'

Jovis rested his head against the side, keeping afloat by gently moving his arms. The minerals and warmth had him suddenly feeling relaxed. 'Not sure I want to share it.' He opened one eye, looked at Caitlin. He was fairly sure this was her handiwork after seeing what she was capable of outside. 'I guess I should give you credit for this, but I still think it was a fluke.' He smiled, both eyes closed again.

'May my flukes make your life better.' She moved beside him and rested as he did.

Artisan floated and paddled about for a bit before coming over to them. Bored, he pulled Jovis, then Caitlin, under the water which began a frenzy of ducking, bombing and tomfoolery.

Caitlin was waterlogged by the time she pulled herself out and sat on the side with her feet still dangling. Her magic had a towelling coat wrap around her, keeping her comfortable while watching her new companions. They had so much strength, and now she was out of harm's way they kept her amused with their antics of who could win the most challenges. Of course, Jovis was stronger and incredibly nimble, but it pleased her to see he let Artisan win sometimes. Jovis laughed heartily each time he lost, showing her he was also a good sport.

He gave Artisan a firm nudge. 'Time out, big boy.' They swam over and pulled their soaked bodies out, then sat each side of her to dry off before they dressed. 'We do need to stop babying you, Cait. I see that now. And we really do need to trust you more.'

Her movement was delicate again, just as it had been that first day they met. Sometimes she was so capable and resilient, yet moments later like now, Jovis wanted to wrap her up in his arms and protect her. Would he ever feel normal around her? So many emotions she dragged from him.

'Everything is fun when you're around. I'm going to hate it when you go home,' Jovis said when she sat quietly. He wondered if she was listening. She seemed far away, and wasn't at all being her usual attentive self. He continued anyway. 'And try as I have, I can't see how negotiations will ever go ahead, after what we have done to you. Let's be honest, when I take you back to Axon, and unless I steal you back, I feel we will never see you again.'

Caitlin blinked and touched his arm. She was listening now and felt his worry. His sadness was visible. 'This worry is because you are only just learning trust. It's not an easy emotion to deal with when that person you want to believe has not grown up around you, like your good buddies Artisan and Rocky. When you're ready to trust what you and I have, it is then I'll go home and sort everything out for you. Sedna has so much potential, but you must have faith in me that I won't lead you into a trap. Also, what I suggest is purely for your long-term happiness, nothing more, definitely no ill gains.'

He breathed in deeply and exhaled with a sigh. *Cait was right.* He had only known her a while. Did he trust her fully, as he did Artisan and Rocky? Maybe not like that, but to build such a friendship he had to start somewhere. 'I don't believe in many people, that is true, but in you, I am learning very quickly that what you say is what you mean. Therefore, if you tell me I need to start listening, which is all I am prepared to do right now, I will listen. For the moment, that's all I can give you Cait.'

She smiled. 'Then I will take what I can get.'

He leant back on his elbows and watched her swirling the water with her hand. She had stayed out of loyalty to him, to help make things better, but only at this moment did it sink in. And even though, like now, she seemed so childlike, he was ready to hear what she had in mind.

'Tell me, Goddess of Peace, how do you see this going down?'

She pulled her legs from the water, crossed them and faced him. 'I just thought a two-day break should give us enough time to do what needs to be done.' His eyes widened, but she continued, surprised he didn't interrupt and call it stupid. 'My reasons include both of us because I want you to do something while I'm gone.'

'Go on.' His eyes were almost closed with suspicion.

'While I'm discussing private matters about you with my husband, I wish for you to go down to Earth and do what it was you were doing before I mucked it up.'

His head went on a slant and he grinned.

'Yes, you get it, don't you? I know you had gone there to... how do I put this, sow your royal oats.' She chuckled, showing her innocence at even talking about such matters.

'And while we are away, you intend to set up a meeting between my men and your friend.'

'Just the three of you. It has to be a trust thing for both parties or Jett will not agree to it, and neither will Axon.' She hurried through that part when his face turned red with annoyance and quickly decided to steer the topic in another direction. 'Oh, and maybe you could visit one of those ice bars while there to get the latest ideas for here. Then when you come to pick me up, and I'm there, you can finally start trusting me and stop worrying about what Axon thinks. It's only then you'll be able to change your future for the better.'

Jovis listened but looked noncommittal. 'What will you say to Axon?'

'I'm not sure yet, but I do know Axon is the only one I fully trust to organise a meeting between you and Jett.'

'You mean the king, who is our sworn enemy,' Artisan huffed.

'Yes. But he would feel more comfortable if you called him, Jett. He hates formalities when in private. Those are just titles and not who we really are.' She watched them both for a reaction.

'We did notice you don't use his royal title. In our kingdom growing up, and as it is on Earth, royal status is always used,' said Jovis.

'And yet we all call you Jovis and not Prince Vador.'

'Okay, I get the picture. Friends are permitted in the heavens to drop the royal titles as there are so many of us. However, at this stage we are not his friend, nor is he ours, so king it will be.'

'The man you met that day is who he is.' She screwed up her lips in thought. 'But on second thoughts, because you took me from him, Hades may be who you speak to for a bit. As I'm sure, he will be talking to Prince Vador and not you, Jovis. Each of you was shocked to find out who the other was, but you are two determined and intelligent men, so I'm sure you will come to an agreement and sort it out.'

'And if not?' Jovis's jaw was set firm.

'If not, I will have to fight you both and force you to give in.'

Artisan wasn't so easy to win over. 'What if the King wants to punish Jovis for what he did… what we did? I warn you, regardless of the rules you lay down, Jovis will one day be our king, and he won't be going anywhere without being guarded. So the king had best be prepared for me, Rocky and our best sentinels to accompany him there to protect him.'

'I agree on Jovis needing protection, and this is why I need time to set up this meeting between royals.' Caitlin's tone became very serious. 'If it's Hades he faces, he may be after blood. But Axon would never allow more than an exchange of words. I trust this, or I would never suggest it.'

'Then, after this get-together, will Axon and your two king friends allow the goddess to come back with the prince?' Jovis didn't feel comfortable with this plan at all.

She shook her head. 'No… The goddess will not be back, but if you're happy with boring old Caitlin, I will come back if you promise to stay as Jovis and Artisan.' She grinned. 'I doubt she will be needed here anymore, do you?'

He held her face in his hands. 'No, she won't. And you have my promise as the future ruler of my people; I will stay Jovis for you, Cait.'

Letting her go, he stared ahead. 'I want to believe in you wholeheartedly, but I'm not quite there yet. Unfortunately for me, the only way to get there is to give you a chance to prove yourself. So this is me trying to be trusting.' He clenched his fists, making a decision. 'Let's say I agree to this, when did you want to leave?'

Caitlin stood up. 'Why not now? It's as good a time as any. Gives you less chance to think negative thoughts. Keeping busy on Earth while I'm gone will help you stay confident in who I really am, a trusted ally and friend.'

Artisan screwed up his lip in thought. 'Actually, if we are to do this Jovis, it's not a bad idea to leave now as she said. That's if we want to catch up with our friends. They are still on business down there, and we both know where they will be tonight.' He stared at Caitlin. 'I intend to put my full trust in you, Glow, but the boss still has some issues. Just remember to let Axon know Rocky and I will be coming too, and we will be armed.'

She grinned. 'You will need no weapons while the peacekeepers are there, but if it makes you feel better to carry a big gun, feel free.'

'You're such a stirrer, Glow.' He shook his head and tried not to smile.

Jovis paced the cave. Now he had sort of agreed, he panicked, stopped and glared at her. 'Can I say it does make me a little suspicious you jumped at the first opportunity to be taken home. You *did* want to stay with us, didn't you? Or was that just you leading us into a comfortable lull?'

'Jovis, it's going to be okay.' She calmly put her small hand in his. The power and worry throbbed up her arm. 'You know, you *can* trust us females too. I have promised my loyalty to you, but if you need more, you can believe this, as a peacekeeper I give my word, and this will *not* be broken.'

Artisan turned to face her. 'I trust you Glow, but given time to think, this does feel like it's moving too fast.'

Caitlin saw he wasn't ready to cope without her, but Jovis was, even if only to prove to her he could. This had to be enough because someone was calling the goddess within, and she had to leave for a time to sort out the urgent matter. 'It looks as if I have a lot of work to do when I come back to Sedna.' She smiled, her eyes alight with compassion for these two men. 'Not only do I have to get your home ready to accommodate and make the women of your dreams happy, but I also need to change your stubborn ways, so you don't chase them away.'

'Good luck with that.' Jovis pulled an unlikely expression.

'Yes, good luck with that!' Artisan had his head down.

Caitlin moved towards Artisan, placed fingers under his chin and lifted his head. His eyes showed past hurt. 'Allow me to heal your pain as you healed me. Please!'

The corners of his mouth moved to give her a slight grin. 'I don't want you to go. Can't you just wait a while? Let me get used to the thought I may not see you again.'

'I will never give you that chance.' Her lips touched his soft cheek. 'For you are stuck with me as a friend always if you'll have me.'

His arms wrapped around her gently in a hug. 'That will get me through the next two days, but after that, I can't promise to be good.'

Jovis hugged them both, 'goes double for me.'

Caitlin wasn't ready to leave them either but was being summoned to go home. 'If you both agree, we best get a wiggle on if you want to catch up with those friends of yours.'

Jovis picked up her hands. 'Caitlin I'm placing my heart that is only just learning to open, in these precious hands. It will go with you, but my body goes in a different direction. Please don't harm it or I swear it will turn to ice forever more.'

She knew he spoke the truth. He surprised her when he turned to Artisan.

'And stop hogging Cait, else you'll never be welcome here again.'

Artisan stuck his finger up and gave him the NAVbird. 'Blatzing hell... Mr Smootho. Way to go giving her your heart like that... Keep trying to outdo me and when she visits me, and I know she will,' he winked at Caitlin, 'you won't be welcome on my Ice World either.'

'Touché, little prick.' Jovis was quick to retort.

They started laughing.

'Do we need to pack, boss?' Artisan let Caitlin go and started gathering his clothes to put back on.

'Hang that. Let's buy new clothes when we get there, my shout,' said Jovis.

'Better splash out too, or I'm spilling to Rocky you've finally lost your balls over the opposite sex.'

'You're such a blatzing loser. Tell him I've turned soft and you're dead, buddy!' After he was dressed in the dry clothes they'd arrived in, Jovis turned to Caitlin. 'Ready, beautiful?'

Caitlin glowed bright, and when it subsided, she stood tall and elegant in a slim-fitted, black skirt with a sheer cream shirt over a lace camisole. Cream, extremely high heels, showed off shapely legs and thin ankles.

Artisan whistled. 'Wow, look how she dresses for Axon, lucky man.'

She chuckled. 'Aim higher, stud. You too could win the heart of a snappy dresser.'

He screwed his face up, 'as if a high-class broad would give me a second look with all these tatts.'

She eyed him up and down. 'Not in those scruffy jeans and tee-shirt.' She turned to Jovis. 'Treat him to tailored pants, long-sleeved shirt tucked in and boots, belt and cufflinks.'

'What! You want me to dress like the boss?' He winced, not at all pleased.

'Trust, there it is again. Try it or not, but you are one sweetheart and need to show off that cute backside and those muscular arms. No girl will be looking at those tattoos, I promise you that.' Caitlin twisted her hair up into a bun and placed a band around it. She smoothed her skirt and put her hands out for both to hold.

'You look stunning, Caitlin. Thanks for everything you're trying to do for us. I hope this is not goodbye,' Jovis said.

'Only if you don't come and get me in two days.' She gave him a charming grin he would not forget for a while.

'Where to?' He squeezed her hand gently.

After giving the coordinates, the cave faded, and seconds later, Axon's castle appeared before them. They stood in the gardens. Caitlin knew it would only be seconds before she was snatched up but wanted to say goodbye first. The alarms already bleated out across the compound and it surprised her to sense Rory's presence close by, very close. *What is Rory doing here on Axon's world?* In fact, she only got to kiss them both on the cheek when she was in Rory's arms and like a speeding bullet they had reached the security of the house. Looking back over his shoulder, she hoped the magic used on Jovis and Artisan to get her here this fast, didn't leave them shocked and riveted to the spot. *Move.* She willed them to go. They were sitting ducks if fired upon, but she breathed out with gladness to see they were way stronger than expected. Both waved before they vanished. It was only then she relaxed. Although did keep her fingers crossed a little longer in the hope the calming given stayed with them until they found their friends. If not, she expected them back causing one hell of a racket.

CHAPTER TWENTY-FOUR

Ancient Voices

A xon appeared in front of them as they entered the castle. His hair was tousled from what looked like a rough couple of hours sleep. For Rory and the team to be there and on watch, something was going on. *And why did Axon look as if he was sleepwalking?* 'What's going on here, Rory? Are we under attack?'

'Hello to you too, Cait.' He stopped her questions.

'Sorry, howdy boss.' She blinked and eyed him. 'I just wasn't expecting to see you, Rory.' She turned and wrapped her arms around Axon. 'Hi, gorgeous, you look beat.' She kissed lips that were warm and delicious tasting. They tempted her to have downtime but she could feel something amiss and turned her attention back to Rory. 'Okay, formalities over, so tell me, what's going on? How come you're here and why is my husband sleeping in the afternoon?' She glanced at Axon who still had not uttered a word. 'This is so not like him to need a nap.'

Axon rubbed his eyes with one hand. 'I'm dreaming right?' He didn't release his grip.

'Not a dream, my love, and although my mission is still a high priority, I have been summoned to come home. Due to this being poor timing, I've had to do some quick thinking to get a couple of days here alone, to come and lend a hand.' She turned back to her husband. 'So what has Axon been up to that has upset the balance enough to warrant this urgent visit?' She figured it must be him. He was far from with it and didn't look well at all.

'Really, you're here!' Axon started to grin, and cuddle in.

'Just one-second sleepyhead…' It was also noticeable he didn't seem aware of what she was saying. She spoke soothingly to keep him calm. 'Rory, can we talk and walk at the same time. Think my tired man needs to go back to bed.'

'Here, let me help, he's too heavy for you if he passes out.'

'What! Why would you think he might pass out?'

'Axon has barely slept since you left Cait.' He put an arm around Axon and helped her get him up the staircase and into bed. 'The team are here too, but on duty. We've only today had clearance to come and see what's going on. I was getting worried. The three of them were sending out some really weird vibes.'

'Three of them,' she repeated.

He took a stronger hold on Axon who wanted to sit. 'Come on big fella.' He got him moving again before continuing. 'Axon, Jett and Calyx have put in a tremendous effort moving all the humans and their houses back to Earth. I tried to warn them they were doing too much too soon, but did they listen… not on your nelly. It took months to settle them in up here, and they've moved them, houses and all, in just a few weeks.'

'Wow, that's huge. No wonder he looks beat.'

'The three of them have worked around the clock. This past couple of days they have captured all the animals brought here, and after sorting out what variety went in what country, they transferred them too. It's been a mammoth job, but they are almost done.' He stopped when they got to the bed. 'Keep going,' she said as she pulled the blanket back.

'Well, after getting the strange vibes I asked Zoren if I could check on them. He held me back saying they'd be fine and convinced me they knew what they were doing. He insisted I would tick them off if I interfered. But after not hearing from Axon for a couple of days, he finally allowed us to check on them and I'm damned glad I did. When we arrived, the three of them were spent. They sat without talking, their vitals were poor and their powers completely depleted.

From what I can work out from the staff, they haven't slept or eaten in days.'

'Axon knows better than that, and so do the other two,' Caitlin huffed.

'For a short time, I allowed them to draw magic from the team. I knew the job they were doing and tried to help, but in the end, I had to sever the output to protect us.' Rory grunted as he helped Axon's large but limp frame onto the bed.

'Maybe, being gods, Calyx and Jett thought they were different to other immortals and had an abundance of power that kept on keeping on.' She spoke up for her friends.

'That's exactly what happened. And when I advised Axon to give it a break and for them to refuel, eat and sleep, my advice fell on deaf ears.'

'If it's self-inflicted and R&R will fix them, I'm baffled as to why I was called back here so fast. You guys can easily handle helping them with recharging their magic.' She stared ahead, thinking. 'What about Calyx and Jett? Where are they and are you sure they are resting and okay?' Caitlin said while tucking the covers around her worn out husband. His eyes dropped immediately. 'Wow, he is out of it already.'

'They're all here and now sleeping. Honestly, talk about babies, I ended up having to use magic on them and forced them to rest.'

'Big call, Calyx and Jett will know what you did and give it to you after they wake,' she warned.

'Well, it was their call to stay connected to us, so they could feel you were okay so that shit comes with the job.' He shrugged. 'You know my team comes first, Cait. They had become a drain on us and had been warned. As you have all learned, I only give an order once; the second time I will take control.'

'I felt nothing my end.'

'You were on a mission, so I blocked them from drawing from you. Glad it worked.' He smiled.

'Thanks, I've needed it all. Especially today doing a flip on them to get home as quick as I did. Poor guys, when it wears off, I hope they're okay.'

'You know what you're doing Cait. Your boys will be all right.'

As they left the room, she looked up the corridor, listening. 'Gee, you sure gave Calyx and Jett a high dose; I'm surprised neither surfaced when the alarms went off before.'

'Mmm… That is strange. I only used a mild imprint, so it didn't make them suspicious. They must have been more exhausted than I thought and it's taking them longer to come out of it. I could wake them, but I doubt it will hurt to keep them sleeping until we at least get time to catch up. They honestly looked no better than Axon.'

'In that case, I won't stick my head in the door. They'll surface soon enough, and with luck, they'll be able to enlighten us as to why I'm here.' She said, and eyed him. 'Surprised you didn't send them home to sleep it off. Wouldn't I be wrong in thinking they gave you a tough time, and nagged for you to man up, ignore orders and come and get me?' She gave him a cheeky grin.

'Believe me, they pushed it a bit far a couple of times, but nothing I couldn't handle.' He grinned knowing he won. 'But when we arrived here today, you have no idea how wrecked they were, so bad in fact, their transporting powers didn't work. I got the guys to settle them into one of the double rooms upstairs. I tell you Cait, they are one big handful when you're not around. I'm not saying to hurry up and come home, but please, hurry up and get home.'

Caitlin chuckled. 'Doing my best; almost there.'

'So, while they sleep to replenish their magic, how about you join us in the tower so we can all talk? We'll try to work out what you're doing here. Not that we don't enjoy a visit from you. But it is unusual for you to end up home instead of somewhere you're needed.'

'And it's unusual for you to have the entire team up in the tower together on watch.'

'Put it this way, these three were enough, and when my lot acting up as well, it was that or put them all to blatzing sleep to shut them the hell up. All they've done today is stir the crap out of each other.' He smiled at the look she gave him. Caitlin never had to say a word, her expression of complete disbelief he would contemplate that had him calm down. 'I'm fair-dinkum,' he said, taking two stairs at a time and trying to still act tough.

'Sure you would, big softie.' Caitlin pushed him and they both laughed.

* * * *

It was late in the evening before Axon surfaced.

'About time you came around.' Rory welcomed him with a smile when he joined them all in the NAVtower.

Dark rings were prominent around his eyes, and Caitlin noted the heavy collapse into the nearest chair. 'Your energy is zapped. Let's see if I can't fix that.' She sat on his knee and wrapped her arms around his neck, giving him a hug. At the same time, she let out a burst of power that had the two of them engulfed in a golden glow of energy. Tiny lights emitted from her hands. These were released as she wiggled her fingers; the glowing mini sparks on impact were absorbed into his skin.

He stared at her, mesmerised by what she had done to him. His eyes brightened as the sparks ignited more than his energy levels. 'Think you may have overdone it.'

She felt his manhood had grown and was firm against her thigh. She chuckled. 'Yep, reckon you're done.'

He wanted a minute with Caitlin on his own and after he got rid of Rory and the team he intended to take the rest of the day off. He hated that Rory would know every detail of her mission by now, but preferred to hear it from his wife. After they talked, he wished to take her somewhere nice for dinner. The plan now firm in his mind, he leant back, 'I'm awake now if you lot want to head home?' He felt renewed after Caitlin's magical fix, and now she was home, and all the hard work of moving Earthlings back home was complete, he couldn't wait to get their life back to normal.

'I have to clear my travel route with Zoren, and after, we'll get going if you can handle it from here.' But when he turned his attention to Caitlin, he saw what Axon hadn't. She was picking something up, looking confused.

Axon followed Rory's gaze and noted his wife's silence.

Caitlin listened, her senses drawn to a particular chamber in the castle. Her worry was for Jett and Calyx who still hadn't surfaced, quickly escalated. Feeling both men stare at her, Caitlin looked up. 'Sorry, my mind is all over the place. I might be over-thinking this, but I doubt Axon, Jett and Calyx merely being tired, would be the reason I was called back.'

'You're not back?' Axon curled his fingers around hers. His mood changed, eyes flashed. 'And what do you mean, *called back*?'

Caitlin spoke calmly as she always did when he got grumpy. 'Ancient voices brought me home.' She shrugged. 'As yet I'm not sure why. Jovis and Artisan have gone down to Earth, so I have two days to find out who needs me and why.'

'If you are on good enough terms for him to let you go, won't visits work from here on in?' Axon forehead creased with worry for her.

'I still have a way to go as Jovis has plans to grow his empire, and we all know how that typically works.

'War!' Axon shook his head. 'Has he confided any details?'

'Not directly, but during the night while I was healing, they use to sit by the bed and either read or just tell me about their day. Not much of it made sense, except for this one time, so maybe it was a conversation I was meant to hear and remember.'

'Go on,' Axon was interested.

'It appears Jovis has been in talks to purchase two of the Ice Planets within his colony. One of them I believe has sold to him.'

'The other?'

'Not sure but there was something said about him previously owning it but his grandfather, lost it in a card game some years back. Jovis has proof they cheated but I think for my sake he is trying to do the right thing and repurchase it. However, when he arrived home last night, I did hear him grump at Artisan to prepare his army. So I figure he's planning to go to war.'

Axon frowned. 'This could have been settled so quickly if Jovis accepts Jett's kingdom and all it has to offer. The swindling culprits would be forced to hand it back.'

'I totally agree, but I get the feeling his trust has diminished because our system has failed him. If it hadn't, Jovis and his family would be living so differently today. So I guess this is why he now struggles alone, his confidence surely lost in a legal structure that obviously refused to help him. And before this, his parent's when it first started many centuries ago.'

Axon straightened, 'if it is our side that caused this, then I will fix it. But all things aside Jovis hasn't told you this directly, so complete trust is not there yet.'

'This I hope to rectify by returning as promised. My relationship with Jovis has grown quickly since my recovery. We have become friends and he has promised he will listen to all sides, but can't give me more just yet. This commitment has opened up the door for this home visit where I am to arrange a future visit to Pluto, and for them to meet Jett. '

'So was this the reason he allowed you to come here?' Axon's brow lifted.

'I said you were the only person I could trust to orchestrate this meeting between the two royals.'

'Royals?'

'I guessed it and surprised Jovis too. You see, the hum of royal magic is almost the same as Jett's and Calyx. He is the Prince of Sedna but I'm not sure yet why he lives as he does in a fortress under the ground, and not in a castle somewhere. He doesn't even trust guards to be around. That's the reason I wasn't found after hurting myself until he returned. But that's another story for later. For the moment, I just need for you guys to promise me there will be no tricks when he visits Pluto, or we will have a war on our hands, and with those boys, it will not be pretty.'

'I will make sure it's as you wish.' Axon agreed. 'But there is one thing you must do for me. You have to make sure only Jovis and his two buddies go to Pluto because this is the only way I can ensure no harm will come to them. If they arrive with armed guards, Jett will retaliate, and it's a real possibility trigger happy idiots will stuff this up.'

'Not a problem. Consider it done!'

'He better do as you say, Cait. I'm still pissed off at how ill you got while there. Hell, honey, we thought you were going to die. As far as I'm concerned, we get this meeting organised and leave Jovis to Jett. If you don't want to go back, it's more than okay by me.'

'What!' Rory's head turned angrily to Axon. His eyes glowed red as his temper boiled over. Rory stared at Axon with steel grey expression. 'Blatzing hell! Axon, will—you—stop—babying—her. What she is doing is what we all do, every—single—day! We put our lives on the line for the good of the universe. Not just Cait here, we all do! And we all get seriously hurt once in a while. Cait could have been riding with us and been injured just as bad, shytzer, she has been. You're getting soft since hanging out with Calyx and Jett. They influence you for their own interests, and it's all to keep her safe. If she was any other team member you know full well you would never give them that option. You'd say, "Suck it up and deal with it," as you have many times before. Love Caitlin, but don't stifle her talent for shytz-sake.'

The walls shook, and it wasn't from Rory's outburst. 'What was that?' Caitlin stood, her head turning every which way.

'What was what?' Axon looked about as she did.

'You didn't feel the room shake?' She turned her head to the side, refusing to believe only she felt it.

Rory snapped his fingers at Bree. 'Feel anything, Breezy?'

'Not a thing. Sorry, Cait.' She was apologetic for not being able to back her up.

Caitlin closed her eyes to try and pinpoint where the sound came from. 'If I'm the only one who heard it, I'd say it's why I'm here. Mmm...' She eyed Axon suspiciously and turned to Rory. 'The comment my husband just made is something Calyx would say, is it not?'

'What are your thoughts, Cait?' Rory moved towards her taking a closer look at Axon who had a faraway look in his eyes.

'Something has my stomach in knots. It happened when I

mentioned Calyx just then. Do you think it strange that Jett and Calyx haven't surfaced yet? Has anyone checked on them?'

Axon turned and lifted his head up. He'd become moody after getting a dressing down he didn't appreciate. 'Well! Have you?'

Rory glanced at him and back to Cait, a frown etched his mouth. 'They said not to disturb them or else. I left them in the twin suite sulking because they had been confined to quarters until they rested up a bit.' He turned to his men. 'Nate! Zeke! Go wake the lads, double time.'

Both were up on their feet and out the door before Caitlin had time to finish what she was saying. 'Aren't they connected to us? Shouldn't we sense them? Even in their exhausted state. I picked up Axon's vibrations as soon as I arrived and that's why I was shocked to discover my friends were here.' She rubbed her forehead that hurt from trying hard to feel them. Suddenly it dawned on her. 'My mind has been so busy concentrating on the occasional ancient chatter I hadn't considered it to be them. What if it's them calling me for help?'

'You may be on to something, Cait.' Axon closed his eyes and suddenly snapped them open. 'I just tried to connect with them, and you're right, even my extra sensitive senses can't pick them up.'

Rory put his hand up to deflect their worry from the rest of the team. 'Settle down you two. They're gods. Please remember this magic that links us is different for each member. I mean, take you for example Axon... you can hide much from the rest of us. Imagine what secrets those two have kept hidden. The boys will be back in five, four, three...'

Next thing Nathen burst in through the door. 'Zeke is scouting the rest of the rooms, I'm going back to check the grounds, but they've gone... not even a wrinkle on the beds, they haven't been slept in, and there's not a trace as to where they went.'

Axon swung into action. 'Rory, Bree, you both stay here on watch. If the gods do decide to make a grand entrance, I'll need you both to keep them busy until we get back.' Axon was no fool, with Bree by Rory's side they had become a powerful duo, enough to hold off a stage three attack. This allowed the rest of them to search.

'Could they have been kidnapped?' Bree spoke up.

Axon put that worry to rest. 'Rory would still feel them no matter where in the universe they were.'

Rory nodded in agreement. 'Sure would.'

Caitlin frowned. 'This is so weird, Rory, I mean how it is possible for them to sever ties with us, with you in particular. In fact, how did I not feel it is more the point? I have a stronger connection to them through working so closely with them.'

'I'd say it's impossible for us not to feel it happen.' Rory kept his eyes on Caitlin. 'So go. You know their royal hum better than any of us. Start in their room and widen the search until you hear it. Once you have them pinpointed, report back to me. I don't want you or Axon to go anywhere without us knowing. I have to assume they are not missing of their own accord and don't need to discover later today that you have both disappear too.'

'Agreed, will keep you in the loop.' She nodded and joined Axon who transported her to the chamber.

* * * *

When they arrived in the luxury twin suite, the last place Calyx and Jett were seen, Caitlin looked baffled.

'I'm sure I can sense something, but it's so slight it could be nothing. There seems to be no sign of their physical bodies anywhere, not even an imprint on the sofa or bed.'

Axon leant against the door, and his frame blocked most of the light from the hallway. Caitlin had switched off the lamp. The dim lit room helped her to concentrate.

'You're very close to them, Cait. Focus your efforts on where they went, and maybe we can pick up their trail.'

She stared at Axon. 'As good as I am, I'm not a dog. What would you have me do, sniff a trail?'

He burst out laughing. 'Sorry honey, but you can do everything else. Your talents lie in many different directions. But I agree, maybe a sniffer dog, you're not. Although that is amusing, you have to admit.'

'Ha-ha funny... keep it up.' She stuck her middle finger up at him and walked around the other side of the bed. She wondered why she suddenly got the urge to laugh, because losing her friends had put her in a crabby mood, and nothing seemed even slightly amusing.

'I've so missed you, funny girl.' Axon grinned at her feistiness. 'Blatzing gods taking you from me again, I should toss you on this bed and ravish you. Make you forget they exist.'

It made her grin widen. 'You're so full of it, hot stuff. As if you'd be able to concentrate on me while your boys are missing. You care about them as much as I do.'

'You ever tell them and I'll have to kill you.' He screwed up one side of his lip, enjoying her mood.

'Looks like I'm dead then 'cause...' She broke out in song and did a funny jig. 'I gotta secret, I gotta secret, and I'm gunna tell them, that you're a softie.' She ran as he headed for her. Both collapsed laughing on the couch. He had her in a better mood and kissed her on the forehead. 'Come on beautiful. Let's go get our boys.'

* * * *

After searching every square inch of the castle and the grounds, Axon and Caitlin left to expand the search. 'We'll visit every planet if we have to, Cait. Someone must know something.' He tried to cheer her up.

While visiting each planet, they spoke to family, friends and staff, but each time they came up empty-handed and with no leads. Frustrated, they moved on. No one had seen Calyx or Jett since their departure the previous morning. The hardest of challenges was to phrase the questions, so the entire galaxy didn't go into a frenzy over missing gods. They had left speaking to the parents until last.

Caitlin turned to Axon as he was about to transport them to Saturn. She wanted him to talk to Cronus and Rhea alone. 'I think you should take me home before you meet with Ted and Honey. For you not to have a clue where they are is believable, but they will be suspicious if I say I don't know. The entire family has seen I'm just as capable of sensing where their sons are as they can me. If alarm bells are raised, Ted won't stop until he finds them. He will leave no stone unturned, and many could die if he loses his temper or thinks someone's lying. Things could get ugly.'

'You're right, of course. Cronus can be ruthless. You haven't the hold on him that you have over his sons. So I agree it's best to play it safe.' He transported her home.

* * * *

It was late in the afternoon when Axon stood to talk to their father and mother, Cronus and Rhea. 'I thought your sons might be here. I wanted to thank them personally for their help.'

Cronus folded his arms. 'You know my boys. If you left them on Earth unattended, and together, it might be a few days before those two come up for air. They love to gamble and down there, too many times they have been side-tracked by the variety of games and gambling houses. Don't even bother searching for them. Trust me, when their credit cards are empty, and they pine for a decent drink, they'll come home.

* * * *

Back on Ara, Caitlin walked into the chamber where Jett and Calyx were last seen. She told Axon she was drawn to the suite, so would go take another look. As she walked around the guest bedroom, Caitlin wondered if they had left her a clue. This time she even checked under the bed. *Not a sign of struggle, nothing.* Deep in thought, she sat on the edge of the bed. *Why do my shoulders suddenly feel heavy?* She stood and swung around. Seeing no one, she shook her head. *I must be losing it.* The weight vanished. She walked into the ensuite, but again, nothing.

'Hello, you still in here?' Rory poked his head in the door.

Caitlin walked from the ensuite. 'Sure am, just poking around, nothing to report. Is Axon back?'

'Not yet.' He took a couple of long strides and sank down into the chair. 'Really great having you back, Cait. The team has missed you.'

She smiled.

'Okay, and I have too.' He grinned.

'I miss you too, Rory. Thanks for not giving up on me.'

'What the hell happened, Cait? That was one close call.'

'It was partly an accident. I had a wash in Artisan's apartment, and Jovis came looking for him. Instead, he was surprised by me getting dry. At that stage, Jovis was still angry with me as he thought I'd deliberately orchestrated the meeting between him and Jett. We had an exchange of some hostile words, he flung some insults and shoved a towel at me before leaving.'

'Insults!' said Rory

'He said I was ugly and not his type. I'm kind of glad in a way because I feel safe around him now I know, but it did leave me with a bruised ego.' She grinned at his expression.

'He must be gay,' Rory scoffed.

'No, he just prefers a stronger physical body, and I liked his honesty. Artisan's the same, so really, I'm in no danger,' Caitlin assured him.

'How then, are you getting through to them if they don't feel any attraction to you? And now I don't get what happened to make you so ill if it wasn't them who hurt you.'

Caitlin took in a deep breath and blew it out. 'Well, Jovis didn't realise how weak I was without powers, and the light shove of the towel had me slam back against the tiles. I bashed my head, and my leg hit a footstool which smashed. It was the footstool that did the most damage as it sliced my leg open. When I realised what had happened, I called for help, but he had transported from the room. I was alone.

'In a daze, I dressed and wrapped up the wound in a towel. Once in front of the fire, I finished dressing and cuddled up under furs. With the head injury, I couldn't get up again, so I slept and waited. What I didn't know was they both travelled back to Earth, to check out my story. Days went by, and when they finally came home and found me, I was apparently unconscious, and by then my leg had become severely infected. The place froze up because I couldn't get up to get more firewood and food... well you know me, can't cook to save my life… Well, it's true!' She shrugged her shoulders at his look.

'What about servants? Didn't anyone come to check on you?'

'I was deep underground, and I mean deep. Guess they didn't know I was there.' She sat on the arm of his chair. 'When they arrived back Jovis was so upset he had hurt me he gave me back my powers. But I was running a fever and too sick to access them. I'm glad you waited and knew what to do, or I may not have made it.'

'Cait, I was freaked out. I thought we lost you. Apart from riding in there gung-ho and taking my chances of being turned to stone by Medusa, there wasn't much more I could do but wait,' he said anxiously.

'Bet you acted all cool, calm and collected towards the others. With your, *'she'll be right'* attitude. You're so good at what you do Rory, but you're going to have to find someone else to confide in while I'm not around. Worrying alone like that's not good for you.'

'I know. I have tried, but with you, it's different. You really get me.'

'As you do me.' She leant over and ruffled his hair. 'You know, I did try to send you love, hugs and thanks for saving me, but this thing you do only goes one way.'

'I'm glad; I can just imagine Bree's reaction. You'd have me in the dog house for a month sending me love if Bree felt those vibes you can put out. She'd be like… *Why did she do that? Why not to all of us? What's going on between you two that you haven't told me?*' He poked her gently while kidding her.

She laughed so hard she had tears. 'You sound just like her… you girl.'

He was just about to grab her when he heard something and stood up. All joking ceased. 'What was that?' He spun around, searching for where the sound came from.

'I heard it too,' Caitlin agreed.

'Sounded like someone yelled out… "Our girl", but we two are the only ones in this room. The door is still closed, and only I know you're in here.'

'Crazy thing happened before you come in here. It felt as if someone had an arm around me.'

'Shytzer Cait, they're still in here.'

'Seriously! You think they're invisible?'

'Or in another dimension and can't get back.' He put his arms out, waving them about, trying to feel them.

'How?' Caitlin walked back over to the bed and put her arm out as he did and immediately felt a tingle against the tips of her fingers. 'I can feel something over here, Rory.'

Rory moved next to her and sensed nothing. 'I think they're overly gentle with you, and so you are able to feel them. Maybe you could get a stronger reaction if I stay still. But first, we have to contact Axon. Get him here to help us find a way to get them back.' Rory closed his eyes; the joys of having direct communication with his team.

Caitlin waited for him to finish his call out to Axon before she spoke. As soon as his eyes opened, she walked quickly to him. 'We can't hear Calyx or Jett, but it seems they can communicate but only ever so slightly.'

Rory decided this conversation needed to be private and spoke telepathically to her. *To get them to strengthen the connection, let me try a little experiment. I'm going to try something to get a rise out of them so stay with me.*

He put his arm around her. 'Maybe it's a good thing they have disappeared for a bit. I want it to be just us, Cait. Those two, pain in the arses can go get their own girlfriend, your mine.' He grinned and continued. 'Geez, no guy can have any time alone with you while those two are around, even stuck in another dimension, they still watch over you. Annoying bastards...' He jumped, rubbed his backside and threw his head back roaring with laughter. 'My little experiment to get a rise from them sure worked. Rotten sods just kicked my butt. Pleased to feel you both... not!' He shook his head.

Axon arrived and had his shoulders sunk in defeat, but his tense expression eased as he listened to Rory. Slowly he glanced around the room as he spoke. 'Glad they're still with us and worked out a way of telling us.' Axon stopped searching and concentrated on

Caitlin, knowing they would be beside her. 'Hi, guys. What the hell do we do now?'

Caitlin moved, and when doing so, she straightened. He was right; the invisible men were both leaning on her. *Mmm... Interesting.*

Her eyebrow lifted with an idea. 'Maybe there is a spell we can use to bring them back. Got any?' She searched Axon and Rory's features to find a positive response.

'Who me? Don't look at me. I'm no wizard,' said Rory.

Axon folded his arms. 'Maybe not, but Woody is, and Nate's his equal. Ask him to search his memory data that was entrusted to him. There has to be something.'

'True! But you know Woody, he only shares what is necessary.' Rory looked unsure.

Caitlin casually tossed her hair over her shoulder and smiled at Rory with full confidence in him. 'You don't need him, Rory, you have all of us. Together as a team, we'll nut this out, and you know where it is we do our best work.'

'In the kitchen.' He gave her a knowing smile.

'Food will get everyone thinking straight again. I mean, when was the last time you guys had a good meal. We might need the energy to create lots of magic.'

'Clever girl, it's been hours.'

Axon relaxed his stance to leave. 'I agree, you guys keep surprising me, and the two invisible ones must recognise this too, or they'd have called on someone else, not you and Cait.'

Caitlin felt both gods next to her, confirming what Axon said to be correct. 'They agree.' She turned her head from side to side and glanced at what she hoped was them. 'Hang in there, guys. You have the best of the best working on this for you.' She put her hand up in an attempt to get a high-five, but instead got two distinct tingles through her hand. She chuckled. 'Oh, one more high-five if you can leave this room.' She got nothing. 'Okay, if you can hear us anywhere in the castle.' She received two more tingles to her hands. 'Excellent. They can hear us.' She spoke to Rory. 'Must have been them that shook the walls when you said earlier they were softies and turning

Axon into one too.'

'So that's why I got two kicks in the butt.' Rory laughed aloud. 'I guess I better watch what I say around here if they can hear us. I'll summon the guys, and we'll meet in the kitchen.' He stopped at the door and smirked. 'Want us to bring back some takeaway, boys?'

He jumped again, and rubbed his butt, which sent Caitlin into hysterics.

Before she left, she held her hand up one more time. 'Any ideas before we put it to the team?' There was no tingle. 'I'll take that as a no. Talk soon. And behave...' She wiggled her finger, tut-tutting them before closing the door behind her.

* * * *

In the galley, Caitlin walked around the other side of the bench to where she always sat to watch. She was talking to Rory and just before she launched up onto the counter, she saw a plaque that said *Caitlin's spot*. 'Aww, you guys. That's so sweet.'

His smile was broad that she noticed. It was the little things he and the team did that made her always want to return to them, and he knew it.

'My idea.' Rory put his hand up.

'I had it made up.' Axon pushed Rory out the way so she could see only him.

'Stop fighting dirty, or I swear this won't end in your favour.' Rory closed his eyes, using mind control on Axon. Next thing Axon walked into the pantry and closed the door. After Caitlin and Rory laughed uncontrollably, Caitlin shook her finger at Rory. 'Now let my husband out. You know he will give you what for later.'

'Why do you think I'm enjoying this now? Hell, the big guy's going to kill me.' He chuckled some more, but concentrated for a second and let him come out.

'You bastard, you are so dead.' Axon laughed with them. 'Well, when my honey love is not here to hear you scream, prick.'

'All jokes aside guys, I'm anxious about Jett and Calyx. Can we try and keep the fooling around until after we've freed my friends from nowhere land?'

Axon and Rory shoved one another. 'Behave, idiot,' Axon growled.

'Just getting rid of your competition; you should be talking about a big bonus. Ungrateful shit.' Rory shoved him back.

Caitlin was about to open her mouth to chastise them yet again when the door flung open. It was Bree and Lisha.

'We tossed a coin to see who stayed to keep watch and wait for the guards to turn up. Nate and Zeke lost. They'll be down soon,' Bree said.

Lisha walked in like a tall model with way too much of a sexy walk for a Rider. Caitlin thought she kept herself in better shape since she and Conor had become engaged. Last time they were together, all she did was flip through wedding magazines and daydream of her big day. Her good mood filtered through the group and the entire team was very happy for her and so glad of the change.

'Hey sis, can you take over making the muffin mix,' Rory handed the mixing bowl and spoon to Lisha. 'This is definitely your field of expertise.'

'What about me?' Bree wore a pouty expression.

'You can help me.' Rory grinned and put an arm out to her. Bree's smile brightened up the room. She was so smitten, just sulky of late that Lisha was engaged and she hadn't been asked yet.

Pigtail bouncing and now wearing a happy smile, she leant over and gave Caitlin a kiss on her cheek. 'Hi girlfriend.' She said before joining Rory in the pantry.

This was one of Caitlin's favourite moments, being in the kitchen with those she cherished. If this, right here, was missing from her food, she barely ate. Over the years she had tried to be interested in the exotic tastes of the many delicacies across the universe, but nothing stood up to the taste of food made with love. She found no comparison.

Once Rory had delegated jobs for everyone, he turned and pointed the rolling pin he held towards Caitlin. 'You're up, Cait. The first question is mine because we all want to know. What was

Cerberus like and how did you befriend him? I'm sorry, but we don't believe the stories Jett tells.' He looked down and continued rolling out pastry. Glancing up quickly to see her smiling, he warned, 'and no bullshitting.'

She was still telling tales of her travels when Zeke and Nate came in and stood to listen. Riveted in her magical storytelling they leaned against the bench with arms folded and never moved until she had finished. Both asked her questions about other events since they had seen her and the entire time, Caitlin sat swinging her feet while happily bringing them up to date. At times, she pulled her legs up and crossed them in front of her when talking about something scary. Like when Cerberus's serpent's tail was aimed at her head, or if excited-scared, she would roll up in a ball with her arms around her legs, enthralling them with the time she went hang-gliding with Jovis. Masterfully over-exaggerated the moment when they got to the edge of the cliff and fell, a drop that was unexpected, and yet as a Rider would seem nothing, so details had to be breathtakingly beautiful and she didn't let them down. 'It took my breath away,' she grinned as saw their faces. With their team link, Caitlin knew they had felt her joy at reminiscing her most epic moment.

At the table, as usual, Rory changed the topic to give Caitlin a rest. She looked worn out after helping Axon regain his powers. Rory leant over to her, 'thanks, we all missed you and needed that, but I know you have more on your mind than pandering to us lot. Let me tell the guys our new findings and see what they can come up with.' He sat up straight and spoke to the team, telling them what they had experienced in Calyx and Jett's room.

Axon sat beside Caitlin and rested his arm on the back of her chair. Not able to leave her alone knowing this was only a short stay, he used his hand to run small circles around her shoulders. He felt her muscles loosen and her persona brighten. Her worry for her friends was evident and he hoped there was an answer soon. After Rory finished Axon removed his arm to allow her to eat in peace.

'I love you so much,' she whispered as they both picked up a fork to put food on their plates.

'I know.' He kissed her cheek. 'And after we've solved this mystery, I'll show you why.' He gave a seductive wink.

Once whispers slowed, Caitlin put down her fork. This they knew would not be picked up again until they had given her a satisfactory outcome. 'So now you know Calyx and Jett are still here, and you've had time to discuss it between yourselves, please share any ideas no matter how ridiculous. Anything on the subject could trigger off a favourable outcome and bring them home, so don't hold back.'

Rory wasn't about to let her leave the table without eating and poked the air with his fork as he spoke. 'Cait, keep eating, or we don't help.'

She frowned, snatched up the fork and stuck it in the air back at him. 'I will, but l want answers. My friends are see-through for goodness sake, and I want them normal again.'

'We know, Cait. They have become our friends as well. Let's hear from the team and who knows, maybe Calyx and Jett will be back with us quicker than you think.' He nodded to Nathen, his second in charge. 'You're up Nate, what you got?'

'Because they are divine beings, no spell is strong enough to bring those two home. I reckon they depleted their powers and until they reboot, they won't be back anytime soon.'

Caitlin sat forward, interested. 'Any ideas how we can help them restart these powers, Nate?'

He shrugged and stabbing his fork into his steak and chips, shovelled a considerable amount into his mouth.

She looked at Zeke. 'Are you with him on this one?' Normally he was.

'Nope, got me some realistic views. The joining with us has altered their DNA somehow. The thread has tangled, and your boys are stuck in another dimension until we can disconnect us from them.'

'Mmm, interesting, what about you Lisha?'

Lisha swallowed her mouthful of food. 'Your boys have turned into ghosts until we somehow break the link we have to them, and if not, reckon we may all end up ghosts.'

Caitlin smiled. 'Fair enough, a bit out there but glad to see you haven't changed, Lisha. Still all doom and gloom.' She chuckled and turned to Bree. 'What are your thoughts, Breezy?'

'I think they've done this to spy on us. GGs are doing the nasties. Catching us out naked and getting their rocks off while watching.'

'What and what?' Caitlin blinked through tears of laughter. 'GGs?'

'Godly Ghosts.' She chuckled. 'Sorry shouldn't joke, but I know they're listening, and they so deserve some payback. Those pranksters have given me hell since joining our group.'

Caitlin collected herself. 'First time I've ever heard you hang it on anyone, Bree. If anything, they have sure brought you out of your softshell.'

'Tormented me at first, but love the lug-heads now. Actually, I had a different spin on it. I think they called you because they saved your life and some of that power they used is still inside you. They need to access it. But that's as far as my thoughts go. Can't come up with the solution how you would communicate with them on their level or in their dimension.'

She turned to Axon. 'Have you any ideas?'

'I'm still on the spell thing. There is a wizard I know who just might know how to reverse this.'

'Aldebaran?' She breathed out and raised her eyebrows. 'Now that is worth looking into. Even Woody wouldn't know the evil that guy has drawn from to prey on the weak or get what he wants.'

'I'll leave after I hear from you, Rory.' Axon nodded in his direction. 'Looks like you're the lucky last. Give me something, or dammit, I'll have to go into work. Gaining entry into Taurus will not be easy and I'll need Kayden.'

Rory folded his arms with a slight stubborn expression. 'I understand it will be a tough ask getting into see Aldebaran, and hate to put you through all that if we don't need to but I refuse to sever the link between them and us. It could be what is holding them to us. Any change and we could lose them forever. As for the ideas so far, none of them has me enthused. Still not sure a spell will help, but if you're willing to follow it up, Axon and it works, all hail you. But Caitlin stays here. I think she is the key and needs to be with us in case we come up with something she thinks will work. So my advice to everyone is buckle in, because it's going to be a long night for all of us.'

'That it will.' Axon stood. 'You know where I am if you need me but one request before I go, I'd like a couple of hours alone with Cait before she has to leave tomorrow.'

'Sure.' Rory saluted him.

Axon stood and pulled his concerned wife to her feet, then gave her a hug. 'I have faith that between us we can fix this honey.' He smiled and winked. 'Can't have my woman go back to work tomorrow worrying about what's going on here.'

She smiled. Thinking about her at this moment was so him. She adored this man who was prepared to go to the ends of the universe to make her life easier. It would break her heart to leave her friends in this ghostly status, but her mission on Sedna was just as serious. Jovis was only on the cusp of goodness. These violent and criminally run worlds drain the light in his life force and if not dealt with, it could become not only a danger to Jett but to all the gods, if Jovis continued to take over more dark and unruly, Ice Planets. The magic he drew from this darkness was getting stronger every day. She was torn and it was not surprising to see Axon saw it too.

'Honey, Calyx and Jett called you here because they knew you would lead us to them. We are aware of their location now so your job might be done here. If tomorrow you don't feel any further ancient chatter, you will have to go back to your current mission. Leave us with ours, okay.'

'You're incredibly intuitive and know exactly what I needed to hear. Thanks, I'll see you soon.' She stood on tippy toes and kissed his lips.

'Love you, honey,' he whispered.

'I know.' She smiled. 'I'll show you why later.' She said back the words he used earlier as he disappeared from her sight. His laughter echoed as he transported to the Alpha base.

* * * *

It was past midnight when Rory broke up the group and made them have a break. 'I want you all to go take a walk, clear your heads and meet back here at NAVtwo-hundred. I'll be in the tower if you need me.' He left the room.

Caitlin got up and walked out, leaving the others to chat amongst themselves. Her mind couldn't slow down, and she knew what she might have to do. *Rory will be furious.* She chewed her lip. *Desperate measures for desperate times.*

The team admired her and wished this once they could have helped. Instead of going, they stayed in the room and had no intentions of giving up.

Upstairs, Caitlin opened the door to the bedroom where Calyx and Jett were. 'Hello, anyone in here? Casper and his brother, are you home?' She chuckled and flopped down on the couch. 'Just kidding, come sit with me.' She patted each side of her. 'Let's find out if I can tune into you both. Give us a chance to discuss it. Maybe together we can work this out.'

She felt a tingle each side of her and knew they had done as she asked. 'I think this will work better if we all lie back, close our eyes and concentrate, not focusing on just me, but the three of us.' She put her hands up and her both hands tingled. 'Good; you agree.'

She laid her head back, lush lashes fanned her cheeks as lids dropped, and glossy red curls fell softly away from her creamy, healthy complexion. Both men adored this woman who had rushed back to help them.

They kissed her cheek before resting back each side of her. She wiggled her nose and grinned, to let them know she felt them.

* * * *

On his scheduled rounds, Rory entered the room to find his team still deep in conversation. So much so they didn't hear him come in. 'It's NAVtwo-hundred; where's Cait?'

Nathen poked his head up first. 'She left the same time as you did. We figured she followed you up to the tower.'

'Nope, haven't sighted her. Have you guys been here the entire time? I told you to have a break.'

'Sorry boss, but we wanted to stay and have something for Cait when she came back. We never seem to be able to help her. This time is different, she wants us to, and we are determined not to let her down.' Zeke sat back and stretched.

'So what have you got?' Rory joined them at the table and pulled a chair around and straddled it.

'Nate, you're up, you can tell him,' said Lisha. Being second in command, Nathen was well respected by Lisha as the team leader when Rory wasn't around.

Nathen leant forward, both hands clenched on the table in front of him. He hoped Rory would go for the latest idea. 'We thought that if their powers were depleted, it could be because they were linked to us. As gods maybe this works in a bad way.'

'Go on.' They had Rory's attention.

'Well, gods are the top of the chain, so to have, no disrespect Rory, a lesser person able to control them, it may have lessened their status, drained their life force that wasn't needed anymore.'

'If this is so, how do we go about reversing it?' Rory sat back, interested. 'And don't ask me to sever the ties with them. I have promised Cait I wouldn't under any circumstances.'

'Well, we believe if we can get them in the middle of us, make a circle around them, and you draw healing from us to send to them, it might just do the trick.'

'And what makes you think this will work.' Rory needed more before going down this path. Draining all of their magic was dangerous. He liked the idea but what if it didn't bring them back. It was a huge risk to leave them as a group, exposed while their power reset. They would be temporarily sitting ducks in a big sky where hardcore lawbreakers were at large.

'I believe it is the best course of action, as do the team.' Nathen continued. 'Axon's situation made us see that even after a good rest, Cait had to sit with him and give his life force a boost. We could all feel it depleted her at the time, and that's most likely why she ate much more than normal at dinner tonight. So we figure two gods are going to need a lot more than Cait can give.'

'Let me mull it over a bit, and when Cait gets here, we can decide as a team.' He put his hand up for quiet when everyone started talking at once. 'Let's see what the holdup is with Cait; she's not answering my telepathic call to join us.' Rory picked up his NAVcom and, swiped the screen which gave a holographic image of each team member and their location within the castle walls. 'Okay, you guys are all here and accounted for, but Cait's light is out. That means she's not on the premises.' He punched in a few more codes stretching the range outside the Castle. 'Nor is she anywhere outside.' He stood and touched his earpiece. 'Give me coordinates of Cait's last seen image.' Up above the table appeared a hologram. They watched Caitlin almost skip to the gods' bedroom, enter with her usual cheery greeting and sit on the couch. Her invitation to the gods to join her was met with a smile, so they knew they were all together. They were surprised and mystified when her entire body disappeared.

'She's with them.' Lisha jumped to her feet.

'Wait, see if she comes back.' Tears stung Bree's eyes.

'That's all there is, sweetie. Rory just called up her last seen image.' Lisha put an arm around Bree. 'Come on kiddo. We can do this, we can get her back. Let's show her how talented we've become.'

Bree stood and wiped her eyes. Her bond with Caitlin had always been sisterly. Caitlin had taken her under her wing from the very beginning and had been Bree's lifeline and best friend. To lose her would be too painful to imagine.

Zeke and Nathen had also stood, leaning on the girls. Bree felt better with the support of the team. This was her idea, and they had all agreed it made sense.

Rory watched them stand arm in arm. He was so proud of them. In moments like this, when they were united, he would back them one hundred percent.

While they headed for the bedroom where they'd seen Caitlin's last image, Rory contacted Axon to try and explain how he had lost Caitlin to the room as well.

'How did you go with the wizard? Did he give you a spell?' Rory was direct.

'I had no luck with Aldebaran. He was off-world with Cassie on business. They're deep in Draco's galaxy where all communication has ceased for security reasons. No one was expecting to hear from them until morning. Blatz you, Rory, can't believe you let Cait out of your sight giving her a chance to get caught up in this mess. She's been through hell. I should have taken her with me.'

'Axon, what's done is done! Let's get together and fix it,' Rory snapped at him.

'Give me a second. I'm with Zoren, updating him.'

'I'm nearly at the suite. The gangs with me and seconds we might not have.' Rory clicked off the NAVcom.

Rory was pleased when Axon shimmered into sight. The team had spaced themselves around the couch and moved to make room for him. Now they were in a circular formation, Rory took control using their positive vibes to build a magical haze in the middle of them.

Let me guide you from here and for goodness sake, calm down. Rory used telepathy, not allowing any of them to continue their conversations. Without their magical rides, he needed the team's full concentration to assist him. Silence helped and with the boost of extra power, Rory kick-started the sequence required to begin the miracle required to bring back Caitlin and hopefully the gods too. To do such a task, he realised he needed more than just them and started to drawing power from the magical horses that were still in their stalls in the barn. None had bridles on, so he let them think they had them on and this transformed them into pegasi, the beautifully winged visions. Once the image of these mystical creatures surrounded them, he had their life force move clockwise on the outside of the circle which the team had created. This flooded the room with the extra boost of magic Rory felt they might need. *Ready guys?*

One by one they nodded.

Explosive colours filled the room, speeding up the winged steeds that moved faster and faster until they blended into a stream of sparkling stars. *Faster,* Rory instructed them, and it looked as if the whole room began to spin. Even the Riders were no longer visible with such a strong force.. Rory had used this technique only a couple of times before, but with the team so motivated and sure this power was what they needed, it changed into sheer beauty. Horses and man worked together in a magical mist now that was so bright, so full of healing that Rory wondered if the team needed the final kick of power. But when the gods and Caitlin hadn't yet appeared, he kept perfectly still and took the only option left. He drew from himself and Axon. It meant the outcome was now in the lap of the gods. He would be too weak to control the power until it ran its course. But for Cait alone, he was willing to give it all he had. He knew once their power was depleted, the room would steady, go back to normal, and he and the team would need to eat and then rest a few hours to recharge. Until all was given, he would not give up.

Axon we're up. Let's give this one more go. Make it a good one; this is our last chance. I've pulled Caitlin's horse in this time, so concentrate, men. Here we go...

With a crack of a whip, the horses shot out laser-like strikes out in every direction, the room shook, and the noise of ancient beings roared as the room seemed to explode out into the atmosphere, the magic so powerful.

Suddenly silence. The room calmed without a thing out of place. Axon, Rory and the team stood looking at the empty couch. It hadn't worked...

'What was that?' Bree squealed. 'I saw a flicker.' She was the only one who caught it.

Rory put an arm around her, 'Sorry Bree, we tried, but that's just wishful thinking.'

Weak and unable to stand with the unbelievable truth they had failed, the rest of the team sat on the edge of the bed, watching Bree stare with passion at an empty couch.

Not taking her focus off the couch she squealed and pointed. 'Look it's working.' The image of the three lost souls flickered then nothing... Then another, and another.

The team caught it now and stood enthusiastically waiting. Cheers of elation erupted when suddenly the image stabilised and there sat Caitlin in between Jett and Calyx. The three of them were smiling.

Caitlin jumped up and in turn hugged them all. 'Figured if I went to them, you'd find a way to bring us back. You guys are ace!' Caitlin was getting hugged by Rory until that comment. He held her at arm's length, his complexion turned crimson and eyes were almost slits. 'What if I hadn't been able to do it, Cait? Don't ever risk your life like that again.'

She smiled. 'But we do it every day. Today's lesson! We are permitted to use our magic for ourselves as well as for others. Rory, you are not only the best person I've ever met but the most talented.'

'Wish I could take credit, but it was actually Bree's idea. She idolises you, Cait and would never give up where you are concerned, not ever.'

'But it was you who orchestrated it.' She grinned admiringly. 'I so wish I was you.'

He shook his head. 'No trying to con me into forgiving you so quickly and no more lessons okay, you scared the bejeezers out of me.'

'Out of us,' the team said in unison.

After welcoming them back, Axon stood talking to Calyx while Cait got a dressing down. 'Looks like Cait's in trouble with Rory again.' He shook his head.

'He should hail her. She's brilliant!' Calyx glared at Rory while he gave her a hard time for leaving them and scaring the bejeezers out of them. 'Cait was not only bright enough to come to us, but she hid her power somewhere. When it wasn't working, she waited for Rory to give the last command, and said to Jett and me, *hold on men, this will hurt.* And blatzing hell did it ever. She pumped into us the same magnitude of magic as the lot of you did. That gal has become one powerhouse goddess.'

'I have to agree.' Jett pulled at his chin growth as he spoke. 'I think Glow not only leaves us with a piece of her but takes a smidgen of us with her when she goes.'

Axon grinned. 'Well let's keep it to ourselves. If she wanted the Riders to know she helped them, she would have said. They did well, and her accolades are their reward. Just look at their faces, they adore her and that's the reason why none of them gave up until they worked that miracle for her.

'And it's likely we won't get a look in for a while until that lot leave.' Calyx grinned. He took his eyes from Caitlin and shrugged. 'We can't complain, we did just have a couple of hours with Cait and we're glad she was able to ease our minds about what's been happening to her. We're pleased to hear she is fine, in fact, everything is fine.' Calyx slapped Axon on the back in a friendly gesture. 'How about we let them be for a bit? I could sure do with a drink if you've got any of the good stuff left. We did give it a good nudge when we got back here if I remember correctly.'

'Follow me to the den. I keep a bottle or two hidden for medicinal purposes, and I reckon this is one of those emergencies. I even have some Cuban cigars stashed away from our last off-world trip to Earth if they are suitable.'

'More than adequate,' Calyx agreed.

Jett stood, finding it hard not to stay and soak in the happiness radiating from Cait. Axon threw an arm around him. 'From my experience, they'll be a while. Don't worry, we'll catch up with her later. She'll make time for us then, and the others will be happy to give her some space. Somehow, she works it out, so we all feel as if we've had ample time with her and when she leaves us, we feel content enough to let her go. You'll see. If you're not feeling it yet, she hasn't finished with you.'

Jett turned to him, 'I'll hold you to that Axon. And any prior grievances I had regarding your team, strike it from the record. They are amazing and do deserve to celebrate considering what they just accomplished. Your right, let's go get some guy time while we can. That was some scary crap, and I need an injection of pure testosterone.'

'Agreed, brother.' Calyx followed behind them. 'That was surreal. Those Riders of yours were on fire! Cosmic Riders, be blowed. They should be called 'Galactic Vanguards' because I've never heard or seen anything like that anywhere.'

'Rory sure is a mastermind. The kid's a genius.' Axon slowed his stride to talk to Calyx. 'He's a true guardian spirit. We haven't had one of them in the galaxy for many centuries.'

Calyx smiled at Axon. 'Not since you! Well, that was until Zoren promoted you to Lord of the Planets. Must admit Rory's a chip off the old block. You're teaching him well.'

Axon shook his head. 'As I said, boy genius; he's worked it all out himself since I've been connected to the group. I refuse to separate from them as I need to feel Cait, so to hell with it, if he can use what I don't need anymore, good on him. I still have my reserves which I've hidden, as I'm sure you two have concealed a lot too. Bet that's why you disappear. Am I right?' He eyed them as he held the door for them.

Calyx gave out a boisterous laugh. 'You can bet your sweet self we have shrouded much, and our super smart goddess came to us knowing that was why. We told her, as we told you lot, we are not breaking the connection, so she had better come up with a solution.'

'After we got a dressing down, mind you,' Jett grinned, 'she set us right. Glow Girl has given us what she calls a chasm, somewhere to keep our private lives. Only we as Jett and Calyx are linked to the team now. When we are working as gods, the Hades and Zeus persona go about their duties inside the Chasm and, it being a bottomless abyss, there is plenty of room to continue our growth as deities without having to share with the team, or have this ever happening again. And man oh man was it worth the fight to stay connected, this feels great,' Jett said, and put his goblet up in a cheer.

'Hear! Hear!' Calyx leant in with his drink in good spirits. 'Feels good all right, but I wonder if Rory is aware of her capabilities.'

'One thing I do know,' Axon said, 'is she tells Rory everything. That closeness they have, that's stronger than any cosmic connection known. Rory has a heart that beats pure and true. He not only saved her life and gave her the will to live but taught her trust. This being the reason why she gives everyone a second chance... because he gave her one. Rory is more than a boss and a friend; she sees him as family in every way. In fact, they are all her kin, but Rory is up on that pedestal and let no man try to knock him off.'

Calyx pointed towards where Rory was. 'What! So you're telling us we have that snotty nose shytzer out there to thank for not being kicked to the kerb by Cait?'

Axon held his goblet up to both, 'Yep, you'll get used to it.' He leant back and closed his eyes for just a second, enjoying the moment. He was happy it wasn't only him who got ticked-off at having to share his woman.

Calyx offered Axon a cigar. 'I think we all learnt a little from this incident.'

Jett had an amused glint in his eyes, 'best not hide stuff until we ask Caitlin how.'

The three of them laughed.

'I'm just mighty glad you're both back safe and sound.' Axon ran the cigar under his nose and lit it. 'Mmm, Galactic Vanguards... There are only two people I would honour with that name, and those two are here in this very room with me. '

Calyx and Jett clunked goblets and winked.

Axon smiled, drew on the cigar and leaning back, focused on the fire in the den. It had been a good outcome, and after this, he intended to go and find his talented wife and for a while, make her forget all these other men.

Chapter Twenty-Five

Promises to Keep

C aitlin stood next to Axon on the lawn outside, waiting for Jovis and Artisan to arrive. She hadn't expected it to be such a whirlwind visit. Much had happened, and she was relieved to have spent the last few hours alone with Axon. The small amount of time they had was as always, packed full of love. 'Thanks for waiting with me.'

'I can see it in your eyes it's time to go back. The planet calls for you, doesn't it?'

She never had to lie to Axon and would never want to. 'Yes.' She nodded. 'I know from my own experience how hard it is to trust after your heart has been shattered.'

Axon's eyes searched hers. 'I hope they know how lucky they are to have met you, Cait. They will treat you right this time, won't they?'

'Yes. You have my word. It was a misunderstanding, not deliberate. I go back as a friend this time.' She leant in with love that radiated through him. 'To have peace in the universe is my passion, to have you one day, all to myself… is my dream.'

Axon touched her cheek, and his eyes glistened. 'Mine too. It can't come fast enough for me.' He gave her one last kiss and let her go. Many things came to mind as he stood to wait with her. He wanted to shirt front them. Tell them if they dared hurt one hair on her head they were dead men… but maybe threatening them was a bad idea; he might never see her again. But how he wished he could do something to forcibly prevent a repeat of her first visit to their world. He wanted to run off with her. Axon sighed silently as Rory's telepathy broke into his thoughts. He forgot big ears would be listening. *Axon, stop being overbearing and quit the bully tactics, those ideas will make it harder for her. Step back now, airspace reports travellers inbound. Let Caitlin do her job and stand down.*

Axon stepped back three paces. His mind was filled with Rory's commands. His own thoughts were blocked for the interim.

Now, when they arrive, be polite to her new charges and bid her farewell, or it is the last time I entrust her to you as a guard. As I've said before, if it were Bree or Lisha you would send them off without a thought. You were warned well of her duties by Zoren and me. Get your head back into the mission in 3... 2... they are here.

Jovis and Artisan arrived. They radiated with joy to see she had kept her word, although they were surprised she was not alone.

'Hi, wow you're on time, but where's Rocky? Thought for sure he'd be with you.' Caitlin sounded chirpy and looked genuinely happy to see them.

Unable to share her with any more than one of his mates, Jovis held back the fact they'd come without him deliberately. 'Maybe next time.' He would tell Rocky about Caitlin in due course. He changed the subject with a grin. 'What matters is that you're here. Glad to see you kept your promise.'

'And always will,' said Caitlin.

Axon watched her draw them in with a charming grin and noted the change in their appearance. The hard-drawn features were replaced with softer expressions.

Caitlin glanced at Axon and saw by the light in his eyes, he was pleased with the mission's progress. She had worked hard to get them to this point and was glad he noticed the difference in the two men. She introduced him. 'When you first met my man it was under an alias, Mr Wolf. However, now we have trust I'd like you to officially meet my husband, and boss, Axon Stanton and yes, the Lord of the Planets. Axon has given me his word he will speak to both gods, and if he feels any resistance to an amicable visit, he will attend. And although he won't interfere otherwise, he will stay tuned to me so if there is even a flicker of worry from me, he will come immediately. That is if you decide to go ahead with talks to become Dwarf Planet status.'

Axon wasn't expecting to be introduced and took a step forward.

Jovis kept his nervousness in check as Axon approached him, but when Axon's arm outstretched to shake his, and he took it, calm came over him. Caitlin felt it too, knew where it came from, and looked up towards the tower and winked. *Nice work Rory.*

'Jovis, Artisan,' Axon said politely, and after he stepped back, he eyed the tower where Rory was and gave a smirk. Rory the sneak was using magic on them all to keep the meeting calm. *Little shit!* He turned back to Caitlin. 'I will miss you!' he mouthed silently before he addressed her new friends one more time. 'Take care of our precious jewel here.'

Jovis and Artisan nodded in acknowledgement.

Axon didn't get time to wait for an answer before Rory summoned him and he immediately did as commanded and transported up to the tower. *Big ears and an interfering shytzer,* Axon grumbled once standing looking out the window at them. He didn't really need them to answer, but they said it with a look which he spotted as he transported away. It was the same protective glint Calyx and Jett had when with her, and she didn't even have her goddess scent turned up. *My wife's magic is getting stronger with each mission.* He stood amazed that even though it hadn't been a walk in the park in the beginning, she was making this look easy. It calmed him to know that for this trip the goddess had stepped aside, and it was Caitlin going with them. His wife was one smart lady, and even though she could be argumentative and stubborn, it was generally for the greater good. If these men listened, they were going to have some memorable moments with her. He smiled; he had chosen well. She was all that and all his.

'Sorry I had to step in, boss, but you've been through a lot lately and worn yourself out to save humanity. Ordinarily, I know you would have done the right thing, but you have missed her more than normal this trip, and I couldn't take a chance on anything going wrong. This mission she needs to keep focused and I don't want her going off worried. If she succeeds, it will save months, maybe even years, of negotiations.' Rory spoke to Axon while they watched Caitlin and her new friends from the tower.

Axon nodded. Rory was right.

Bree had her nose pressed hard against the glass. 'She's so gutsy going on these jobs alone. Turn up the sound Nate; I can't hear what he is saying to her.'

The sound was fed through their NAVcom earpieces. 'Stickybeak,' Rory lightly chastised but didn't say they couldn't.

Bree grinned. 'You want to hear too.' She put her hand up to stop him talking. 'OMG, are they dancing with her? How cute!'

* * * *

Outside, Jovis stood talking to Caitlin. There was no rush to snatch her up and run because Axon had given permission for her to visit with them. He was a little overwhelmed. 'Axon was so charming in his manner.' Jovis scratched his head. 'I wasn't expecting that reaction. He's obviously a good man, Cait; how can you stand to leave him.'

She smiled. 'Because I made a promise to you.' She put out her hand to him.

He laughed and pulled her in, swung her under his arm and with a twirl leant her back on his arm. 'You would have to be the best female friend I've ever had. I think I have a lot of work to do on my trust issues.' He lifted her.

Artisan stepped in and stole her from him. 'My girl; not yours.' He made a couple of slow dance moves with her and grinned at Jovis.

He was unimpressed. 'Share or I'll drop you off on your own Home World.'

'Okay spoilsport.' Artisan finished a move that had her between them.

Caitlin laughed, having so much fun she barely noticed they

argued. By the time she stopped still, Jovis had transported them back to his planet.

Chapter Twenty-Six

Ice Planet Sedna
(The Deception)

Landing on the icy surface on Sedna, the gale force winds whipped up tested Caitlin's strength while waiting for Jovis to enter the code to his fortress. Once inside, Caitlin was given a rug and instructed to stay warm until the fire was lit. 'I could help,' she protested but was glad when it was met with a hearty laugh. Caitlin sighed silently, she was almost depleted of magic. Her trip home was exhausting and was why her clothes didn't change to keep her warm enough. As if Jovis felt it in her he insisted him and Artisan get the dinner on first, before they settled in for a chat.

'Stay there until it warms up in here.' Jovis saw her lips were blue and turned to start the fire.

'Don't think you're getting a free ride, Glow.' Artisan gave her a warm smile while he unpacked food from the large bag he carried inside. 'You can tell us all about your weekend to entertain us.'

'I can handle that.' Although Caitlin could never divulge the real reason for being called home, she did have a lovely time with everyone after the gods were brought back. These were the moments she would share.

Now feeling warmer, she pulled back the blanket to enjoy the heat of the fire that Jovis successfully had burning. Occasionally she would stop talking to watch the routine of these two new companions as they went about business in this bygone era that still existed in these worlds off the NAVgrid.

'Would you like a hot drink, Glow?' Artisan asked as he pumped water by hand to fill up a billy.

'Love one.' She watched him walk with it to the hearth where hot coals had formed. Here, Artisan carefully hung the container full of water from a hook that protruded from the unique stone construction.

'How long has it been since you ate?' Jovis observed the lack of energy in her movements.

'Last night.' She decided to be truthful. It was a crazed trip home, and the food was the last thing on her mind while there. 'Food was offered, but I wanted to eat here. I figured you guys possibly hadn't eaten either.'

'You're starting to know us well.' Artisan raised his eyebrow at her and moved back into the small kitchenette. Whistling, he washed the fresh vegetables and after chopping them up, tipped them into a pot.

Inquisitive, Caitlin got up, ambled over to him and leaned on the bench watching. This time Artisan was the one who talked. He told her of their adventure while on Earth but deliberately left out the saucy bits with the girls. He didn't feel right discussing these details with her.

Caitlin picked up on his shyness and stirred him until she got a few truths. Once she was sure they had enjoyed their time on Earth she left him with his secrets and changed the subject. Her interest shifted to food as she watched him pull a chicken from the cooler bag. 'When did you get time to buy all this fresh food?' She grinned.

'We wanted to eat with you too, so instead of going to breakfast we went to the market instead,' Artisan admitted. 'I think we got all your favourites but it's only a quick trip if we've missed anything. The rest will be delivered through our normal NAVtransport.' He gave her a grin while stuffing the chicken with onion, lemon and a sprinkle of natural chicken seasoning. 'Taste this.' He took the lid off a jar, and while he waited for her to tell him if she liked it, he tucked the wings back, before spearing the bird with a rod.

'Mmm, sweet and delicious.' She licked her finger.

'And it's all natural. So if I have your approval, is it okay to baste the bird with it while it bakes?' He carried the chicken over to the rotation device attached to the fireplace.

'It gets a big tick from me.' Caitlin followed with the jar and a basting brush he had handed her.

By then Jovis had put up a tripod stand, and after hanging the pot of vegetables over the fire, he helped clip the chicken in brackets attached to each side of the hearth. Artisan had planned hard for their first night together and wanted everything to be perfect. He happily listened to Caitlin chat to Jovis while he basted the bird which rotated over the hot coals.

'Prep dishes and mess clean and we are ready for service.' Jovis called to them while he put out clean bowls and cutlery ready for them to dish up. 'So while we wait for dinner to cook, how about I make us a mug of hot chocolate?'

'Count me in,' Artisan called from the fireplace.

'Anything with the word Chocolate in it sounds good to me.' Caitlin put her hand up to agree while she stood watching Artisan brush the turning roast until it looked glossy and delicious. 'You guys have surprisingly got this down pat. It shows how long you've been together?' She leant closer to warm her hands.

'Sure have. We do this every night after work.' Artisan sat beside her.

'Does Jovis always make the drinks?'

'Hell yes! He makes the best hot chocolate you'll ever taste. Bet the boss shows off tonight and makes it super special to impress you. Well, I'm hoping so, anyway.' He rubbed his hands on a damp cloth to remove the sticky residue while watching her. 'Guess you thought our life would be all booze and two men that couldn't take care of themselves.' He nudged her.

'I'm suitably impressed so far, but haven't tasted the spoils yet. Who's the better cook?' She was enjoying this new side she was seeing of them.

'Me of course,' Jovis called out from the kitchenette.

'He knows I am; why do you think I do the food preparation duties, and he lights the fire?' Artisan was not letting Jovis take all the credit.

'Okay, he can cook, but who makes the better meat pies?' Jovis called out.

Artisan gave him two thumbs up. 'Okay, hands down, your pies are awesome.' He turned to Caitlin. 'My chicken shooter pies are pretty darn good, but his battle beef orbit pies are to die for.'

Caitlin licked her lips. 'Mmm, this calls for a cook-off, and because pies have to be one of my favourite foods, I vote to be the judge of this debate.'

'What do you think Jovis? We do a pie bake-off, and settle this lifelong debate.' Artisan sounded competitive.

'If we do this, Cait has the final say.'

'And if she chooses mine?'

He screwed up his lip, thinking. 'Cait won't chose yours, so you need not worry about the what ifs.'

'Don't get too cocky, I won't be taking it easy on you this time.' Artisan stood up and headed over to him.

Jovis grinned and pointed the spoon he was stirring the chocolate with towards Caitlin. 'You! You are evil.'

By the time the drinks were ready, Caitlin's sides hurt from laughing so much at the testosterone based arguments in the kitchenette. This was only the start of many more challenges she would set. Her mission was to make these men happy and contented enough in their own lives not to need the title they wished to rob from Hades. Only then would the universe feel harmonious once again, and she would be free to go home. As she quietly sipped the best hot chocolate she had ever tasted, Caitlin looked forward to a new start for herself and Axon as well. She wanted to wake up with her man every day and intended to work hard to make it happen. As for this situation, Jett was a worthy king and deserved honourable rulers in his kingdom. These men were that and more. If she could make this happen, a more genuine partnership between men would never be more rewarding than this prince, his men, and the King of the Dwarf Planets.

After dinner, Caitlin watched intently as her new friends cleaned up. She wondered again why they chose to share in this lonely existence in a fortress so far under the ground. It wasn't normal and was no life for anyone, never mind two eligible and very single men. She understood now why titles and real estate were so important. It gave them focus, but even she knew it was no substitute for a loving home which they sadly lacked. *Where are their friends, family? Surely, they have servants!* She knew all rulers had them, so why not Jovis. Was there not a single soul they trusted to keep the fires burning while the master of the house was away? Hearing a break in chatter, she took the opportunity to speak; it was time to prove their trust in her. 'Where is your help, Jovis? Shouldn't they be the ones cleaning up for you? Maybe have the fire lit and a meal ready for your return each day?'

Jovis stopped and stared at her, not expecting her to query him and yet if she hadn't, he would have deliberated why. She was astute and intelligent. He smiled.

'Why? Are you bored waiting? You can come over and join us. Just thought I'd leave you by the warmth.'

'I'm not bored, and you're right, it's lovely by the fire. It's just… well…'

'Well… what? Spit it out.'

'It's only us here, Jovis. I hear no other heartbeats, and my hearing is sharp due to the work I do. Apart from the nurse I recalled being in the room while I recovered, I haven't seen or heard anyone else. Neither did I see or hear anyone a few days ago when we walked to the caves. Could it be you still don't have confidence in me as a friend and have chosen this location to keep me many miles away from your home? You can be truthful, and I won't take offence if you tell me to mind my own business.' She turned to him, lifted an eyebrow and gave a slight grin.

'To tell you the truth, I did have a couple of maids here in the initial stage, who attended to you when we first found you. But once the nurse arrived there was no reason for them to be here, so I sent them back to the barracks to continue their normal duties.' Jovis put the tea towel down, walked the few steps to the fireplace and poked at the fire. It blazed up high into the chimney. The warmth was instant. Jovis was choosing his words and was in no hurry to rush an answer. Finally, he faced her. 'I have huge trust issues, but no, not with you Caitlin. It is, however, with everyone else... except my two comrades who rule my other worlds of course.' He saw Artisan nod in agreement while drying up the last of the dishes.

Jovis eyed her through thick dark lashes. He liked her, liked her a lot, and because of this, made a decision to disclose some information. After all, who would she tell? By the time he was ready to take her home, he would have won the war and moved back to his real abode.

He moved closer and leaned towards her. He had learned, since knowing Caitlin she held no grudges and preferred honesty even if it wasn't favourable.

'To tell you the truth, this is my place of business, not my home base. We are currently a few hundred NAVhoysts from my family's castle where I do live, and currently three NAVhoysts underground.'

She nodded. 'I figured this was a secret location and now it makes sense and stands to reason why you have no need for an army. But I assumed you would still require some staff.'

Jovis sat back. 'The war between Ice Planets has taken its toll; not only of my family but my people, and drastic measures have had to be taken to save them. As far as anyone is aware, the royal army dwindled due to capture and death. But in natural fact, they are safe on my other Home Worlds and will return to their families after the war is won.'

'Who guards your family while they are gone?'

'I left the glacier guards and what is left of the royal battalion to protect them. None remaining has full bloodline except for me, so they are not in any immediate danger. Before beginning this quest, we came up with the plan to remove all my family valuables and wealth, hiding them away, leaving those remaining with only the essentials. This was accomplished, and afterwards, it was blamed on those who were already held for high treason. Lack of wealth has put the castle into disrepair, and while it's in such poor condition, the threats have stopped towards them. Sedna, at last, appears underprivileged and not worthy of a full takeover, which has kept it out of trouble for now. If anything changes, such as the army returns or expensive repairs are made to the castle, alarm bells will ring out to my enemies monitoring us. They would immediately know royal blood and riches had returned, and consequently, we'd be under threat again.'

'But you are their prince, in line for the throne no doubt, it is sad you are not enjoying a better lifestyle. As to the threats on your life, you have three Ice Planets now, and I'm also aware you have ample security. Even, Jett, who is a god, could not visit, so how are these criminal land grabbers getting in?'

'It's complicated, and I have four Ice planets now. Signed off on another the day you woke.' He saw her look of concern. 'It was amicable; the swindling swine's allowed me to purchase it back after stealing it in the first place.'

'Why did you not report them to the authorities, asked for help? What they did was obviously illegal.'

Both laughed, but not in a good way, at her suggestion.

'So you were on your own with this one?'

'I had an entirely different way I was going to handle the takeover before I met you, Cait. For you, I changed my tactics and for this Ice Planet, a financial takeover worked. Therefore, because of your influence and also for giving me a second chance, I have decided to change the name, Asbolus, to the Ice Planet Kaih.'

Caitlin grinned, 'Kaih means new beginnings, very appropriate. You have endured more than most Jovis, so I only hope now you are four Ice Worlds strong and have the bodyguard Medusa, you can finally shift back to your castle?'

He breathed out. It felt good to talk to a woman who was smart enough to fill in the blanks. He could see in her soft, caring eyes she didn't mean him or his people any harm. He trusted those eyes like no others. 'I'd like that too, but why it is not possible just yet is lengthy to explain.'

'I have time. I'm going nowhere.' She smiled.

He sat back, stretched out his legs to get comfortable and watched as Caitlin tucked her legs under her and turned to face him. He loved the way she made him feel the most important person in her life.

'It all started some years back when my father, the King of Sedna and my mother, were murdered in their beds.' He saw tears spring to Caitlin's eyes, and her emotional reaction to his heartache encouraged him to continue. 'As if that wasn't hard enough to deal with, after the funeral, my eldest brother disappeared. It was then my closest allies and friends warned me of the threat against my life.'

Caitlin turned her attention to Artisan, guessing he was one of the allies.

Artisan put his hand up. 'Guilty as charged. My buddy Rocky and I overheard a courtier speaking to someone we had never seen before.'

'They saved my life.' Jovis gave him a grateful look.

'So where did you go. I assume this fortress wasn't here then.'

'Actually, it was. You see, many years before when we had almost lost the war to those planets I know own, my father came up with a plan if we were overrun by the enemy. He figured we were best to hide here and build a new army, one to fight the thugs from the inside and in time, take back what was rightfully ours. He had this fortress built although we never ended up needing it.'

'How did you keep a construction of this magnitude a secret?' Cait sat forward intently listening.

Rocky and Artisan would pick up outside contractors and transport them to this location each day. To get paid the men had to work hard and abide by our regulations. Our number one rule was absolutely no handheld devices that might give the location away. They were all checked each day before leaving the pickup point. Anyone found with a tracking device of any description were left behind at the pickup location and never given a second chance.' He shrugged, 'my good friends took no chances and were extremely thorough to ensure the secret was kept.

'This was built by then?'

'Yes. Well, almost. As you can see we ran out of time to spruce it up but it's liveable and all I need.' He paused and shifted uncomfortably. It was the first time he had ever told anyone, yet Cait wasn't just anyone so continued. 'For the moment my family's valuables are safe and this gives me a quiet place to work. Here, Artisan and Rocky have helped me take back what is rightfully mine and I intend to stay here until all those who oppose my family and killed my parents have been pursued and dealt with as I see fit.'

Caitlin felt his raw hurt and anger when she first arrived on Sedna but also saw he had changed and not just towards her. He was still not there yet but she could see he wanted to be that man again, the person he was when his parents were alive. 'Your mother and father would be very proud of you. You did it without bloodshed, and I also find that very admirable.'

'That may be so, but I have one more Ice Planet earmarked. After I take it back, all is how it was before, when my father was ordained, King. But this last one will not be an easy win, and I feel you and I will be at loggerheads if you condemn my final quest. This last world must be taken and once it's mine, I can, at last, search for my brother who was last seen there. I pray he still lives and when I bring him home he will take the throne as my father would have wished.'

'What if your brother is not there?'

'In that case, the search goes on. I will not accept the position as king until I know for sure he's not coming back.'

'You are a good man Jovis and will lead your people well, regardless of status.' She was horrified by what he had dealt with so far.

His jaw jutted out with pride. 'I look forward to just that, to sleep in my own bed and begin my new life out of hiding. By then, I will be five Ice Planets strong with the largest army in our ice sector. Let the thieving criminals come for me then.'

'Has any other Ice Planet offered to help?'

'Just one, but he prefers to stay nameless until the last World is secured.'

'You trust him as you do Artisan.'

'Hell no, but he does seem harmless.' Jovis went quiet, his eyes clouded with thought.

She said when he got up and shook his hands and arms as if

releasing the anger towards others.

'Are you okay to continue?'

He nodded and took a breath.

'While you are here, who runs the day to day issues in the castle and tends to your people?'

With his composure recovered he sat back down. 'After my parents were put to rest, I asked my father's half-brother to run the kingdom. He has taken over many of the royal duties and holds the fort until the return of my brother, dead or alive. One day, if my brother is dead, it will be me who becomes King of Sedna, but this is not my time. I want retribution first before I can even think that far ahead. This last Ice Planet I fight is all that stands between me and my rightful place in the palace, supporting my brother, the king. You have to know, Cait, I will not rest until I have my revenge and get back what is rightfully mine and my brother's.'

Picking up on Jovis's sudden mood swing, Artisan turned and spoke to Caitlin. 'When Jovis is done, he will be hailed as a hero, but as yet, no one knows of his successes. He hasn't shared any of his conquests with his people. They have no idea it is he who has won the war against Quaoar and Orcus. Nor are they aware Rocky and I are the rulers of these Home Worlds. As for Jovis's plans, we support him all the way. Rocky and I have a score to settle with them too. You see we never knew our own parents, but Jovis's family took us in and treated us as they did their own kids. They even gave us both a good education, and we are now thankful they did. It has given us the good sense and brains to help their son. They were our family too, and we want, as Jovis does, to see the killing bastards responsible, get what's coming to them. There will be no peace for any of us until we win the war against Varuna. We believe the Varuna brothers to be the instigators of not only the attacks on Sedna, but also the ones who put out the hit on Jovis's parents.'

Jovis had a glint in his eye. 'So now you know why we live here, alone, and I think we have said enough.' Jovis stood abruptly and leant against the mantel with his arms crossed, watching her.

'What just happened, Jovis? You snapped shut like a book.' She frowned.

'I look at you as a friend and speak of things as I would to a good friend. But you aren't just that, are you, Cait? Your priorities are as a peacemaker first, and we both know that will always be between us. You are a law-abiding citizen and the Goddess of Peace.' His mood had gone sour. 'As Artisan has just disclosed, we will go to war. I hate with a vengeance this last ruler and intend to make him suffer at my hands!' He breathed out and dropped his arms. 'Rocky and Artisan have their armies ready and waiting for the go-ahead. Yet I hesitate, waiting for your input, needing your approval, and yet know what you will say. The thought of losing you over this, Cait, drives me crazy but I have no other option. You have me dreaming of a family, a wife, a child and yet to get what I want, I will need to reclaim what's mine. I have to go against your wishes, or I will never have a safe harbour for them to live. I already know that no woman will come and live in this fortress, but if I lived in a castle, well things would be different.'

Caitlin's features softened. He was finally thinking ahead. A dream for a better life gave her a warm shiver, but the way of getting there was something he still fought her on. 'To choose love over greed is a commendable quality, but to choose love over the safety of you and your people is not. As the acting ruler of the land, you have a job to do. If you have tried to sort out the conflict with your enemy and have been met with blatant disregard and hostility, then I agree further talks are senseless. However, there is a higher power that could help prevent a full-blown war. Eliminate your enemies, not the innocent.'

He sat beside her. 'I don't want to start an argument, Cait, but you must understand I will not accept Hades as my King.'

Artisan passed them both a cup of brewed tea and sat cross-legged in front of them. 'Maybe you can talk some sense to him. I've tried and given up.'

'Zip it blockhead.' Jovis put his foot out and nudged him backwards in a playful manner.

Artisan chuckled and sat up straight again. 'Get him, Cait.'

Caitlin chewed her lip. 'Mmm.' She turned her head to the side and eyed him. 'Hades is ruthless, unkind and has little patience. You two would butt heads for sure and yet!' Her eyes lit up. 'With you as Jovis and he as Jett...'

Jovis put his hand up. 'Don't go giving me reverse physiology, young lady, because it won't work.'

'I saw you almost smile. Did you see it, Artisan?' Caitlin stirred him.

Jovis shook his head, trying to keep a straight face. He adored her, but she was way off base. 'Don't, Cait.'

She smiled. 'What!'

'You think you're always right and will change my mind. Not this time, curly.' He strode away from her.

'Is that so!' She tossed back the throw rug covering her legs and chased him with a stick she grabbed from the fireplace.

Laughing, he picked up a wooden spoon from the kitchen bench and drew it like a sword. '*En Garde*!' he called and shaped up, impressed at how Caitlin fought bravely with one arm behind her back. She had him pinned. 'Artisan! Stop laughing and help me yield this woman into submission.' He grinned, enjoying every minute of this side of her.

Artisan was on his feet and choosing a solid stick he moved towards her. As quick as lightning, she somersaulted over him, grabbed another stick and wielded both pretend swords, fighting both of them off. Finally, with Artisan on the ground with a stick to his throat and Jovis against the wall, she moved her first stick skilfully. Jovis's weapon went flying in the air and as she caught it, she smiled. 'Hey, me hearties, you're both dead.' She chuckled and tossed the three sticks over her head. They all landed in the fire.

'You fight well my lady.' Jovis inclined his head. 'You're a worthy opponent indeed.' He reached out and took her hand smiling. 'Your magic gave you a glove and was the only reason I played your little game. Clever girl aren't you.'

'To do what I do you have to have some tricks up your sleeve.' She was pleased he hadn't thought her too delicate to have some fun.

Seeing she was okay, Artisan looked for revenge. 'That was a hoot, well except me on the ground. Let's see if you can beat me now I know you cheat and wear a protective glove. I won't be taking it so easy on you this time girlie.' Artisan was on his feet and snatching up another stick from the hearth. He stood facing her in a fencing position. He barely saw her move before she was back with a new weapon of choice, this time a carrot from the basket on the bench next to her. He laughed and lost some of his concentration as she used it to keep his stick from striking its mark and finishing her off.

Jovis watched on in stitches as she finally pinned him in the corner of the room.

Artisan dropped his stick. 'I give up crazy lady. That carrot is just too dangerous for me.'

Jovis had laughed so hard at this stage tears streamed down his cheeks. Never did a female have such an effect on him. He felt a boy, not a man; he enjoyed this child-like game so much. Suddenly he wanted her with him always. She turned and faced him, with a smile like that of an angel. The fierce fighting spirit was gone. 'We need you, Cait. Thanks for coming back with us. You have given me hope and brought laughter into our dark world. How will we ever repay you?'

She took the few steps between them and put her hand on her chest. 'There is no payment in the universe for friendship.'

He was remorseful for only moments ago being a dick. 'You are more than just a friend, you are my saviour. Ignore my outburst; my emotions seem as if they're on a rollercoaster. I laugh one minute and am sad, and worry you may want to leave the next.'

'I will stay until trust returns and those feeling you experience pass. This I promise.' She hugged him.

'If you were to leave now it would destroy me.' He spoke in almost a whisper.

Artisan joined them and put an arm around them both. 'Destroy us both!'

They stood for a few minutes in a group hug, until Caitlin raised her carrot in the centre of them. 'Pick up ye swords me lad's or be slit from gut to ye throat.'

Both men jumped back away from her. Jovis grabbed a long candlestick holder, and Artisan grabbed her blanket. He threw it over her and picked her up in his arms. They could hear her laughing.

'We have her caught, captain!' Artisan had her well wrapped up. 'Time for this lassie to walk the plank.'

'Arrr! Me lad, let's show her who ye captain is and what happens to insubordinate pirates.'

Jovis transported them to the cave where they had found the hot springs.

Caitlin could smell the steam and minerals and knew precisely where they were. Using her magic, she lifted up and out of their hands. Up high the blanket fell to the ground. Both men stared at her with gaping mouths. Her magic amazed them. She flicked her hand once then twice. The movement flicked them off their feet and, still fully clothed, they landed with a loud splash into the water. They both came up with a cough and splutter. It had happened so quickly. Caitlin lowered herself and placed her hands on her hips. 'Arrr! Me lads, two mistakes, hold me better next time... and secondly, never let a pirate smell where ye are, no quarter given!' She chuckled.

As if a hand had picked her up and held her, she was now standing over the water, her feet not quite touching the surface.

Jovis had his hand out, using his powers. 'Arrr! My lady, ye never trust a captain of his ship. Ye walked the plank, suffer the bite.' He let her go and dumped her in it too.

She came to the surface, laughing. 'No more magic, I promise. Only games with strategy from now on... Truce.' She put out her hand and Jovis shook on it.

Getting to the side was a struggle. 'What's with this coat?' She couldn't wiggle out of it. The weight was dragging her under, but she managed to get to the side and hold on. Even her own magic wouldn't remove it. Hearing chuckles from behind she knew Jovis had cast a spell on it. She turned to Jovis. 'Ratfink.'

He couldn't stop laughing. 'Last time for me too. I had my fingers crossed, but I give my word now as well.' He removed the coat for her.

'Repeat it and show me your hands.' He did, but she didn't trust him. 'Arrr! Me lad, those toes below better not be crossed or tis ain't over, captain sneaky pants.'

'Who doesn't trust who now?' He put his hands on the sides of the pool and lifted quickly from the water. Artisan was right beside him, still smiling from having this much entertainment in one night.

'I trust you now!' She yawned.

Jovis grinned. 'You didn't get much sleep when we took you home, did you, party girl.' He saw how tired she suddenly looked and instantly transported them back to the house.

In front of the fire, Caitlin's body glowed bright, causing the other two to take a step back. They were amazed when her wet clothes were replaced by PJs and a long fluffy black and white, lion-hood dressing gown, complete with ears on the hood. Her slippers were also in the shape of white lions. Her hair was dry and brushed out to full length.

The glow dissipated and Jovis blinked. 'How do you do that?'

'That is so cool.' Artisan grinned and walked around her. He and Jovis stood in a pool of water, both dripping wet.

'My little secret.' She smiled. 'Guess it's telling me I could do with some rest. And to your question, Jovis, less than an hour just before you picked me up. Big dramas at home but all good now.' She yawned again.

'I'll show Simba her room. It's on the way to the shower.' Artisan smiled at her. 'Come on little lion, I promise not to scratch or bite.'

'Grrr,' she growled, following. 'I might though. I get ticked off having no control over these stupid outfits.'

Jovis couldn't stop grinning. She looked so exasperated at looking like a lion, yet so adorable at the same time. 'I'm heading to my room to shower too and calling it a night. It's been fun, Cait, but please, try to dress more grown up while you're here. You know I'm not opposed to a French maid or a nurse's outfit if you need some ideas.'

She was halfway up the staircase when he finished his stirring.

Not expecting it, he saw her turn, claw the air and hiss at him before continuing to follow Artisan.

Jovis put his head back and roared with laughter. The echo lingered, and his fortress, at last, felt like a home. 'Night Cait,' he finally called out, and whistled happily while bounding up the stairs to his own room.

* * * *

The next couple of weeks flew by quickly. Games, teasing and much laughter filled the walls of the fortress. Jovis whistled a lot and Caitlin could hear Artisan singing during his shower.

She had just woken and laid thinking. While they were in such good moods, maybe she could broach the subject again regarding a meeting with Jett.

Throwing back the blankets, she shivered, glad her magic covered her feet in slippers the moment they hit the icy tiled floor. In the bathroom, she brushed her teeth and shuddered as she splashed freezing water over her face. Later she would bath in the warm water from the underground spring. They went there every day now instead of having the usual icy cold shower. With her smile wide and a spring in her step, she had high hopes this would rectify itself soon. As their king, Jett would share with them many secrets, including how to generate power on their Ice Planets.

Dressed conservatively for a change, in warm slacks, knee-high boots, thick polo-neck jumper and jacket, Caitlin headed downstairs. From the kitchenette drifted the aroma of bacon. Bouncing through the door she was about to spread good cheer when she spotted Rocky. It flashed through her mind that he still thought her a bad egg. She backed away when he stomped towards her. She had no choice; he had stripped her of her powers. *Shytzer he knows who I am, and he's reacting badly.*

'Is that who I think it is?' he said, walking over to get a better look at her.

Caitlin backed against the wall. *These rulers that have learned to block magic are really becoming annoying.* She got her legs moving and ran from his grip. She saw Jovis smiling. He obviously didn't know Rocky had taken her magic and had a feeling he most likely didn't know yet that he had done the same to them. Not having her sharp goddess skills, they would not know they'd lost their powers until they went to use them. *Why would he take their powers?* She wasn't hanging around to find out, and maybe get swiped by the big bully before they saw she needed protection. *Bruised cheek, hell no!* She ran and hid beside the bookshelf by the stairs.

She heard him bluff them with a kind tone. 'I must have scared the little thing.' He blew out the candle in the hallway. 'Oh, and the light just went out. I hope she's okay.' He didn't sound at all convincing to her. Why didn't they pick up his lying tone? Had they been friends so long they just didn't notice when he wasn't sincere?

Artisan's voice was high pitched, worried. 'Out the way big guy, she'll hurt herself now it's dark,' Caitlin heard him say. A torch shone towards her, and once Artisan was in sight, she spoke. 'You should have told him I was here,' she called to him. Still at the kitchenette door, he swore and growled at Jovis, 'She's scared of Rocky. I told you we should have told him she was here.'

Jovis called out in a friendly voice, trying to make her feel safe. 'Rocky get in here until she feels better. Come and butter the toast.'

Even though Rocky had stomped back into the kitchen, Caitlin's feet were riveted to the spot; literally felt stuck to the floor. He was using weird magic to make her stay. She stayed still and waited.

'Don't move Cait, I'll come to you.' Artisan realised something more was going on. This woman he had got to know over the past few weeks was no pushover. She would stand up to a Rocky twice his size. He was beside her in seconds and put a hand on her shoulder in a soothing manner. 'You're shaking.' He changed his position and put an arm around her shoulder. This broke the hold Rocky had over her. Apparently, he wasn't strong enough to remove all Artisan's powers plus Jovis's and an unexpected extra; her.

'I'm confused, Cait. I swear you're safe with us. And you've met Rocky before. You must know I would never let him hurt you. Jovis would kill him. What's scared you?'

'There's something wrong with him. Evil has a hold of him. Please don't make me go in there. I need you to take me home immediately.'

'What! Hell no, Glow, please wait and let us sort this out.' He yelled out to Jovis. 'She's terrified of Rocky. I don't get it. He wouldn't hurt a fly. She wants to go home.'

Jovis joined them and put his hand on her head, attempting to calm her. She felt nothing. This didn't feel right to her. Jovis definitely had a block on him too. What was going on here? Only evil could do this magic. She didn't believe Rocky was capable of this. It was as if he had been gifted with a dark power to use on them.

'Come on Cait, he won't hurt you, honest. We're both here and quite capable of protecting you. And anyway, you have your own powers. You have my permission to zap him if he gets out of line.'

'That's what I'm trying to tell you, Jovis. He has conjured up some ridiculously strong magic to use here today. The only ones capable of removing my powers are those who wish me harm, and he took them from me, the moment he realised it was me. Please, I'm begging you; just take me home until he has gone. Rory will know what to do to get my powers back. Whatever is going on, I'll need them to help you. Rocky is too strong while this angry so until we find out who is helping feed his rage with their magic, we should steer clear.'

'What the hell! What is he doing?' Jovis cursed. 'So even now you have nothing?'

'He has blocked them and possibly many of yours also, Jovis.'

There was a brief silence, then Jovis said, 'I've never had mine blocked before. Don't know what it feels like. Just know I've got none because I tried to transport you away from here.' He turned to Artisan. 'You still got yours?'

Artisan tried to lift the vase of flowers with his mind. He had picked them only hours ago off-world, to surprise Caitlin. 'Mine are gone too. What is that fool doing?'

'We're sitting ducks and vulnerable, so let's slip outside and hide until he's gone,' Caitlin whispered.

Jovis shook his head. 'This is ridiculous, surely a

misunderstanding. Take her to the cave Art, she'll be safe with you there. The hot steam from the underground spring should keep you both warm until I come get you. He grabbed Artisan's arm. 'Take extra skins from the mudroom on your way out just in case it's colder without your powers. In the meantime, I'll find out what the hell is going on.' He saw Artisan's concern. 'Don't worry, he wouldn't dare hurt me.'

'I know. This must be about Glow. I'll get her out, and he'll calm down.'

Stepping off the lift to exit the fortress, Artisan and Caitlin sifted through the snow equipment in the mudroom. Geared up with thermo jackets, gloves and boots, they both put on the breathable helmets before grabbing skins for extra warmth. These, Artisan rolled up and secured on the back of one of the snowcross NAVbikes. Once Caitlin was on, he kicked over the motor, opened the volt door to the outside world, and sped off towards the ice cave.

It was a quick trip, and once Caitlin was settled next to the hot spring, she begged Artisan to leave her. 'I'm all right now! My fear is more for Jovis. You must go back and help him. Even without powers, I can feel something is very wrong.'

'Jovis told me to stay and look after you, Glow. He would kill me if I left here.'

'And what will you do if Jovis is killed because we left him alone to deal with your friend who has obviously lost his mind? The man was acting crazy.'

'He'll be pissed I left you here!'

'And I'll be more pissed if you let anything happen to him.'

'I am concerned. But I shouldn't be. I've known Rocky all my life. This is unbelievable.'

'Then you need to check,' she said with more urgency. 'You have made me very comfortable here, and no one knows of this cave. We only just discovered it recently, so it's secret, now go!'

He kissed her cheek. 'Be back in twenty.' He ran out the door.

Chapter Twenty-Seven

The Goddess of Peace

Caitlin waited in the ice cave by the warmth of the heated spring for what was surely a couple of hours. She began to pace, as her mind conjured up demons and she started to really freak out. Where were they? Something was *very wrong*.

It was at that moment her powers were returned. She knew Rocky had now left the planet. Thankful for that, Caitlin waited to be collected but they didn't come. Her stomach was twisted in knots by the time she faced up to the fact she may be here alone.

It had started to snow again outside, but that didn't stop her determination. *Where are my friends?* Caitlin trudged on, following the tracks the snow vehicle had left. The snow had almost covered the tracks by the time the fortress was in sight. Luckily for her, Artisan had left the entry unlocked in his haste to get back to Jovis. Inside, she closed the door behind her, but not having the code she was unable to lock it. 'First things first,' she muttered and grabbed the lamp in the entrance way. 'Find Jovis and get the code.' The kitchenette was her first thought but once there her heart skipped a beat. There were tables and chairs smashed and droplets of red blood on the floor. Frightened for her friends, she ran through the fortress checking in every room, looking for someone, anyone, but there was no one in sight. 'Hello, where are you both, Jovis ... Artisan ...' she called to them, while double checking each room yet again. It was then reality hit; she was on her own. Jovis and Artisan had either been taken or killed and their bodies, either way, had been taken to Rocky's Ice Planet.

Freaking out about the idea of anything that disturbing, Caitlin collapsed by the fire in shock. *'What will I do now?* Suddenly she got up and headed for the exit. Her best chance was to alert Rory she needed help. A rocket with a simple "Help" would do.

She knew Pluto was the closest planet to Sedna. Pluto's army monitored the sky 24/7. Luckily, Jovis had pointed it out when they were outside one day. She had her powers back. Her plan didn't take much thought. If the men were nowhere in sight outside, the rocket was her only hope to get Rory and the team and maybe an army here to search for Jovis and Artisan.

With her mind settled on what to do, Caitlin stood, and shook off the wet jacket and shoes, allowing her magic to re-dress her. Once dry and feeling warmer, she took a waterproof coat, gloves and ski mask off the coat rack. Not trusting to keep her powers in case Rocky returned, she made sure she had plenty of warmth on. The sheer worry for her friends had her rush. Her hand had just reached the door handle which would lead her outside, when she was gripped on the shoulder from behind. A chill ran down her spine as he spoke.

'I knew you'd be hiding and come back here. Why in such a hurry to go back outside? You're such an underhanded, sneaky bitch. I should have stayed out of sight a little longer to see what you had planned. I hate that he forgave you! I hate you!' He shook her angrily.

The minute his hands touched her she reacted by attempting to electrify them. She knew when it failed that Rocky had now taken her powers for the second time. In an attempt to pacify him, Caitlin spoke calmly. 'When I came back and saw Jovis and Artisan had gone, I decided to look outside.'

He stared at her, eyes glowing with anger. She doubted his ears heard a word she said. 'Rocky, what have you done?' She whispered, hoping a quiet tone would get through. She felt so tiny against his giant stature.

His eyes burned into her. He thought he'd never see her again after trying to con them. How could Jovis forgive her after all the lies she told him, them? He knew nothing of her except that Jovis had said she was a lying traitor and would not allow her name mentioned. *Now what, they are best buddies? Glow Girl, what does that mean… stupid name if you ask me.*

She felt his anger grow as he stared at her.

He now wondered who she really was… *why is she here?* He felt even more ticked off… *why has she been kept a secret from me?* This here was the last straw as far as he was concerned.

'I know you are that girl called Glow that we met on Earth. Only down there I couldn't feel your powers; you masked them from us to make you seem like a human, didn't you. I thought only rulers could do such things.' He tapped his chin… and repeated his words. 'A girl called Glow.' Suddenly the penny dropped, and he gritted his teeth. The muscles flexed in his jaw as he growled. 'I remember now, your friends slipped a couple of times and called you Cait. You're Caitlin. Glow Girl is bloody Caitlin Stanton, Axon Stanton's wife.' His voice rose in anger. 'I should have known he and his Riders would be in on this coup with Jovis. Well, let's see how tough Axon is without his damned wife to fight his battles.'

'Rocky, you're angry and not making sense. What do you mean the Riders are involved in a coup with Jovis against you? I know nothing of this. I swear I was only visiting. If you'd calm down for just a minute and talk this through, you will see it's one big misunderstanding.'

'You're a blatzing liar. Someone tried to blow my planet out of the sky last night. Those two bastards that call themselves mates want me gone. They have been secretive for weeks and I know they have been planning something against me or they would have let me in on it.' His voice lowered, deadly serious. 'You may have twisted Jovis's ear to get back in his good graces, but I,' he eyed her with a deathly glare, 'will not be such a pussy of a pushover.' He grabbed her shoulder. 'Be glad I don't kill you right here and now. What saves you this moment is leverage. Keeping you alive will motivate those two traitors in my dungeon, to tell the truth. If not…' his laugh was evil, 'you will beg for death.'

She tried to shake him off and run from him, but his grip was ironclad.

He shook her roughly. 'Quit it stupid,' he said before he transported them both to his Ice World.

Caitlin guessed it was Orcus he spoke of and worried now for all Jovis's Ice Planets. They landed on the hard floor of a dungeon. 'Cripes, take it easy Rocky,' she cried out as he dragged her by the arm past a couple of cells. 'What is it with these cold dungeons, and what happened to the old-fashioned judge and jury? Not cool Rocky.' She was not about to show how truly frightened she felt at ending up back in one of these icy cold dungeons again.

Opening the cell door, he roughly turned and glared at her. 'You might as well enjoy your boyfriends because they will be the last people you'll ever see if this isn't sorted out, and fast.'

'Well, you're not giving us much of a chance. How about we go back upstairs, pour a nice cup of tea and chat calmly about this. It will be fixed in no time.'

He met her remark with a scoff as he pushed her into the cell and slammed the door shut behind her. The key turned, and the loud stomping ceased for a moment when he stopped to speak to the guard by the door. 'If she doesn't shut up, kill her. And if her husband doesn't tell us what the blatzing hell is going on here, I'll kill her to save you the bother.' His gruffness was loud enough for her to hear.

'Kill her!' Like hell you will!' She called out to him. His moodiness thickened the air. She wondered if she had pushed it too far. A silent pause had her worried.

She breathed out, hearing a sharp squeak of his boots as he turned away. 'You have your orders,' he said as he walked through the dimly lit door and slammed it shut behind him.

The guard called out. 'Quit it, lady, he ain't himself today. Give it a rest, or you'll make me do what he ordered.'

She threw her hands up in frustration. 'Has he gone stark raving mad?'

The guard went to get up and she put her hands out in front of her protectively. 'Okay, I'll shut up.'

He nodded and sat down by the door again.

Ticked off she was yet again locked up, Caitlin squinted in the dimly lit cell to find Jovis and Artisan. In the darkened corner leaning up against the stone wall, she caught sight of them and walked quickly towards her friends. Not hearing a word from them, she dropped to her knees and began feeling for their vitals and checked for possible injuries or broken bones. 'What did he do to you both?' She was annoyed when finding Artisan unconscious. And Jovis, well, Rocky had sure done a number on him.

'How's Artisan?' Jovis asked when she moved over to him. His voice was almost a whisper.

'He has a nasty lump on the back of his head, but he's alive. That lunatic must have hit him with something and knocked him out when he went back for you. He has no other lumps I can feel. You, on the other hand, are not in good shape.' He groaned with her every gentle touch.

'I'm sorry Cait,' he whispered. 'I should have listened to your instincts. I just never believed he would turn on us like this.'

'I'm so sorry too. I was meant to save you. Instead, I'm here with you and no one knows. He caught me before I could send out an SOS. Oh, and he has worked out who I am and has decided to use me as leverage. If Axon doesn't tell him who tried to take him out last night, he says I'm toast.'

'Take him out? He kept yelling that at me before knocking me unconscious. As if I'd destroy what I own! But I couldn't get a word in. He was out of control.' Jovis moved and grimaced with pain.

'Hey, keep still and let yourself heal. We'll get through this.'

'I have no powers to help me get better.' He groaned through gritted teeth. For the first time ever, he anguished feeling so much pain and felt helpless to do a thing about it.

'Well, I know what that's like.' She smiled.

'Don't Cait, I am really so sorry.'

She chuckled. 'Just keeping your spirits up.'

'Gee thanks, friend.' He tried to smile but even that hurt and he moaned instead.

With a grunt and a tug, Caitlin dragged Artisan next to Jovis. She wiggled between them and once far enough back, this allowed Artisan's head to lean on her shoulder.

'What are you doing, Cait? If knucklehead comes to get one of us, being together will not stop him dragging us out. In anger, he might hurt you too.'

'This huddle is not for protection. It's to help you heal.' She struggled to flip one end of her coat over Artisan, the other over Jovis. 'I've learned over time that heat and rest help heal our kind. It's slower but has worked on me a few times.' She tapped her other shoulder. 'Give it a go. You have nothing to lose. Lean on me, hug in as close as you can and put yourself in a trance. It has to be deep enough not to feel pain or this won't work.'

'You've done this?'

'How do you think I stayed alive waiting for you? Now shush and do as I say. Trust me... no one dare better come in here and disturb you or they will have me to contend with.'

'Little softie. Where is this coming from?' He coughed and groaned as his aching head moved against the rough stones behind him.

'Others can hurt me, but don't you dare hurt my friends. Mother is pissed. Now sleep, while I try and work out how to fix this mess.'

'Good luck with that. Like so hear how?' he whispered.

'Not sure... leave that to me. Come,' she patted her shoulder. 'Rest your head... here,' she patted the crook of her neck. 'It will hurt, but not for long.'

He moaned as he got into a position. 'I doubt if I will sleep, but will try to rest.'

Caitlin touched his forehead; he already had a fever and she could feel a cut still weeping. 'Do as I say, you're panting in pain. Let me teach you a little trick I learned. Try to breathe with me.' Once his breathing slowed, she spoke more softly. 'Good, now go deep within you, where there is only blackness. What can you hear?'

'Us breathing,' he whispered.

'Deeper.' She waited a few seconds. 'What can you hear?'

'The ice underground moving and groaning,' he said.

'Can you still feel your pain while you are there?' She checked, and he had stopped bleeding. This was good. He was mighty powerful. She liked that about him. *And he listens.* She smiled.

'No.' He said it so softly she only just heard him.

'Then stay there and let the sound of water relax you so you can get better.'

She turned her attention to Artisan and covered the lump on his head. She hoped the warmth of her hand would be enough to comfort and keep him sleeping. While he slept, he would heal too. With Jovis's fever, she was heating up. It reminded her of the times Jett had used this healing method on her.

Jovis's breathing had totally relaxed and Artisan's was almost normal again. She leant her own head against the wall, wondering how you could go from a bounce in your step to this. How a day can turn on its head.

It had been a few hours when she felt Jovis tremble. Caitlin lifted his head gently, leaving him lean against the wall. Luckily, he was deep in the trance. She wiggled out of the way and scrambled on the floor, finding some pieces of an old ripped blanket she had almost stumbled on earlier. Caitlin rolled these up, which made a perfect pillow to lay Artisan's and Jovis's heads on. Once she had manoeuvred Artisan and he was lying down, she tended to Jovis. This she did ever so carefully so as not to bring him out of his trance. Finally getting him lying flat, she slipped the rolled-up rag under his head. She pulled her long thick snow jacket off her shoulders and quickly placed it over Jovis's shaking body. Carefully, she tucked it in to keep his temperature elevated. This was her only means of caring for the two men she had grown so fond of. The entire time, her mind wrestled with a way to get them free when she had no power... or did she? She smiled and tapped her top lip, thinking.

With both men now settled, she moved to the bars and called out to get the attention of the person on watch who was pacing the floor near the door. 'Excuse me, guard, I insist you give Rocky, I mean your boss, Torin, a message immediately.'

The guard's steps were loud as he came towards her. 'This should be good. Go on then.'

'Tell him that just because he has taken me captive, there is no reason for him to be a poor host. I want blankets and pillows for three.'

He walked towards her, his glare wild enough to kill, but stopped in his tracks when her voice cut through him. 'You heard me young man, or whatever your name is, don't make your goddess repeat herself.' Her voice was so strong and regal that he shivered.

'Sel miss. They call me Sel.'

'Well, Sel, you have your orders. Tell your boss that the Goddess of Peace is waiting for a bit of hospitality and will be very cross if she is kept waiting.' Her tone was impatient as all gods and goddesses were known to be.

He bowed his head. 'Sorry miss... I mean... Goddess, I had no idea who you were. I will get right onto it.' Sel scurried out the room.

It was less than a few minutes before Sel came back with three pillows and some fur rugs. 'Apologies Goddess, I came back as fast as I could.'

'Your apology is accepted with thanks, Sel. Now get back to your post! That is all.' Caitlin put on her best royal tone. He shook as he handed to her the items she had requested. She was glad so many still feared yet respected even the mention of a goddess, never mind having one so close. It was very bad luck to refuse the request of a goddess. This she had banked on to get what she needed.

'Thank you, Goddess.' He bowed low as he backed away.

Caitlin moved quickly, exchanging the dirty rags under Jovis and Artisan's heads for clean white pillows. The fur rugs she laid over them and after, put her hand gently on Jovis's forehead. He was cold and clammy. Without a thought she climbed in between them, and hugging into Jovis, she pulled the last rug over them all. She knew no other way of projecting heat into him other than direct body heat. Gradually he stopped shaking. The warmth had Caitlin's lids close while she was wondering how the hell she was going to get them out of this pickle. She begged the gods to give her strength and drifted off to sleep.

She was unsure how many hours the three of them slept.

It was Jovis who finally stirred and turned to face Caitlin. He wrapped his arms around her. 'You did it,' he whispered. 'I am so much better.'

'I'm glad.' Her eyes flicked open, and her struggle to grasp where they were, became apparent. *No... It hasn't been a dream.* 'Is Artisan awake yet?'

Artisan groaned from behind her. He too had wiggled in close and she was one hot lady. He spoke sounding in a pain. 'I'm awake, but I have the worst headache. What did Rocky hit me with?'

They heard loud footsteps from what sounded like giant feet before the entry door to the dungeon squeaked as it was flung open. The clump of steel cap boots on stone began heading towards the cell.

'Shh... You two must pretend you are still unconscious. If they touch you, make your body limp and floppy so they leave you alone. I don't want them roughing you up further. I will do the talking,' she whispered. She got up quickly and was at the bars before the two loud stomping guards got to the cell. 'And who are you?' she asked in the same uppity tone she had used earlier.

The two guards were as large in build as Rocky. *Gee, they grow them big on this planet.* Her mouth was wide as she looked up higher and higher until she reached their faces.

'I've been told to come and get one of the prisoners.' The bigger one with the patch on his eye spoke with authority.

'Well, you can go back and tell Torin he has done too good a job on his best friends and they are still unconscious. You can also tell him that because of his uncomfortable quarters, the Goddess of Peace has a headache and requires two painkillers... and I will not be amused if you dare bring them down without a pot of coffee and cups. The service here is most unacceptable.'

He stood looking at her, dumbfounded.

'What is your name, lad?'

'Um, it is Lisk, miss.'

She knew this firmness had increased her goddess scent by the mere change in their posture. 'Well Lisk, you have your orders. Tell Torin the goddess is waiting for further hospitality and there is no need for him to make her go thirsty or be in pain.'

'And Lisk…'

'Yes, miss.'

'Yes who...Lisk?'

'Oh… I'm sorry, Goddess?' He inclined his head respectfully.

'Lisk, your goddess will be very cross if I am to be kept waiting much longer.'

'Yes miss, I mean Goddess,' he said as he still stood staring.

'Well run along, that's all.' Caitlin fluttered her fingers at him as an impatient goddess would. Both guards slumped off, looking confused.

She went back and sat between the boys and sighed. 'Bluff number two. Last night it worked, getting a pillow and rugs, this morning... not too sure.' She heard chuckles under the blankets and lifted the corners up to look at their faces. 'Don't you two give me away. Torin has a guard stationed in the far corner by the exit.'

'Sorry miss, I mean, Goddess. You crack me up, Cait.' Jovis was in silent fits of laughter. 'If you'd used that on me, no way could I have kept from laughing at you.'

'I'll remember it next time you get all crazy-eyed and cranky at me,' she whispered.

Jovis stuffed the corner of the rug into his mouth to stop from laughing out loud.

'Shh... Someone's coming.'

She jumped to her feet and stood at the cell door. This time Rocky had come. His face had reddened with contempt.

She spoke, before he could, only this time really turning on the regal tone. 'Well, my dear boy, haven't you made a nice old mess of your best friends? Now correct me if you dare, but are you not a mere caretaker for this planet? Are your transportation powers not given freely by the Prince of these Ice Planets for loyalties served?'

He went to speak, and she put her hand up, commanding silence until she finished. 'So, pray tell, if he is unhappy with your rulership, why would he try to attack your world? Wouldn't he just remove you? And lastly, young Torin,' she continued, her voice pitched higher, 'why destroy his own army and friend when he needs all the power he has to fight against his enemy, the King of the Dwarf Planets? I mean, have you gone insane, boy? If you were my employee, I would have you horsewhipped for your insolence. Now, where are my painkillers and the coffee? Honestly, if you have to keep me in such filthy quarters, I demand you allow such a simple request. Now go, I have no interest in discussing anything further until I get my beverage.'

Caitlin walked away from the cell door and paced as if she was really annoyed. She felt his eyes burn into her, but he left. She sat between Jovis and Artisan, shaking, 'I thought he was going to horsewhip me. I could feel his rage thumping through me.'

'I think you might have pushed him a little too far Cait,' Jovis said, 'but let's wait and see.'

The three of them sat quietly... and waited.

The look of surprise on Jovis's and Artisan's faces was priceless when they heard the tinkle of china and smelled the aroma of coffee, as Caitlin's demands were met.

'Wow, it worked. Never pulled the goddess card before,' she whispered as she got up and stood at a distance, waiting. She had her arms folded, foot lightly tapping.

Inside, a card table was quickly erected, and the guards placed a decent sized pot and three mugs on top.

Lisk saw her impatience. 'My apology it took so long, miss... Um... Goddess. The fire had to be lit to boil the kettle.'

'Then you have done well... and, Lisk!'

'Yes, miss... Goddess.' He was nervous and kept forgetting to address her as she requested. Drips of sweat lined his forehead.

'Always remember, when the Goddess of Peace is happy, we can all rest.'

He inclined his head, backed out the cell door and after checking it was locked, both guards turned dutifully to leave her to enjoy her beverage.

Caitlin began to pour the coffee and paused. 'Oh and... Lisk...' She heard him stop. 'Do tell Torin he may have an audience with me in half an hour. I shall be ready to discuss matters a little more civilly by then.' She lifted the cup to him indicating she meant after the painkillers and coffee began to work.

'Yes, miss... Goddess.' He looked embarrassed that he couldn't get it right.

She tut-tutted him and shook her head. 'That will be all, Lisk.' She made sure she dismissed him, instead of the other way around.

He stood staring at her and with a short, sharp military turn, he stomped off.

Caitlin poured the coffees and took the two painkillers and hot drinks over to Jovis and Artisan.

'Can you sit up?' she whispered.

Once they had wiggled up and leant against the wall, she shared the painkillers between them, before handing them cups of coffee to wash it down. 'That will have to do for now. Otherwise, they'll know it's for you and how can it be for you when you're still unconscious.' She tossed her hair over her shoulder with attitude. 'I'll just have to fake another headache later to get more pills.'

In the dim light, she noted Jovis was staring.

'What?' she said.

'Just wondered where you're getting your strength from Cait. When I snatched you, sorry not sure how else to put it, you were so upset and miserable.'

'Yes, that's true, but it was not the capture that upset me, it was taking me deep under the earth where I had spent my whole childhood. Memories flooded back like a smack in the face. I thought I had let go of all that stuff, but I wasn't expecting it and the fear of yesteryear made me weak and angry.'

Jovis breathed out deeply. 'Of course, I didn't understand, but that makes perfect sense now. I didn't feel you tense up until we started going down the elevator shaft. I must admit the first time I did it as a kid, it frightened the life out of me. I should have warned you.

Bloody hell Cait, you should still hate me. That was really mean.'

She put her head on the side and grinned. 'But that was Vador, not my friend Jovis. My Jovis would never hurt me, not ever.'

'I wouldn't.' Jovis smiled. 'I would sooner die than hurt you now I know you. Although I can't say the same for Torin.'

Artisan agreed. 'I can't believe he allowed the coffee. It looked from here as if his head was steaming and about to blow. Never seen him so angry. It actually rendered him speechless.'

Caitlin stood calmly and reached for their cups to take them back to the table. Two of them, she wiped clean with the napkin left, so they didn't know her friends were awake yet.

When she sat back between them, Artisan faced her. 'You may be all soft and sweet smelling on the outside, but there is a whole other thing going on when the redhead fires up. Rocky better hold on tight, because I think he has met his match.'

Jovis chuckled.

'Stop it you two,' she whispered. 'I'm just a woman looking after her friends the only way she knows how. Now get back under the covers and play unconscious for me. He'll be back soon, and I have some more work to do.'

Seconds later, Rocky slammed in, the door to the dungeon almost flung off its hinges by his momentum. His heavy footsteps echoed on the cement floor as he strode with purpose towards them.

Caitlin was already up and on her feet again. She didn't have to act aggravated, as that was how she really felt. She glared at him. It was time to scare him a little. 'Have you contacted my husband yet?'

He didn't answer straight away. She kept saying things that were out of left field, leaving him to wonder why.

'Well, let me tell you, young man, he will have you court marshalled for locking me up like a mere peasant. And Rory and his Riders that you dare scoff at as fools, have the authority to remove a planet if it cannot be reasoned with and is out of control. If you kill me, you will certainly be signing your own death certificate. Well now, speak up. Tell me what you are going to do about this mess you have just caused. I can only help you to a certain point; if you go over that line and harm my friends or me any further, that line will be crossed. After that, I will not use my authority to assist you further.'

Torin crossed his arms defiantly. 'I am waiting for instructions from my boss. You are not he! And although you have made me see I've made a grave mistake, the damage is now done, and you can do nothing to help. As for me, I will take my punishment from him when he comes around. If you can call me when Vador wakes up, I would appreciate it.

'Well!' She threw her hands in the air. 'Thank goodness you have come to your senses, it's about ruddy time. I will call when I'm able to wake him.'

He didn't leave, just stood staring.

'Off you go then.' Her hand movement dismissed him. 'Give me room to work here. He isn't going to respond to me with you loitering about.'

He stood, still riveted to the spot.

'Is there something further I can help you with?' She eyed him with an uppity glare.

'You're so different to the person I met at the resort. I thought you were nicer.'

'And I you, but I guess neither of us turned out to be very good judges of characters.'

Torin hung his head. 'I guess not.' He turned and left.

Once he was gone, she walked back over to Jovis. 'Well, he's broken. Still not the Rocky I know he can be, but better. Now it's up to you. My work here is done.' Caitlin smiled and fell into them both.

They groaned as she dropped on them.

'Oops, sorry, does that hurt?' she said, and poked at Jovis gently. 'Payback can be such a bitch.'

'Look at you!' Jovis poked back playfully. 'The fiery little redhead that brought the giant to his knees. And let me say, he did deserve everything you said to him. His fault for not believing one word of what came out of our mouths.'

Artisan grinned. 'I've got so much rug in my mouth and my gut is aching I've laughed so hard. This story is going to continue to be a doozy even after it's been told for several thousand years.'

Jovis looked at Artisan. 'True, but now it's our turn to handle this. We must sort this out quickly. Get Cait out of this jail and home to some comforts before her husband finds out about this and comes marching in here with the cavalry to take her home. What are your thoughts?'

'I want to kick his derriere back to Earth and find someone more trustworthy.' Artisan gently rubbed where he had been hit, the lines on his forehead deep with pain.

Caitlin sucked in her breath. She could understand that while in pain he would still be cross, but she wondered if he would later regret this rash decision if it went ahead. She moved away and leant against the wall, her eyes closed.

'Cait, what's wrong?' Jovis eyed her sudden change of mood.

She stayed in her relaxed state. 'I'm giving you some privacy to discuss Torin.'

Jovis took her by the hand and she opened her eyes. 'I can't think without you, so don't ignore me. I get that comment upset you so tell us why?'

'You will not like my answer Jovis. You said it yourself, I am a peacekeeper first, and admit, I do find it hard to think like you.'

Artisan looked up. 'Then teach us, peacekeeper.'

Caitlin moved and sat in front of them. On the cement floor, she sat cross-legged, her hands relaxed and rested on each knee. 'Your friend may have got confused, but it did show how passionate he is when protecting this planet. In the end, he showed his loyalty by listening to reason. His thought pattern must have been corrupted somehow; by someone meaning you harm is my best guess. But we already know how he became vulnerable enough for that to happen, don't we?' She raised an eyebrow.

They shook their heads, not getting it.

'Well let me clear that up. You both sit here sore and sorry for yourselves and angry that he let you down.'

They both nodded this time, agreeing.

'And yet it seems to me that it is you two that have let him down.'

Both glanced at one another, their eyes wide.

'What! Come again!' Jovis sat up straight and noble.

'Correct me if I am wrong, but I have been with you for a few weeks now, give or take. I bet during that time you haven't contacted him, and I bet you didn't even ask him to go on that weekend trip to Earth, did you?'

Jovis screwed up his face. 'Truth is I had trouble getting my head around what I was going to do with you, once I had you. Then I really got to know you and it was nice...' He saw her grin. 'Okay, it was great. And at that stage, I didn't want to share you. Artisan understood, felt the same and kept my secret.'

This she understood. She had enjoyed their company too, but this was about their friend. 'So, you can see how your neglect must have affected Torin. I'm also assuming you didn't even contact him to see how he was, as you would normally have done.'

'I guess not,' Jovis admitted.

'For a long-standing friend, as he has been, it's easy for me to see why he went crazy on you. And here lies the problem. If it was him and Jovis doing this to you, Artisan, and you felt they were planning stuff behind your back, how would you react? Not now as you are, all gorgeous and adorable, but before, when you were evil and mean?' She smiled.

'Well, I would have gone ballistic at Rocky first. I doubt I'd say a word to Jovis... but maybe?' He shrugged.

Caitlin turned her focus to Jovis. 'I think you have your answer. Artisan's not as hot-headed, that's all. Now for what is serious. He has hurt you and for that and only that, should he be reprimanded. But never forget, he has shown his loyalty by admitting his stupidity to me, someone he doesn't like. He already stood down, still called you, boss, and showed good character waiting for the worst when he could flee.'

Jovis eyed her, interested in her further thoughts. She fascinated him. 'And if you were me, what would your punishment be to fit this crime?'

She blinked and chewed her lip. 'There is only one thing to think about before working out a suitable punishment. As friends and immortals, we are all going to be together for a very long time. In these many centuries together, we are all going to hurt one another at one time or another. What will determine a special relationship will be the ability to forgive one another,' Caitlin shrugged. 'Do you think we would be sitting here chatting like friends if there had not been forgiveness between us?'

'This is true.' Jovis leant back against the cement wall, thinking.

'One last piece of advice if I may,' she said.

He looked at her. 'My head is aching while working through this Cait, but your words soothe me. Continue, please.'

'It seems your Ice Planets are in trouble right now. If you aren't the instigator of these threats, then who is? And who's next?' She glanced at Artisan. 'Maybe yours, Artisan.' Her eyebrow lifted. 'Think you men need to stop bashing heads and put them together, and quick smart.'

Artisan sat up straighter. 'I hadn't given that any thought. We better rethink this, Jovis. We need to talk with Rocky. Glow is right. What if I'm next? I must get my men ready. We have to find out what he does know. This isn't good.'

'I know, little buddy. I've been thinking exactly that but needed to hear what Cait thought about it, and she is one smart girl. We do need to sort this out with Rocky, and quick smart. What do you think, Cait? If I promise not to kill him as I wanted to a while ago, will you organise the guard to bring Rocky here for a chat so we can get out the hell out of here?' He smiled. 'You really are a true friend to us all, Cait.' He put his arm up. 'Now help Artisan and me up so I can act like the prince you believe me to be.'

'Sure will.' Caitlin jumped to her feet and helped both to stand. Leaving them to lean against the wall, she went over to the bars and called out to the guard.

'Lisk, oh Lisk are you awake?' She called a couple of times before he shook awake and walked to her. 'I need you to take a message to Torin for me. You are to repeat it exactly how I tell you.'

'Yes, Goddess.'

'Tell him, the Prince of the Ice Planets will see him now.' She shooed him away. 'Now off you go.'

He bowed, and his large boots clunked as he turned and left.

She gave Jovis a grin. 'Couldn't help myself; had to do it one last time.'

'Don't go thinking that attitude will work with us my lady,' Jovis warned. 'When we get out of here the Goddess of Peace will be grounded for not doing as she was told. You were to stay in the cave.' He bit his cheek to keep from laughing at her indignant stance.

'Why you ungrateful...' She stopped as the entry door to the dungeon flung open. She leant against the wall between them. 'Gee, that was quick. Rocky's here already. You boys are up.'

He peered in through the bars as he walked to the door of the cell. His hair was all ruffled from obviously running his hand through it while stressed. The second he unlocked the latch and the squeaky bars opened, she felt her powers return. Confident they all had them back and it was now even kilter between these men, she moved away to give them room. She wasn't about to be in the middle of a fist fight, and figured after the way Rocky handled the situation earlier, this was how folks here must go about solving misunderstandings.

Rocky stood still, staring at Jovis and Artisan. 'I want to know why you have both shut me out and... If you weren't planning anything sinister, why all the secrecy?' Rocky raked fingers in his hair before dropping the hand to his side. 'I know you went down to Earth for a couple of days and didn't invite me. I don't understand.'

'Maybe we all have a bit of humble pie to eat,' Jovis said quietly and finally opened up and told his friend why he had been so distant; that he didn't feel he could share Caitlin at that moment. He wanted time to get to know her.

When he finished, Rocky's complexion was red and livid. 'We can see who your favourite is! Art was allowed access. And anyway, why would you want her to stay with you? She is one nasty piece of work, Jovis. How could you trade our friendship for such an absolute bitch?' Rocky glared at her.

'That's enough, Rocky. Art found her in the holding cell down in the dungeon. He ignored my orders and gave her warmth and comfort. Look, it's a long story but believe me, there is no favouritism between you men. You are both my confidantes, and family to me. Well, you were, but if you can't refrain from calling Cait names, this conversation ends now.'

'Whatever.' Rocky folded his arms and dismissed it, not even wanting to discuss her. As far as he was concerned, she acted just like any spoilt goddess. Nothing would change his mind about that.

Jovis grimaced and walked closer to Rocky. 'Now that's said, there is the little matter to address of what you did to me last night.'

Caitlin saw him pull his arm back, but the hit was so quick she didn't see it move. He had punched Rocky in the face. His head smacked back against the wall and the cement behind it crumbled and scattered on the floor with Rocky as he was knocked off his feet. Rocky brought his arm up to protect him but it was too slow, blood gushed from his split nose and lip.

Jovis had hurt his hand and shook it out. 'That feels better already,' he said, smiling.

Rocky looked up at him from the ground while holding a broken nose, not the first one by the looks of the angle it was earlier. 'Okay, I deserved that.' He clicked it back into shape and groaned with the pain before pulling out a rag to soak up blood which gushed out from the nostril adjustment.

Jovis put out his arm, and Rocky pulled himself up. 'Sorry boss,' he said, apologetically, 'I was out of control and wasn't thinking straight.'

'You've got that right. But under the circumstances, I guess I can understand.' Jovis had his hands on his hips.

'You can?' Rocky seemed shocked. 'What... is that it, you forgive me?'

Jovis rubbed his knuckles that still pained him. 'Yes! And the person you should be thanking for that is Cait. If it were up to Artisan and me, we would have kicked your butt back to Earth, and bloody well left you there. You're just lucky you had someone in your corner because we weren't, and I think you still have some major sucking up to do to your other mate over there. He still sports a pretty bad headache from the crack on the head you gave him.'

Rocky drew his brows together. 'Awe I've given him worse than that! He'll get over it. I'm sure in time he'll give me worse.'

Artisan kicked off the wall. 'You bet I will buddy. That busted jaw I gave you last year is nothing to what you'll get for giving me this prize frigging egg on my head.'

'Bring it on baldy.' Rocky's eyes were alight with amusement. 'I swear, living with a sheila has turned you soft.'

Artisan grinned. 'Give you soft when my lady friend is not around blatzing shytzer.'

Caitlin was amazed as she stood listening to how men get over disputes. A smack in the mouth and it's over.

Jovis put his hand out to her. Rocky backed away as Caitlin walked over to join Jovis and Artisan. Facing Rocky's hugeness, she bit her lip. 'I doubt you'd have listened if I acted a mere sheila, am I right?'

He screwed up his lips, summing her up and inclined his head to the side in agreement. 'You look smaller between my boys.'

'I am,' she said.

'You don't look as nasty.' He scratched his head.

'Neither do you.' Her eyes lifted to view him.

'Glow Girl is half your size, you big galoot. She wouldn't hurt a fly.' Artisan put his arm around her protectively.

Caitlin put her hand out to Rocky, and Artisan let her go so she could take a step forward. 'Let's start again. Hi, my name is Glow Girl.' She gave him a smile and because she had forgiven him too, she glowed brightly for just a second.

His head moved back slightly. 'Whoa! Now I know why you get called that.' The surprise over, he held her outstretched hand. 'Wasn't expecting it to be baby-soft.' He noted her cool response. 'Your hand; I thought it would be harder and more powerful.' He let go of it and eyed her. 'I swear you're definitely not the goddess that was here earlier. Where have you hidden her?' His eyes swept the cell.

'Sorry about that, but I protect my friends like a tiger would her cubs. This is just little old me now. Bells and whistles are all gone.'

'You were just acting!' Rocky's mouth was open, eyes wide.

Jovis winked at her and turned back to Rocky. 'After that little performance, I reckon she missed her calling as a world-famous actress. Believe me; she shook like a leaf after you left. Little softie.' He touched her nose affectionately.

Rocky threw his head back and laughed heartily. 'She was shaking.' He slapped his leg. 'Damn girl, my undies needed changing.' This made them all chuckle. He fake-tipped a hat and bent in respect. 'You won, my lady, a pleasure to finally meet you, the real you!'

She glowed again.

'Umm… you're doing that thing again.' He stepped back.

She shrugged. 'It means I'm happy.'

'Really, I have finally pleased the Goddess of Peace.' Rocky grinned before addressing Jovis. 'Hope you guys are able to stay for breakfast. I mean, if the goddess has to wait until you get home, light the fire and cook, she will be one temperamental deity.' He turned to her. 'She hates having to wait, so I'm told.'

'You're very astute.' She used the regal tone. 'Yes! Your goddess will be most displeased.'

They all laughed at her doing the voice and she knew it would not be the last time while dealing with these three rascals. Caitlin linked her arms through Jovis and Artisans. 'Let us follow young Torin to the galley.' She made them smile one last time before she knew it would get serious again. *This might look like it's swept under the carpet, but the culprit who wants Jovis's blood is still at large.* She had more work to do here before they could leave Orcus.

In the dining room, the table was laden with food. Rocky stood with arms folded. 'I figured if the goddess was a ball breaker to me, she would never let you two leave either without us discussing who did attack and why, so I got my chef to cook up a feast.' He pulled out a chair for Caitlin. 'Thank you, Goddess. You sure know your stuff. Glad you didn't give up on me.'

She smiled as she sat. 'You snatched my powers, or I could have made it less painful.'

'I was shocked, even without powers that scent was... well let me just say it really had my men entranced. They pissed me off, they were so in awe of you. Even when I flatly refused to give you anything, they still got you what you wanted. I ended up coming down to tell you no myself. Instead, I stood there powerless against you. Wow, even with your magic gone, you were amazing, that's all I can say.'

Jovis put an arm around her. 'She is; we've never seen her in action before and if that's a glimpse of her peacemaking skills, us bad guys haven't got a hope in hell of getting away with evil doings. Artisan laughed so much I thought he was going to give her act away at one stage.'

Artisan patted Rocky on the back. 'Close your ears, Glow.' He turned to Rocky. 'She had you by the balls, mate, and we loved it.' He laughed again. 'Now let's eat, I'm starving.'

Chapter Twenty-Eight

Medusa

Caitlin was pleased the men had a chance to bond while having a quick bite to eat. It also gave them a moment to discuss the attack more logically. They had only started talking about who could have planned and orchestrated such a hit when Rocky began to look around anxiously. He stopped the conversation. 'Sorry guys, I hate to ask you to eat and run, but I'm getting a feeling this might not be over. My hackles are up, and I can hear a strange buzz, the same sound I heard before this first attack.'

As Jovis stood up, his chair scraped back on the tiled floor. 'What the hell? Why destroy Orcus? It makes no sense. It's blatzing well crazy! Why not take it over?' He held out his arm. 'Caitlin, it's time I got you out of here.' He turned back to Rocky. 'I'll help sort this out when I return.' Facing Caitlin, he frowned. She had stayed seated and shook her head at him, and her stubborn stare bothered him.

'If there is something more headed this way, it's best I stay and help out.' She ignored his second gestured attempt to take her hand.

'Cait, I know you're a Rider, but I believe this is way out of your league. That last hit took out half of Rocky's village and wiped out a quarter of his army and their barracks. The next hit could break up or possibly blow up the entire Ice Planet,' Jovis warned.

She sat back in her seat and folded her arms. 'I hate to burst the male egos here, but this is what I do every day, I save worlds with my team. Trust me. Until we speak to Axon and find out what did happen, he will expect me to stay.' She turned to Rocky who had said he was contacting Alpha Site. 'Did you get that call into Axon? Is he on his way?'

Rocky shook his head. 'The NAVcom system is still down. Have a team working on it but might be a few hours yet before they can get it going. The entire area has sunk. We're still digging men out from under the collapsed tower. It's a mess out there.'

'Sorry mate.' Jovis looked as worried as Rocky. But suddenly his worry was more for Caitlin. *She shouldn't be here, this is too dangerous.* Yet he noted she personally showed no fear. *She must be unaware of the seriousness of this attack. Axon had better get here, or I'll transport her out kicking and screaming.* No way would he allow her to be within cooee of this world if there was another attack coming.

Artisan was worried about her comment too, yet calmed when he saw Jovis's creased forehead when Caitlin said she wanted to stay. Artisan knew Jovis would never allow it. Feeling she was in good hands, Artisan stood. He could now put all his effort into helping his mate Rocky. 'I'll head off now and bring some of my men back to help out.'

'Good idea, Artisan.' Jovis agreed. 'Put the rest of your men on standby in case whoever they are hit your world next.'

'I will.' Artisan transported out. He faded slowly, blew a kiss and waved at Caitlin. She thought it sweet. Even in a crisis, he cared. She had been lucky it was him and not Rocky who found her in the holding cell on Sedna. She was almost sure Rocky wouldn't have given her a second thought. Now knowing the three of them as she did, Artisan was definitely the softie.

'While he's gone, I'll take Caitlin home, so she can speak to Axon in person.'

Again, Caitlin shook her head. Her red curls glittered with sparks showing how serious she was about staying. 'I'm not leaving until the Riders arrive. And I know for a fact if you haven't contacted Axon, he would *not* have deployed them. Small attacks like this are monitored by Alpha Site, but if nothing else is picked up and the ruler doesn't lay a complaint, it's classed as a Home World domestic.

Therefore, Axon needs to be informed if you want his help solving this attack. It's you that needs to do this, Jovis. We both have our strengths, and mine keeps me here to protect Rocky and his men. It's what I do. Well, when I'm not lazing around visiting friends.'

'Axon will be worried sick about you, Cait. I bet he also felt your anxiety last night and won't be happy with any of us. You should come with me in case he thinks it's a trap or something.' Jovis didn't give up trying to get her as far from this danger as he could.

'Axon is no fool and can pick up a lie a mile off. He knows better than anyone why I cannot leave my post and any concerns he has with what went on here will dissolve once I speak with him.'

Rocky interrupted. 'Jovis, we haven't time to argue and let me tell you from experience, she will win in the end, so you may as well give in now.'

'Sorry Jovis, but Rocky's right. You won't win on this one. I'm not leaving my post.' She had a stubborn tilt to her jaw.

'Fine, I'll be back shortly, but we leave as soon as Axon says to, deal?'

'Deal.' She crossed her arms, not moving.

'I should pick you up and take you with me!' He put his hands on his hips.

She grinned. 'But you won't, because deep inside, you've started to trust me. You're starting to believe in my abilities. Am I right?'

'Yes,' he said.

'I'll be fine, seriously.'

'Then no hero acts while I'm gone.' He was still not convinced this was what he should do, but other than carrying her off kicking and screaming, he had no choice. Rocky was right. Time was ticking.

She rolled her eyes at such concern. 'I'm no superwoman, and so you're safe to go.' She smiled and put on the regal tone that made him so amused earlier. 'Now toddle along Prince Charming, the Goddess of Peace hates to be kept waiting.'

After Jovis left she marvelled at how quickly his injuries had all but healed. Caitlin could feel his power surge when worried and was almost positive the energy of magic he projected matched Jett's. To have these royals meet before Jovis was ready might be dangerous for both parties if they don't see eye to eye. She shuddered at the thought.

While her two friends were gone, Rocky received some images saved from an overhead NAVcam. It was the only one not destroyed in the blast but it had been disabled, so knew the images weren't going to be as good as he hoped. 'Well, this seems to be all we have at the moment if you want to take a look Glow.' He showed it as a hologram, so they could both watch.

Caitlin peered into the image. 'Can you enlarge that area?'

'No problem.' Rocky lifted his arms and used his hands to enlarge the image in the air. 'How's that look?'

Caitlin squinted and stood to view it closer. 'There!' She pointed. 'Shards of ice and debris; this is all too familiar to me. A comet did this.'

'I was sure it was an asteroid. But clearly, I was wrong,' he agreed.

She turned to Rocky. 'My guess is it came from an enemy somewhere in the Oort cloud region. It looks like you've really ticked off a ruler from one of the ice bodies, outside of Kuiper's belt. It's out of our solar system but with luck, still in our jurisdiction.'

'Cait is correct, and yes still zoned under my authority.' They both swung around to see Axon, who surprised them with his answer.

'You're here!' And within a few steps, Caitlin was in his arms getting a hug. 'I missed you!'

'I missed you too, beautiful; are you okay now?'

'For a change, it wasn't about me... it was these men fighting. I ended up playing the goddess card.' She winked.

'Pulled out the big gun to fix it did you?' Axon's eyes sparkled at his gifted wife.

'Yep! Damned if it didn't work. Unfortunately, I can't do any more here so was hoping you'd help me.'

He smiled. 'It's so unlike you to ask for my help. I'm flattered.' He let her go. 'So let's see what Rocky's found that we haven't.'

She followed him back to the table where the image still projected.

'Doesn't look good, does it.' She watched for his reaction.

'Actually, it's worse.' He moved closer to view the damage and saw it was apparently an earlier image.

Jovis had joined them too and stood beside Rocky. 'You might as well tell him, Axon. 'He has to organise his men and quick smart.'

Axon gestured towards the outer regions and overlapped the original with images he'd brought along, which opened up the damaged area considerably. 'Sorry to be the bearer of bad news but there was considerably more destruction than what we see here. There were also several ground blasts. A traitorous criminal is amongst you working with an outer Oort Ruler. They planted bombs which were timed perfectly to go off at the exact moment the comet hit. The worst of it is they have taken out your underground NAVbase completely. We have data showing it's destroyed. There is no repairing that one, Rocky, the entire tower will need to be replaced. This is the reason your men have been unable to fix it for you.'

'Are you positive? Blatzing hell, Axon, it's my only line of defence, I need that tower.' Rocky crossed his arms.

'Agreed and that's why it was the first thing I discussed with Jovis when he came to me. He gave us permission to order a new one.'

'Thank the blatzing heavens for that.' Rocky breathed a sigh of relief.

'A team made up of consultants and professionals in this field of expertise will be arriving shortly. They have been given orders to help with the construction of a new one. I'll leave you and Jovis to work out who you can spare to help them and where you want it placed.' He lifted his arm and motioned towards the damaged area they viewed. 'Whoever did this, wants you unable to communicate with anyone.'

'They didn't plan on us knowing Glow and asking for your help. Alpha Site is the last place they would have expected us to get support from. I mean considering we're not actual planet status yet.' Rocky spoke gratefully to Axon. 'That's why I really appreciate what you are doing for me Axon, thank you.' He smiled and put out his hand, wanting to shake the hand of the man who had come to help, no questions asked.

Axon responded and shook it. 'I hope this convinces you we aren't the bad guys and that you'll allow my team entry into your airspace. Can't risk them coming up against the dark destroyers that Jovis here, keeps as extra security around your worlds.' Axon smiled at Rocky, but it was Jovis that intervened.

'Can't say we've ever needed help before, or will again. But we do appreciate you giving us a hand on this one. Normally we know who our enemies are and our spies alert us to any pre-planned attacks. But this, if you are right, and it did come from the outer Oort cloud, has got me stumped. What would someone out there want with this planet?'

Axon knew by Jovis not yet giving him an access code right then and there that he was far from being ready to seek more help or speak to Jett. Something big would have to happen before he trusted them further. He turned to Cait, and could see in her eyes she already knew this and wouldn't be coming home anytime soon. He missed her like hell, yet had to agree she was good at what she did. These men had lost the harshly irritable lines that creased their foreheads when they first met. The dark eyes and untrustworthy glares had gone. Artisan had just transported in, and if it weren't for the tattoos and bald head, Axon would not have recognised him at all. Her mission was still going, and he knew by her professionalism in how she addressed them and spoke to them while he contemplated doing more of a sell, that she had this. What Caitlin did need of him was to help find the criminal behind the attack. He was glad she did, as it gave him a chance to see her if only for a while.

His eyebrows suddenly pressed together. Usually, the criminals came to her. So if Jovis and his boys weren't the problem, who was? His stomach flipped and he took a silent deep breath. This mission had only just begun for her. He was going to have to be strong. He suddenly realised they were both in for one bumpy ride.

'Hi Axon! Wasn't expecting to see you here. Thanks for coming mate.' Artisan shook Axon's hand and smiled as if they were old friends.

Even though Axon showed there were no hard feelings between them, he did have a long memory. For now, he had to remember Cait was not only making them accept her, but he came in the package as her husband. It was nice to be welcomed with a handshake, though. *Maybe Artisan is different.*

'Glad I can be of some help. It's not only here on Orcus we monitor, but we have eyes on Quaoar and Sedna. Anything heading for them should be picked up by Alpha Site, but there is always a chance the criminals will tamper with our satellites. If this happens, I have my best man on the job right here.'

Artisan looked around. 'Who's that? Do I get to meet him?'

Caitlin put her hand up. She was listening to them as well as talking to Jovis and Rocky. 'That would be me!'

'What!' Artisan stared at Axon. 'You're kidding me. Sure, I've seen her do some fireworks, but that's child's play. We're talking meteors and supernovas deliberately slammed into our worlds. That's not funny, Axon. You're kidding, right!'

Suddenly an alarm went off and within a split second, Axon transported Jovis, Rocky, Artisan and Caitlin outside. 'Highest point Rocky, think?' Axon yelled at him.

Rocky pointed. 'That mountain where the tip is lost in the cloud.'

Again, Axon transported them. It was time they saw how valuable Caitlin was to the universe... Time they took better care of her if she was going to be with them for a while.

Upon the hill and between the broken clouds, they had a clear view of the damage below. Jovis had heard Artisan's comment and knew Axon had included them to see Caitlin in action. He was excited. Had never seen a Cosmic Rider at work and his hands were sweaty in anticipation of what they were about to witness. This was the first time he didn't worry. Axon was here too and would take care of their Cait.

As far as Jovis could see, the sky above was clear, yet Caitlin stood still and stared up into the emptiness. *Was she even breathing?* There was absolutely no movement. He glanced at Artisan and Rocky who shrugged, seeing nothing either, and back to Axon, who stood calmly beside her. His arms were folded, and he watched her and occasionally glanced up too.

'Got a lock on it yet Cait?' he finally asked.

'Hang on, there's a problem. The team has readjusted the hold on the weapon, and it's beginning to spiral out of control.'

'Why?' Axon stared upwards, trying to see what she could.

'The entire team has been ordered to avert their eyes from trouble heading straight towards them.'

'What trouble?' He watched her, surprised.

'Medusa is on her way. She must think they're the threat. The noise up there is preventing me tuning into Medusa to see if I can pull her out.'

Axon swung around, annoyed. 'Jovis, call your beast off. Medusa is heading for my Riders.'

Jovis only now understood what Caitlin watched. Axon's team of Riders had arrived, and somehow, she could see what was going on without using any NAVequipment. *I'll be damned, she has superhuman vision.* What else was this woman capable of? With no time to think further, he transported to Sedna. There he rushed to get the unique siren he kept to call Medusa back. It was supposed to work on all the dark destroyers, well, so he hoped. This was the first time he ever needed to use it. Medusa would inevitably turn Axon's Riders to stone if they looked into her eyes.

Fumbling and heart racing, he keyed in the security code to his hideout. The elevator seemed to take forever, but his powers to transport didn't include travel that far underground. Only Hades had power enough to go through earth's crust.

By the time he reached the hidden room in the dungeon and located the switch behind a loose brick, sweat poured down his forehead and stung his eyes. He wiped them with his sleeve so he could see the panel. Finally, with blurry eyes, he punched in the code... nothing happened. 'What the hell!' He wiped his eyes again, allowing him to re-enter the code. Ear-piercing squeals sounded out. Both hands went to his ears. The noise so intense it brought him to his knees. It lasted a few seconds and switched off. He prayed it was enough. *Next time I'll use NAVtect ear silencers.* His ears still rang as he grabbed the hand whistle and dashed to the lift which took him topside. Locking up before he left, he transported back to the top of the mountain.

'Cait, has Medusa turned around?' Jovis called to her and waited for a response.

Axon shook his head. 'She started to leave, but something drew her back. She's almost there again.'

'I don't get it, we have a deal. Medusa must stop and return to the cave if the warning is sounded. It means I'm okay with whomever it is she has bailed up, and they are to be given free passage into our airspace,' Jovis growled. He was cross and not sure what else would stop her.

Axon pinched his lips, unimpressed. This was his team in trouble. 'Caitlin, I know you and Rory have something special you do that you have always kept secret from the others. I understand you want to both keep it a hush-hush as Rory will lose control of the team if they could use telepathy back, but this is life or death. I want you to use it now!' he barked. 'Call the team off; get them to land here on this mountain.'

She swung around with her mouth open. It surprised her that he knew.

Axon was flushed, and his gut churned for his team. 'You must complete the mission from here. There is no time for Rory to relay your message. Cait, I want them out of Medusa's line of sight! And I want them here, where Jovis can protect them. Now! And that's an order.' He yelled to get her to snap out of her surprised state.

Without a word, her body gave him her answer. The sharp snap of her head, just one nod and like a trained soldier she turned stiff and confident. Her eyes closed, and all was deathly quiet.

Jovis figured she must have been communicating with the team. To learn that was what they did was a massive disclosure on its own to share in front of him and his boys. It dawned on him at that moment, how much Cait trusted them. Jovis felt a pang of pride he

He smiled for the first time since the ordeal had begun. 'Bravo,' he applauded.

His boys did too. The three of them whistled and cheered until Caitlin and the team was done.

'What a show.' Jovis stood in awe of them. The three men had arms around one another, and the thrill still shook them.

The horses landed, the Riders somersaulted off them and ran to Caitlin. The team and Axon were in a group hug when Jovis noticed Medusa struggling, almost free. He whistled and called out, 'Hey! Guys, what's the decision about my security. She's about to rid herself of the net.'

The rest of Caitlin's friends moved from her as she put her hand up and removed the magic that encased Medusa. None of them looked up, not even Caitlin. Her trust that Medusa would not harm her fascinated Jovis because he saw real fury in the creature's eyes. *Or did she trust I would protect her?* As she swooped in close to the top of Caitlin's head, Jovis put the magic whistle in his mouth and blew hard. It was so high pitched only she was meant to hear it. It was the only way he could think of to snap her out of her rage. When the creature stilled, his arm went out, and he pointed towards Sedna. 'Go now!' he roared.

His focus shifted to Lisha, who groaned at the same time as Medusa, and covered her ears with her hands.

'Sorry Lisha. That was meant for her ears only. Didn't know your hearing was supersonic on top of your other gifts.'

'Just me, freak,' Lisha yelled at him. 'Try sticking headphones on and turning your NAVboom up full blast. Then triple it... blatzing hell!' She rubbed her ears.

He grinned. 'I'm sure you can handle it after what I've seen you do.' Then he glared back at Medusa who still hovered overhead. 'I swear, Medusa, you ever disobey me again, and you will pay dearly! I'll destroy you myself!' He lifted his fist in the air.

Medusa took one last glance at Jovis, smiled at him and slithered off, back to where she came. Was it a polite way of her apologising or was she smiling because he had also hurt another? Either way, he would want more than that when he went to see her. *She had better have a damned good explanation for ignoring an order to stop and return.*

Caitlin saw Jovis, Rocky and Artisan looking up at her. 'What! How come you guys can look at her and not turn to stone? I don't get it.'

'We found a spell that prevents any of the dark destroyers influencing us. That's the reason we work so well with them. Medusa is a loose cannon, so she stays with me on Sedna. I like crazy.' Jovis grinned.

Caitlin was curious. This was the first time they had spoken of the dark destroyers. Jett had told her a little of them, but after seeing Medusa from a safe distance, she wondered where the others lived. She closed the gap between them. 'But I have heard the Avengers are worse. They sound even creepier. Is it true they are winged women who dress in black robes, blood drips from their eyes and snakes twist in their hair? Now *they* sound hideous.'

Rocky let out a deep low throated laugh. 'They are the furies and are mine. They live in caves many miles from here. They are loners and really, apart from, as you say, looking hideous, they are really very nice. But do the crime, they will hunt down the guilty and show no mercy.'

She eyed Artisan. 'Are you serious? You have the smelly Harpies. I'm told their sound is ghastly and the smell they give off is nauseating. Yet you smell nice all the time. Where do they live? Obviously not near you.'

He put up his hands. 'Hell no! They have wings and huge clawed feet. They are not allowed anywhere near my home or village. Those screamers live high up in the mountains. They watch the skies for me but if they are upwind, they know to head underground, or they are in big trouble. Mess with me, and those screamers cop it good. I reckon mine are the worst, but Jovis insists I keep em' around. Glad I do now.'

Axon joined them. He had to go, but before that, he wanted to make sure Jovis understood what he allowed him to witness was a sign of good faith. 'Duty calls, but there is one thing I want to make perfectly clear, Jovis. I could have ordered Cait to kill Medusa.' Axon stared at him. 'There is no good reason why I should let you keep this creature of doom. The dark destroyers were the reason I couldn't bust in here and take Cait home. And you do know they will not be helpful for these death star attacks.'

The muscle in Jovis's jaw moved as the conversation touched on his capture of Caitlin. He'd known it had to happen but hoped it wouldn't be now. Caitlin had told him Axon didn't mince words. If he had something to say he would. He needed Axon's help and trusted him after this, as Axon had trusted him sharing the magic of his superior group. He stood unwavering. 'I do appreciate you keeping my pet alive, and agree totally, we will need more help. I can clearly see your team is very capable of stopping these attacks, but we still need to get to the bottom of who is doing this and why.'

'Alpha Site will have monitored that last attack. If we have the direction it came from, that's where we'll start searching. As for my team of Riders, they can't fight what is coming as well as your out of control security. Keep your dark destroyers restrained, Jovis, or I'll pull my team out.'

Jovis gave him a nod. 'Understood. I have no clue why Medusa ignored me. But I will get on it as soon as I'm back on Sedna.' He looked at Caitlin. 'Why are you smiling? Medusa could have ruined everything.'

'I'm smiling because I know why... Medusa is the mother of Pegasus.'

'You're kidding,' Axon and Jovis said together. They stood with mouths wide open.

'I was able to communicate with her once she was caught. Medusa wasn't chasing our guys, she was inquisitive, that's all.'

'Hey Rory,' Axon called out, sounding amused. 'Medusa wasn't after you guys at all. She was checking out her grandkids. She gave birth to Pegasus.'

Suddenly a severe situation went from evil scary to intriguing. The team had fun with it, and Rory called back to Axon, 'Great Grandmamma Medusa, who would have thought.'

'Okay, well that solved that mystery.' Axon put an arm around Caitlin's shoulders and gave her a squeeze. 'No wonder you didn't attempt to hurt her. I should know better. There is always a reason for all you do, or don't do.'

Caitlin smiled. 'Are you sure you have to leave? You can't visit for a while?'

He touched her nose. 'When I look into those adorable eyes, I wish I could play hooky and stay. But this won't fix itself.'

Rocky stepped forward. 'You and the Riders are welcome to come back later, Axon. We're having a dinner party tonight.'

'Love to but maybe next time. The Riders and I were on our way to an outbreak in sector 3 before we diverted here. When Rory gives me the nod it's safe, we'll have to head off.'

'If you do sort it out early and change your mind, better head over to Sedna. This venue is far too unstable to host.' Jovis entered the conversation. He spun around to Rocky. 'Hell, with everything going on I forgot all about it. Can it be cancelled?'

'Not on your nelly,' Rocky insisted. 'That's an owner you don't want to tick off. I'll transport them across when they arrive. Best to get ready after you send your little lady here home. She's best away from our wingding. In her own bed, she'll get a better rest and a much-deserved one after her big day.' He eyed Caitlin. 'No disrespect Cait, but it will be a big night and us boys tend to loosen up after a drink or two, and the company will certainly not be of your standing if you get my drift.' He winked.

'What if you get attacked again? Shouldn't you be on duty?' she asked.

'We have our procedures, and I have good men here that are well trained in combat. Axon has a team coming to give me eyes; they are rebuilding my communication tower, and until then I will be leaving a skeleton crew here. It's just too dangerous to leave my planet unprotected like that. I don't want anyone else killed.' Rocky shared his next planned movements with her.

Jovis breathed out heavily. 'Sorry, Cait. I didn't give it a thought. We would have come here for dinner and left straight after. Now I'm hosting, and Rocky's right, this dinner can't be cancelled at this late date, and it will likely be a big night. Go home with Axon, have a good night's rest, and I'll come and get you tomorrow. Maybe when you're fresh, you can help us nut out our next move.'

'Sounds good to me,' Caitlin agreed.

Artisan pushed past Jovis. 'Don't listen to those two fools, Glow. Stay for the party, I'm not even interested in any of what that big-noting, loud-mouth owner ever offers. I don't even like him. Be my date.' He smiled with innocence and caring.

'I'm not interested, either.' Jovis frowned at Artisan's effort to secure Caitlin's full attention. 'I was trying to be polite and give her an out if she wanted some time with Axon that was all... Idiot!' He pushed Artisan out the way. He smiled at Caitlin. 'You're most welcome to stay. I hope you know that was just me doing you a favour after what you just did for us. That was beyond being a good friend. No one person has ever laid their life on the line like that for me before.' The pure tone and gaze were something none of them expected. He turned to Axon. 'Is she allowed to stay, or do you need her where you're going? We've just witnessed how valuable she is to you too.'

Axon shook his head. 'I insist she stays. Caitlin is the only one who can help you at this stage while the Riders are busy. Party or not, my girl will keep your three worlds safe.' He snapped his fingers and summoned Rory over to them.

'What's up boss?'

Rory's manner was friendly and yet, there was an air about this leader of the elite team. His eyes glowed brightly as they had when he first arrived. His magic must have been powering up ready to lead his team off their world. His entire aura was pure in spirit and Jovis felt a little out of place in the presence of such greatness. Caitlin, Axon, Rory and his team were terrific. He was royalty himself but felt like bowing to these angels of the sky. He was fascinated, and instead of wishing them gone, he found himself wanting them to stay awhile so he could get to know them better.

Axon folded his pocket-size NAVcom and slipped it into his

cargo green shirt. 'Jovis has to leave to organise a dinner party. I'm sure you agree it's best Cait stays.'

Rory nodded.

'If your team feels it's safe enough now, I'd like us to get going too.'

'Lisha has been listening and just relayed it was all clear. Was about to saddle up the men when you called. We're good to go.' Rory folded his arms. 'You be right here alone, Cait? I can leave Nathen if you need back up.'

'I'm fine now, but thanks for the power boost. Do you want some of it back? Didn't use its entirety.'

'All good, keep it. We came directly from training with the Cloud Riders so had plenty to spare.' He grinned.

'That explains why you were loaded.' Her eyes and tone of voice gave away what good friends they were.

With that, Rory winked at her before turning to shake Jovis's, Artisan's and Rocky's hands. 'Leaving me best Rider here so you shouldn't need us, but if she gets in any difficulty, you now know where to find Axon.' He stared at Jovis, his eyes menacing. 'Do—Not—Hesitate! You have now seen how important she is to us, so *don't* stuff up our *trust* in you.' His warning was heard loud and clear.

'I won't let you down again, that I promise,' said Jovis. His arm rested on Caitlin's shoulder. 'I get it now and fully understand.'

'Good man.' Rory turned and playfully ruffled Caitlin's hair. 'Don't be a stranger, Red, you know where I live.' Then he inclined his head to Jovis, 'Prince, boys.' He included Rocky and Artisan, and with the swiftness he arrived he was back on his horse and had the team in the air.

Axon gave Caitlin a hug and while still holding and smiling at her disappeared from sight.

'He'll have to teach me that.' Artisan slapped his pants leg excitedly. 'What a cool exit.'

Caitlin shook her head, grinned and eyed Jovis. 'Guess we have a party to organise.'

CHAPTER TWENTY-NINE

Mysterious Magic

On Sedna, they landed in front of the fortress with many of Rocky's staff. Unable to host it in the castle for fear of enemies still at large, Jovis opened up his dining and ballroom which had never been used. The door was hidden behind a large bookshelf, and once Jovis unlocked the security door, Caitlin saw why the room had been kept secret. The magnificence of it with the scale of treasures displayed behind glass was most impressive, and in her field, she thought she had seen it all. Jewels set in gold ornaments and massive ancient sculptures and figurines were cased and filled every wall. With the roof so high and tastefully decorated, the grandness stopped Caitlin in her tracks to admire all she saw. *So this is where he stored the family heirlooms and treasures.*

Off to the left of the room was a dream kitchen and this is where Chef Kully used his size and weight to push past them. Ignoring Jovis's glare, he grunted and proceeded to throw orders to the staff he had brought with him. Rocky grinned and shook his head. 'He can be a right pain, but you'll never eat better vittles than he dishes up. Chef's just moody because we took him from his comfort zone. Best leave him to it.' He held the door open so they could leave.

Jovis didn't look impressed. 'They're your people, Rocky, and you may trust them, but I don't. I want this room out here guarded. If one thing goes missing, I hold you responsible.'

With no more said, Rocky turn and whispered to the man beside him and within seconds the room filled with guards.

Jovis looked happier. 'Once they're done with serving I want the place left as it was before you came. As soon as they're finished, all these people had better be gone and this room locked. Understood?'

Rocky bowed his head. 'Goes without saying.'

As they walked back to the dining room, the table was being laid with candelabra, fruit bowls and delicate gold-trimmed china. A tall, thin gentleman dressed in tails ordered around a few middle-aged women dressed in traditional maid attire. Caitlin grinned at them scurrying around getting organised. 'Now this is how I would expect a prince to live.' She yawned. The power used to eliminate the treat only moments before had taken its toll on her. 'Sorry about that.' She had covered her mouth politely. 'Seems you're all sorted, I'm heading to my room to get some rest. That's of course if I'm not needed.'

Jovis held her hands. 'We slept most of the night while you cared for us and bet you didn't get an ounce of rest yourself. You must be exhausted from that alone, never mind fighting my pet and saving a planet straight after.' He smiled and released her hands. 'You look pale, so how about I send up some hot chocolate to help you sleep better.'

Caitlin yawned again and waved a hand as she headed to the door to go to her room. 'Not needed, but thanks for the thought.' She suddenly stopped and turned. 'Forgot to ask, what's the dress code?'

'Formal,' Jovis said and grinned at her look of horror. His unheated home was hardly the temperature for such attire. 'I promise to crank up the fireplaces and have the dining area toasty warm.'

'You know my magic will change my dress if you're telling fibs,' she playfully warned. 'And no more fighting.' She waved a finger at them. 'Not unless you want the Goddess of Peace to return.'

Rocky laughed. 'Hell no! Keep her under lock and key. I'd sooner face the Kraken.'

Caitlin chuckled as she left. Rocky was a funny man. She was glad they had sorted out their differences. Jovis needed his two friends. They were opposites yet centred him perfectly. She looked forward to a good night with the three of them.

In her room, she flung herself on the bed, and her clothes changed to warm PJs and thick bed socks. Too sleepy to crawl under the sheets, she wrapped herself up in the bed cover and now warm, drifted off to sleep.

Upon waking, she heard water splashing and went into the bathroom to investigate. A maid poured the last buckets of hot water needed to fill the tub. 'Oh, wow, not used to such luxury here, thank you.' Caitlin was thrilled someone had thought to boil water enough to fill the tub.

After a nice long warm soak without being disturbed, Caitlin finally got out, and after drying herself, allowed magic to dress her. But tonight, it left her looking … well far from how she wished to be clothed. The room wasn't as warm as they promised, so the after five cocktail dress she hoped for wasn't going to happen no matter how hard Caitlin tried to change it. The deep green velvet evening dress, although fitted exceptionally well, did remind her of a saloon girl in the old westerns she used to watch, right down to the low-cut bustline and bolero that did nothing to hide her girls. 'Looks like you two are out to play tonight. Who are you out to impress?' She attempted to tuck them in further to no avail. She had to admit these gowns were a style she was becoming accustomed to since merging with the Rider magic. With a shrug, she walked from the mirror, and the long skirt opened and revealed fishnet stockings and black high-heeled boots. 'All I need now is a whip!' She picked up one of the lanterns and went back into her bedroom. Here, on the bed, the servants had left her a long black fur coat. She was warm enough in what she had on, so she left it to put on later.

Near the toasty open fire, she lifted her leg and rested her foot on the stool. As she bent to adjust the laces that did up the side of her boot, she heard a little whistle and straightened up.

'Nice look.' Artisan smiled.

'Thanks. I couldn't change it, so I'm going with the saloon girl look. Hope it's okay.'

'You have your goddess scent turned up again. You're damn near irresistible, but trust me, you won't need it. We've entertained this ruler many times before and never had an issue with him or his entourage he drags everywhere with him. He can be quite funny and has helped Rocky out numerous times with staffing.' Artisan tried to help her calm down.

If the guests were credible, Caitlin now worried the power she had used destroying the death star might have set it off unnecessarily. 'I'll try and tone it down,' she said, closing her eyes to concentrate.

'Don't.' He spoke quietly. 'It feels so good being this happy, so don't spoil it for me. Jovis won't care either.'

'If you're sure you're all right with it. I think I overused my powers and my mechanism is thinking I will need protecting until they are fully recharged. Some good food and it will sort itself out.'

'Then let's not feed you,' he joked and, picking up her fur coat, put his other arm out to escort her downstairs. As he walked out with her, he gave her a charming smile. 'Have I mentioned you look a knockout?'

'You're just saying that because I have that goddess thing going on,' she teased. 'I have... you under my spell.' They both laughed, and Caitlin was left wondering if she was also under a spell tonight. She felt good and was very happy. Like Cinderella, she looked forward to this night with an eager step.

At the top of the stairs, she noted the guests had already arrived. A group of three women walked in first, then Rocky, who held the door for another four men and a woman. This was a group of people he would have just transported from his Home World to the party here.

'I wasn't expecting so many guests.' Cait leant in and spoke to Artisan.

'Nitarn never travels alone.'

'Who are the girls by the fire?'

'Nitarn brought them as entertainment for us, even though me and Jovis have insisted we're not interested. I guess this is his way of thanking us for this dinner in his honour. You can see why I said I'd look after you, although these three are slightly better than the ones he brought last time.'

Caitlin saw beyond the tacky dress code, too much jewellery and way too much make-up. They could be so much more than entertainment but her mission was these men and she had to stay focused.

Artisan leant closer. 'I've been told those three men just entering now are rulers of our guest of honour's other Ice Planets.'

'So out in this quadrant in these dark, icy corners of the universe, are there many of these multi Ice Planet owners?'

'It is only those with merciless natures or a selected few who have good business skills that become multi-owners. Our honoured guest is one of the good guys. Come, and I'll introduce you.' He took her hand. 'You may as well get to know as many of the Ice Planet rulers as you can while you're here.' Then he leaned in close and whispered, 'after all, you are their Peace Goddess too.'

She put a finger to her lips and smiled as she hushed him. 'Best keep that a secret for now.'

When they reached the dinner guests, Jovis put out his hand to Caitlin's, kissed it and turned her to face the visitors. The gesture made her feel like a princess, and she received a warm welcome when introduced to his friends. The last introduction was the man standing in the shadows. She could feel his eyes devouring her, and when he stepped forward and was under the brightness of the chandelier, Jovis introduced him. 'Caitlin, this is our good friend, Nitarn. Like me, he is a multi-owner of other Ice Planets, and the wisdom he has imparted to help me acquire my last Ice Planet is the reason for this dinner party. Tonight, this is to celebrate that deal and also a thank you for the time he has invested helping Rocky.'

Feeling something amiss, she quickly summed him up as untrustworthy and not such a likeable character. But her opinion changed for the better once he was closer to her. Nitarn's complexion was dark, much more so than Jovis's, yet it was his eyes she was drawn to the most. They were so black; they tinged purple as he stared at her. Caitlin found him to be entirely different to how she first perceived him to be and liking his vibe now, put out a hand in a sociable gesture. 'Pleasure to meet you; I look forward to getting to know you.' She blinked when he moved to shake her hand, surprised when his pitch-black hair shone purple under the candlelight. He fascinated her, and once the introductions were over, she stood beside him, engrossed in the way he spoke about his Home World. He was so forthright it helped ease the last niggling first impressions.

He was attentive and while in a conversation with Caitlin, the other three men and one of the women stood quietly beside him. At first, Caitlin tried to move away to give them space, but Nitarn was not having that and ignored the others, keeping her captivated by divulging secrets regarding his four Ice Planets, Ixon, Varuna, Vesta and Pallas. Caitlin was aware he was over sharing but had a feeling he did so to make her feel comfortable around him. Because of his honesty, she lingered beside him. Interested to find out more about this unusual man she was actually starting to like.

'With four to choose from, it must have been hard to decide which world to call home?' She was intrigued after he said he had acquired them all at the same time.

'I chose to make Ixon my home because my favourite sport is skiing.' He shrugged as if it was a no-brainer. 'The continuous snow falling over the mountain ranges ensures perfect conditions to ski all year round.'

Caitlin related to that as Pluto gave her the same enjoyment, although she kept those thoughts private.

He broke off the conversation when his friend, the woman, became restless. Caitlin couldn't help noticing she had one icy stare.

He turned from Caitlin to speak to the friends he had put in charge of Varuna, Vesta and Pallas. It was now she realised the woman who wouldn't leave his side was from his Home World, Ixon. He addressed her as his commanding officer, but from the way she threw daggers towards Caitlin, it was apparent there was much more to their relationship. Caitlin watched as she acted overly interested in his every word and demanded his full attention, flipping her hair and moving, so she was directly in front of him. This action pushed Caitlin back from them. The sneaky manoeuvre kept her entirely out of the conversation, and the frozen smile flashed at Caitlin as she did it, which made her shudder inwardly. *I'll stay clear of you tonight.*

Caitlin took this as her cue to leave and headed towards the three sleazily dressed ladies by the fire. They were having fun, and before long she was laughing again and enjoyed the banter between them. She liked them. They were down to earth and at least showed no jealousy.

When Nitarn joined them, he astounded her by his persistence. He had given the others the flick and joined the fun group. Without frozen lady, he was even more entertaining. He had Caitlin and the girls in fits of laughter telling stories of his travels to Earth and what he and his mates got up to while there.

While listening to him, Caitlin glanced over to see what his ruler friends were doing. Jovis and Artisan had joined them, and it looked as if the visitors were finally having a good time. They even had ice lady laughing. *What!* Maybe it was her goddess scent that was getting her mad. Perhaps ice lady could smell it, but that was unusual as the fragrance was only ever picked up by men. She smiled inwardly. *To look as she does, maybe frozen lips has too much testosterone from all that bodybuilding.* Her voice was deep and those arm muscles... *so not normal.*

Nitarn turned to see what she was staring at and put his drink down on the table. He had lost her interest. 'Come.' He put his hand out to Caitlin.

She accepted and followed him into the main dining room. She thought it enchanting and magical as the flames from burning fires and candles flickered and reflected in the crystal on display. To the left was a quaint dance floor with a trio playing; a piano, harp and violin, no singer, just music. It was here they stopped, and Nitarn bowed.

'Would you do me the honour of having this dance?'

Two of the rulers must have seen him take Caitlin into the other room, for they picked partners and moved on to the dance floor before she had even agreed. She was about to say no, but instead shrugged. 'While in Rome...' She smiled.

'What does this mean?' he asked.

'Yes, it means yes!' She chuckled as he swung her into the unfamiliar dance the others were doing. He was a skilled dancer and moved her efficiently while teaching her the dance, which was a lot of fun once she got the hang of it. Before the number had finished, they were interrupted.

'May I?' Jovis cut in on Nitarn who didn't look impressed.

Halfway through the next dance, the head waiter called for them to be seated.

Jovis pulled out a chair for Caitlin. Ignoring table etiquette, Nitarn slipped into the chair next to her. Jovis rolled his eyes at Caitlin. He was ticked off he had to sit two seats from her as the seating arrangements alternated males and females. He kicked himself for not using card placements. Not liking the idea of Caitlin associating with someone he hadn't known for very long, he watched like a hawk. He noted that during the meal, Nitarn kept her glass full of wine and every chance he got, stole her attention. After dinner, a few of them got up to dance. Jovis was irritated with the ruler who wouldn't allow them a look in with Caitlin and took this opportunity to ask her to dance.

Nitarn looked up and saw Jovis's gaze go from Caitlin to the dance floor. He guessed Jovis's plan and turned back to Caitlin. 'We were interrupted earlier. Would you come back on the dance floor with me? We were having so much fun.'

'I think I've had a bit too much wine for dancing.' She smiled politely, hoping he couldn't read minds. She was fine, just wanted time to catch up with some of the other guests.

He stood up. 'Come on, just one. I promise to look after you.' His smile was charming.

Caitlin took his hand and allowed him the pleasure of one more dance since he asked so nicely. This time he was surprisingly careful and being so light on his feet and with his movements so gentle, he had her relax into him.

'You're a very nice dancer,' Caitlin commented while easily following his steps any which way he wished her to move. Looking over his shoulder her smile brightened when seeing Jovis and Artisan.

Both danced with a couple of the ladies she had befriended. All four couldn't have seemed more suited to one another. However, Nitarn had taken up much of her time, and she decided to break from him to try to chat with the other rulers. This was her only opportunity to learn more about their worlds, and Nitarn was too often off topic, talking about his travels, mostly to Earth. She looked over at Nitarn's female companion and saw she was speaking to Rocky. This was her chance to approach these guys and build relations with other Ice Planets. As a Rider, she needed to be friendly no matter what the reception.

At the end of the number, Caitlin stopped dancing and smiled. 'Time we joined your friends.'

'That lot, they'll be fine.'

'Come on, they don't look as if they're enjoying themselves at all. Let's go brighten them up.' She pulled his hand, giving him no choice but to follow. 'You do all get on, don't you?' If she ever went to their Ice Planets, it would be nice to have some type of connection. 'I feel I'm dragging you over to your enemies.'

This comment changed his entire attitude. He straightened and put a spring in his step as he walked beside her. *What was his deal with these three men and this woman?* Why would he ignore them most the night and choose to be with her instead, considering it really ticked off the female in the group? *He didn't seem a snob, yet sure acted like one...*

'Hey, where are you off to,' she heard Jovis call out.

Caitlin stopped and turned to see Artisan and Jovis standing with their dance partners.

'I thought we'd go chat to Nitarn's friends,' she called back. She could see their eyes were a little glazed. It was a party and she wasn't surprised they were letting their hair down. She, on the other hand, had stuck to drinking the Moonjuice, a beverage that didn't affect her judgment if later she needed to work. Since Nitarn didn't know this, Caitlin used it to act slightly intoxicated to manipulate him into leaving the dance floor. She was glad when she was no longer in the circle of his arms. In them, there was a strange controlling vibe that made her feel uncomfortable.

'Too late, they're leaving.' Artisan gestured towards Nitarn's friends who, in the meantime, had moved quickly through the corridor towards the door and stood waiting for Rocky to let them out.

'They're going… without saying goodbye, even to you?' Caitlin spoke to Nitarn.

'Sorry Caitlin, they can be quite unsociable. They obviously didn't want to disturb us while we were dancing.'

She thought them so rude. They had almost shunned her during dinner, not making eye contact once, except ice lady. And even now she threw Caitlin a cold, uninterested stare as she stood with the other rulers while Rocky struggled with the code. He must have been here dozens of times, and she wondered what was going on with him to be so forgetful. Caitlin found this unnerving and somewhat strange. Finally, the door swung open. Frozen lips gave Caitlin one last glare before leaving. She glanced at Nitarn, who didn't seem to notice what a cat his friend was. Artisan had said her goddess power was up high but she figured the fragrance must have settled down after eating. If it were still intense as before, Artisan and Jovis would not have left her side, yet they seemed happy with their dance partners and came nowhere near her. As far as she was aware, the bouquet generally calmed evil. *Surely that includes witches that are frozen bitches.* Her thoughts were interrupted by Jovis and Artisan who joined them; still with arms around the two they suddenly had taken a keen interest in. And after only just one dance.

Jovis had a big grin and now up close Caitlin noticed his eyes glazed over even more. She was shocked that he and Artisan had consumed so much booze, considering they may well be the ones under attack, and at any moment would be needed if that happened.

'The girls want some fun.' Jovis ran a hand down the side of his partner's face. 'Now there's only a few of us left, we're taking the party to the hot springs out in the cave. We told Rocky about it, and apparently, he had the servants fix it up real nice for us. We figured we may as well check it out. Rocky will join us after he transports the visitors and his staff from here and security is back in place.' He turned to Nitarn. 'Would you like to join us, or are you leaving with your buddies?'

'It's been a while since I indulged in a midnight swim. If it's heated, I'm in. Wouldn't miss seeing something so rare, should I say unheard of, on an Ice Planet.' Nitarn seemed completely happy to join them.

'Cait... What about you? Feel like letting your hair down?' Jovis smiled with a faraway look in his eyes. It didn't seem like him.

This gave Caitlin no choice. She could stay and seem like a party pooper to the four rulers or follow them and try to keep them out of trouble. The way she saw it, this looked like big trouble if anything was to attack them and if so, she would need to draw power from them. She wasn't sure how she'd go taking magic from drunken men and worried the power may be too unstable.

This was turning into a frat party, and just like those, she could see this one spiralling out of control.

By the time the girls had gathered their coats and bags, Rocky had joined them. Seeing him fling his arm around the final girl without a partner had Caitlin unnerved. What were the odds of the three women invited being a match for Jovis, Artisan and Rocky? That meant she was left to entertain Nitarn. And the way the other girls were wrapped around their man and acting far too easy, she hoped he didn't expect her to be like that with him. She eyed them disapprovingly. *Girls please, have some decorum!*

'Well, are we going for a midnight skylark or what?' Rocky had that same glazed look as Artisan and Jovis. She figured it must be just the female influence, nothing more and she was reading too much into it. *Men!*

Jovis smiled. 'I guess we're all in then; ready guys?' He transported them to the mouth of the ice cave.

Caitlin shuddered. It was instantly freezing, and she ran into the cave. Inside, the temperature was better, and she shrugged off the thick warm fur coat that had been tossed over her shoulders seconds before they left the house. The others ran in with her, giggling and making the experience less painful. She was amazed the men had lost all concern for their worlds entirely. Still, that was their concern. If Jovis lost an Ice Worlds, he would only have himself to blame. Caitlin decided to loosen up and try to stop worrying so much. If something did happen, one of the men would just have to transport out and bring back Rory and another Rider so she could use their magic. With this plan in mind, she relaxed and turned to Nitarn. 'If you don't mind, I will need someone to hold on to while in these boots. The ice becomes quite slippery closer to the hot spring.'

'Of course, my lady.' He was as he had been all night and very charmingly held out his arm.

As they stepped into the spa room, at least a hundred candles were burning, sending a strange glow on the cave walls. The red cultured soil that seeped through the icy walls made the room glisten in shades of pink and crimson. Thick luscious towels were stacked on shelves that had been erected, and each side, towelling robes hung ready for use.

The three women wasted no time, not bothering to sift through the swimwear displayed on a table. Instead, they discarded their clothing and jumped straight in. Deciding to swim in knickers only; lacy underpants that barely covered what they had been designed to cover.

Jovis, Rocky and Artisan dived in only seconds behind them. Jovis and Artisan were always so attentive this seemed out of character. They would normally wait and have her join them. Caitlin was happy they had a girl each for the night, but this was hardly the way to act, this dinner party was becoming more risqué than she was used to. She was dealing with the dark side of the universe where evil lurked. Now she felt she would be getting a lesson on a different side of life; after all, she had to remind herself, these rulers were no angels. Rocky had tried to warn her. She suddenly felt like Mother Theresa and wished she had taken up the offer to go home for the night. Since she'd stayed, she had to suck it up and not act such a prude. If Nitarn did get frisky, her powers were strong enough to sort him out. *Loosen up girl* she instructed herself.

'Coming in?' Nitarn eyed her, interested in what was going through her head as she stood staring uncomfortably at everyone. He held a hand out to her and waited.

Nitarn had taken off all but underpants that did look like shorts, so it wasn't as bad as imagining chatting to him half naked.

'Sure.' Caitlin was for a moment out of her comfort zone. Going in didn't feel right, but backing out was not an option. Something was off kilter and she decided to join them all to see if she could find out just what. Not even she could control this many people at once, so she knew it wasn't Nitarn. He seemed too relaxed and nice to be that devious. Was it something they ate? *That's it, maybe they're drugged.* If this was so, she felt sure it would wear off in the water.

She gave Nitarn a smile to make him feel at ease with her. It was time for her to go to work. This was not just an ordinary dinner party. Removing her clothes her magic enabled her to wear a swimsuit. But not just any swimwear. *No...* The white material glittered, and the one piece fitted snugly, too snugly and off the shoulder straps draped delicately, giving the costume further sex appeal. *Why, oh why, is my magic doing this to me?*

'Oh, my dear girl, you look like an exquisite goddess. You are very beautiful, Cait.' Nitarn took her delicate hand, slipped it around his neck and picked her up in his arms. 'You are more than I ever dreamed of finding.'

'I'm married,' Caitlin squeaked out. She had no idea why her magic was doing this, attracting another man. She didn't want this, and yet she was unable to speak. Instead, she stared at him as he carried her into the water. Not even Jovis spoke or seemed to notice this man was taking control of her.

In the water he lay with her in his arms, while his gaze roamed her entire body, slowly taking the image of her in. He got back to her face. 'You are so incredibly perfect, Cait. Leave that idiot man of yours who would carelessly leave you here. Come away with me. I will treat you like the goddess you look at this very moment.' His eyes sparkled, and his voice was rough and lustful.

She wanted to yell out for help, but again her words were

silenced with this man's magic. She had to fight it, use the water to give her strength. Similar power had been used on her once before. Calyx had this capability, and if she could beat a god, she could beat this man. Yet because her friends and his had ignored her, she had lost confidence. This loss of willpower had made it easy for Nitarn to win. *He is doing all of this, but why?* She had been affected by his magic differently. She managed to avert her eyes to Jovis; he was genuinely captivated in a passionate kiss. *Can't any of them see me! Or get I would not like this situation? Hello guys, this dude is romancing me, strike that, looks as if he wants to devour me.* Worst of all he had no idea who he was doing this to and was in for one big surprise very shortly. *Sorry Jovis and Rocky, but I need to steal some of your powers.* She closed her eyes to help her concentrate.

She knew Nitarn felt her shiver. He frowned; worried for her; little did he know it was due to the extra powers that filled her delicate frame, but it was still not enough to stop him.

'Best we go back inside by the fire.' Nitarn carried her out. He wrapped a towel around her and threw the coat over her shoulders before transporting her back to where they were.

Once inside, Caitlin remembered all the servants had gone home, and it was just them alone, sitting on the floor on soft cushioning and furs, in front of the fire. This was good. He was unable to hurt anyone if nobody was here and with that thought, her powers kicked in now she was warming up. *I'm back... and this cunning sod is about to get angry... very angry. Game on!*

CHAPTER THIRTY

Scent of a Goddess

In front of the fire, Caitlin could feel Nitarn let her go, or was he unable to keep the hypnotic hold since she sneakily soaked up of some of Jovis and Rocky's power? She failed to take much of their magic in her state of limbo, but it must have been enough to set her free. She could feel Nitarn struggle now he was unable to control her further.

His eyebrows furrowed together, annoyed, yet he was not a man to give up. 'You were cold. Your friends were enjoying themselves. I brought you here to sit and chat in private.' He placed a fur over her legs. He would have preferred to take her to his Home World, but keeping the party in a trancelike state had drained his powers. To break free of this world and get past Medusa he would need to sit a minute and wait for them to reboot. Until they did realign, here was as good a place as any to stay, especially with such fine company.

Setting eyes on Cait tonight had changed his plans on how he would take over Jovis's Ice World. If he was to impress this woman, he couldn't go killing off all the guests in front of her. She had him by the balls, and he didn't like the feeling. He eyed her, and couldn't work out how this happened. Her skin was far too soft and what was that fragrance? He would have to treat her so carefully and yet didn't care. Meeting her had sent him into a spin, made him want her so badly, he was barely able to breathe while near her. One thing he was sure of, she was going home with him. He hoped one day she would want him as he wanted her. He had all the time in the world and all the money one would ever need, and he was confident she would choose him. *She will be mine!*

'I think we need to talk.' Caitlin saw lust in his eyes. 'We have a few things to sort out.'

'Like what?' He looked rattled.

'I'm sorry if you feel I have led you on, but it was not my intention. Your stories were of travel on Earth, with humans. I enjoyed listening but didn't realise this signalled I wanted you romantically. I think we should call it a night.'

'Look, love!' Nitarn answered moodily. 'You have tried to lure me in all night so don't give me that prim and proper bullshit. That overabundance of perfume, that dress you wore during the night and then those bathers you had on tell me a different story. Face it, they were to lure in a man tonight. Well, you have my attention, and lady, let me tell you, it has worked.' He leered at her.

'You're acting sleazy. Stop it.'

He sighed and gave her a smile used when he first met her. She liked it and once again, he saw her calm down. 'My intentions are not to anger you, I am merely tired and you're right, being obnoxious. But be clear on one thing, Cait, I am taking you home with me after I sit a minute or two and catch my breath. Once you have seen my world and what I have to offer, it will be me you choose. This life, with these weasels, will never enter your mind again.'

'I'm sorry to burst your bubble, but I'm married and not available. Even if I wasn't taken, trust me Nitarn, me loving you; that ain't going to happen, not ever.'

'I beg to differ, and you are coming with me. Oh, and I hate to point out the obvious… But no one's around to stop me!'

'I will if you don't calm down!' Caitlin was over his bullying behaviour. 'And, not to mention Jovis will kill you if you did, never mind what my husband will do.' She hoped mentioning Jovis and her husband might snap him out of it.

'Jovis!' He put his head back and laughed. 'You think it was a fluke that all three girls were completely compatible and able to keep your friends from remembering about you? Think again, sunshine. I thought you were some kind of royalty, the way they guarded you, but you have no stuffy accent, so if you aren't royal, it can only be one thing; you must be damned hot in bed.'

Her eyes widened in disbelief at his outburst. 'For a start, we are just friends, and that is all. But those poor girls out there... how could you use them like that? It's disgusting of you.'

'They belong to me, and I use them however I wish. Mind control works better if a man is happy. With your friends out of the way, it has given me time to play with you, my feisty new love. How else was I going to get you away from them?'

Caitlin tried to defuse the situation that was getting out of hand. 'Look, I promise to keep from telling what happened here between us if you leave now. There is no way I will be leaving with you Nitarn, and that is final. We have begun a friendship that is sure to be destroyed if you don't stop this nonsense right now. In the morning things will look different and you will be glad it went no further.' It upset Caitlin the night had ended so badly.

His eyes pierced hers. 'So, you're telling me you have no desire for me whatsoever? That's such a lie and you know it.'

Caitlin was finding it difficult but wanted, if possible, to finish the night without hostility. Had no clue why her magic had dressed her in that way and was unable to explain it. Even so, he was overreacting to mere clothing choices and not being mindful this was inappropriate behaviour towards any married women. The ladies he brought with him were more scantily dressed than she had been. He was acting completely different to the honourable man he had been during dinner. Most likely this was the real Nitarn and she wondered why she did not see through the fake facade during the night. 'You are very charming, but my husband is the only man I will ever desire. I'm sorry, Nitarn.'

Suddenly his brows pulled in tight, and his eyes were lustful and wanting. 'Then I will just have to change your mind. Come, we are going home and there, you will see I am the one for you, trust me.' His arm stretched out and steel grip fingers snatched for her.

She was shocked by the extent of his confidence that she would eventually fall for him. *There is no talking sense to this creep.* She didn't care who Nitarn was anymore. She didn't have to put up with his cave man conduct. Maybe on the Ice Planets way out in the Oort cloud, this was how it was done, but not here. She was no cave dweller nor was she from the Stone Age, and as far as she was concerned, he was acting like a self-centred, arrogant pig that needed to learn some manners. Caitlin readied her wits for his attack.

Woody had warned her that one day, her goddess scent might work the opposite way. Instead of calming evil, it might heighten their sexual desire. But try as she did, she couldn't snap out of his magic hold to turn it down. Struggling with this man's god-like power had left her quite drained. She knew this next move would take everything she had, and hoped someone would come to her rescue soon or she would be playing Wilma to caveman Nitarn in Bedrock way out in the galaxy somewhere.

With speed Nitarn had not expected and power he had no idea his lady friend possessed, Caitlin put up her hand. From it shot a burst of heat that propelled him backwards.

For the first time, Nitarn felt the power she'd hidden from him. *Ah, the feisty witch has magic...* It only made him want her more. He had wasted too much time already with this unnecessary chatter, and it was time to take home his prize find. Only to his further surprise, she dared raise a second hand to him. As soon as this realisation hit, he blocked her powers to prevent an additional attack, but it was too late. This one single burst of her magic was so intense he couldn't even duck out the way. The energy-driven strike threw him backwards. Nitarn somersaulted through the air and slammed into the cement wall behind him.

Caitlin saw him in the air and knew if it didn't knock him unconscious, she was in big trouble. She was done; he had taken away her powers and she was unable to fight further. *What is it with these Ice Planet Rulers? How have they learned the biggest secret kept by the gods?* To take a goddess's magic was unfair. She intended to find a way to stop this from ever happening again. In the meantime, she needed to run… her feet barely touched the floor as she wasted no time heading for the stairs. Stretching to take them two at a time, she hoped he would not get to her until she had dressed, so as not to lure him further. In her room, she tossed aside the coat to cool off and cursed when she saw her magic clothes had gone.

From the room, she heard Nitarn groan. As fast as possible, she opened the chest of drawers and pulled out some pieces of clothing. Still intent on listening for her aggressor to burst in at any moment, she preferred to be fully dressed and quickly slipped on pants and shirt that must have belonged to Artisan. They did nothing for her figure. 'Good.' She hoped the baggy grunge look would deter him. In the closet, she had found a pair of runners. They were slightly bigger and wider but geeky. His footsteps came closer. She knew now it was not alcohol, but Nitarn, who put that glazed look in her friends' eyes. She prayed his extra use of magic to block hers would set her friends free. She hoped Jovis would snap out of it and make it to her before Nitarn did. Just in case she was wrong, Caitlin quickly grabbed a face washer and while washing off her makeup, ruffled up her hair, making her look a mess. She hoped the messy appearance would have him run the other way. *It couldn't hurt.*

On the stand alone mirror she scrawled the word "Nitarn," and threw the towel she held over it.

She stared back at her wild features in the wall mirror. *Please let this buy me some time. Hurry Jovis!* She willed him to her but without powers had little hope it was working.

Suddenly, Nitarn smashed through the door, and she covered her eyes with her arm as the solid wood shattered with his out of control force. 'I could smell you in here.' He glared at her, his eyes wide. 'Hell, what are you wearing?' He rubbed his sore head and stood looking confused as if the bump on his head was giving him hallucinations. He couldn't believe how genuinely young she looked without makeup and hair done. *She is only but a girl!*

At that moment Jovis transported in and called out, 'Cait… close your eyes and don't open them until I tell you!'

Caitlin did as she was told. She knew by the smell, recalled from the sky earlier that day, Jovis had brought Medusa with him. The thump as the creature landed shook the floor.

Jovis scooped Caitlin up. 'I got you, beautiful, everything's going to be okay.' Nitarn went to snatch her up, but she faded and slipped from his grip. Jovis reappeared with her on the opposite side of Medusa.

The beast glared at Jovis. 'This deluded fool is the one who dares bring harm upon you?'

Jovis nodded. 'The blatzing mongrel tricked us all into thinking he can be trusted.' He kept Caitlin in his arms at a safe distance. He could move her in an instant if need be, but wanted to stay to see this lying bastard get what was due to him. He saw on entering that Nitarn had smashed the door down and was about to try to harm, or maybe even abduct, Caitlin.

'Kill him!' Jovis was furious.

Medusa lashed out with her spiked tail. Nitarn rolled from the sharp plunging hit towards him and pulled out a dagger; an ancient weapon Jovis recognised.

'That will not kill her!' Jovis moved Caitlin away as Nitarn thrust the knife towards Medusa's underbelly, his eyes evading her glare.

'After I kill your monster, then you, Cait is mine.' Nitarn swiped at her and slashed the snakeskin. Medusa screamed angrily and, keeping her body away, used the serpents while she gained control. The serpents snapped and kept Nitarn busy while the body of Medusa raised its tail behind him, in the strike that would have killed her opponent.

Nitarn knew he was out of his depths with this vicious beast and was just about to transport out of the situation when everyone froze, him included. Though unable to move, Nitarn saw the two gods, Zeus and Hades, shimmer into sight. He was done; he could not fight both brothers. One god maybe, but two... he had no hope. He felt an invisible box go around him and seal him in. Nitarn was so angry, he was steaming up the jailer's chamber. He could barely see, but what he did get a glimpse of was enough for him to realise he had been set up. Medusa was there to play with him; keep him on Sedna and alive until the gods arrived. But who called them? Jovis hated the King of the Dwarf Planets... *Or did he?*

The gods shook his hand... What the hell, was going on? *Jovis is friends with them.* This was bull. *No!* He screamed as Zeus and Hades gave Caitlin a group hug. Zeus then swung her up into his arms, and she linked her hands around him as they faded from sight. Hades stood speaking with Jovis for a couple more seconds then shook his hand again before the unexpected scene before him faded. Hades was taking him somewhere, and he had a good idea where.

* * * *

Calyx took Caitlin home to Ara where Axon waited for them, his mood livid as he paced back and forth. He had felt Caitlin's shudder of disgust as she told them of Nitarn's intentions to have his way with her.

Axon knew the creep, and it made him wonder if she'd hidden some details. Caitlin's recollection of events left some missing hours of which she seemed unaware. *Did Nitarn's magic still linger?* Not wanting to startle her he decided to give it time to wear off. He hoped she'd work it out eventually because the time frame was questionable and it was important they worked out what went on.

'You can tell us the truth, honey, all of it. None of this is your fault.' He gritted his teeth. *I'll kill that bastard with my bare hands if he has laid one sleazy hand on my wife.*

Caitlin glared at him, unsure what he was getting at and why. 'Honestly, there is nothing more to tell!' she assured him.

Calyx stood with arms folded when Caitlin looked to him for support. He smiled kindly at the woman about whom he cared above all others. Even distressed and teary-eyed she captivated him with her loveliness. He wished it was him who would be drying her tears tonight. But all that aside he also had doubts as to the time lapse between going in the water and ending up back at the house.

He turned to Axon. 'You know, after what we have learned from Cait, it wouldn't surprise me if Nitarn was behind the attack on Rocky's Ice World, Orcus.'

'My thoughts exactly.' Axon sat in the armchair near where Caitlin had knelt to dry her still damp hair. It was apparent she had no powers, or she would be dressed and her hair perfect by now.

Caitlin nodded. 'That I'd believe. He's so cunning how he gets people to do things, like using the girls to keep the men busy while he used his magic to try and pursue me.'

Calyx snatched up three shot glasses and the star shooters decanter from the sidebar. He sat heavily in the armchair the other side of Cait and poured them a shot each. After he passed one to Caitlin and one to Axon, he gulped his down and poured a second. If he couldn't control his temper, Caitlin would shut down on him as she had done many times before until he calmed down.

Axon twisted his drink in his hand. He wished he could down the entire bottle, but one of Caitlin's boys falling apart was enough. He had to keep level-headed and help her work this out so she could come home. 'Let's say Nitarn is as smart as we think. What if he wanted to get onto Jovis's Home World for a reason? Cunning would have him blow up Rocky's world, hoping Jovis would choose him as an ally, and want his help badly enough that he would host the party, not cancel. What if the men that came to the party were hit men and not rulers? That might be the reason he kept them from you, Cait.'

'Well that's true, Cait would have picked up in a minute, by the vibration of their magic when close enough, that they were imposters.'

'That makes sense. I thought them so rude for ignoring me all night. But what was up with his commanding officer, she honestly acted as if she hated me.'

'That should have set off bells and whistles right there. You're not easy to ignore, little one.' Calyx grinned. 'As for your ice lady, Nitarn would have told her the plan had changed, and she guessed it was because of you. That news would not have sat comfortably with a hired gun, so I assume she has tried to move you along through intimidation.'

'It didn't work. Nitarn wouldn't let me out of his sight for me to make myself scarce. Come to think of it, his commanding officer left the same time as the men. I mean, they had permission to be there and leave so if they really were rulers, why didn't they transport out by themselves? And where did Rocky take them? He was gone and back in no time. Surely if he had taken them to their worlds, it would have taken him a bit longer. He seemed to get on well with them, so I assume they would have chatted before he left. This would surely have held him up.'

'Maybe Rocky just dropped them back on his world with the staff? They might say they would make their own way home from there. Instead, they stayed and waited for Nitarn to pick them up?' Calyx aired his thoughts.

Axon agreed. 'Sound feasible and explains the time loss.' The words were out before he could stop them.

'What time loss?' Caitlin swung round to face him.

Axon lowered his tone. 'You told us you got in the spa at around eleven. Give or take an hour of arguing with him, and that takes you up to midnight. Sweetheart, you got here half an hour ago. It's almost four in the morning.

Caitlin swung her head back and forth to both men. 'He had me, I mean us, like that for three hours?'

Calyx leaned over and put a hand on hers. 'Don't worry Cait, we'll work this out.' He sat back in his chair, staring at her. 'So let's look at what he could have been doing in that time. Let's see.' He squinted. 'So far, we know Nitarn and his goons were given permission by Jovis to be there. With no fear of being attacked by Medusa, or being stopped by guards, why not use this time to do a little scouting and work out a foolproof plan to take over the three worlds? You can do a lot of ground surveillance in that time.'

Axon's eyebrows rose. 'You think Nitarn might have picked up his men and his lady friend to do some recon, and maybe left something behind to help them with an invasion later?'

'Anything is possible.' Calyx frowned. 'Why else would he put everyone in a dreamy state? It had to be so he could duck away. He is no ordinary immortal ruler being able to spellbind someone as strong as the Goddess of Peace. That wicked slime had conjured up deep dark powers to be that strong. No way are we ever letting him walk free with what he has learned, or by the time he is done there would never be enough goodness left to help keep the natural good and evil balance within our universe. To keep that mongrel where he is we'll need solid proof, and somehow I will find it or so help me, my brother's Kraken can come out to play.'

'Holding us in a magic bubble must have really drained him because he did eventually lose his hold on me once we got back to the fortress. My clue was when he said he needed to sit a minute and catch his breath. It was my one and only window and took it. You see I'd taken some magic from the boys while in the water, but in that mesmerised state, was only able to seep it into me a little at a time. It was enough to help fight him and once free from the weak state where I was confined, I was able to use the magic I'd sneakily locked away.' Caitlin admitted.

'Being clever enough to do what you did under the circumstances is commendable.' Axon held her hands. 'On Nitarn's return, it would not surprise me if he planned to kill you all. He could easily pull everyone under the water, one at a time. There would be no noise, and this was possibly the reason he didn't need to bring any help back. But was not counting on you glowing from that power you drew on. You would have caught him by surprise and while he stood looking at you Cait, shining in all your glory, it would have stopped him in his tracks. The sleazy bastard's insane greed and urgency to have you was obviously what put a hold on his ploy to kill you all.'

Calyx butted in. 'You saved everyone's life Cait, well, temporarily until he got what he wanted. After, he would have returned to the cave and finish the others off. My best guess is while you lay in the water looking so sexy and smelling desirable and with everyone still in a trance, he must have decided to enjoy you for a bit. After, he'd either kill or take you for himself. He wouldn't decide until he had seen how you performed for him.' Calyx steadied his voice as the thought came to mind. If he had a top, it would lift, allowing the steam to escape that came from a roaring fire of pent-up hatred for Nitarn.

'At least that now explains the dress and bathers because

seriously, I looked like a saloon girl trying to attract a badarse, and now I know why — I was meant to. Oh, and did I curse the bathers for making me bare it all but if it worked, "thank you magic" is all I can say. But it was scary at the time wondering why.' Seeing the look she was getting from Calyx she gave a slight smile. 'Geez, don't tell me, you want me to attend a class to teach me some lady etiquette, right.'

He breathed out heavy, 'Cait you are perfectly in tune with all your powers, and I'm proud of how you handled the situation.' Calyx calmed. 'And no, you don't need etiquette classes, but so help me, creeps like Nitarn will never get a second chance to be graced by your presence. Not while I still breathe.'

She smiled and flushed crimson from receiving the compliment.

Axon lifted her hand and kissed it. She was so Caitlin right now and was glad no one, not even Nitarn's treatment of her, tainted or changed his virtuous wife one little bit. He turned back to Calyx. 'As we know, Caitlin is powerful and it sounds as if he didn't take control of her fully until Rocky had transported the staff, guards and the hit men from Sedna.'

Calyx tilted her head thinking. 'It is quite possibly this was when he was able to finally take full control as the group was smaller. It would then be possible for a demonic like him to easily cast a spell and put a magical bubble around who was left. Those inside the bubble would be kept in a sleepy state and therefore not able to cause him any problems while he went about his business.'

'Goodness knows what else he had time to do while the lousy low life had my wife and her friends in stasis for what... I'm thinking around three hours?'

Calyx finally downed his second shot. 'It's not good that such a man who has become so dangerous has managed to skilfully fly under our radar. The magic needed to not only hide his ability from us gods, but do what he did to Cait and her new friends is unbelievable, yet it happened. When my brother and I arrived, Nitarn had in his possession the secret weapon known to kill all dark destroyers and their rulers. So he was well equipped and had everything planned, except you Cait.

'We can thank Jovis for that. He kept me a secret from Rocky otherwise Nitarn would have learned of me and my powers too. Seriously, I was cross at Jovis and Artisan from doing that to Rocky and yet now I could hug them. Nitarn was surely using Magic to get every bit of info out of Rocky he could. Obviously the night of the party Nitarn felt he knew all and could foresee all, and didn't need anything more while being transported to Sedna. Well, that was a blessing.' Caitlin's eyes were like saucers when she sighed with relief.

Axon nodded. 'It was a close call tonight Cait. A couple of seconds more and he would have transported you to who knows where.'

'Sorry I scared you and in future, I'll keep you informed if I ever come across another Nitarn or the likes of him. I do get the dissimilarity now. Woody tried to warn me, but you have to meet a pure evil one before you know the difference.'

'Good to hear,' Axon turned to Calyx. 'I guess I can't stop her leaving and going back there, but can sure as hell kick out my competition while she's home here with me.'

'I get the hint. Can I give her a hug goodbye?' Calyx eyed him. *Blatzing girlfriend-stealing husband.*

'I guess so,' Axon grumbled, and picked up the shot glasses and the empty decanter and sat them on the sidebar to be washed.

Caitlin stood up and gave Calyx a hug.

He whispered, 'Your powers are back, aren't they?'

You bet. Leave me to cheer up grumpy pants, and we'll talk after he drops me off at Jett's in the morning. She spoke telepathically. *Thanks for saving me!*

'My pleasure.' He turned to Axon who had given an impatient cough. 'I know when I'm not needed. I'll see you both for breakfast at Jett's.' Calyx didn't want an answer. He faded from sight with a royal wave.

Axon got it was an order. 'He can be such a god.' he shook his head.

Both chuckled.

* * * *

The next morning, Axon and Caitlin arrived on Pluto just in time for breakfast. Taking a plate each they filled them full of fluffy omelettes bacon and hash browns. At the table, they buttered toast and chatted to Jett while he reached over and poured them both a coffee.

'Worked up a bit of appetite did we?' Calyx put down the paper he read and picked up his own fork.

Axon grinned. 'None of your beeswax. I liked it better when you had your nose in that paper. Anything interesting?'

'Not particularly, just checking if the story about us holding Nitarn had broken yet. It seems he isn't important enough to include in the NAVdaily.'

'Actually, we locked the story up in case any of his sympathisers find out where he is and try to break him out.' Axon dug his fork into the omelette.

'Yum, nice.' Caitlin folded her toast in half and dipped it into her soft egg and took a bite and chewed it while smiling.

'How was your night Glow, did you sleep well back in your own bed?' Jett liked seeing she wasn't dwelling on what had happened.

She nodded, 'Can't talk, eating.' She gulped the mouthful down while filling her fork again.

Axon passed her a slice of his buttered toast. 'She didn't eat dinner last night. Apparently, Rocky's chef cooked, need I say more. Only found out before we left home or I would have fixed her a snack when she got home.'

'Cait, do be more careful.' Jett frowned.

'You know better, what were your words to us when we didn't replenish our powers after a drain just recently?' Calyx was concerned she hadn't told him she was hungry either.

'I called you ding dongs.' She grinned.

'Exactly.' He ruffled her hair.

Axon was late for work and had already given Caitlin a hard time on the topic. He was pleased Jett and Calyx backed him up and agreed with him. 'Look guys I have to run, but before I go, has anyone heard from the enemy camp?'

Calyx put down his knife and fork. 'After Jett got back from delivering Nitarn to the universe's maximum prison on Saturn, I had him report it back to Jovis.'

Axon shifted focus to Jett. 'You guys actually spoke... and it was civil?'

Jett moved his head from side to side and cracked his neck to relax. 'He's not as ready as I had hoped. Glow's done a good job with him; at least he talks to me now. But ready to sign up as a Dwarf Planet, not so much.'

'Cait, where are you at with Jovis?' Axon raised his brow.

'It's taking more time than I thought. Jovis has been let down too many times. All he has ever known is war and trusts no one. So-called friends and many staff have all turned out to be traitors of the kingdom. After his parents were murdered in their own beds, he could take no more. His heart hardened and as time went on it became as cold as the ice on his planet.'

'Did he find the killers?' Axon sat back to listen further.

'They did, but not who was behind it. The criminals never told who sent them. Then his brother went missing and seemingly he was next. That's when Artisan and Rocky stepped in. They took charge and got him out of there as soon as they heard there was talk of another assassin hiding somewhere within the castle. You could say that since then, Jovis has been undercover and after years of his family not getting any help when being robbed of much real-estate in the sky, he has become self-sufficient, self-reliant and a very proud man for his achievements. Now he has finally got back what was rightfully his and his brothers, he doesn't need or want anyone's help. The only problem I have with that is he has this huge growing empire but no real family to share it with. If I can't make him accept help, and in turn open him up to other joys, his heart will continue to grow dark. If that happens, with royal blood in the mix, Nitarn will be a pussycat compared to Vador if he comes back out to play.'

'Then you have much to fix Cait.' Axon spoke caringly. 'It must make him livid every day having to give up all royal privileges and those he loves to live in a cold fortress, stuck deep in a mountain somewhere. It must be a very lonely life.'

'He couldn't even trust one servant enough to take them with him, and after what happened last night, he'll be even more closed off from having others around him. I just hope he still has trust in me or I may be on the outer now too.'

'Really? Surely not.' Axon was surprised with her comment. 'He moved mountains finding me last night to have me help save your life.' Axon turned and spoke with a renewed respect for him. 'He even threatened Zoren. Cheeky shytzer. Never seen the angel so dumbfounded with a man's passionate plea. I was off-world and in a secret location handling a very delicate matter. Jovis transported in with Zoren and almost gave me a goddamned heart attack. Luckily it didn't affect the talks. As for him not wanting to see you anymore, I find that hard to imagine after seeing him so worked up.'

'It's all making sense now.' Calyx's jaw muscle relaxed. 'Medusa was to protect him, not keep us out.'

'Then why the dinner party after all this time?' said Jett.

Caitlin bit her lip. 'It was my fault. I guess he felt relaxed. I was teaching him trust, something he struggled with and now I fear this has ruined everything.' Caitlin blinked and took a deep breath. 'Of all the people in the universe to invite to your party, he chose an evil, no-good liar. I have no idea how I'm going to fix this mess.'

Axon put his hand over her clenched knuckles that rested on the table. 'Why don't you invite him here, honey? I bet he is at this moment trying to work out how to approach us to ask for you. Make the first move, I'm almost positive he is busting to see you no matter where you suggest.'

Jett leant forward and spoke softly. 'You deserve to win this one. He has tested your very soul. But here might not be the best place to meet. He is only just starting to speak to me without that look of hatred he had in his eyes.'

'I know there's a lot to consider if he was to come here. You must still hold a huge grudge from his threats, so maybe that look of hatred went both ways.' She grinned. 'But I honestly believe all ill feelings will dissolve once you get to know him better. He's a good egg. If I can get him here, and patch this up, you will like him, Jett, and I know he will definitely like you!' She looked confident.

He lifted a brow. 'We'll see, but I have my doubts.'

Caitlin ignored his tone of animosity when speaking of a possible friendship with Jovis. This feud had almost pushed Jett over the edge so to have him allow Jovis here was a big deal. In the earlier day he wanted to see Jovis, now she felt him hesitate and hoped it wasn't too late. Giving them time to digest what she proposed, Caitlin stood to pour tea from the elegantly engraved silver teapot on the café bar. 'Giving this more thought, I must add, if Jovis does receive an invitation to meet me here on Pluto, it won't seem strange to him. I have already told him I'm on holidays, and Axon drops me here each day before he leaves for work. He is mystified why I prefer to spend time here on an icy-cold world and not sunning myself on an island somewhere. He knows nothing of the outstanding changes you have made here, Jett, and he wasn't interested in hearing it from me. So this will be a total surprise. This here is sure to make him see why it is a wise move to accept you as the king. If you really don't mind the inconvenience, I agree with Axon; this is the perfect place for us to meet.

Jett squinted, his face twisted in a sneer. 'It's no secret of late I have wanted a meeting with him, but that was to beat him to an inch of his life, strangle and then throw him in the underworld and let him burn in hell for eternity.' He gave her a wicked grin then shrugged. 'For you, Glow, and only you, I am willing to try talking and being civil one last time.'

'Then it is settled.' Calyx stood up and put his hand out to Caitlin. 'Say your goodbyes to lover hubby and let's get you up into the NAVcom tower to contact Jovis. Jett, you have company coming. Tell the commander to ramp up security to NAVcode-red. I want the castle ready for any situation that may arise.'

Jett nodded in agreement.

Axon and Caitlin grinned at each other. When Calyx acted all officially, each knew what the other was thinking. *He can be such a god.*

She hugged Axon. 'He is so worthy of our time. I just hope I haven't lost Jovis by running out on them. I thought Jovis would have come and got me by now yet we haven't heard a word. Most likely he felt I had no trust in them after what happened. Hope I get a chance to explain that I needed to reconnect with my goddess powers stolen by Nitarn. I couldn't do it on their dark world. Well, not until they make many changes.'

'Axon held her by the shoulders and gazed at her bright green eyes. 'If they are smart they will come the moment you call, and allow you to explain. If not, seriously, none of them is worthy of you.'

'Hope you're right.'

Axon kissed the hand he held. 'My promise to oversee this reunion still stands, however, it will be best supervised from afar. A silent call out from you will have me come the second you need me.'

She nodded in agreement. 'I guess less is sometimes best.'

'Thought you'd agree. Miss you already.' As usual, he never stayed to hear any response. He didn't need to because when they were alone, she sure had a way of showing him. *Mine!* He grinned as she faded from his sight.

* * * *

Axon floated on a cloud when he arrived at work. An unexpected night with Caitlin and the luxury of a meal with her this morning was a perfect way to start his day.

Zoren waited in the satellite room for him to arrive. Pale blue eyes watched through long white lashes, and majestic white wings delicately rested either side of him. The archangel of the heavens glowed white when he turned. Axon closed the door behind him and walked over to the window to see what he was observing. There was a battle going on in the distance. Zoren glanced at him. 'I need not inquire where you have been.'

'It is unreasonable to deny me a night with my woman.' Axon crossed his arms, keeping his eyes straight ahead. If Zoren was in true form, he was about to intervene. The huff he just heard was to make Axon feel uncomfortable for not being at work earlier. Zoren was annoyed he might have had to step in and fix a dispute in Axon's quadrant.

'I am a man first.' That was all Axon would give him today. He was too happy to argue. 'Now, who's out there trying to break through the security of Saturn and why?'

Zoren changed back to male form. They had both put in many hours already this week. They looked out over the sky knowing much had been fixed, but they could feel this uprising of Nitarn's followers was cutting edge. Even though he was in custody, these rebels would not be giving up anytime soon.

Zoren eyed him. 'They are Nitarn sympathisers trying to break him out of jail. No clue yet how they knew he was there. I thought we had his whereabouts top secret.' He folded his arms. 'Caitlin is going back to Sedna, I hope?'

'Yes, organising it as we speak.'

'Good, her little playmate is the key to much calm amongst these Ice Planets. Nitarn's reign of terror has to end, but until she has control of Jovis, we are in for a perilous journey forward.' Zoren slipped the Mini NAVcom from the desk into his pocket. 'With everything else going on out there, this is a headache I will leave with you and your team. Ignore this mood of mine, my friend, it's not easy watching NAV4 platoon cop a hiding out there. They have lost a Rider from his horse and need to go collect him. Another two are seriously hurt. I'm pulling them out to regroup and heal them. They're blatzing mummy's boys compared to Rory and his team.' He patted Axon on the back. 'Not sure if I ever praised you on your choice, but good job finding them, Ace. Now go out there and show these old dogs of mine how it's done. You must put a stop to this evil sect Nitarn has put together. Not sure how many fractions will come at us, so be ready for anything. We cannot allow them to take Nitarn, he has grown far too dangerous. Track the ones that run and unless you have a better idea, which I'd love to hear, take the lot of them out. Heartless souls with no light can never be rehabilitated.'

'Are you sure?' Axon had never heard him give an order to wipe out any criminal before, never mind an entire group. These thugs who were currently trying to blast their way onto a planet must have really got under his skin. They must be beyond even Caitlin's help, or Zoren would suggest she be pulled from her current mission to sort it out.

Zoren moved from the window. 'First time I've stood looking at so much darkness. Those souls no longer live, so why allow evil to use their bodies so dangerously.'

Axon nodded.

'Bless you for choosing my side.' Zoren slid his hand on Axon's shoulder and squeezed it before he turned and pointed back to the battle. 'You had better get out there, buddy. Rory and his team have just arrived.' He stared into the distance and to the left. 'Took it upon me to call them. Although I must say, that commander of yours is a very strange lad to speak with. Cheeky sod calls me *arch buddy*.' He turned to Axon, his brows pulled in firmly. 'The language is hard for me to understand. He asked who was having the blue, was I on my Pat Malone and said that you must be knackered after bringing the sheep back to Mary.'

Axon laughed heartily at the look on Zoren's face. 'He asked who was fighting, were you on your own and alluded to me being exhausted after putting the Earthlings back on Earth. He was saying he understood why I hadn't turned up yet.'

Zoren's crinkled brow smoothed. 'Well I had no clue, and instead of doing my head in working it out, I gave him the coordinates and logged off. Please send my apologies.' Zoren inclined his head respectfully and faded from sight.

* * * *

Caitlin walked briskly back with Calyx to tell Jett the excellent news. She burst in the door eager and happy.

'Jovis and Artisan aren't mad at me and instead waited patiently for my call.' She couldn't wait to share the news. 'Because they felt guilty they invited a criminal to dinner, and this bad judgment on their part had almost got me raped and possibly killed, they were willing to agree to anything as penance.'

Calyx stood proudly beside her. 'And did she give it to them!

They were so remorseful by the time she finished. Didn't know our girl had it in her.'

She nudged him. 'Eavesdropper.'

'You bet I did. Wouldn't have missed it,' he grinned.

'Anyway, they're coming. All three rulers.' Caitlin slapped the hand Calyx held up to her. 'But then again, you read minds, Jett, so you'd know that, right?'

'Unlike my brother, I can give you some privacy.' He shook his head at Calyx before addressing Caitlin again. 'So when can we expect these friends of yours?' Jett didn't look thrilled but was happy for Caitlin. She had worked hard to get Jovis and his boys to this point.

'Well...' she played with her fingers, taking her time to answer.

Jett worried she had picked up the sudden change in him, she seemed suddenly nervous to continue. But her worries were way off base. Never did Jett question her loyalty; the indifference came from pure jealousy. His Hades side was possessive, greedy and downright nasty when it came to sharing Caitlin. It would take all his might and newfound happiness as Jett, to restrain that tyrant inside if she wanted to go back to Sedna with Jovis. He eyed Calyx, who stood with a sly grin. He could hear he was thinking the same thing. They both fought tirelessly over her. But this was much worse than having to share her with one another! *What if she starts to like them more!* Caitlin's voice that suddenly commanded his attention brought him out of the mood he had slumped into, and shaking off the anxiety, tuned into what she was saying. He hid a grin, she was going all goddessy on him and he wanted to hug her for making him always feel better.

'Our guests will be here late this afternoon to join us for cocktails. This should give us enough time for a tour of the grounds and after dinner, maybe some fun on the slopes.'

'Seriously Glow, you think they'll stay that long?' Jett's eyes were wide.

'If they want me to go back with them... yes.' She folded her arms with a stubborn pout.

Jett was as shocked as Calyx looked when she confirmed their worst thoughts, she was clearly thinking of going back with them. They had hoped while Axon was at work they could talk her out of that plan and come up with a better one. Maybe just have her visit from now on. Jett's voice caught in his throat. He didn't like Jovis. *Was this why?* Jealousy was the way they were. If Caitlin had taught them anything, it was trust, which was now what she was trying to show Jovis and his friends. She had nearly died during this mission trying to save his kingdom, and he was acting a brat. He listened to his brother's thoughts which were similar, but his heartfelt love for Caitlin had him want to make her happy first. Jett admired this new quality in his brother and was so proud of the well-respected god and brother he had become.

Calyx's expression softened and put his arm around her. 'I'm glad you're not going to make this easy on them. What those boys did was careless. Personally, if I had a say in it, I would not allow visitation until they have learnt how valuable you truly are, Cait. But, this is Axon's call, so I will support you in any other way I can.'

Caitlin opened her mouth, but Calyx put up his hand to stop her. 'I will hear no excuses for them, Cait. They should have known better. When you have stayed with Jett or both of us, have we ever had anyone outside family visit? My brother won't even allow his commander to come in the house when you are here. We would never dream of putting you in danger. These guys had better learn quickly, or even Axon won't be able to stop me stepping in and make it law they do as they're damn well told or lose all they have to the gods.'

'You wouldn't rule so unfairly.' Caitlin swung around and faced him. Her green eyes shone in dismay, which made him grin.

He tapped her perfectly shaped nose. 'No... But the threat might make them all think twice. Make your job easier.'

Caitlin's lips spread in a soft smile. Her lashes closed with thanks he was joking, and she now knew he would never do any such thing without her approval.

'Oh, you!' She pushed him playfully. 'You had me for a minute.' Her hand was quick and slapped his arm. 'Jett needs you to be on your best behaviour. So behave.'

'For you only.' His voice was soft and caring.

'Then for me.' She used his arm as support and stretched up and kissed his cheek. 'You are both my favourites and always will be, so no need to act all tough and jealous.' She knew she could never kiss one without the other, so, turning, she did the same to Jett.

They were not expecting a kiss, never mind her saying what they needed to hear. They grinned at one another and back at her.

'Now, if you can spare me for a bit, I have hardly slept. If my room is still made up, I might take a bath and rest up before the guests arrive. You have no idea how I have missed a hot tub with a splash of some aromatherapy.'

'Seriously!'

'First, you have to collect wood to light the water furnace. With everything so cold, wood is scarce, so usually, it's a warm wash with buckets of water heated by the fire or a cold shower. Well...' she smiled. 'That was until recently when we found a warm spring that had miraculously appeared in one of the caves. You know they didn't even know it existed until we discovered it one day.' She spoke innocently.

Calyx's lips parted, and his eyes glistened. 'You little sneak, you cracked the ice to the heated core and created it, didn't you? Thought as a Rider it was not allowed?'

She chuckled. 'Me, do something to help make the prince happy? As if...'

'Maybe you've been hanging around us too much.' Calyx raised a brow.

'You are a naughty Glow Girl for using our style of magic to make other men happy.' Jett grinned.

'I am the goddess of peace and can be as naughty as I want.' She stuck her nose up high and laughed as she ran past them, but stopped at the stairs. 'Oh, and the goddess will be hungry after a bath so I would like roast chicken and scallop potatoes for dinner,' she called back.

'Are you serious?' Calyx stood firm. 'You abandon us, invite friends over and then go sleep and leave us to do all the work. I have news for you, young lady, and it's not good.'

'Jett will get me what I want!' She stopped and put her hands on her hips cheekily.

Calyx was off after her.

She squealed and ran towards the steps.

Jett headed Calyx off, giving him a hard knock out of the way. He picked up Caitlin and transported her to his bedroom. 'He won't find you here, and anyway, my bath is much bigger and already filled with clean hot water. Calyx disturbed me early so only got time for a quick shower. Take your time and have a good soak, I'll make sure you're not disturbed... goddess.' He bowed and grinned playfully.

'Is that right!' Calyx bellowed behind him. 'He won't find you here.' He repeated Jett's words with amusement. 'You're so soft with her brother.'

Caitlin's magic changed her from the outfit she wore and into bathers. Aware she would get an earful from Calyx, she jumped into the water with haste and pressed the button which set off the jets. The motor cut in and bubbles shot from them. The noise was enough to allow her reprieve. With a hand cupped to her ear, she made out she couldn't hear.

Calyx wiggled a finger at her. 'You'll keep!' he mouthed, and chuckled as Jett transported them back to the den.

Nobody, not even my brother, disciplines my girl.

Chapter Thirty-One

Royal and Divine

After an afternoon of water therapy, and rest, Caitlin was finally ready to great her guests. She felt very graceful walking down the stairs wearing an elegant pale-gold gown. Her hair was swept up on one side, and long luscious curls fell gently down her backless dress. She had accidentally thought about dinner with the prince and try as she did, she couldn't change her outfit. She shrugged at her reflection. *Could be worse, at least the girls aren't out.* The thought amused her as she headed down to the group.

Jovis turned and smiled as she came down the stairs. He didn't take his eyes off her as he stood part-listening to what the king said.

Jett saw Jovis's attention had diverted and guessed why. Not allowing him access to her just yet, he moved quickly to walk Caitlin to them. 'Here she is now.' Jett put out his arm, and she slipped hers through his, and he liked getting a smile for his chivalry. Unfortunately, his devious plan to keep her from them didn't work. Caitlin dropped his arm and hugged Jovis, then Artisan and Rocky.

After greeting them, she stood back. 'Missed you guys, but wow, what a cool send off. Medusa was a nice touch.'

Jovis grinned. 'You'd met her previously so thought you'd be okay with my security dropping in like that to help out.'

'I thought I'd met the universe's most unusual pet when I was introduced to Cerberus, but yours is off the charts.' Caitlin grinned. 'I never thought I'd be so happy to have a visit from Medusa. I was really in a bind and had to have faith that Nitarn's hold on you guys would lift while he tried to block my magic. I really gave it to him, so he'd lose control, but it almost backfired. Glad you got to me in time, as I trusted you would. That was one fantastic entrance.

'You can always trust me to be there for you, Cait,' said Jovis.

She nodded. 'Like now, trusting me to come here, thank you.' She smiled.

'We are all, really sorry Glow.' Artisan frowned. 'It was foolish to have let that lying creep, Nitarn, and his friends, onto Sedna. A mistake that will never be repeated while you visit with us and that's a promise.'

Rocky agreed.

Jovis just wanted to get this over with quickly and be gone from Pluto as soon as possible. He had no idea why she would want them there and worse, now found she had the gods here listening while he begged for forgiveness. 'Seriously Cait, we have learned our lesson and absolutely assure you we have all agreed never to allow another soul to enter the fortress while you're with us.' He wanted to get down on his knee and beg, but in front of the gods, he thought not. 'Please forgive, me, in particular, and come back with us. I feel terrible for what happened, and maybe after you kick our butts for being so stupid, you'll give us a chance to take away the unhappy memories and replace them with good ones. In fact, we thought we could begin your stay with a trip to the hot springs first. That always puts you in high spirits, that's if you feel up to it.'

'It's not that I'm not up to it, but I'm already waterlogged.' She held out her delicate fingers. 'See still wrinkled from having a spa upstairs?' She glanced at Jett. 'And Jett has had his staff slave all afternoon cooking my favourite foods. Surely we have nothing to rush back to, so how about we have a nice dinner here first? It will save you cooking tonight, and after we've eaten I promise I will come back with you?'

'He has a spa here?' Jovis's eyes were wide with disbelief.

'Yes, he has two, and both are heated.' Caitlin grinned at their faces. She wanted to reach up and close their jaws. 'Would you like a tour before dinner?'

'Hell yes!' Artisan and Rocky said together.

Jovis tilted his head. 'I was hoping we might get going if you will do us the honour of coming with us. I would much prefer us to be talking in private.' He gave her a steady gaze that demanded her time to be with them, not here. The two gods looked protective, and he wasn't sure how to get her out of there except throw her over his shoulder and take her kicking and screaming if she did not agree to come now.

Both men stood with arms folded, unsure if the night would go ahead at all. Suddenly their nostrils filled with Caitlin's goddess scent. Jett and Calyx glanced at one another. Their girl had expected this response, and it was apparent she had no intentions of them leaving just yet. They breathed in deeply. It was strong. She was divine and in charge.

Jovis stood still, staring at Caitlin. He shook his head. 'Sorry, I lost my train of thought.' His eyes were glazed over with her magic.

'Artisan and Rocky wish to see what I would like to show you too. It's outside and will only take a moment of your time.' Caitlin started to walk towards the double doors that led outside. She stopped and put her hand out for him to take. 'Are you coming with us, Jovis?'

Jovis was hesitant until Calyx and Jett moved and stood each side of the double doors leading outside. *What are they up to? The blizzard outside will snap freeze her with no jacket on.* But he cheered up knowing if it were that cold, it would give him reason to transport her to his place. He would explain to Axon later that the losers didn't have a clue how to look after her. Happier with that thought, he put out a gentlemanly arm for her to take. 'Tell me why we're going out into the icy darkness with you dressed like that.'

'I want to show you something and promise if it's that cold you can hug me and keep me warm.' She smiled and slipped her arm through his and moved in close.

He tried to shake off the dreamy happy mood only she could put him in, but had no choice and gave in to her. 'If you allow me to walk with you, does this mean you have forgiven me?'

'If the Prince of the Ice Planets is willing to keep an open mind, I would enjoy nothing better than to walk beside him.'

His grin was all she needed.

Artisan came up and slipped in between them, steering her away from Jovis. He turned his head and smiled. 'Mine.'

Jovis's eyes squinted. 'Artisan, share, or you can sleep on your own planet tonight.'

'Okay.' Artisan was reluctant but moved her over to him. 'Ours, then.'

Jovis grinned and put his arm around her. 'My Glow,' he whispered to her.

Calyx looked at Jett. 'We aren't that possessive, are we?'

Caitlin heard him and glanced over her shoulder. 'Worse.' She smiled.

It was at this moment Rocky barged in and lifted Caitlin up into his arms. He was so quick no one had time to stop him.

'Bloody goddess power has us all under her spell, even the big guy,' Calyx whispered to Jett when Rocky and Caitlin reappeared not far from them.

'She's mine,' he said in a gruff voice.

'Rocky,' Jovis warned. 'Bring her back, or you are banned from Sedna for a month.'

Rocky's eyes softened as he looked at Caitlin. 'Just wanted to thank you for helping me, you know, seeing the light and then saving my planet. You're the coolest woman ever. But I'm still on Jovis's naughty list for whipping his butt, so I'd better take you back to grouchy, or your friends over there will have to witness us two fighting again.' He grinned as he walked her back. 'Here you go, boss.'

Caitlin chuckled. 'Now truce, or we'll never get outside these doors,' she said teasingly.

Jovis gave a sigh of relief when she slipped her arm back through his. 'Ready Prince?'

'Ready.' He patted her hand kindly, but his mind was not that easily controlled by his lovely companion. He knew she was special and was doing something, but he was still on tenterhooks, so ready to take her the hell out Hellsville.

Jett stretched out his arm and flicked his fingers. The slight twitch of magic opened the big double doors. The bold display had Jovis's brow raise and eyes widen. To move matter from one's path was a rare gift.

Outside, Jovis stopped suddenly, for the view was not what he expected. 'What the hell?' He gasped at the sight as tropical warmth filled his nostrils and a slight breeze messed up his hair. The sound of water splashing into a pool and birds chirping had his glance go towards the sound. A bee buzzed past him and he took a swipe at it while he blinked several times, sure he imagined it all. Turning his head, he looked back inside and back outdoors. This time, he looked up at the clouds and tall trees that swayed in the breeze. *But how?* Water ran down a wall of creepers and moss-covered jagged rocks. Glistening, crystal-clear water splashed into a huge swimming pool that shaped around a bar with seats deeply immersed. At the deep end, lifted high, was what had to be a spa. The bubbling water that overflowed ran gently down more rocks and greenery and back into the pool below. Further from them, the landscape switched from tropical to manicured gardens with blooms and shrubs shaped into many of the star constellations.

The three visitors stood with mouths still gaped open.

'Wait for it...' Caitlin turned to Jett. 'Can we have the night view?' she said while releasing the hold she had on everyone.

Jett nodded and clapped his hands.

'Hey guys, you'll love this,' she called and pointed upwards. With mouths still open, they followed her gesture. 'Watch what it does.'

Suddenly a motor cranked above them and the shutters moved on the roof and opened up. They saw the blizzard swirl around in the real sky before the shutters settled in place in the opposite direction. Strategically placed coloured lights lit up the roof, taking it from a cloudy summer day to a magical night sky. Each formation of lights gave the illusion of looking at moons, planets, stars and even galaxies. In front of them, floodlights switched on, highlighting an outside kitchen complete with a barbeque and comfortable seating. Beside this, rainbow lighting picked up the magic of a waterfall which sprayed softly down on the roof of a tropical bar and into the massive pool. The ambience was set to give romance to any moonlight swim under the stars.

'You have to admit this is pretty cool, Jovis.' Artisan pointed towards the entertaining area. 'Check it out, it even has a stage and small dance floor.' He put an arm around Caitlin. 'No wonder you dressed like that, the temperature emulates a perfect summer night on Earth.'

'Hot damn, what a ruddy cool chick magnet,' said Rocky.

Jett clapped his hands again, but twice this time.

Caitlin took hold of Jovis's hand, keen to see more. 'Two claps, that's new. He's added something extra.'

No sooner did she say it than brightness illuminated a path. Nobody moved as it was too intriguing not to just watch. The walkway was adjacent to the entertaining deck and trailed alongside the pool until it reached the outer edge of the tropical garden.

'Jett!' She was wide-eyed. 'You've already put in an arboretum?'

'And shaped the trees.'

'I can see that, but how did you grow them so quickly?' Suddenly it dawned on her, and she snapped her fingers at him. 'Don't tell me. They were the excess trees and plants from the Earthling habitat you helped Axon move.' She grinned when he nodded. 'I'm impressed; what a great idea. So pleased you could use them. They grew super crazy in the atmosphere on Ara. Axon thought he might have to destroy what couldn't go back.'

'On my request, Axon now grows them for my Dwarf Planets. He has hired a horticulturist to tend to them.' Jett looked proud she had liked his new addition.

Suddenly a burst of lighting stopped them talking as laser lights that resembled fireworks shot off in all directions. The display was better than Caitlin could have ever conjured up while in her playful moods. He had outdone himself. This new designer laser display was just as much a surprise to her as it was the men who still stood amazed.

Leaving Jovis to speak quietly with his men, Caitlin moved closer to Jett. 'It's so beautiful.'

'That last bit was inspired by you and those creative sky shows you put on,' he said, pleased she liked the expansions. He put his hand out. 'Will you walk with me, Glow?' He had saved this moment for her. He had not even walked the new part of the grounds with his own wife. She was his inspiration, and this was his tribute to his friend. He clapped his hands and brought the dome back to daylight.

'Of course, love to.' She took his arm.

He inclined his head in thanks. His old worldly charm always made her smile. He liked that about Caitlin; she appreciated everything. He strolled beside her, trying to concentrate as she asked questions. To go with him, she had turned up her pleasant goddess scent so the others would follow. He didn't care. This was one moment he wished to share with her first. *Selfish, hell yes!*

Caitlin's delight had satisfied Jett and after the tour of his high-end botanical garden, she surprised him when she asked him for a moment to select some flowers. He turned to chat to Jovis while Caitlin knelt between the flower beds.

Her true aim was to force the men to talk. The only way she knew how was to keep busy and force them to stand and wait. Maybe this would give them time to get to know each other a little better.

The strategy worked, and after a reasonable break, she started heading back towards them but stopped when a tall, thin servant appeared in front of her.

'Can I take them from you madam?' He bowed.

Caitlin knew Jett must have been aware of her ruse and telepathically summoned someone to give her a hand so she could re-join them. This meant all had gone well, but it was time for her to retake charge of them. Her wish was for them to stay for a meal and allow them to get to know Jett, and become a little more comfortable in his presence.

Caitlin handed the arrangement to the servant. 'I want them to go on our dinner table. Oh, and in a low vase, so they don't hide any guests.'

'A perfect location, madam.' The tall servant hurried off to find a bowl-shaped vase to display them in.

When she reached them, they appeared to be quite civil with one another. Undeniably they were not friends or mates yet, but talking without her using magic was a start and it pleased her.

'If you have finished picking flowers,' said Jett, 'I thought I'd take Jovis and his boys up to the cabin for a look around. Would you like to join us?'

Caitlin was even more surprised at how the events were moving along. 'Sure, count me in.'

Once she was with them, the lovely tropical warmth changed to teeth-chattering-icy-cold conditions. The lovely gown was immediately covered by a long white furry thick coat with a hood, and her shoes became boots made from the same alien fur. It pleased her that she no longer needed a horse to dress her. Shargan's magic she now carried within.

Jett clicked his fingers, and the wood in the hearth crackled and burst into flames. Caitlin ran to it, placing her hands near the heat. 'Brrr... that was a cold snap.'

'Better?' Jett put an arm around her.

Caitlin leant in and smiled. 'Now I have you next to me, radiating even more heat, I'm much better.' She glanced up and saw the dark gaze of Jovis. He had taken offence at their casual affection and didn't look impressed by the displayed closeness of their relationship.

He's still hurting, Jett. He hasn't found happiness in his own world yet and clings to me. She had to quickly change this situation around. *What about some drinks?*

Jett heard her thoughts loud and clear and removed his arm from her. 'What about a round of Starstarter shooters to warm up your guests?'

'Sound good,' Cait thanked him and then privately asked him to take Calyx with him.

As both men went over to the mini bar to pour the drinks, it left her free to see how the other three were faring. They couldn't see outside as it was dark and had no idea why they were now standing in a small room with nothing much but fire going in a fire place and four walls. They had a lot to take in and this she knew had left them feeling confused on top of being overwhelmed.

'Jovis?' She pretended she was still cold and gave a shiver. 'Do you mind keeping me warm until this fire kicks in and heats the room?' She noticed his eyes were almost closed and he was looking cross. She hoped he wasn't planning anything silly or if he was, that he would register what she was saying quickly and snap out of it.

'If you don't I will,' Artisan pushed him.

Thank goodness for Artisan! She smiled as Jovis moved close.

'Sorry; my mind was elsewhere.' He didn't take his eyes from hers.

'Jett's just grabbing us a drink to have while he finishes off the tour. In the meantime, I hoped you might share your power to keep me from freezing. The fire is taking forever to heat this room.' Her teeth chattered as she put her arm through his and leant into him.

'Sure... warmer?' His temper calmed.

'Much.'

Artisan took a couple of steps between them and stood the other side of her. 'She needs me too, dork, so stop hogging.' He held up a bent arm which Caitlin eagerly accepted and put her arm through his. 'Yes, I definitely feel I have an electric blanket wrapped around me now.'

Jett was amused at how easily she handled these men. Yet he was annoyed he had been sent off to get the drinks. Calyx shared his expression as they glanced at one another while they carried them back.

'Cheers to all your magical Ice Planets!' Caitlin raised her glass. She knew these men needed a tradition straight off the bat to link them. 'Down the hatch!' She gulped the drink and threw the empty shot glass into the fire. On the sound of smashed glass, she cheered.

The three visiting men, including Calyx and Jett, shrugged and holding up the shot glass repeated after her, 'to the Ice Planets,' they said in unison and gulping down the amber liquid. With a grin, they too tossed their empty shot glasses into the fire. The sound of them smashing against the brick walls of the hearth magically sent a vibration of ease through them. Warmed by a load that would possibly be shared, they felt somehow lighter and together hollered out a hearty cheer.

Jett eyed Caitlin. *Oh, you're good, girl. Your magic gets better with each quest.*

Caitlin winked at him before getting the attention of the men again. 'Let's make this an Ice Planet tradition from now on. When we meet, no matter the reason, good or bad, we have a drink together first. The liquid represents that dampness beneath your feet that links you as brothers. Broken glass is the ice wall you comfortable smashed down to allow one another inside. The fire is the flame in your bellies to want more than you have, but also means the light of knowledge you will find together. From this day forward your journey is made easier by the camaraderie as a collective. "Stay wise and stick together, no matter what," is the Ice Planets new motto.' She turned to Jett. 'Let's show our guests my favourite room before we show them what you did bring them here to see. She took Jovis by the arm. 'Come and see my most favourite room in the entire kingdom.

Jett opened the door, the lights flicked on, and Caitlin couldn't wipe the smile off her face. 'You've renovated.'

'You like?' He eyed her.

'I love it!' She strode in, excited.

Jovis was already blown away by what he had seen so far, but Caitlin was right. This room was world standard. Jett had all the mods and cons of a Modern Greek bathing house. There was a large-size, blue-tiled, rectangular pool in the centre and a smaller pool each side. He assumed one was a hot spa, and the other therapeutic, as the jets looked different. Each pool had been sectioned off with stone walkways and broad stone steps leading into all three. Past the mineral spas, matching blue-tiled-pillars stood tall against a backdrop of embossed stone panels, which led the eye to further opulence. Matching lush-white and gold cushioned lounges softened the decor and behind them, clearly marked, were showers and a sauna. Jovis lifted his eyes. The roof was an artist's delight as he admired a painted mural of dwarf planets and where they fitted into the solar system. Jett's unique place in the heavens had made its mark and the artwork showed the massive imprint he had accomplished in this short amount of time since becoming the King. Each domain was emblazoned with bold gold lettering and included names such as Eris, Pluto, Haumea, Makemake, and Ceres. In amongst this elaborate artwork, a cluster of dark shapes hung from the roof. Inside each one, lighting threw images of bright galaxies, the patterns shining down onto the water below. He wondered if the mood could be changed in an instant from this daytime effect, like outside, to a soft romantic glow, if entertaining a loved one. He looked for a dimmer switch. *Nope, a clap of the hands.* Jovis shook his head slightly as Jett did as he thought, and changed the mood to romantic.

Caitlin placed her hands to her mouth and squealed with joy. 'It's nothing like what I recall. You've extended the walls and roof. It's double the size, and this is... well... I just love it, it's perfect, Jett.' She ran her hand over the pillars that stood nearest to her and grinned. 'This is one massive project. How did you keep this a secret from me?' She slapped his arm.

'Ouch.' He chuckled. 'My wife swore me to secrecy.'

'Melita did this?' Caitlin's eyes were wide and so was her smile.

'Sure did, well with a bit of help from yours truly.'

'And me,' said Calyx.

Jett folded his arms, looking very pleased. 'Melita wanted you to have somewhere special and private to bring Axon. She worries you don't see enough of one another. You know what my wife is like.' He grinned. 'Wish she could have been here to see your reaction. She's worked tirelessly on the décor and will be thrilled you like it.'

'Love it!' Caitlin corrected him.

He liked her being happy. 'I know that playful look, but this room is out of bounds until Axon is with you. Melita left strict instructions that you two must be the first to use it. So out you go.' He turned her around, ignoring her pout. 'No!' He chuckled when she protested, and he walked out behind his guests, turning off the lights with a wave of his hand.

Jovis was taken back to the lengths Jett and his wife went to make Caitlin this happy. He was starting to like this Jett. He was nothing like the Hades he had been warned of all his life. He blinked and finally got it. Jett was not Hades around her. Calyx didn't act at all like the almighty Zeus, God of all Gods, either. As for him, he was a warlord, a prince and feared by many. Yet since he met Cait, he knew he had changed too. Her friendship and happiness were infectious. It was almost as if he had found love, but a different kind. She made him happy to be who he was, yet strangely, more so under his new name, Jovis. Even he had started to like who he was becoming. They had all changed and would continue down this path to find... He wasn't sure. He knew it wasn't love, as he could clearly hear in Jett's voice how in love he was with his wife. Calyx was married too, yet they wore the glow of happiness. *That was undoubtedly all Glow Girl.*

Suddenly he wanted to flee with her and not ever share again. But, wanting and doing was not an option. He enjoyed her laughter so much that it captivated him, and his two feet felt glued to the floor.

Jett started talking, and he turned his head to see what he was pointing towards. He felt Caitlin take his hand. He was moving towards the door and stood out on a wooden deck. It was pitch black. Suddenly the outside world lit up. He looked at Caitlin and back at the view. It was a snow resort, complete with ski-lifts.

Jett was still talking. This time Jovis was interested as suddenly it all made sense. Caitlin had been trying to get him to listen and understand there was more to his planets than ice and snow. Well, he was finally paying attention although he was not yet sold on needing a king to show him how. Did he need help? The pig-headed side of him was still saying, No!

Jett pointed. 'Beside us, we have ski buggies, and that hut is full of skis, toboggans and snow-gear.'

Jovis had never thought to do any of this. His heart leapt. The people to help him were all here. He held the hand of the girl who brought him to this point. He trusted her, but did he trust Jett? That, he could not answer.

It was Calyx who suggested they break for dinner, and before anyone could argue, he transported them back to the house.

When back inside the castle walls, Jovis was polite but insistent. 'We have to head back. There are continued threats to our worlds. Please accept our apology for us not staying to help you eat this wonderful spread.' He eyed the table. 'But duty calls.'

As he finished speaking, he heard a noise from behind him. Everyone spun around to see what was happening. Axon had arrived.

'Have you been waiting for me?' He walked straight to Caitlin and, putting an arm around her, headed for the table.

'Actually, Jovis was just saying we had to leave. The men are worried about their Ice Planets.'

Axon stopped at the table and pulled out a chair for her. 'Bulldust! You're eating something decent before you leave in case you are needed, my lady.' He winked at her and turned his head to Jovis. 'My team is there and will stay until Caitlin returns. Sit, eat!' he insisted. 'My wife must be taken care of first.'

Jovis stood for all of a second in silence before he spoke. 'Fine, but no stalling… My loyalty…'

Axon stood up straight. 'Your loyalty had better be to Caitlin before that real estate of yours, or she stays here. I can replace your Ice Planet if it blows up. I can't replace Cait. Now sit and enjoy a meal with us. '

'Thank you,' Caitlin mouthed as he sat her down.

He turned back to Jovis, who stood smiling. 'You can do that?'

'You have no idea the lengths I will go to keep my wife happy.' He pulled out the chairs each side of her and looked back and forth at Jovis and Artisan. 'Now get your butts over here and entertain our girl, so she eats up big. Not sure what's been going on today, but she's almost depleted of power.'

'You can tell?' Jovis said as he and Artisan moved quickly at his command. If she had to stay, of course, they would too and to sit next to her, well that was a bonus they were not expecting.

Calyx and Jett secretly knuckle-punched. They knew now

why Jovis had said he was leaving. Caitlin had used her powers up keeping them controlled all afternoon. She had nothing left. They were so pleased Axon knew her so well and had swooped in and saved the day. A meal together was a chance to chat freely and get to know these boys better. They sat.

'Rocky, you're with me, big boy.' Axon smiled. 'I need someone to talk to that isn't in goddamned love with my wife.' It cracked everyone up and broke the ice. From then on, the conversation and jokes flowed freely.

During dinner, Jovis told them how Caitlin had become bored and wanted to explore a cave that wasn't too far from his home. 'With her, it looked so different. Her stories had us captivated and we didn't realise how deep into the cave we had gone.'

'Her tales are most intriguing, I agree. For someone that's barely lived, she is one remarkable storyteller.' Jett grinned at Caitlin. 'I too become engrossed in her experiences; the details she recalls of the events are quite fascinating.'

'One was that of an ice bar that had me and Artisan travel to see. Since then, I have designed one similar for the ice cave where we found the hot springs. I've already started work on it.' Jovis sat back, looking chuffed he had something Jett didn't.

'It's coming up a treat.' Artisan placed his fork and knife down while he talked. 'The steam from the hot springs caused us some major headaches, but we think we've found a solution using … well, maybe I better keep it secret until we test it out and make sure it works.'

Rocky spoke too, but with a mouth full of food. 'My idea.' He spat food when he talked.

'Manners, buddy,' Jovis growled at him. Everyone else laughed.

Rocky's face when he looked at Jovis was so innocent. *What did I do wrong?* 'Geez Jovis,' he said after a gulp, 'you can be such a princess, mate.' This made even Jovis laugh.

Insults continued for a few minutes until Jovis turned his attention back to Jett. 'But in all fairness on who did what, we would never have known about an ice bar or that we had readily available hot water it if it hadn't been for Caitlin. And seeing what you have done here, Jett, I understand when she tells us we could have it all. You have captured a piece of normality in a cold and icy dark existence. If I hadn't seen this with my own eyes, I would never have believed it possible. You have done a remarkable job, and I take my hat off to you for the innovation and execution of work completed.'

Jett was genuinely pleased he finally shared his thoughts and the nature of them. 'Thank you Jovis. But I have only one person to thank for this. If Glow hadn't had the innocent vision of doming the grounds of my castle to warm it, I would still be on the warpath to take over a warmer planet. This dome allows Melita and me to enjoy outdoor living all year round, and now when we invite family and friends, they like visiting and want to stay over. Maybe a bit more than I would like...' He grinned at Calyx.

Caitlin sat forward. 'This was all you, Jett. The dome might have been an idea I threw around, but it was you who worked out how to add power to it and give the roof night and day shutters. Oh, and the pool spa combination and plant life! I had no idea they would even grow in these conditions.' She chuckled as she looked at Jovis. 'I swear, I did nothing to help build any of this. This planet was so cold back then, I lived up by the fire in my room and read all day by the window. I watched it from afar, but help? You know me I'm about as handy with a hammer as I am with a kitchen knife. My friend is kindly trying to give me some credit.'

Jett eyed her with a love that they all saw. 'You gave me my life back. I am eternally grateful.' He inclined his head then turned to Jovis. 'Do not underestimate our clever Glow. Talk to her and don't hold back. She does this thing, kind of like a nose twitch. Watch for it and allow her to think. This is her changing negatives into a positive.'

'I've seen her do that!' Artisan sat up straight looking at her. 'I didn't know I should shut up. Bet I've missed some doozies.'

'I do not!' Caitlin argued.

Jovis nudged her. 'You do!'

'Well, I disagree. But just in case, no looking at my nose, ever!' she said.

'Can't help it, that is such a huge nose,' Artisan stirred. 'Each time you tell a fib it gets bigger.'

'Does not.' She squeezed at it, feeling to see.

'Gotcha.' Artisan laughed with her.

Axon could see how they interacted. Artisan was the humorous one, and Jovis kept it real. He smiled, but the entire time, he watched out for her. He made sure she had food on her plate and stopped the games every now and then to encourage her to eat. He liked seeing she was well cared for, although he would much prefer to take her from these stubborn men and have them sort out their own problems.

He heard in their tone at times when asked a business question that they held back, which meant they were not yet ready to take on Jett as their king. Therefore, it was time to bow out until he was needed to help with negotiations. 'Well,' Axon said as he stood up, 'it's time for me to get back to work. Hope you men have enjoyed your visit here on Pluto. Cait, can I see you for a minute before I go?' He looked towards the end of the table. 'Jett, Calyx, thanks for dinner.' He then glanced over at Jovis, Artisan and Rocky. 'Men, keep in touch. And no more guests while Cait is with you.' He gave them all an informal salute. 'Gentlemen, later!'

Caitlin got up and joined him in the foyer. He wrapped his arms around her and kissed the lips he loved. 'Wanted to do that all night.' He smiled, his eyes alight with love for her. 'Do what you need to do. I'll wait for your return.'

'Because of a passing comment by Artisan, I fear the girls who were involved with Nitarn are locked up in their dungeon. I'm guessing this might be the reason Jovis kept trying to rush back. You better give me a few weeks. These men need a lesson on how to treat a lady. Maybe I should send you back with them, and I'll go home.' She grinned.

He pulled his hands from her and put them in the air as a sign of, *hands off*. 'No way! I have better things to do than pandering to a spoilt prince and his men. Not my field of expertise, beautiful.' He took her hands and kissed them. 'As your husband, I'm already missing you. As your boss, you know I have faith in your abilities to fix the waring Ice Planets, but I'm not sure you'll be able to sort out the women situation.'

'What am I up against?'

'Until they sign up under Jett, they operate under the old laws. What the girls did was to aid and abet a criminal. In their world, the crime is punishable by death. Good luck with getting them out of that charge if this is what you are thinking.' By the faraway gaze, he knew no matter what he said, she would fight Jovis on it, and he admired her immensely for being able to see the good in all people.

'Mmm...' She tapped her chin, thinking. 'Talk soon, sweetheart.'

She was already lost to him as he bade her farewell.

She held her hand up in a goodbye gesture and turned once he was gone.

When Caitlin walked back into the dining room unaccompanied, her three new friends were standing.

'Are you ready?' Jovis said as she walked towards them.

'Sure!' She gave Calyx a hug goodbye and instantly her clothes were covered with a floor-length warm fur coat, her shoes disappeared, and were replaced by fur boots. 'Can't have you catch your death out there.' He grinned.

'Thanks, Calyx.' She hugged him one last time for being so sweet.

When she went to Jett, she felt his hands shake when they went around her. 'I hate handing you over to them. Are you sure you'll be okay? And don't just say yes because I'm worried,' he whispered.

She spoke by telepathy. *I'm so proud of you and Calyx. The visit went better than I imagined. And please don't worry, they look after me so well and have learned a big lesson. I trust them and know it won't be repeated.' She grinned, 'If anything does go wrong they're on good terms with you now and won't be nervous about bringing me here if I ask them.'* She glanced towards the backyard. *'By the way, I love all the improvements... and you.'* She gave him a nudge and after, rolled her eyes. *Geez, you better tell Calyx that I love him too, or we'll both be in the shytzer.'*

Jett couldn't hold back his grin. He leant in and whispered as she gave him a hug. 'Keep safe, beautiful, we love you too.'

CHAPTER THIRTY-TWO

Learning to forgive

Caitlin was glad Calyx had wrapped her up in his own designer furs. When they shimmered onto Sedna, there was a blizzard, so for once she felt appropriately dressed. She could barely see the door Jovis was opening, and it was only a few metres from her. Inside, they stood on the elevator shelf.

'Where's that noise coming from?' She heard sobbing and calls for help. Her question was met with silence. 'Seriously, who's down there?' Caitlin pulled her brows in tight, as her fears for the girls were made real. 'I don't care who it is down there, but if they have been in that dungeon since you left, they will be frozen with that blizzard going on out there. The cold air travels down this shaft even when the door is closed. Trust me, I remember.'

'Those criminals have broken our laws and are waiting for my decision as to their fate. They deserve no better, but to appease you, I can tell you they have ample warmth, so don't concern yourself with their welfare. Artisan and Rocky will check on them after we get you settled. The fires will be out, and I need them to help me warm the rooms for you first.' Jovis brushed it off as nothing, but she knew better.

The sobbing sounded like a female's, and Caitlin was almost sure her intuition was correct, and it was the women they had recently befriended. 'If those criminals you speak of are the ladies I met at your party, I can tell you know, they have no special gifts as you men do and it will be far too cold for them in your dungeon, Jovis. You know that I know this first hand.'

'Cait, please… they have committed a crime, and we have our laws. You must respect them and not interfere. The lads will see to them shortly.'

'I accept and understand you have to uphold the law, but in fairness to me, as Goddess of Peace, I need to see if they are okay. You can't surely think I'd just go inside and not worry? Especially as it seems they are where I was not so long ago, when you thought me guilty too.' Her voice rose with annoyance and at the same time had her hands firmly planted on her hips. 'I want to see them now!'

Jovis knew how Rocky must have felt when Caitlin was cross at him. He stared intently, but not a muscle did she flex to show this was her acting tough to get what she wanted. He needed her, but not like this. He shrugged. 'Stuff the girls. They aren't worth us arguing over. Fine… go visit them. But I warn, they'll get no special treatment.'

Rocky's forehead creased, showing his agreement with Jovis. 'Those women down there were invited to keep us three busy, and give Nitarn's hit men a chance to catch us unawares and kill the three of us.'

Artisan turned to her. 'It was you who saved us, Cait. He saw you and called the hit off, and that's why the hitmen left. The girls don't know why. Their part in it amounts to treason, though. To assist in such a hit on the prince or any of the royal family is punishable by death.'

'That is the only thing waiting for those three,' Rocky chimed in.

Caitlin stood firm. 'I'm not going anywhere until I know they are humanely treated.'

Jovis shrugged. 'Fine.'

When they got down to the dungeon, an elderly guard was leaning back in a chair, sleeping through the noise. He jumped to attention when Jovis forced a cough and woke him. 'Sorry you caught me dozing Your Royal Highness, but them gals have been acting up and kept me awake all night. Even gave 'em extra blankets and still, they complained.'

'We'll take over from here. Go have a coffee, man, and wake the hell up,' Rocky dismissed him.

'Sorry boss,' he mumbled to Rocky when passing him to head over to the far side of the dungeon.

Caitlin glanced over and saw the man sit at a table where he opened a thermos and poured coffee into an oversized mug. He looked a gentle, kind man, and she was glad Rocky had left someone compassionate to care for them while they were away. Her attention was soon back to the girls. She stared through the bars and saw the three women from the party huddled up together on a big mattress they'd been given. The younger one that Artisan had been with was the one crying. Caitlin glanced at him watching her sniffle. He was such a softie. Even though she had done wrong, his expression showed empathy and concern.

He felt Caitlin's eyes burn into him. 'I've given them bedding to keep them warm and plenty of food, but she keeps sobbing. I don't know what else to do.' Artisan shrugged helplessly.

'A good slap might help.' Rocky sounded unusually cruel, but she felt he was just acting tough in front of his mates.

'It's Glow!' The girl stopped shedding tears and lifted from the bed. With only a few steps she was at the bars where Caitlin stood. 'Please help us, Glow, you remember me, don't you? I'm Sienna, from the party. I was with Artisan.'

'Yes, I remember,' said Caitlin, unmoving and showing little of any emotion.

'Well, Loray over there was with Rocky.' She pointed to her. 'And Jana...' The third woman had stood up, and her tall, slender frame leant stubbornly against the wall. 'Well... well she's just a bitch, so don't worry about her.' Sienna turned back to Caitlin. 'Honestly, none of us knew what Nitarn had planned. He had put us under a spell. He's always doing stuff like that. He had your friends there under a spell too, didn't he? Yet it looks like you forgave them! Please forgive us and ask them to forgive us too.'

Caitlin turned to the men that stood protectively around her. 'Can I have a moment alone with these ladies?'

'What! Hell no!' Jovis glared at her.

'Look at them, they're behind bars and have no powers that I can sense. Even if they did, they are no match for me. You know this. I'm perfectly safe. Geez, even a furry rat has more self-respect than to hide down here.'

'She has a point. Nothing lives down in this chiller,' Rocky agreed.

'What! You want us to just go upstairs and leave you down here... with them?' Jovis thought this irrational.

Her brows rose. 'Do I have to beg?'

Jovis was unsure if she was acting again or not, but she looked different, more controlled and ticked off. He knew she couldn't be harmed here and although he didn't like it, he wondered if a few minutes back down here might change her attitude. 'What you feel necessary to discuss in private with these trashy criminals is beyond me. But if it is what you wish, then so be it. I will give you fifteen minutes and no more. Get the guard to call me if you finish earlier.'

'I'd appreciate that, thank you!'

They didn't move. She put her hands on her hips and stared at them. This was a pose they knew well. She was dead serious and without another word they turned to leave. Three sets of boots stomped loudly to showing their leaving was under protest. They couldn't believe she was kicking them out.

Caitlin turned back to the girls.

'Wow, you can do that, you're so little! No man has ever listened to me like that.' Sienna's eyes were wide as she watched them leave and slam the stronghold door behind them.

Caitlin had already chosen their fate, but taking it up was their choice. *Laws of the land indeed...* it had been a long time since any statutes here had been followed. Jovis hid from all who knew him. For security, he broke a number of laws by giving homes to Dark Avengers, who in return, fiercely protected his worlds. On top of this, he bought real estate, which was poverty-stricken due to his own raids and artillery, and fought laws to prevent the many worlds he now owned from becoming Dwarf Planets. Nothing was legal on these Ice Planets yet. She could, therefore, operate in accordance with humanity laws and sort this out in-house.

If she was ever a good judge of character and had any understanding of matters of the heart, these were going to be put to the test. She felt Jana's strength from where she stood. As she was the strongest of the three, Caitlin worried about her the most. It was going to take more than a man to break through the wall she had built around her.

Caitlin would have to be smart, smarter than the three of them put together. As one, they would figure her out quickly and game over. She ran her eyes over all three and stopped at Jana. She was perfect, but no man would want her as she stood. Sienna was sweet but easily led, and as for Loray, if she and Rocky were friends, it was for only one reason. She had a dark side, but however shady her past, Caitlin was not able to gauge her, and couldn't work out why. She sighed. This was going to take a miracle to pull off, but she was willing to test her abilities and people skills.

It was dead silent while she continued to assess each girl, coming up with a strategy that would work for all three.

Finally, Caitlin spoke. 'This is my one and only offer to you, ladies, take it or leave it. I may be able to get you out of this cell, but there will be consequences, and you must do as I say, or I shall have you all thrown back in here for good. Regardless of who was under what spell, you were Nitarn's girls and knew he must have been up to no good. You used your charm and assets to draw Jovis, Artisan and Rocky into a web of deceit. This, as you know, is a severe crime, especially against royalty.'

'You know what she wants of us; surely you're not that pathetic!' Jana stared at the other two girls. 'I know already, she'll keep us caged like animals until we are needed to pleasure the men upstairs. Kill me now!'

'No Jana. That is far from what I was suggesting. I simply wish you to take up residence here for a while and do your time working as servants.'

'What!' the three girls yelled out in unison.

'It's the only way I will get you out of here and back into comfortable quarters. Surely you would prefer to pamper the person you betrayed rather than stay here and meet your fate?'

'But we didn't know Nitarn was going to kill or kidnap anyone, or we would have fought him. Usually, we are just company for the odd man who is without a partner. Maybe we went a bit far because these guys were hotties, but we didn't ever want to hurt them. I swear none of us knew Jovis was royalty,' Sienna said, and sniffled.

'Then prove to these men how sorry you are and that you can be trusted! I am trying to give you an opportunity to get out of these freezing conditions and in doing so, hope to prevent you from meeting your maker too soon.' Caitlin breathed deeply in frustration. Her outburst was met with silence. This was to be their only salvation. Nothing else would Jovis go for, and even this was going to be a tough ask.

'Go on, I'm listening.' Jana finally spoke in her no-nonsense tone, her arms folded in a guarded pose as she came closer to hear what Caitlin had planned for them.

'Yer, so tell us what yu proposin'?' Loray lifted from the bed and came closer. She spoke with such a thick dialect, and so quietly, Caitlin only just caught what she said. How she was able to attract Rocky amazed her. He was so loud.

Caitlin paced, thinking, and then stopped. 'If I help you, I expect you to abide by all my rules. They will challenge you to your very core, but follow my wishes and your freedom will be granted.'

'Not sure if I believe you can give us our freedom, but amuse me!' Jana sneered.

Caitlin would have preferred to slap her snobby face rather than continue, but in a way, she liked her straightforwardness.

'I propose you take care of the men you deceived. Not just washing and ironing; I'm talking about pandering to their every whim.'

'Till when?' Jana curled her lip.

'Until I say otherwise, and I insist these following chores are adhered to without one word of complaint. These duties will include organising washing and ironing, cleaning and picking up after them, and any other reasonable request.'

'Like?' Jana huffed.

'If they want their backs washed, bodies massaged, food or drink, you will grin and bear the task. If you can promise me you will abide by this and pay your debt by hard work...' She stared at Jana who swore and went to argue.

Caitlin raised her hand. 'I've not finished. There is one last personal detail I wish to share with you, and it is not negotiable. Also, it is never to be discussed with the men, so do I have your word as honourable women?'

'Yes,' they all said together.

'Good, but if I find you have lied to me regarding this, you are straight back here, in this cold pit of sadness, and I will not accept any excuse.'

'Just tell us and quit the threats. We're not stupid. As if we want to be back here!' Jana shifted from one foot to the other.

'None of you will sleep with my men.' Caitlin's final demand hit them like a bomb.

'You're blazing kidding me, right!' Jana dropped her shoulders in surprise.

'As their goddess, I lay claim to these men as mine, and I am the only one that will sleep with them.' She had hands on hips. 'Do I make myself perfectly clear? Your duties will not include you ever being easy prey. You must refrain from teasing or any attempt to charm my men into your beds, or I swear, I will bestow my worst wrath upon you.'

'What could be worse than being thrown back down here?' Loray sounded irritated.

'Try my patience, and you will find this cell is Pleasantville compared to where I could banish you too, my dear girl.' Caitlin raised her voice with an air they were not expecting. 'So you have my proposal. You leave all sluttish behaviour behind and no matter what the task, you will answer politely and take on the challenge with dignity. Am I making myself clear or would you prefer to stay here and wait to be put to death? It's your choice.'

Sienna started to cry again. 'Please I will do anything, it scares me down here.'

Loray's eyes were wide as she realised Caitlin wasn't kidding. She was ready to wash her hands of them, and it was apparent by the glare of impatience in her eyes. 'I too, agree to do as you ask. Just get me out of here,' she muttered.

Jana stood glaring at Caitlin. 'You… sleep with Jovis!'

Caitlin nodded. 'He is my man, and don't you forget it. We have not been formally introduced, Jana, but I am the Goddess of Peace, and I vow to declare my wrath on any women who dare to take what I lay claim to or who may abuse my good nature.'

Jana was the first to break the thick, uncomfortable silence that followed. Her moody tone was not shaken by Caitlin, not one bit. 'What would Jovis want with a fragile thing like you? Well, if that is what he prefers then so be it. I'm fine with wiping his nose until you say. Just don't make it too long; there is only so much boyish behaviour I can stand then I would much sooner come back here and face my punishment.'

Caitlin had to hold back laughter. Jana was perfect for Jovis. He must have felt something when he was with her, but he certainly wasn't showing it.

'So be it.' Caitlin snapped her fingers and with the goddess tone, she had found entertaining after using it on Jana to get her attention, called for the guard. 'Inform Prince Jovis that his goddess has finished speaking to the women and tell him I have made my decision on their fate.'

Shortly after, the door swung open, and it took everything she had not to smile when Jovis, Artisan and Rocky stomped cantankerously onto the concrete floor. Caitlin held her ground, although taking one look at how furious they were with her, she almost ducked behind the guard who followed them in. She should have guessed they'd be up there stewing that they were not involved, but there were secrets shared here that were not for their ears. They stood glaring at the women, and she saw they had every intention to stick together and refuse any request she made on their behalf to make their stay in prison more comfortable. *They are sure not going to like this proposal.*

'I'm not happy with this Cait.' Jovis gritted his teeth and waited for her to reply to this behaviour he had not seen from her before.

Caitlin could feel the air was thick and hoped begging wouldn't be required. She eyed the girls. *Are they worth fighting for?* She didn't like upsetting Jovis, as he was at a very vulnerable stage. Still, this would prove how strong their friendship was at this point. She politely addressed them to get their attention. 'Jovis, Artisan, Rocky; as you know, this is no place to keep a lady.' She put up her hand to stop them from interrupting when their mouths opened to argue. 'Let me finish, then you can debate my proposal. I do not mean for these ladies to be set free; oh no, far from it, as they have much to prove. Therefore, I propose they are given a room up in the main house where I can keep a watchful eye on them.'

Their jaws dropped. They had no comeback; nor did they guess this was what their sneaky goddess was planning.

Caitlin continued. 'They have promised to attend to the men they have injured by their crime. This means every chore or need of yours is met until they have proved themselves to be worthy members of society.'

'What if they do us in while we sleep?' Artisan said.

'You have me to protect you, as no doubt, there will be some teething problems.' She turned to the girls to show them who was going to be the boss here. 'It's nothing I can't handle.' Her tone emitted confidence.

Jovis ran his hand through his hair and moved uncomfortably from foot to foot. 'I'm not happy about this, Cait; I would prefer us to discuss this in private.'

She put her hands back on her hips.

Here it comes. Jovis half expected it. Her eyes glowed like exquisite jewels, and her hair sparked red flames. He'd found out even Jett feared this stance. He'd told them at dinner; *once our Glow has her mind made up, there is no talking her out of it.*

She stared into Jovis's eyes. *'Trust me.'* Her voice was clear, yet her lips didn't move. *'And you owe me!'* She spoke to him in telepathy.

He stared back, eyes almost closed. *She so has me over a blatzing barrel.* A smile suddenly gleamed in his eyes. 'Okay, I'll play your little game Caitlin, but only until we are even. Nitarn being here was my fault, and you're right, I do owe you big time for you trusting me and coming back here. But no more favours, ever.' He dropped his hands and held hers. 'I hate us arguing. I guess for you, my angel, I can handle it for a bit.'

'Oh, please!' Jana coughed out, covering her displeasure at Jovis sucking up to Caitlin.

Caitlin heard it but only because her hearing was astute due to Rider magic. She knew Jana was going to be a handful. *I think she's jealous.* Was Jana already smitten? *Sure sounded like it!*

* * * *

For the next few weeks, the girls fussed over the men and with nothing else to do, the men fussed over Caitlin. Inside the fortress became a happy place during the day. The men had begun to relax, and she'd hear giggles from the girls, instead of the first stiff and uncomfortable interactions. At bedtime, it was a whole other mood. It amused Caitlin how she'd feel the burn of Jana and Sienna's eyes when their men and Rocky would accompany her upstairs to bed.

Loray would turn and walk off without a word. She was far too quiet for these boys, though she and Rocky seemed to be friends.

The men were totally unaware that the women were left with the lingering thought they were upstairs making love to this goddess who had some weird sort of harem thing going on.

Jovis would lift Caitlin up and playfully throw her over his shoulder. 'Bedtime, beautiful!' He'd smile and take her upstairs with Artisan and Rocky right behind them, leaving a grumpy Jana and Sienna to finish cleaning up the night dishes.

This behaviour happened often; one of the men would carry Caitlin upstairs, while the other two joked around, trying to steal her from them. Once in her room, Caitlin always made sure the key in the lock had been turned so the women, if wanting a peek at what went on, were unable open the door. It meant she couldn't fall asleep until the men left, but this was a small price to pay to keep the secret.

Kept hidden was the innocent sight of her much-loved friends who sat on the sofas and chatted to her, sometimes until early morning before they retired to their own rooms. It was their time alone together to plan their future and to talk about private matters they kept from the women, who were not yet trusted.

In the mornings, Caitlin always stayed in her room until the men went down for breakfast.

'I'll meet you downstairs in a minute,' she would yell out when getting a wake-up call from them. Little did any of them know, that before she did come downstairs, she'd make Jovis, Artisan and Rocky's beds. Caitlin, however, left her own bed messy. Going as far as tossed covers and pillows on the floor to make it look as if they had one fabulously sexy romp. If she had to go to her room while the girls were cleaning it, Jana would tut-tut it when she walked in. Her gaze never left the bed for long. It was as though she was reliving it, only in her mind it was just her and Jovis.

Caitlin was not looking forward to the day she would have to come clean and tell all. *No lie is a good lie.* However, these girls had to stop throwing themselves at men and disrespecting themselves. They had built up walls and were not attractive to any male suitor. The men, on the other hand, wanted women but from what they had told her, they used them for sex and weren't at all interested in getting to know the women they lived with. They acted like single men determined to continue living their lives as usual. *They also have a lot to learn.* Their lesson was simple; treat a lady as she should be treated and allow not just a female, but love, into their heart and life. Although she felt riddled with guilt for removing the one thing that prevented them getting to know one another on a more spiritual level, it did make them interact as ordinary folk do. She was more than pleased when it worked. Slowly but surely, they had become friends. *Would love follow?*

CHAPTER THIRTY-THREE

Lesson of the Heart

U pon waking, Caitlin's mind was on Axon, which was unusual when on a mission. It made her wonder if her time here on Sedna was almost done.

As she came down the stairs, Jovis waved at her to join him. He held a NAVreader up to her and by his nervous fidget; she could only surmise he had received his plans for the new and improved living conditions on Sedna. The project included his entire Kingdom, and she flooded with proud emotions he had allowed Jett to help.

'Coming, just give me a second.' She stopped to pour coffee. As she did so, her eyes darted towards Artisan and Rocky. Neither wore the same look, so she assumed only Jovis's plans were ready. She knew Jovis still had security in the sky, so she figured he must have been up very early to go and collect them himself.

Her thoughts went quickly to the development stage; the hours of planning and researching ideas to make their Ice Planets a better place to live. Under Artisan's dome was to be a sports arena to house competitions between the three worlds, and Rocky was determined to build a casino. *He's such a party boy.* Jovis wanted a family to share his life and had settled on a similar plan to Jett's. The changes Jovis made were to the far end of the kingdom. Instead of the botanical gardens, he figured in a soccer field, tennis court and beside it, housed in a bowling alley. He felt sure this entertainment would be fun if he were lucky enough to ever have a family. This was the most complicated of designs and stood to reason it was worked on first. That was unless she was wrong... *never!*

'Look what's come back!' Jovis held up a NAVreader when she entered the dining room. 'This little baby holds the key to a new life, and I wanted you to be here with us to see it for the first time.'

'Oh wow, that was quick. Just yours?' She smiled, chuffed she had a small part in helping, even if it was just to contact Jett and plead with him to help.

'Just mine. The boys said they were happy to wait, so I got the call late last night to say I could pick them up this morning.'

'If Jett sent you the same architect as the one he used on all his other Dwarf Planets, I can understand why you have them so quickly. The guy is brilliant at design, and with Jett's mastermind behind the ingenious constructions and how these work best, the two make an awesome team. I know for a fact that all Jett's Dwarf Planets now have all year round outdoor living, and under their domes have become thriving metropolises.'

Jovis nodded. 'Credit to him. In such a short time he has revolutionised his empire, and it's become the most talked about innovation within the galaxy. I finally have to admit, he was the right man for the job after all.'

Caitlin was not only thrilled to see how happy Jovis looked, but delighted to hear the outstanding accolades for Jett. 'He would be thrilled to hear you say so.'

He grinned and ignored the comment. 'Come; sit.' He pulled out a chair for her, and after she was seated, the men joined her. Jovis's hand shook a little as he unlocked the device with the secret code he'd been given. In clear view, a holograph of the architect's design, as per Jovis's instructions, lit up above the table where the device was positioned. The four of them were stunned at first, too busy staring at the intricate images. It gave such a vivid impression that it was as if it were already built and each movement of Jovis's hand to adjust the angles, gave peripheral views of inside the buildings as well.

Jovis paused his hand and rested it on the table so he could talk. 'Look Cait, he even found space to add that tree and swing we spoke about. The whole thing is so perfectly symmetrical and detailed.'

'This guy sure knows his stuff, boss.' Rocky scrutinised it and raised his hand to enlarge the tree.

Caitlin slightly tilted her head. 'Jovis, don't spoil the yard with a tree that big to accommodate a swing for me. You could fit a basketball court in its place. It takes up so much room.'

'That big tree I chose is a symbol, and it represents the huge impact you have had on the three of us. It, along with the swing, will always take pride of place not only here in my yard, but also here in our hearts.' He smiled, placed a hand on his chest and patted.

Artisan and Rocky agreed.

'But the swing! It's pink. Seriously, are you really going to leave it that colour? What if you have a boy, Jovis?'

'When I asked, your answer was pink. And although we gave you such a hard time about it, kidding or not, it will always be a reminder of the fun we had putting this together. And we three agree, in a way it reminds us of you, all cute and curls, and I will sit proudly upon it while swinging with my first born, telling my little one stories of how this tree and all around it came to be.'

'Awww… that's so beautiful and exactly what I wish for you.' She rubbed his arm.

His eyes filled. 'I love what you have done for me, Cait, for us. If this is all I'll have of you after you leave here, then let it be a big reminder, so the three of us never go back to the way we were.'

Her eyes filled too. 'Stop that now; you're going to reduce me to tears.'

'Happy tears I hope.' He smiled and took her hands. 'Did you know, to get these plans, your husband made me sign my life away?'

'He did? You did? When?'

'We've just come back, actually.'

'From Alpha Site?'

Jovis nodded. 'I got word my plans for Sedna were ready, so we didn't waste a minute. We went in early this morning while you slept and after we signed on the dotted line, my plans were given to me on the spot. Oh, and a message from Jett. He said it's time to come home.

He's missing you.'

'What did you say back to him?' She eyed him with a slight grin.

'He might be the king, but you belong to all of us, so we told him to go blatz himself.' The three men started laughing.

'He took that well?' Her eyes widened, knowing Jett would not take kindly to such an insult.

Artisan laughed the loudest. 'He turned him into a goat until he agreed to send you home.'

Jovis had a glint in his eye. 'Don't worry, revenge is sweet, and he will get his just deserts when we have our boys' night out we agreed on.'

Caitlin chuckled. 'So basically, just another day at the office. You guys are so bad. Will I ever be able to stop worrying about you?'

Jovis smiled at her. 'We worked out a lot of issues and to tell you the truth, I like your friend when he is simply being, Jett. So no more worrying, it's just boys having fun. And I didn't inform you about the meeting because I wasn't totally sure of the outcome. When it did go well, you were the first person I wanted to tell and just to see your reaction right now shows me it was worth keeping it secret from you.' He put a friendly hand on hers. 'I want you to know, we didn't give in just because we wanted help. I could have done this alone, but as I told Axon, we want you in our future, Cait.'

Artisan butted in, saying, 'It was either accept the king or never see you unless we played up.'

'And we don't want to play up.' Jovis's voice was almost a whisper. 'We want you to be proud of us from now on.'

'Seriously, you have accepted Jett,' she squealed. 'Wahoo!' She high-fived the three men. 'Now I can see you guys anytime I want; this is the best news ever!' She flung her arms around Jovis and cried, before doing the same with Artisan and Rocky.

'We don't want any special privileges Glow… like hell!' Artisan teased.

Rocky bent low and steadied on one knee for his hug. 'I was busting to tell you Jovis had seen the light. Well, should I say he finally saw your light and what you were offering? You had me back in the jail.' He chuckled in a low vibrating tone.

When she stood alone, she took a deep breath and wiped her eyes, drying them with the backs of her hands. Her job was done, and she was proud of what she had managed to pull off this time. Caitlin's home was with Axon, and now the mission was at an end, she felt it time to come clean about the girls and leave Jovis and his men to enjoy this newfound happiness.

Jovis smiled. 'I know what just ran through your mind and it breaks my heart you will be leaving, but I knew by signing those papers you can no longer stay here as a friend. You are now a Rider again and can only visit. No special privileges, right?'

She nodded. 'Although the friend's bit will never change.'

'Thank heaven for that! But how can we stay close friends like now when you are out there looking after that big arse piece of sky?' Jovis sat on the table, looking a little forlorn.

Caitlin shrugged. 'Easy, we get together once a month. Maybe have a BBQ, sports day or, possibly just hang out together. Oh, and to make it fair, we should take it in turns to host, but it has to include—'

Jovis cut her off. 'We have to include your other good friends, Calyx, Jett, their wives and of course, Axon and your Rider teammates.'

She grinned. 'You know me too well. But let's just keep it a planet gettogether. My team live on Earth and have their own friends to hang out with. Too many people and it becomes a party. Not sure about you, but the best part of having close friends over with the same things in common, is this; you can sit back and chat about topics you enjoy. What do you think?'

'Cool, we get a turn!' Artisan high-fived Rocky.

'Sweet... visitors,' Rocky agreed.

Having an issue with it, Jovis screwed up his lips. 'The problem with that is you'll be busy with Axon, and the others have wives. We will be as we are now, single and standing on our own. Can't we have a day for just us?'

'I swore not to leave here until you were happy and was hoping you three would see by now the true happiness that's right here, under your very noses.' She noted their stunned expressions. 'I'm talking about the strong bond you have formed with the women here. If true love is what you search for then it's time you manned up and took charge of the woman you adore. Then you will have a partner to bring.'

'Firstly, we do not hold you to such an unrealistic promise.' He looked confused. 'And as for the girls, and sorry to burst that bubble, but they will leave the minute you set them free.'

'I beg to differ.' Caitlin wasn't ready to tell all, but it looked to be time.

'Why would you think they'd be interested in us? I agree we have become friends, but they have no romantic interest in us whatsoever. We've tried everything, and they almost run if we attempt any affection.' Jovis scratched his head, puzzled.

Artisan was just as baffled. 'We talk, yes, but that's as far as it goes. We are men, Glow; don't think for a minute we haven't tried. But we get nowhere; they don't like us that way.'

Caitlin pressed her lips together and took a deep breath. 'Umm, I think that naughty redhead you're friends with may have been very bad.'

Jovis stood up, his face reddened. 'What did our little redhead do?' he bellowed.

He didn't scare Caitlin anymore and she stood up to him. 'Well, she might have led the girls into believing she was Goddess of Peace and had laid claim to you men. She might possibly have implied she had a harem thing going on upstairs at night with you all.'

Jovis threw back his head and laughed, all tension now gone. Artisan and Rocky stood up and threw an arm around one another in hysterics. In fact, the three of them laughed so hard they had to sit down and catch their breath.

Jovis finally ceased the laughter and put his hand up to silence his men. He stared at Caitlin, realising the severity of these implications. 'Seriously, you really did say that! Hell, no wonder Jana has shied away from any affection.'

Caitlin nodded. 'I know it was evil of me, but you never got a chance to really know one another. Maybe you were well suited, but

Nitarn's magic blew any chance of love developing with his conniving tricks. All I did was remove one portion of the relationship to give you time to get to know each other. Yes, I weaved a web of deceit, but in my defence, if I had not, it would have been wham-bam, thank you ma'am, and they'd have been tossed aside like the former girlfriends brought here. That behaviour was never going to bring true love to your door.' She stared at them, all wide-eyed and innocent. 'So, if there is already a spark and it leads to more, then it was worth all the secrecy and I am sorry, but you did need help.'

Jovis went quiet. He knew she was right but wanted to strangle her for playing him. 'Jana is feisty enough to fight for what she wants. Has she had a shot at you or anything along those lines that would prove she gives a damn?'

'Jana never utters a harsh word, but her eyes burn holes in me when you take me up to bed at night. Well, so she thinks. Particularly the nights you carry me.'

He shook his head. 'So this has been a game from the start. All I can say is, well played Cait. I can't believe we fell for it!'

'I'm sorry I had to keep this from you, but I couldn't bear the thought of leaving you all without a companion. I adore you guys, you must know that by now. And I have wished for so very much for the three of you, including love. But I have no crystal ball and unfortunately, I've done all I can. Your hearts are open and so the rest must be left up to you.'

'Fair enough, but I still have questions. You must have said a great deal to the girls that day you sprang them from their cell. I know them now, in particular, Jana, and I bet she would not have agreed easily.' Jovis had to know. 'What did Jana say when you told her you and I were sleeping together?'

Caitlin took a deep breath and rolled her eyes. 'She was a tough cookie, let me tell you. I had to pull rank on her, but still, it didn't faze her. She said to me, and I quote; "what would Jovis want with a fragile thing like you? And, if you are what he prefers then so be it. Told me she'd wipe your nose until I say, but I better not make it too long, because there is only so much boyish behaviour she could stand and after that, she would sooner go back to the cell and face her punishment." I nearly started to laugh, thinking how perfect she was for you.'

He beamed. 'That sounds so Jana.'

Caitlin eyed the three men staring at her. 'I really hope what I've done will not change your opinion of me. All I wanted was for you to be happy. Please try not to stay cross for long.'

Jovis leant forward. 'How could I ever get cross with such innocence and sweetness? You have tried so hard to make me happy. Once you have gone, I will miss seeing your beautiful face every day and honestly, I don't really know what I ever did to deserve such devotion.' His affectionate retort melted her. They had become good friends and not showing anger at a time she thought he would, showed her how much he had grown as a good person.

'You respected and pledged your loyalty, and in the end, trusted me,' Caitlin said, returning the compliment to the man who had earned her admiration. 'I leave you with a woman who doesn't only love you as I do but is *in love* with you, unconditionally. She is gorgeous, Jovis; give her a chance to prove her devotion to you. She is of good breeding and will never be an embarrassment to your royal status or kingdom.'

He hugged her. 'You're not staying, are you?'

Cait shook her head. 'You'll be far too busy going over this project and getting to know those women on a different level, so I'll contact Axon after I've finished telling the girls what I've done, or not done.' She gave a sheepish grin. 'He'll be happy to come get me.'

'What do you mean I'll be too busy? I will never be too busy for you, Cait.'

Caitlin didn't want to muck up Jovis's chance to find true love. After she spoke to the girls, she preferred to leave so her magic wouldn't change fate in any way. She wanted the men to concentrate only on love. How could they do that with the captivating scent she gave off? No, this would work better if she was gone and for some reason, she needed to be gone from here quickly. Her heart raced, and beads of sweat trickled down her back. It was cold here, so her reaction was stressing her out further. 'After I speak with the women, and I know you will agree, they will be free to leave. If you want the woman who has cared for you all this time to stay, then it's time to ask them. If they choose to leave after knowing how you feel, they are not the girl for you and as a curtsy for all they have done, I will ask you to kindly drop them off at a location of their choosing.'

She waited for them to agree and after answering a few more questions, left the men so she could summon the girls. Looking back at them she saw they were okay, maybe a little quiet, but not sad. For Jovis and Artisan, she saw their future and got a shiver of happiness for them. As for Rocky, she smiled, he didn't now, or in the future, need anyone's help in the love department.

* * * *

Jana, Sienna and Loray entered Caitlin's bedroom when she summoned them.

'You may want to sit for this.' Caitlin gestured towards the couch.

Sienna gave her a bright smile, and her light complexion flushed as she sat. Loray had her head down while going past Caitlin. Once again, she found it hard to read Loray as she never used eye contact, and nor did she speak very often. This was why Caitlin wondered if there were two sides to Loray. There had to be something more to entice men like Nitarn and Rocky, both powerful in character. Jana was the last to sit. Her bright blue eyes glared at Cait as she flipped her long dark hair in a twirl, so she didn't sit on it. Although slim, she was taller than the other girls which made her presence that much stronger.

'I called you ladies here to share in a secret.' Caitlin told them the story of how she met Jovis, Artisan and Rocky. She described her near-death experience and how Jovis and Artisan nursed her back to health.

'We had no idea. The boys have never mentioned anything. We were never allowed to speak of you, and nor did they. They're very loyal to you,' said Sienna.

'And it was my loyalty to them which made me tell you they

were my men and hands off.'

'What do you mean? You didn't really lay claim? My Artisan has been available all this time?' Sienna squeaked out.

'Blatzing liar!' Jana wasn't buying it as usual. 'Don't think we didn't hear the laughter and noises. Sometimes it went on until the wee hours in the morning before they left your room. And then the kissy kissy hug hug... please!'

'They hug me goodnight, yes! But as for the kisses, they were generally on the forehead or cheek, nothing more. Sorry to disappoint.'

Jana shook her head; her face drawn and upset. 'Why would you lie and continue this charade for so long?'

'It started as a way to show the boys you had class. Under a spell or not, the three of you acted as easy prey when you jumped into the hot spring, almost naked. The men had no respect for you then, and why should they. You invited them to have sex before they had a chance to get to know you. Maybe the spell influenced you, but I am sure Nitarn would not have a spell strong enough to make you act so improperly if it wasn't part of your habit. That's why the men held such little regard for you, treated you as liars and why you ended up in the dungeon and not in their beds.'

'Then why did you save us if you thought we were lying whores?' Jana huffed. She straightened her skirt, looking suddenly uncomfortable in the outfit she'd chosen.

'I saved you because I saw through that promiscuous behaviour. What I put you through these past weeks and how you conducted yourselves, proved you were worth the trouble. You have shown not only to me but to the men, that you are commendable ladies and not at all what they thought you were.'

'It's been so hard watching you go to bed with Artisan every night.' Sienna's eyes filled.

'I hated you, hate you!' Jana stood up. 'And I don't believe you. Jovis has been getting it from somewhere. A man like him would have taken me weeks ago if you weren't fixing him up.'

Caitlin stood and leant towards her with big questioning eyes. 'Do you really think he is the man you are now trying to make him out to be? If you don't believe in him, then you're not worthy of the beautiful soul he is. You said it when you first met me; what would he see in a fragile thing like me, and you were right. A man like him needs a strong woman and one who is available. You see, I am not, as I'm married to a wonderful man who happens to also be my boss. Jovis and his men have become close family friends, and for this reason, I could take time off and come here to assist Jovis with renovations to his Ice Planets. That is my true reason for being here and I was certainly not expecting to deal with you three.'

Jana gulped. 'You're married.'

My husband is Axon Stanton, Lord of the Planets. I am Caitlin Stanton, one of the peacemakers under his command.'

'I know of Axon and his Riders. I never connected the dots. I heard them call you Cait, but never imagined you were the one they call Glow Girl.' Jana put her hand to her mouth. 'You really are a goddess, the Goddess of Peace. We thought you were joking. You're... You are so... so fragile.'

'Yes, but fortunately not in power.' Caitlin smiled.

'So where to from here?' said Jana, collecting herself. 'I mean, why tell us now?'

'My time here has run out, and duty calls. I asked you here to let you know you are free to pursue the man you have fallen for or free to leave. I no longer stand in the way. Your fate has been reset. If there are true feelings in your hearts for these men, then chase your dream. Those men you chose to care for may not show it, but I can see they have developed real feelings for you too. If you want your man, stay. If not, ask, and they will take you anywhere in the galaxy you wish to be dropped off, with no ill feelings.'

'So you're not staying, even to share one last meal with us. The guys will be devastated... and I will be too.' Sienna shed a tear.

Loray threw her hands up, frustrated. 'Great! They will be missing you so much we won't have a chance in hell with them while they sulk about.' For someone who rarely spoke, this was an outburst, and everyone stared at her for a few seconds before collecting themselves.

'And what will we talk about without you at the table leading the conversations as you do?' Sienna's shoulders dropped.

Caitlin chewed her lip, thinking before she answered. 'Allow them to spoil you for a change instead of me, and I have a feeling I won't be missed as much as you think.' Caitlin turned and picked up her jacket. 'Farewell ladies. It's been one fascinating experience and so glad to see you finally got your well-deserved freedom.'

'What, you're leaving now, right this minute?' Sienna cried out.

'Jovis now has the plans to upgrade and improve his home. It was the true reason for coming back here. The four of us have spent hours working on it.' She smiled. 'It was a project deliberated and debated while you girls thought we were having sex.' She paused to allow them a moment to take in what she was saying. 'As for you ladies, the men have allowed all charges to be dropped which means you are now free to begin a new life. And if you have learned anything from this experience, I hope it's to now make smarter choices and stay as far away from men like Nitarn as you can get.' She eyed them and shrugged. 'So my work here is done!'

It surprised Caitlin when Jana responded kindly. She stepped towards Caitlin and wrapped warm arms around her in a hug. 'I'm sorry, Glow. I've been terribly ungrateful. You're right, without you, goodness knows what would have happened to us. I have been so busy disliking you because *he* loved you, I didn't see what was going on. Now, thinking back, it was so innocent when I watched you. I was a fool. Can you forgive me?' Her eyes were glassy with tears. She dropped her hold and stood back. 'Is Jovis sad you're leaving?'

'He has found real happiness right here.' Caitlin put her hand on Jana's heart. 'You're perfect for him, but please don't hurt him.'

Jana glowed. 'Me... really! He chooses me!'

Caitlin grinned and wiped the tears that ran down Jana's cheeks. 'Yes. But don't tell him I've told you. He will be stubborn and cross instead of allowing his feelings to shine.'

'Oh, how I know that side of him.' She grinned. 'Thanks, Glow. I promise I will take good care of him now you have taught me how.'

'What about Artisan and me? Does he know how I feel?' Sienna pushed in tight next to Jana and stood waiting in anticipation.

Caitlin held her cheek. 'How could he resist those eyes? This is why I have held you from him, so he learns. Does he make you happy now?'

'So extremely happy,' Sienna swooned.

'Then only you know how to stay that way. I can teach no more.' Caitlin kissed her forehead. 'You are my favourite. I will miss you.' She hugged her before heading for the door. 'Goodbye, my friends.'

Only before she could touch it, the door swung open. Artisan and Rocky barged inside. Both stood frozen for a second, not sure who to go to first. They had come to see Caitlin, but this was the first time they had seen the women on equal terms, and they wanted to show them how they really felt.

Artisan's tattoos stood out against his complexion that had paled from his obvious distress. He had red rims under his glassy eyes from holding back emotions. She knew he was upset she was leaving but he had Sienna now. He wrapped his arm around Caitlin. 'We can't let you go like this. You must stay for dinner, have a few drinks and let us give you a proper send-off. Please Glow, this feels so... so sad.'

Caitlin put out her hand to Sienna and brought her in next to them. 'Artisan, I'm not leaving you... ever! Just won't be sleeping over anymore unless it is with my man.'

His gaze fell upon Sienna and he dropped his arms from Caitlin.

'Artisan, you don't need me as you did before. Sienna is who you are in love with and who you now need by your side. It is what I have wished for you. It's time you let me go and let her know that you love her the most.'

He looked up, his eyes full of sadness. 'I do love her... you know I do, but my heart is ripping apart. You could have warned me. You can't just walk away like this without a proper goodbye.'

Rocky had slung an arm over Loray's shoulders and hugged her while he talked. 'I agree with Artisan. Please don't just leave us this way Glow. You might be the most fragile person in the universe, but you've been our rock. And if I know these girls, they must be in shock as well and will feel a great loss if you leave so abruptly. Let us at least put on a goodbye dinner party for you as a parting gesture.'

She honestly felt it best to move on and allow them alone time to find love naturally, without any of her enchantment. She hoped her fragrant goddess power was not what had them begging her to stay.

Jovis arrived, and Caitlin looked at him for support. She figured he'd stayed back to lock away his plans before joining them. She noticed he stared at Jana and was fixated for a few seconds. Jana nodded, and Jovis broke the stare and turned to Caitlin. She was amazed how much like her and Axon these two were; they knew each other so well they could talk without saying a word.

Jovis leant against the wall, his arms folded. 'I think you're outnumbered, Cait. You may have plans for us, but our plans will always include you.' He grinned. 'I have a solution; how about if I go and pick up Axon and we make it a couples' night? Doubt he'll say no to a celebratory dinner invitation with three of his newbie Ice Planets who only today, came under his jurisdiction.'

She bit her lip. There was no backing away from this suggestion, but it still didn't feel right... *why?* 'Fair enough, if you can talk Axon into it, then I'm in.' She had no choice. They had outsmarted her, and she hoped, if it was Axon who really did need her, he would come up with a good excuse.

Artisan whipped her up in his arms. 'Thanks, Glow.' He chuckled as he swung her around before he put her down. The next move was towards Sienna. He swept her into his arms and kissed her lovingly, and being so close, his power even sent shivers through Caitlin. He had so much love to give, and Sienna was getting it full blast. When Artisan let her go, she hid her flushed face as she melted back into the arm he kept around her. The other he put back around Caitlin. 'Now I have my two favourite girls for dinner I'm the happiest man in the universe.' He glowed.

This was how Caitlin saw him. She was glad fate kept her there to see this moment of utmost joy on his face. In love or not, she was welcome to share in their lives; a blessing that had her body glow brightly.

'Oh my god, is that why they call you Glow Girl?' said Jana, her eyes wide.

Jovis walked over to Jana and pushed her long dark hair back. 'You are the only woman glowing brightly in my eyes.' He slipped an arm behind her and leant her back while he kissed her, firmly and passionately. Lips released and came together with a softness that had Jana tremble in his arms. He stood her up. Her eyes shone like jewels, her adoring smile made him smile. 'Wait here for me, beautiful, because if I have to chase you for one more second, it won't be pretty.'

She gave him the most stunning smile. 'I've been waiting far too long already. Hurry back... or I will be gone.'

He held her chin, softly kissed her farewell and disappeared, zapped out of sight as he transported to the Alpha Site to find Axon.

* * * *

Later that day after they had all gathered downstairs to discuss who was going to cook the meal for the dinner party, Axon and Jovis appeared.

Axon wrapped Caitlin up in his arms. 'I wasn't expecting to see you tonight. It was a pleasant surprise to get an invitation. Can we talk for a minute?' He took her to the far side of the room to get some privacy. Nobody seemed to notice them move away as Jovis had joined his friends and entered into the boisterous debate over the dinner menu.

Caitlin spoke quietly. 'I was going to call for you to pick me up, but the guys had other plans. They want us to join them for dinner, you know, one last meal together before I leave. Now you're here I don't feel the urgency to go. Maybe I just needed a dose of you.' She grinned feeling much happier.

'Well I'm very pleased to hear that and I have to admit the feeling goes both ways. I've really been missing you too.' He glanced over at the others who were conversing as if they were very good friends. 'I take it those are the girls they had locked up. Not sure how you did it, but good job getting them to at least communicate and get on.'

She gave him a wink. 'Why have a great new tomorrow when it can be kicked up a notch to a fabulous one.' She turned her head to the couples chatting and smiling. 'Not sure about one of the couples, but the other two... I did well.' She hugged her husband. She had missed the exquisite cologne, the firm bulging male wonderland beneath his suit, and his lips. 'Mmm, this is what I need.' She floated in his heavenly aura.

He lifted her chin, not having to say a word. He could feel her happiness. 'You could have spent a few more days here. I would have understood. But Jovis said it was urgent I come as you were not yourself. He's got to know you well. He said without me he didn't think you would stay another minute, but he wanted the chance to thank you properly. Yet here you are, as happy as a kitten. Whatever it was, I'm glad it was me being with you that calmed your unsettled heart.'

'It has, so thanks for coming.' She spoke quietly and somewhat seductively. 'I had to rush, to end my time here. No idea why. I had this strange urge to be with you. Together, anywhere, that was the need.'

'Keep that up, and there will be no dinner for you, gorgeous. I'll be taking you home.' He had a cheeky grin.

'Her work is not yet done, or she would be home now. Take a number, Casanova.' Caitlin's eyes were cloudy.

It was unexpected to hear the goddess of whom Calyx was confident he had sent packing. Axon stared at Caitlin and waited for her eyes to clear before answering. He distinctively knew this voice, but as quick as it came it was gone, and his Cait was back. She smiled at him as only she knew how and melted his heart. He took the quick opportunity to let her know how he felt before his wife was lost to him again on another mission. 'I have missed you, sweetheart.' He ignored the change and while he held his wife, he bent his head and kissed her soft lips. *But oh how he had missed them.* Wrapping her up in his arms he delved deep into her luscious mouth. The magic of her love unravelled his every nerve end. All thought of others around him disappeared while this seductive poweress moved deliciously in motion with him. For a moment he was lost in her loveliness, the others far from his mind as he kissed his magical wife. When he came back to reality and let her go, what looked like coloured laser lights surrounded them.

Jovis clapped and gave a cheer, 'Now that, you just have to teach me.' He shook his head at Axon.

Rocky whistled. 'No wonder she's never interested in any other man, geez Axon, you just put us all to shame.'

The lights evaporated the instant they walked towards the others. Joining them, Axon apologised. 'Thought you were all busy… sprung!' He smirked.

'Well we were busy, but wow, that light show sure got our attention.' Artisan chuckle. 'But on the serious side, glad you could make it.' He shook Axon's hand.

'Nice to feel welcome, look forward to a home-cooked meal… It's been a while.'

Axon accepted the goblet of Moonjuice Jovis handed him.

'Actually, the men and I started to cook for the girls, but we burnt most of it,' Jovis admitted. 'They're heading to the kitchen to see what they can salvage for us while we have a chat. After signing those papers today to apply for Dwarf Planet status, it has left us with some questions regarding the build. Maybe after the meal, you could help us out with a couple of ideas we've had before we take it to the king to be signed off.'

'Well, if it's the legal side, Axon is the perfect person to speak with,' Caitlin agreed. 'I'll make myself scarce, so you can have a chat now if you like. Dinner will be a while by the sounds of it.'

Jovis lifted his eyebrow. 'Forever the martyr. First, you sacrificed yourself to save me, then our planets. Just a little heads up Cait, like it or not you are part of our dysfunctional unit now and very much loved. There is nothing we would hide from you, so I insist you stay.'

Jana had come out of the kitchen to retrieve oven mitts from a drawer and, hearing the conversation, walked over and took Caitlin's hand. 'Glow doesn't need to be involved in work tonight; she's done enough for us. Come and help us girls get our men their dinner. I swear it will be more fun for you than being out here.'

'Did I ever tell you I can't cook?'

'There is no such thing as can't in my book. Maybe we can teach the teacher something for a change.' Jana patted her hand.

Caitlin grinned. 'I would like that Jana.' She followed her into the kitchen, but after only ten minutes, Jana escorted Caitlin out to the men.

'She may be a whiz kid at sorting out the universe, but in the kitchen.' She shook her head. 'She's chaos.' Jana turned on her heels and left Caitlin with the men who roared with laughter.

Axon put his arm around her. 'That's my girl. Goddess of love and peace, but would starve a nation if she had to feed them.'

Jovis joined in. 'You're just perfect Cait, don't let them tell you any different. If you had to feed a nation, there is always take away.' This made them laugh more at her expense.

Artisan put his glass down on the marble table. 'Well it wouldn't worry Axon, with those kisses she saves up for him, he wouldn't know what he was eating. She could feed him up raw rice, and he'd think it caviar.' This cracked them up with laughter again.

'Keep it up, and you'll be sorry.' Caitlin held her lips tight, trying not to show it was kind of funny.

Axon saw her indignant look and decided to warn the lads. 'Jett, Calyx and I all woke up not long back, and she had us up in the air, over a hot tub. She dumped us all in it for our cracks from the night before. I would think twice about pushing her buttons any further unless you want to wake up somewhere you wish you hadn't.'

Rocky's eyes lit up. 'That might be worth seeing. It would give me a great deal of pleasure to see Jovis butt first in the snow.' He made the others laugh.

Jovis eyed him with half-closed lids and a slight smirk. He didn't like the focus on him so turned it back to Caitlin. 'Sweetie, don't let them upset you. If you were to starve the world and everyone died, you'd still have a job. You could stop the dead fighting and keep the peace while their souls are on their way to Pluto's underworld.' He chuckled and set the others off again.

'Come here gorgeous,' Axon comforted her when he stopped chuckling. 'You know I was just joking, right. But this lot wasn't, so when you take your revenge, I had nothing to do with it okay, sweetie.'

Caitlin closed her eyes. She'd fix these stirrers, her husband included... *give him sweetie*. With her power running stronger than usual, thanks to Axon's kiss, she opened the shaft door which took them to the fortress entrance. Here, Jovis's threatening voice activated the voice code, and the door popped open without needing more. With a grin, she lifted the four annoying men up in a cloud of magic and sent them sailing through the air until they were outside, chuckling at the cries of protest. 'We give in... You wouldn't dare... We'll shut up.'

Ignoring them, she did what had to be done, but wished she was able to watch their faces at the realisation she had dumped them in the snow.

Outside the men laughed at first and once on their feet Jovis looked for revenge. 'Okay, two can play this game.' He started trudging back to the entrance.

'I wouldn't.' Axon tried to stop him until he got a sour look from Jovis. He put his hand up. 'Okay, dig out, but don't say I didn't warn you.' He followed the three cranky men with amusement. His girl could sure push their buttons. But he also wondered if she was doing this deliberately, so they didn't miss her once she was gone. They accepted her as one of their own, she was family, and at the moment she was the annoying little sister on whom they wanted revenge.

Jovis entered the dining room first. Caitlin bolted when she saw the look of retribution, but he caught her halfway up the stairs. She giggled so hard she couldn't run any further. 'You are so in for it young lady.' He scooped her up, and once they had her outside, Jovis transported them all to the hot spring in the cave. 'What are you going to do now?' He juggled her, pretending to almost drop her.

'This.' Caitlin held him tight, and, flicking her hand allowed a bit of power to escape. The action had both ended up in the water. When they surfaced, Axon, Artisan and Rocky were leaning on one another laughing. With a flick of her wet hand she pulled them off balance and one by one they fell in too.

'Axon!' Jovis shook his head, his mouth screwed up at one side. 'Your wife is out of control; what was in that kiss you gave her?'

Axon knew it was all Cait; maybe this was the first time she had shown them this side of her. He wasn't surprised, she had been dealing with many personalities here. Not being blood they were all so different. She had kept her wits about her instead. So not to spoil her game he played along. 'Mischief... I figured she needed some fun. Maybe I overdid it a little.'

'A little, we have our gold spun threaded suits on, and they're wet, most likely ruined.' He grumbled and eyed Caitlin. 'We had these made especially for your last night here.' His eyes softened.

Artisan pulled himself up on the edge and helped the others out. 'We wanted to look worthy, so you'd miss us and come back. Now we'll just look the same old us, and you may forget us.'

Rocky lifted Caitlin up and out with ease. 'So what are we to wear now to please our woman you have worked so hard to get for us?'

'I bet those women are just like me. So long as you are in them, it wouldn't matter what clothes you wore. It's not how spruced up you are that will bring me back time and time again, it's the memories we have made together. Like this...' She glanced from one to the other. 'And because no matter what I do to tick you off you'll always twist it to make me feel loved and wanted.' She spread her hands out. 'But in saying that, I better dry you off as I do want you to make a good impression on your first date.' Her voice softened. 'Now close your eyes.'

They did as she instructed and stood quietly waiting. Cait went quickly behind them and, using her magic, pushed them one by one in the water again. 'Oopsy,' she laughed, 'wrong magic.'

They were laughing so much they nearly drowned.

Once they were out, she put her hand up. None of them could move if they wanted to, and her power vibrated the cave. Using the warmth from the steam, she whipped a wind up that blew around them, stronger and stronger. At the extreme speed it moved, it should have been blown off their feet and tumbled them along the ground, but they stood firm. Once their hair dried and their clothes had unstuck from their bodies the hurricane winds calmed. The last flick of her hand tidied their hair, and it was then she switched it off. 'Better?'

'Better.' Jovis grinned. 'But you look a bit windblown.'

She felt her hair that stuck out in all directions. She chuckled. 'Sad for some, but not me.' She snapped her fingers and not only did her outfit change to a lavishly rich, gold and white gown but her hair and makeup looked photo shoot ready.

'Beautiful.' He eyed her. 'Axon is a lucky man.'

'Jana is a lucky girl. Just promise me you won't stop having fun like this with them too,' she said affectionately. 'Love can be fun. Promise me you'll give it a go.'

'I will.' Jovis finally got what she was showing them. Her last ditch effort was to teach them yet again.

Axon had worked it out too. She amazed him... *hang on, what's happening.* He felt his wife charge up with more goddess perfume than he could handle. He battled to stay calm but had to try and stay with her. He put his arm around her and struggled to say a word. Instead, it came out as a growling sound as he spoke to Jovis, 'Time to get inside, now!'

Jovis nodded, aware of the sudden scent, and transported them directly to the fortress.

Once inside he turned to Caitlin. 'What's going on? Axon's gone all weird, and your goddess aroma has just escalated.'

Caitlin put her hand under Axon's chin. 'I don't know.' She snapped her fingers but got no reaction.

'He didn't even blink.' Jovis was worried.

Caitlin took Axon's hand. He quivered with her touch. 'It must be extreme to do this to him.' She bit her lip. 'Jovis,' she whispered, 'something terrible is about to happen.'

'Hell, what now?' Jovis motioned to Artisan and Rocky. 'Go to your homes and check for any security breaches. Find out if something's heading our way. I'll check in with Medusa. Cait's picking up real trouble and if we have learned anything, it's to trust her instincts.'

'Give us a minute or two to check.' Artisan and Rocky split up to check in with their commanders and dark angel security. Jovis went to see Medusa.

He was back in no time. 'We can strike Sedna off the list. Nothing going on here. Medusa was sleeping, so I have woken the beast, and it's now on high alert,' Jovis informed Caitlin.

Artisan and Rocky returned, giving the same report. It was all quiet on the home front.

Jovis turned to Caitlin. 'I'm sorry Cait, but I'm not taking any chances. Your perfume is even stronger than before we left and even I'm having trouble being okay around you. To be on the safe side, I'm getting the two of you out of here. We can't afford for Axon to get caught up in any of our troubles. He's just too vital to the future of our planets.'

'This is all wrong. It's unlike me to have pulled Axon into something like this. I don't get any of it, fretting to have Axon where danger may be lurking doesn't make sense. My super strong instincts have always kept him safe.' Caitlin rubbed her forehead, confused.

'We can work it out later. I'm taking you home, Cait! Ready?'

'Jovis wait!' Caitlin yelled. 'No, not home, please. I want to go to Pluto; Jett will know what to do.'

'Fine, I don't care where. But we are getting you away from here and now!' Jovis transported Axon and Caitlin to Pluto.

Chapter Thirty-Four

Planned Breakout

Jovis held a distressed Caitlin and Axon when they reappeared in the grand entrance of the castle on Pluto. Jett's guards met them first, guns at the ready. Caitlin was confused why she was being greeted this way. 'Why is his security back on high alert? Have I brought Axon to the wrong place?' she whispered to Jovis.

'Stand down, they are good friends. You know them.' Jett came out from the study with charts of some sort rolled up in his hand.

'Not that one.' His commander eyed Jovis with caution.

'Jovis is a good friend of mine.' Caitlin spoke up.

'Very well, if you can vouch for him, that's good enough for me.' The commander of Jett's army lowered his weapon. The hefty canon-like gun dropped fast with its weight. The giant of a man gave an order, and the dozen or so royal guards marched out with him following.

'What's going on?' Caitlin eyed the men. Their heavy boots clanged loud upon the ultra-shiny tiles.

'Calyx is in the NAVcom, hang on, he's yelling at me, wants to know what's going on.' He touched his earpiece to talk. 'Axon has turned up with Caitlin and Jovis, he is fine. Better get down here.' He walked closer to them. 'It doesn't look good.'

It was then she saw he held one of many ancient sky charts she saw he had in his study. She wondered which zone was of interest enough to be looking up their laws, and figured it to be a very old coordinate because he knew all the ones she did.

'Jovis…' He nodded. 'What brings you here?'

Calyx appeared and stood beside Jett as he spoke. 'I was just about to ask the same thing, brother. Axon and Cait certainly don't need a chaperone.'

'My apologies for intruding at this hour without warning, but Cait's goddess scent went up really high, which put Axon in some kind of trance.'

'What was he doing in your world?' Calyx sounded annoyed.

'Out of nowhere, Cait decided she was leaving and wanted Axon to come and get her. We asked her to at least have dinner with us so we could say a proper goodbye, but she was unusually stubborn about not spending one minute longer with us. Finally, I suggested I'd go and get Axon to join us, and it calmed her. So all went well until a few minutes ago. We were having some laughs when Caitlin surprised us by powering up her goddess scent as she does when evil is around. We checked security in all three Ice Planets but came up empty-handed; nothing on our radar, either. As a security measure, I wanted to take them to Ara, but Cait freaked about going home I so brought them here. But it looks like you guys have got problems too. Should I take them to Rory's on Earth?' Jovis was unsure what he should do after getting this strange, off-putting reception. He wanted Caitlin safe. Here didn't look or sound safe at all.

Calyx moved closer and studied Axon before talking to Jovis again. 'I didn't mean to be rude, but Axon has been reported as kidnapped.' He turned back to Axon and snapped his fingers in front of him. 'He's gone all right, and not sure what you're reading, brother, but Cait looks in la la land too.'

'I feel she's tracking something.' Jett agreed she wasn't with it either.

'Who thought Axon was kidnapped? What's going on?' Jovis was wide-eyed. 'We didn't kidnap him if that's what you thought. He came of his own free will.'

'We didn't mean you, Jovis. For once you're not on our hit list.' Calyx grinned. 'You see, not long before you turned up here, Zoren had me investigating a burglary on Ara.'

'Axon's home?'

'Yes. The alarm went off, but by the time the response team arrived, the rooms had been trashed, and the perpetrators had left. Of course, there was no sign of Axon, so it was presumed he had been kidnapped. Thank goodness that's not the case. I just wish he had followed protocol and let someone know where he went. So unlike him.' Calyx again snapped his fingers in front of Axon's eyes. 'Yep, he is in deep. Thank the lucky stars us lot can still be evil bastards at times, or we'd be useless to help work this out.'

'Cait said Axon reacts differently to us, and that's the reason she knew something was going down. She said it must be really bad if it overpowered him physically. She worried for his safety and wanted to get him away from the danger. .' Jovis couldn't stop watching and hoping Axon snapped out of it soon. He felt uncomfortable here and wished he could just leave. But something held him to the spot and he had a feeling it was Cait, so he stayed and didn't fight her. She had gone quiet and stood still. It was her he worried for now.

Jett smiled. 'They will both be back with us shortly. Something is still going down, and until our goddess is ready to spill, I can guarantee she will keep us all out of harm's way.'

Jovis breathed in deeply before speaking. 'Something is definitely still going on because her goddess fragrance is way stronger than we are used to.' He was pleased he was able to judge this now and heed the warning. When they first met, it was only very mild to his senses. He smiled to himself… *I was very evil.* Suddenly it made sense to him why Axon was bedazzled by it. *He works with an angel and is pure of heart.* Of course, it knocked him around as it did now with Jovis since he had decided to walk in her light. 'Glow Girl, are you with us yet.' He hoped the sound of her heavenly title snapped her out of it.

At the sound of her name, Caitlin shook herself out of the hold this experience had put her in. 'Sorry, what were you saying?' She still held Jovis's hand tight.

Calyx noticed and motioned for Jett to look at what he was seeing. He knew his brother was tuned into Cait and would hear him think too. *Look at the grip she has on Jovis. Her knuckles are white. Is he in trouble also?*

Jett nodded, showing he agreed with him, and had already noticed. 'How are you feeling, Glow?' He got her attention. 'Try to relax, your powers will calm when the danger subsides.'

'Sorry, I'll try. What's this about our home being burgled? What was taken? Have you any idea who it was?' Caitlin gave a frustrated sigh. 'They better not have touched anything in our room or I won't be happy.'

'It appears with the mess they made, the intruders were looking for a single item, and it was of the utmost importance. Zoren is almost certain it was Nitarn's forces. If so, we wondered if Jovis had previously given Axon a device to enter his airspace,' Calyx said. 'It had to be something they couldn't get any other way.'

Caitlin chewed on her lip, thinking. 'Jovis?'

Jovis shrugged a shoulder. 'Axon didn't want the NAVcodes. Told me to give them to Rory as he was going to be the one visiting with Caitlin in the future. But Nitarn wouldn't know about the Cosmic Riders. The boys and I have never mentioned them for Nitarn to do a search for them.'

'Good to hear.' Jett checked his handheld NAVcom, flicking through menus to get the latest news. 'There is a clean-up crew in your home right now, Glow. Going by these reports, nothing has been stolen. But the damage was done to all living areas, and that included the main bedroom.'

Worry lines etched Jovis's forehead. 'My deepest apologies that you and Axon have been dragged into my troubles, Cait. You must feel violated. There is nothing worse than someone forcing their way into your home.' He eyed Axon, his brows almost touching. 'Sorry to drop off and run, but I'm a bit anxious about my friends. If those thugs are looking for a way into Sedna, I'd better get back there in case they try and muscle their way in. Will you be all right now?'

'Sure I will.'

'And Axon?'

'I can answer that.' Jett smirked. 'Axon could break the magic hold she has over him by moving away, but for some reason, is refusing to leave her side. Also, my brother and I are Glow's sworn guardians, so rest assured, if he hasn't moved he knows we aren't enough. I'm guessing he senses more is to come and intends to help out.'

Calyx felt it time for Jovis to leave. If Jett was right, they didn't need someone extra with them that had to be looked after. 'Now you know Caitlin is in good hands, we bid you farewell and thank you for bringing her to safety. If Zoren is correct and this is about Nitarn, then it is our problem, and we are well equipped to handle things from here. You have guests that I'm sure are wondering where you have got to.'

Jovis shrugged. 'They will be edgy and sure to come looking for me if I'm not back soon. I have only one request; could I have my hand back, Glow?' He grinned at Caitlin's uncertain stare. 'I can see you're in perfectly good hands, so I'll bid you goodnight. But please call if the boys and I can help in any way. You know we enjoy a good knuckle fight, especially if it's to get back at Nitarn and his band of narcissistic criminals.'

'Because you're heir to the throne, I hope to always keep you away from trouble. Go with my thanks for proving your loyalty by doing as I asked under such unusual circumstances.' She released him and hugged him goodbye. 'Sorry I spoiled the night,' she called to him. She was unsure if he heard when he quickly shimmered from sight.

Jett snapped his fingers, and a servant bustled out of the side door. 'Yes Your Majesty?' He bowed low.

'Coffee for four,' Jett instructed.

'In the den, Your Majesty.'

Jett gave a nod of his head before he turned to his guests. 'Come, let's talk.' He motioned to Caitlin and Axon, who both followed.

A slight tingle of stress and noisy footsteps running had Caitlin reopen the door and look out. The soldiers had quickly marched back into the entrance way, guns at the ready.

'What now?' Jett walked out past her and into the hall entry, waiting for the appearance of the unauthorised visitor.

Calyx stood in the open door next to Caitlin. He was taking no chances and would get her and Axon out if there was a problem.

'Jovis.' Jett acknowledged him as he materialised.

Jovis's natural dark olive complexion looked ghostly white. 'They've all gone!'

'Who?' Caitlin raced to his side.

'The entire dinner party... Artisan, Rocky, the girls. Someone has taken them but why?' He was in shock and ran a hand roughly through his hair. 'I didn't know where else to go.'

'You were right to come back here.' They heard Axon's voice and turned towards him.

'You're back with us!' Calyx gave Axon's shoulder a friendly squeeze. He turned to Jett. 'This is good news, brother. It means Caitlin has finally powered down.'

'Which means?' Jovis was unsure where he was going with the comment.

'It means the danger to any of us here seems very unlikely at this stage. Unfortunately, it doesn't help your friends, but does give a reason why Cait held your hand so tightly and wouldn't let you leave straight away.' Calyx glanced at his brother.

Jett eyed Jovis. 'Calyx is right; Glow is very intuitive and protective with those of importance. She must care about you a lot to have kept you out of danger. She knows as we do that lessons are the best teacher and would not have changed your fate for no reason.' He winked at Caitlin. 'Guess the motive for this will come to the fore soon enough.'

Axon shook the cobweb of magic from him and confronted Jovis. 'I can't imagine anyone getting past your security, Jovis.'

'Well they must have but has me baffled how. The secret to deflect Medusa's true glare is known only by me. I've never breathed a word of it, not even to my men. How the intruders got a hold of this information has me puzzled. Even drunk I would never give this secret away. And it had to be intruders that did this because it doesn't look like any kind of struggle took place at the dinner table.

Caitlin moved and stood beside Axon. 'We're involved somehow, aren't we? Our home has been ransacked and now this.'

'I believe so, Cait.' Axon was able to hear what was going on but helpless to talk while she had her power up so high. He worried the break-in was to find this type of information he kept hidden. 'In a secret room, I keep ancient scrolls. The criminals may have been searching for these to find guarded secrets such how to get past your pet, Jovis.'

Jovis's eyes were wide. 'You knew?'

But before he could answer Calyx temper flared.

'Seriously, you've known all along how to get past Medusa, and you never told me, or my brother?' he roared angrily.

Axon grinned. 'I have faith in Caitlin and didn't need you two overprotective, brother-figure, sooky shitheads, charging in there and ruining the friendship she had already struck up with Jovis.'

Jovis shook his head. 'You are some silent warrior, Axon, damned if that doesn't make me like you even more.'

'Blatzing rotten... sneaky, untrusting, secretive, mongrel of a friend he is,' Calyx said to Jett, and both laughed.

Caitlin disciplined them. 'Come on guys, this is serious, stop the name calling. We all have secrets. It's why we trust each other to help fix the things we can't. Let's work together and sort this out quickly.'

They all went quiet. 'You have secrets from us?' they said together.

'Well, not me... but you guys have, and that's okay. Just don't act on the bad ones or the Goddess of Peace will come out and sort your arses out for being wicked.'

Axon breathed out a sigh of relief, as did the others. They were glad she had no intentions of using her goddess power to make them disclose any. He spoke first. 'So we can be almost certain this is the work of Nitarn's men. How the hell is that evil sadistic felon able to plan all this from prison?' Axon rubbed his forehead before straightening with a thought. 'Okay, you mentioned there was no struggle. Could they have been drugged?'

'Possibly.' Jovis shrugged. 'They had started eating entrees, and some of the plates looked as if their heads had fallen in their dinner. There was no blood, not even a trickle, so I've eliminated the idea they were hit from behind or shot.' Jovis cracked his knuckled thinking.

Caitlin frowned. 'And it would not be an easy feat to knock everyone out at the same time and with just one punch. There would have been a scuffle. If I were attacked from behind, they would have worn my plate of food for sure. The girls would have tried to make a run for it. The struggle would have broken something, knocked over a chair, did you notice anything like that, Jovis?'

'There was nothing out of place. It was like something out of a horror movie where people had just disappeared. Except for where it looked as if they face plunged into their dinner plates. All was perfectly set up.'

Caitlin tapped her chin, thinking. 'If my memory serves me well, Loray was the only one of the girls that went off-world.'

'You're right, but what has she got to do with anything? Rocky took full responsibility for her, and I trusted him. Are you questioning Rocky's loyalty to me?'

'Not Rocky's, but could Loray have used those trips to contact one of the traitors who are still at large?' She was suddenly overly suspicious of this one girl she never really got to know. 'Could this someone be the same person that turned Rocky against you, Jovis? Possibly, someone he trusts and classes as a friend.'

'Because her goddess charm only works on men, it's more than likely she didn't convert under Caitlin's tough love and still works a hundred percent with Nitarn.' Axon felt this feasible. 'No doubt after the deal was made with the girls, Caitlin had no need to be in control as you men were happy with the arrangement. This would have allowed her magic to be powered down to enjoy time with everyone, but in turn, it switched off her keen senses.'

'Quite conceivable,' Jovis agreed. 'We didn't fight her on it because, in the beginning, we just wanted to spend quality time with Cait. The girls made this easy, so it was a win-win. And Cait is also correct; Rocky would never have flipped out on Artisan and me unless he had someone in his ear.'

Calyx and Jett listened with interest but had kept out of it until now. Calyx's thoughts were fixed on what Jovis said. 'If there is a traitor still on Rocky's Ice Planet, it stands to reason he or she knows it well, and this would be close enough for Nitarn's band of guerrillas to plan their next attack on Sedna. My guess is you'll find your friends there.'

Jett unfolded his arms. 'I agree, the absolute last place you'd look for them is in Rocky's dungeon.' He took a step closer to Caitlin. She was going nowhere without him this time.

'Then we must go now or stand to lose their trail.' Caitlin grabbed Jovis by the hand.

'Hang on Cait.' Jovis took her hand in both of his. 'You sure you want to get involved in this? It means going back to Rocky's dungeon. It took a lot out of you last time, and I might be strong, but my magic is limited; nothing like the members of the team you ride with. Protecting you won't be easy against these thugs.'

'I'm coming.' She flipped her hair up, twisted it into a bun, removed a wooden hair-spike from her pocket, and secured it into place. When Jovis hadn't moved she smiled. 'I'm ready.'

Jovis looked at Axon for help.

Axon wore a slight grin. 'I can see you have cared for her well as Cait's a powerful weapon when she's healthy like this. She's also the best I've got when it comes to combat, and I assume the kidnappers might try to escape if muscle arrived. Once again, Cait is the only team member who can prevent them leaving.'

Calyx and Jett inclined their heads at each other and stood the other side of Cait. 'Be that as it may, Axon, but we are Glow's guardians, and where she goes tonight, we go.' Jett gave Axon and Jovis no opportunity to say no to them.

Axon shook his head and eyed Jovis. 'You might as well count me in too. There is no way I'm missing out on getting into a rumble alongside these two blokes.' He was stoked to be involved in some actual action for a change. 'With two gods and a goddess, this is a party I want to attend.'

Calyx laughed. 'And to see these terrorists get what's coming to them, I bet, will make the reprimand you get from Zoren for tagging along, well worthwhile.'

Jovis smiled. 'You sound like you don't get out much, Axon. Glad to have you on board.'

Caitlin gave a chuckle. 'Zoren will go off his nut we've put his golden boy in harm's way twice in one night.'

'Bring it on.' Axon rubbed his hands.

'So now we're all in, what the plan, Prince?' Calyx said and melted with the smile he received from Caitlin.

'If you guys are right, it's best if we check the dungeon first. If they are there, be prepared for a fight. If not, we'll head upstairs through the secret corridor.' Jovis scratched his chin. 'If my guys are there, I'd say we will have to take out the guards before setting them free, so get ready to use those fists.'

Axon bumped knuckles with Calyx and Jett before he winked at Jovis. 'Put Cait in the middle, and we're ready to go.'

Caitlin was quickly surrounded, and with their backs to her, the castle foyer on Pluto faded...

Chapter Thirty-Five

The Traitor Trap

Cait readied herself as they landed on Rocky's Ice Planet, Orcus.

As soon as they appeared fists and guns were raised as the guards in the dungeon began to protect their prisoners. With no time to fire their weapons, the guards closest swung the firearms with a savage thrust which released a large dagger. Calyx and Axon were closest. Each grabbed for the barrel of the gun nearest to him and snatched the weapon before tossing it aside. Caitlin jumped at the sound of the firearms hitting the stone wall beside her. Their fists were up, and both punched with force as the guards did their best to defend themselves. Caitlin almost chuckled. Her husband and Calyx could have turned the guns on the guards, *but no, that would have been too easy.* Both took on the biggest and mouthiest of the guards and were settling the dispute regarding them giving up, by having a fistfight. They had seemingly chosen not to use their superior being powers, instead electing to resolve it as men.

Axon was distracted for only a moment to see how the others were doing when the guard he fought, swung a punch and it connected. Axon was taken by surprise when he received a fist to his cheekbone. Blood splattered, and he grinned. 'Lucky punch shytzer for brains.' He slammed a hard one back into the guard's nose.

The guard glared.

'Payback can be a real bitch,' Axon gloated as the two of them continued to spar.

In the meantime, Jett and Jovis had knocked out the other four guards with just one hard slam to the side of the head. Leaving them, they went in search of the Jovis's men.

'The hardened criminals are kept down here, and I have a feeling we will find them there.' Jovis led Jett down to one of the underground tunnels to the left.

Jett hissed at Calyx and Axon as they passed them, for dragging it out and using the fistfight to relieve pent-up stress. 'Come on boys, stop fooling around. We don't know how many are upstairs. Finish them off and tie that lot up.' He pointed to the unconscious guards he and Jovis left on the cobblestone floor.

Calyx turned and grinned, and his guard punched his knuckles hard into the side of Calyx's jaw and kicked him in the leg. Calyx held his jaw for just a second and, with a crack, adjusted it back into place. No dislocated jaw was going to stop him now taking his revenge, the old-fashioned way. 'You want to play dirty do you?' He lifted his fists and gave his opponent one fist after another until he had him against the wall. He glanced up and saw Caitlin, and knew he had lost his cool in front of her, which was enough to snap him out of killing the dirtbag. Instead, he threw the practically unconscious bag of bones into one of the empty cells, slamming the door shut.

Axon did the same with his guard before turning to Calyx. 'That was fun, but we'd better secure that lot before bossy britches gets back.' They looked around with nothing but mischief in their eyes until they saw Caitlin with her hands on her hips.

'Behave, or it's the last time you come.' She spoke with conviction.

'Bossy britches stayed,' Calyx stirred, and both grinned but decided to get serious and quickly placed the unconscious men in the cell with the other two.

Under Caitlin's supervision, Calyx and Axon gagged and tied the guards up. The entire time, Caitlin lectured them for fooling around. After she was satisfied the guards wouldn't wake and be able to scream or bang the bars for help, they raced to find Jovis and Jett. By the time they reached them the door had been ripped off the hinges, and Jovis was inside the cell waking up Artisan and Rocky.

'What the hell!' Rocky sounded groggy and stunned.

'Where are we?' Artisan blinked his eyes in an attempt to focus and slapped his cheeks. That seemed to work better. He jumped to his feet. 'How did we get here?'

Jovis crossed his arms. 'Let's ask Rocky; he should be able to answer that.' He turned to him. 'Who the hell have you been consorting with now behind my back? Whoever it is, he has that conniving wench, Loray, in his back pocket and not seeing her here, well, we can assume she is the culprit who drugged you lot!'

Rocky looked around, still a bit dazed. 'Seriously! Loray is working against me!'

His tone helped in his defence. Jovis softened. 'Sorry mate, she's dark matter.'

Rocky shook with anger. 'You're telling me that Aravik is behind all this. The commanding officer of my army!' He scratched his head thinking. 'Come to think of it I did notice he was always where Loray was, but at the time thought nothing of it. I figured he was nice to her while I was busy. Where is the traitorous bastard? I swear I'll kill him with my bare hands!' He was so filthy livid, his tone rumbled painfully in their ears.

'It's not just him, Rocky. It was obviously Loray's plan to spy on us and take back information all this time. My guess is she watched you key in your secret code to my fortress and took a recording of your voice recognition. There is no other way the intruders could have entered once she had drugged you all. And what else have they done while there?'

'But even if she did…' Rocky's eyes were wide with worry. 'The enemy still had to get past Medusa. How could they have…?' Rocky's voice trailed off. 'Don't tell me, they used mirrors, right!'

Jovis was suddenly livid. 'You knew? How?'

'Shytzer, this is my fault.'

'What did you do Rocky?' he roared.

'It was innocent on my part, I swear. I got drunk one night and was fooling around with Loray. She kept putting up scenarios of how she would get around Medusa if I left her behind with the girls next time I travelled here. She didn't like the others and always nagged to be where I was. I forgot until now I even mentioned mirrors. That blatzing parasite... honestly, I said it in jest. I was just referencing the movie we watched on Earth once. You remember? It was about a demigod who once used mirrors. We all laughed at the time, we agreed it was a great comedy, but she must have taken my tale literally. I can't believe it actually worked.'

'Well, none of us is laughing now. And if you had come to me in private, I would have come clean and told you the truth that is wasn't just a movie cliché, but real. Now that it's out, it means we're sitting ducks, and any chump can now access our worlds and take them from us. Shytzer Rocky, you're worse than I am at reading women. And that's saying something.'

Caitlin slipped her hand into Jovis's. 'I also misread her, we all did. That award-winning performance of shyness was to conceal her dark side. Not once did she look at me directly or I would have seen what lurked behind the cunning façade. For the moment...' She stopped and gulped. *Something's not right!* 'Can we save this conversation until we are out of here?' She stared ahead listening.

Jovis felt her shake, his mood softened as he worried what was going on and why her mood had changed. Her eyes were cloudy and she sounded somewhat far away. His hackles went up and glanced quickly from side to side but could hear or see anything out of the ordinary.

Staring at Jovis now she spoke with urgency. 'I must ask you to please leave Loray and the rest of your enemies to the Cosmic Riders. She and her co-conspirators will get what is coming to them, but right now I need us to leave. Can you get the boys to wake up the other girls? If they can't, just pick them up. Something feels terribly wrong here, and I'm getting a warning that we'd best move quickly to safer grounds.'

Jovis lifted her hand in his. 'This delicate hand can't protect us forever. You lot leave, this might be a battle we have to fight alone.'

'No! Jovis we all must go.' Her voice was unusually high, and she shook her head. 'I'm trying not to scare everyone, but something is happening, and we are in grave danger. Blatzing hell, it's too late to even argue, it's happening now! Move it!' she yelled out. 'And I mean… all together! Get us off this Ice Planet right now!' She roared the word out as loudly as she could, and began to scream when hearing a familiar sound. Felt relief when the dungeon began to fade.

Chapter Thirty-Six

Escape to Pluto

When they reappeared on Pluto, far away from harm, Caitlin's cries snapped off, and her head swung around to see who had come with them. Axon had his arm around her. Faithful to the core, he'd responded to her sudden hysteria without question and transported everyone safely out.

'It's all right, honey,' Axon said softly. 'I managed to pluck the girls from the corner as well. But the guards were too far from me. They will meet their own fate for being traitors to royalty.'

Caitlin still had hold of Jovis and now out of danger, let him go. 'We're safe here, but I beg you to stay with me until Axon clears it's okay to go back. Zoren has eyes everywhere, and from what I was hearing, something terrible was about to happen. It was far too dangerous for even you men to handle.' Her face was still flushed and her breathing was still fast and erratic.

'I'll stay if you calm down. You're freaking me out, Cait.' Jovis wanted to give her a few minutes to calm down further before he told her he was going back. He moved over to speak with Rocky and Artisan who both looked bewildered.

Axon turned to speak with Jett and Calyx. 'Keep an eye on Cait for me while I'm gone. I'll be back in five.' Axon wanted to get to the bottom of what had spooked Caitlin enough to make her scream. Last time he saw this was when a bomb went off in Kayden's shed on Earth. He took no chances for fear of her being that hurt again. Last time they also nearly lost some precious magical horses. He couldn't believe a bomb would be set off with so many of Nitarn's men still there. It didn't make sense. He kissed her forehead. 'Keep your boys here,' he whispered to her, and vanished.

In the meantime, Jett and Calyx thought it time to question Caitlin on what she heard that frightened her.

'Now you've caught your breath, Glow, what was going on back there?' Jett moved closer to her.

'It was a bomb.' She shuddered, still reliving the sound that caused her once to almost die.

'But we heard nothing.' Calyx eyed his brother.

'Are you sure, Cait?' Jovis and his boys joined in on the conversation.

'Positive! Trust me, I've had first-hand experience with a bomb such as this on Earth. It almost killed me.'

Jett corrected her. 'It did kill her, but my brother interfered with the process of passing and sent the sun god to heal her shattered body and revive her. I give thanks every day for his meddling nature.' He smiled at Calyx.

'And my brother nursed her back to health as no other could have, so ditto, bro.' Calyx's eyes showed great love for his brother, so many of these experiences had brought them closer than he could ever have imagined.

'What's going on? Nurse who back to health…, and where are we?' Jana insisted on knowing. She and Sienna had woken and although they looked groggy and a bit out of it, Caitlin was glad they were going to be okay.

'You were both drugged, along with Rocky and Artisan. We found you and brought you here to safety.'

'Where's that bitch, Loray? It was her wasn't it.' Sienna looked furious as if she already knew who had done this to them.

Caitlin nodded then put her hand up when an alarm sounded. 'Hang on, there's a traveller about to enter our airspace.'

Soldiers covered every inch of the room around them, guns ready. Jett's army was taking no risks and apparently had been put on full alert.

It was at that moment Axon shimmered back into focus, his complexion pale, his eyes full of empathy when he turned to Jovis and his boys. 'This is not going to be what you want to hear so I'd best show you. He set up the NAVcomHV that doubled as a hologram viewer.

Jett waved away the soldiers, and once the room was cleared, Axon addressed them. 'What you are about to see must stay top secret until we have finished our investigation.'

Once they had given him confirmation they'd keep it quiet, he switched on the NAVcomHV.

The hologram lit up above them, and with eyes wide with disbelief they viewed the actual events that happened milliseconds after they transported off Rocky's Ice Planet. Axon spoke as they watched the recorded incident. 'They thought they were clever in blocking us and taking our eyes from the sky, but Zoren's team is now using NAVmotion and heat sensors.'

Suddenly the picture came into view, and they watched without sound as stars and spheres sped past at an incredible rate while the satellite tracking system headed directly to Orcus. The explosion that happened next had them all gasp and watch helplessly as a large chunk of Orcus's crust broke off and blew out into the atmosphere. Dirt and rock began forming a ring around the planet.

Axon had seen the footage and watched Jovis in particular as he put his theory into words. 'Is it possible the explosion was an accident, Jovis? We thought maybe a nuclear power plant or a large ammunition bunker blew. Apart from explosives, strategically placed, nothing else could do that much damage. Unless of course, you men are holding back secrets.'

'I'm disappointed you felt I would keep something like that from you, Axon. I have been nothing but honest with you since I found out who you were, but to ease your mind and to help with the investigation, I can tell this; all our explosives and weaponry is stored off-world in a secret location, far from our planets and for this very reason. As for us having our own power source, we've only just learned of this technology since visiting Pluto. There is nothing on Orcus that would have done that damage, and as for secrets, I tell Caitlin everything.' He folded his arms, annoyed. 'Not sure if you have noticed, but Cait has become our confidante and advisor, and we would never hide anything from her. And for your information, I happen to trust your wife more than anyone else I know.'

Caitlin still had her hand to her mouth, holding in the fright of what could have been them had she not ordered them out. At the time her sensitive hearing noted something sparked and another sound of something igniting freaked her out. This was proof she had not caused a panic for no reason. They would have all died, been thrown far out into the atmosphere or buried deep underground where they were, in the dungeon. She glanced at Rocky, who had gone white and shook with the shock.

'Blatzing hell, I swear I had nothing to do with this, boss. I would never disrespect the gift you gave me to rule Orcus.'

'We know that buddy,' said Artisan and put an arm around his mate.

Jovis stood, arms still folded, finding it hard to keep his cool in front of everyone. 'I know, Rocky. But rest assured, friend or foe, whoever in your world had a hand in this treachery against us... I will kill.'

'I'm with you on that decision,' Artisan agreed.

Rocky put two thumbs up, which was all he could muster for now. With each blast, his world had started to collapse around him, and so had his plans for the future. He was devastated, and it showed.

Axon glanced at Caitlin. She was listening, he was sure of that, but her mind was somewhere else, so he left her in thought. 'Sorry to add to your worries, Rocky, but it gets worse.' He motioned towards the left of the Ice Planet. 'This blast took out your entire army base, underground headquarters and the castle above. Your home is gone and so is almost a third of Orcus. What didn't get buried in the rubble, as you can see, has been blown out into the atmosphere.' He pointed to the area of concern. 'At this stage, the explosion was so intense we thought your entire Ice Planet was going to shatter into pieces.'

'Thank the lucky stars it didn't.' Jovis breathed a sigh of relief when the shaking stopped. He felt sick, and wished he could throw up but stayed strong for Rocky. He could see he was only just holding it together, and if he lost it, so would his mate. Jovis glanced over, not wishing to take his eyes from the scene unfolding. He saw the full extent of Rocky's emotions show in his eyes. They were of a man ready to collapse after losing so much of what he held dear. He knew how he felt; this was a punch in the gut like no other.

'My men... my friends... my home. They're all gone.' Rocky could take it no longer and slumped into a nearby chair, his elbows on his knees and hands holding his head so as not to collapse.

Jovis and Artisan went over to comfort him.

'I can't believe someone would hate me this much. I'm good to all my people,' he muttered.

'It's not you, buddy.' Jovis felt compassion but wished to leave and search for the mongrels right now. Yet, somewhere inside, he heard Cait's words... 'Please wait; give me a minute.' He sighed, seeing Caitlin was distant he turned his attention back to Rocky. It was important when the time came that he had both his men in the right frame of mind. 'It's the greed of one man that has done this. I can't bring back your people, but we will rebuild. We have Caitlin and her friends. They will help us build it better and stronger this time. Come on buddy, you know Nitarn is behind this, so don't let him win. Stand with me, because I swear he will not run us off. I will fight to the death before giving away my fortune to that tyrant.'

'I feel this is entirely my fault but you know me, boss, I won't give up if you are sure you still want me as a ruler.' Rocky put one hand up, and Jovis gripped it tightly.

Artisan stepped in and put his hand over both of theirs. 'It's our fault. We got careless, and it is time to rectify that, together. If my Ice Planet is next to be hit, how about, we go there now and put a stop to the scum who dare threaten our entire existence.'

Axon leant on the table. 'Hang on guys, let's not get ahead of ourselves. You can't go in guns blazing until we know there are no more bombs planted. I have my team on the way, and you must allow them time to go in and scout for explosives. Thanks to Cait, we escaped with our lives this time. Our hearing is not as superior as the Cosmic Riders'.'

'What do you propose then?' Jovis pulled out a chair and sat at the table next to Rocky.

They all followed his lead and sat to discuss it calmly. Caitlin shook herself from thinking, and on seeing how composed Jovis was compared to how he would have handled this mere months ago, felt a wave of pride sweep over her. No more storming off in a rage, instead, he acted as a true royal who listens to all sides of an issue before making a decision.

Axon straddled a chair opposite Jovis. 'You're right, this could be none other than Nitarn. That being said, we have to assume after what has happened on Orcus, it's possible they have something similar planned on your other worlds. And I'm sorry to be so blunt, but similar weapons may have been planted and ready to detonate if you don't hand all you own over to the lawless mongrels. Nitarn and his criminal lot have terrorised the outer regions for the last time and that's why I'm asking you to give me permission to send my guys in and report back before you take action.'

'We can help.' Jovis wanted to join them and knew his boys would not allow him to go alone.

Axon shook his head. 'It will make it harder for my Riders if you get in their way. You don't realise this but even if you say not to worry about you three, they will, because it's their job to protect the innocent. Being distracted for only seconds could mean a bungled job or death to you, a Rider or both. Trust me, if there has been deliberate sabotage, they'll get to the core of it quickly without causing panic to your people. When they find out who else is working for Nitarn, well, they will be joining him in the high-security prison where he is being kept until trial.'

Jovis's jawline squared. 'I don't trust him not to escape. Vermin like him will find a way out.'

Calyx intervened. 'He, my friend, is locked away where no living soul has ever escaped. He deserves what's coming and, believe me, he and his band of followers will suffer the full force of our law for their actions here today.'

'Death is too easy for those heartless killers.' Rocky looked up. 'I want more justice than him and his goons dangling in the heavens by their scrawny necks.'

'I'm sure the heavenly council will come up with something satisfactory to fit the crime.' Axon sounded reassuring.

'You must appreciate, Axon, it's not easy to do nothing. At least give us your plan and where we fit in.' Jovis pressed his lips tightly in frustration.

Axon sat back and eyed him before speaking. 'Okay, I can see you disobeying my orders if you're not involved so I will include you, but you must promise me you'll follow my orders to the letter.'

Jovis nodded. 'Done!'

Axon gave him a sly grin. 'If you don't, you will find my hands are not soft like my wife's.'

Jovis grinned back. 'I saw that when you introduced your knuckles to the guard's face when you helped to rescue my boys here.'

'Fair enough.' Axon got serious. 'I wasn't going to share this in case you get worked up further, but we have a gentleman's deal, so keep calm and listen. The Riders have already been notified and are calling in here to pick up a team member they can't do this without.' He looked up at Caitlin. 'Rory has asked for you if you're up to it.'

'Up to it!' Caitlin grinned from ear to ear. 'Try to keep me away. And if a certain someone crosses my path, I'm so ready to kick that ice bitch's butt.'

'I assume you're referring to Loray.' Rocky raised an eyebrow.

'You bet, she made this personal by hurting you, my friend.' She reached over to hold his hand for a moment before standing up. 'She and I have a little score to settle. Loray will find I can play just as dirty.'

'Careful Glow, if she's with Aravik, he will protect her and is one nasty piece of work.' Rocky looked worried.

'Cait, this isn't your fight.' Jovis leant forward on the table. 'I don't want you getting hurt. Just do what Rory instructs you to do and leave her to Axon or us after Rory gives the okay to come join you.'

'Whoever gets to her first,' Rocky growled.

'Don't underestimate Caitlin's abilities,' Axon butted in. 'None of you have had the privilege of seeing her in combat yet. With her team, the Riders are able to share their magic, which supercharges their strengths. If Loray has bragged how useless Caitlin is to her buddies, it gives her an advantage. They won't be expecting the Caitlin I know, so to let their guard down for even a second could be their downfall.'

Caitlin smiled at Jana and Sienna. 'Sorry, ladies. I hope this doesn't spoil our friendship knowing I'm not quite as dumb as I act.'

'No female is that useless, Glow. We figured you out after a bit but kept quiet as we had started to like our men. But Loray wasn't our friend. We spoke of nothing in front of her,' said Jana.

Sienna agreed, 'Told that cold witch nothing. She suits that mongrel, Nitarn. Her words were venomous towards every one of you. We wanted to tell you guys, but she told us they had people on the outside that would kill our families and us if we dared.'

'Seriously, you kept that from me?' Jovis snapped at Jana.

'I was too busy trying to work out how to stop her killing you lot in your sleep. You have no idea what pressure we two were under. She threatened us every night. We weren't sure if we'd wake up from one day to the next. After we were locked up in your dungeon and you threatened to kill us, it took a while to trust you guys. We couldn't understand how Rocky could put up with her. We honestly figured you were all pure evil too. Obviously, sitting here now, we see Rocky had no idea and neither did the rest of you.' She smiled with a glint in her eye. 'I'm happy you turned out to be the man I fell for... Well, in the end.'

'I'm also pleased to find you turned out to be the woman I...' He blinked and realising where he was, coughed, embarrassed. 'We can talk in private a bit later.'

Artisan reached over and put his hand over Sienna's. 'Sorry

kitten, you spoilt me too much. I didn't take notice of Loray. She acted so quiet and shy it hid her real character. Slap me silly for not picking that up.'

'Later,' she whispered, her grin wide.

'Bit off track guys!' Axon stopped the chatter. 'Geez, Cait. I sent you to help these guys design a new future, not to play Cupid.'

'Sorry boss, you know I'm a hopeless romantic, your fault.'

'Well you didn't do a very good job. Rocky has lost out on all accounts.'

'Hang on.' Caitlin put her hand up. 'Rocky needs no help in the love department. He is not near ready yet to settle down. He has his hands full at the minute with Patina from Mars on Friday, Saturday night he is with Olga from Makemake and his new one, I'm fairly sure her name is Krista, is from Earth. I think that's all, is it not, Rocky?'

Rocky sat up. 'How do you know about them? I've never told you… in fact, never told anyone.'

'My hearing is super cool. Those phone calls you went out of the room to take, maybe next time text if you don't want me to hear.' She chuckled.

'Now you tell me,' he grumbled and sat back with his arms folded.

'You dirty dog.' Jovis punched his arm.

'Totally!' Artisan agreed. 'How long has this been going on?'

When Rocky just sat there close-lipped, Caitlin answered for him. 'A long time! Sorry Rocky but wowee… what a stud!' She knew secrets were being kept here which would make Rocky feel better if they came out now before she left.'.

'What about them Glow? I'm sure those two have secrets too!' Rocky lashed out, pointing towards Jovis and Artisan.

And there it was. 'They have.' Caitlin was quick in her response. The argument when she first got to know these guys exculpated over a secret, *her*. She had no intentions of letting any of them walk away today without full knowledge of what each of them hid. 'Your mate Artisan said he wanted to build a sports arena, but what he didn't tell anyone is he has almost got it completed. Now he knows how to dome it, he was going ahead without telling you. Oh, and not to leave Jovis out, he has just purchased another Ice Planet.'

Rocky had his mouth wide open.

She turned to Axon. 'They so didn't know I always tell the truth, about everything.'

'One of the many things I most love about you honey.' He touched her cheek lovingly.

'You're building a sports arena?' Jovis and Rocky said together.

'Can't wait to show you, we're finally going to have our own soccer matches against one another.'

'And you have another Ice Planet?' Rocky gaped at Jovis and Artisan.

Jovis nodded. 'That's why I'm not that worried about where you will live, Rocky. I was going to move you anyway. This one has a modern palace with servants and everything. I knew as soon as I saw it just how fitting it was to your lifestyle. I was stoked when they decided to sell to me. It will give us plenty of time to rebuild Orcus; a project the three of us can now sink our teeth into... together!'

'Why wouldn't you give it to me?' Artisan brooded.

'Because I can't get rid of you and this new Ice Planet actually needs a ruler 24/7.'

They all laughed.

Artisan punched both of them in the arm. 'Rotten blatzing stirrers!'

Jovis winked at Caitlin. 'You make everything all right. I love that about you, honey!' He was a little sarcastic but meant to be funny by almost repeating Axon's recent words.

'Cheeky shytzer!' Axon picked up on it straight away. He leant over and took a playful swipe at him, but Jovis ducked. The electrically charged movement that wafted in the air made his hair stand on end.

The lot of them erupted in laughter as Jovis licked his hand and smoothed his hair down. He was by no means expecting Axon to fool around and now understood what Caitlin saw; he wasn't just a stuffed shirt after all.

'Don't think because you're a prince I won't deck you one for giving me crap.' Axon continued to stir and glanced at Caitlin. 'Keep your boyfriends in line or else.'

Caitlin chuckled. 'Sorry my love, but they're all yours. My ride is here. I can hear Rory talking. They're just about to land.' She ran off, leaving them.

Axon called after her. 'You created these monsters, and now you're leaving me with them!' He headed off after her and stopped, looking back at them. 'Well, if you want to see her off, you'd better not be waiting for an invitation. Wife bloody stealers.' He was going crook as they ran past him. Calyx and Jett slowed and walked beside him.

'She best not bring any more of her boyfriends' here or I'll start introducing them to Cerberus,' Jett grumbled. Axon and Calyx roared with laughter.

'Sure you don't want us to go tag along on this mission as chaperones?' Calyx asked.

'You and Jett are too valuable on the front line, and you know Zoren would never okay this crossover. Gods stepping in could mess up the universal order and is totally frowned on. You had fun on Earth together on a mission when Cait was unwell, which was the reason why it was permitted. I'm grateful for that help, but Cait is back and healthy again. It's time she went back to Rory and joined the team. This is what she does, and she loves it. Did you see that look on her face?'

'How could you not,' Calyx said.

Through the door to the outer edge of the dome, it was icy cold and only wearing light summer clothing, they all pulled on thick jackets handed to them by the butler. It was out in the snow they finally caught up with Caitlin, Jovis and his boys. After what sounded like a dispute with Caitlin, they turned and stared at Jett when he got closer to them.

'What's going on, why so serious?' Jett stared at Jovis.

'We asked when we would see her next. She said at our end of the month BBQ. Apparently, we're taking it in turns... and of course, no guessing the golden boy who gets to host first.'

Jett looked pleased.

'Yep, you're first up Jett,' she grinned.

'And who else is to be invited apart from all us? Don't tell me I have to suffer your Rider mates too?' Jett added.

'Nope, they have their own friends back on Earth. This is just my sky friends.' She looked happy. 'I should have organised a monthly get together years ago.'

Jovis moved closer to Jett. 'Guess us two had better bury the hatchet, or she'll ban us both no matter where it is.'

'You bet I will.' Caitlin became serious.

Jett folded his arms and spoke to Jovis. 'You're okay once you let a man get to know you but I have to be honest, it will get competitive. I don't like sharing Glow.'

'Me either.' He squeezed in between him and Caitlin and smirking at a stunned Jett.

'Little prick!' Jett eyed him.

Axon joined in and with a hand on her shoulder pulled her in close to him. 'You will have me on 24-hour watch if you don't stop making friends.'

She chuckled but pointed up when a shadow came overhead. 'Look, they're here. My favourite part is seeing those horses in flight.'

'Sure is a magnificent sight?' Axon hugged her while waiting.

Jovis had seen them before, but this was a sight he could see again and again. The V formation of majestic beasts and their Riders, all dressed in white and black, the yin and yang of the galactic heaven.

The glow of the divine magic that surrounded them suddenly surrounded Caitlin as she moved closer to where they would land. 'They brought Shargan for me.' she clapped her hands excited to see her horse.

Jovis did as Axon had, moved back to give her space as her horse broke formation and flew gracefully towards her. Caitlin glowed so brightly, Jovis shaded his eyes, and as it dissipated, Caitlin had changed. Her glorious red hair was braided and up in a twist knot at the top of her head, well out of the way and combat ready. He blinked twice at the corset top that covered little and black leather-looking pants and boots. *How come she's not cold?* He tried not to whistle. She was one very sexy woman. This was the Caitlin he first met on Earth, yet she had hidden her body in large dowdy shirts and casual jeans. He smiled. She was never meant for him, and he was in love with another woman now. But just once if she had of emerged like this in the earlier days, well, the world would be missing their angel. He could never have let her go.

As if Caitlin read his thoughts she turned and smiled. 'Rider magic will keep me warm now. And as for this,' she gestured towards her outfit. 'My horse is very naughty,' she said directly to Jovis. 'She dresses me when she is around. I have not learned to speak horse yet, but when I do, she is getting reprimanded.'

Jovis loved her smile of pure delight as she turned back while the horse landed. Her arms went quickly around the mare's neck in a hug. The horse didn't move a muscle, not even a wing, while she spoke quietly to her. Shargan's markings on her side were of the tattoo he remembered seeing on Cait. They apparently shared a very close connection.

Her head went up as Rory landed and Jovis felt a pang of jealousy as she ran to him. The guy was so large, he used just one arm to lift her up on his horse for a hug.

'We have to go, Caitlin,' they heard him say. 'Are you okay to leave now? My nerves are jumping. Something big is going down.'

She saluted and jumped down. Running back to her horse she called out to the friends she was leaving behind, 'Catch up with you all when I get back.'

The horse's height had Jovis contemplate how she would mount it and didn't need to wait long to find out. As she neared, the horse bent its leg and in a single leap she had lightly stepped on it and now sat comfortably in the glowing saddle.

Axon stood at Shargan's side and smiled when she bent and kissed him. 'Love you, sweetheart. Come back safe.' He held her hand for a moment before letting her go.

'I will.' She waved goodbye as Rory directed his magnificent grey stallion, Ghost, to take them up into the sky.

Cait had explained how it all worked to Jovis and as they left, she could hear him telling Artisan and Rocky what would be going on.

'At the moment, Rory will be relaying coordinates to his horse, Ghost, who in turn, takes charge of the rest of the horses. And while Ghost controls the herd, Rory's free to concentrate and use his magic to open up a portal for them to go through.'

She liked knowing he took an interest and could still feel them watching as the team of horses, with wings out, soared high into the air and headed straight for a low-lying cloud.

Now out of sight, Rocky whistled. 'It looked too small to fit them all in and yet check it out, one after the other, like magic, they are gone from sight.'

Jovis was amazed. 'How she stayed with us in my small fortress with nothing to do but chat, when her life is that exciting, is beyond me. I mean, that was one cool exit.'

Axon smiled. 'Cait will make huge sacrifices to help those she cares about.'

'Be grateful my boy.' Calyx walked beside him as they trudged in the snow, back to the castle entrance. 'Not many of us are touched by an angel. And like a true angel, she will never leave us. We are the privileged.'

'Please… let us hope we are it, the last of her recruits.' Jovis was blown away to be a part of this new future he had not given in easily too, but which now felt so comfortable.

Jett came up the other side of him. 'That's what we said and now there's you! Any more and this get together she has organised will just become a goddamned competition for her attention.'

'It's already begun!' Axon said, running a hand through his thick dark hair. His dark eyes squinted with concern. *What the hell will Zoren say when I turn up with this football team Caitlin's goddamned left me to look after?*

Chapter Thirty-Seven

Cosmic Riders Mission

A *wesome to have you back with us, Cait.* Rory said telepathically, *but we're almost in range, and as you know it's critical we don't get picked up on alien scanners, so button it the lot of you.* He'd allowed them to chat freely while in the safe zone but now close to Quaoar, which was their destination, he requested silence. As always with his team the silence was immediate. Next, he aligned the horses.

Ghost! Have the team take up defence formation. Lisha, you're with me.

When Lisha was up beside him, he nodded once. *It's just you and me this time sis; I need the rest of the team to stay put, and cover us if it gets heavy down there.'* She nodded, and hand signalled. *Is Red coming?*

Cait stays, now keep your mind clear and ready yourself, I want all weapons disarmed. Nathen, you're my eyes, so keep the team alert until we return. Rory glanced at his sister, knowing her better than she knew herself at times. He had trust in her ability to disarm bombs of any kind, and it never wavered so when her eyebrows went up, and she straightened, he knew something was up. *Lisha, talk to me.*

She turned and using hand signals, pointed along the outer regions of Artisan's fort. The castle had walls surrounding an entire village nestled within. Outside the walls, were four substantial lookout posts that had armed soldiers on watch? They had not yet looked up so for now, the team was safe. *Is it just the guards' weaponry you're picking up or armed bombs under one or more of the lookout posts?*

Once again, knowing words could not be spoken, she hand signalled there were bombs under each one. It was as Rory had first assessed, it would be him and Lisha going it alone and certainly not a job he could give to Caitlin. If she blew up the lookout towers, the population would go with them. They were too close, and he could see hundreds of townsfolk below. His hawk-like sight clearly viewed the men in the towers. He knew they'd been spotted when they swapped light weaponry for hand-held rocket launchers. He was taken aback with how they could have seen them until he saw one of them using an older style NAVscanner. It had enough range to see them from this distance but he doubted they could see much further with the outdated equipment used.

Nathen, you've got the reins. Rockets have left the launchers so proceed with manoeuvre tactics to hide us. Instruct your team to keep the guards busy and their eyes off Lisha and me. We're heading for those lookout towers to disarm bombs under them. Once we're ground zero, move to the clouds to the left of us and stay quiet and alert in case I need you. I'm not getting a good vibe from down there.

Nathen nodded, and figured that was why Rory was going instead of him and Zeke. Four bombs and only two Riders… It was going to be a hard task, but under those lookout towers, he already knew from experience the tunnels were tight. Three would be one too many.

Nathen tapped his earpiece. 'We've been spotted so we can talk until I say. You know the code.' He turned in his seat to see if Caitlin was powering up. 'You got eyes on them, Red?' he saw she was omitting sparks and was getting ready.

She gave him a nod, not taking her eyes from the enemy's missile fire.

He saw her acknowledgement. 'To give Rory and Lisha cover, we need smoke and lots of it. Can you blow the suckers as close to us as you can get them? I'll cover us when you're done.'

'You're right to go, Rory, camouflage is on its way,' Nathen spoke to Rory and Lisha.

Rory put thumbs up and took off with Lisha in a mad dash as

the first missile whizzed past them. Caitlin waited, and touched her earpiece. 'Use your hearing blockers; this will be loud,' she called out. Her hand went up, and flames shot from them, followed by a cloud of smoke. They all touched their NAVsonars to shield the thunderous noise from their ears. The little addition to the earpieces was the ingenious work of Zeke, who tinkered and tweaked all their equipment. This allowed Caitlin to have the weapon fire come as close as she could, and once her countermeasures had been fired off, Nathen covered them with Rider magic to prevent them being blasted off their horses and stop the winged beauties from getting knocked around.

Still working through Nathen's magic, Caitlin moved her hand with easy control to create hot thick vapour swirled with the embers that spun slowly like a tornado, allowing Rory and Lisha to ride it to the surface. With her other hand, the second, third and fourth missiles were destroyed the same way. Only with their fumes and smoke, she whipped up just enough wind to stream it across the sky, blocking the rest of the team, giving them time to make their exit into the clouds.

Moments before, Caitlin saw Nathen's signal to now stay silent and using Riders hand language turned slightly in her seat towards him. 'Did they make it?' She watched him intently.

Nathen put his hand up for her to give him a second. Finally, he grinned and signalled back. 'All good, now stay steady. Rory wants us out of sight until he needs us. Let's hope they think they got us and don't come looking for us using NAVsatellite heat imagery. Although doubt they have that technology after what I saw them using down there.'

Suddenly cheers and yahoos from far below could be heard once the smoke settled, and now out of sight, they overheard the enemy claimed victory.

* * * *

On the ground, Rory saw thick bush where other horses grazed. He removed the bridles from their horses and threw them over his shoulder. Doing so allowed them to transform and fit in with all the other horses. *Don't go far,* he whispered as he patted Ghost. *When I call, I'll need you urgently.* The horse shook its head, snorted and stomped a foot. *I know you know, but this makes me nervous.* He grabbed Lisha by the shoulder. She'd been keeping watch. He shoved the bridles in her backpack. *Ready!*

She nodded. Both ran to the hatch that looked to lead into the tunnels underground that was sure to connect the four towers.

He snapped the lock with one twist of his bare hands, and they slipped inside so quickly, you would have had to slow down footage to see the break-in.

They didn't bother climbing down the ladder. With hands and boots on the sides, they slid down. Having possibly only minutes before being discovered, they weren't wasting any time. Rory hit bottom and jumped out of the way. Lisha touched down with hardly a sound. *You're so light on your feet sis. Which way?* He communicated.

She knew talking would give them away, so pointed at the tunnel to the left of them. Feeling no motion sensors, she sprinted ahead with Rory a step behind. She wished she could ask why he came and not one of the boys, but was sure glad she had the best of the best backing her up for this job. Unable to take one moment longer to ponder, she kept moving, her mind on the task at hand.

Her stop was so sudden, Rory literally had to jump over her as she dropped to the ground and started digging. *Bit of notice next time, crazy lady,* he stirred and got a sour sneer. He shook his head and bent down next to her. *Sorry, my fault, I was listening for the army.*

She didn't react, busy digging into the dirt with her hands. Feeling the weapon, she motioned for her brother to help. Uncovering the bomb was made easy with Rory's large hands. Once the head was exposed, she snatched hold of his hand and shook her head. Wiping her hands on white pants, she flicked her fingers to remove the dirt from under the nail she wanted to use. They were as tough as steel and she worked quickly, using them and a few tools in her backpack to unscrew the head and disarm the bomb.

Done? Rory was pleased when she nodded.

Lisha stood up, swung her head around and pointed to a new tunnel. Slipping her tools into her bag, she had already begun to jog while zipping it up. She slung it over her shoulder, and quickened her pace, reaching the next within seconds. With her hand up to warn him she was stopping, she slid on her knees to the spot and located the weapon before Rory even bent to join her.

This time Rory knew what to do and worked fast to uncover the bomb. Her hands worked so swift they faded in a blur, and the third was just as quickly located and disarmed. It was when they were running to the last location that a siren went off. He could hear panicked yelling and the sound of heavyset men scrambling down the ladder. *They know we've disarmed them. They could try to set the last one off to kill us. Can you do this, Lisha? Otherwise, I want us gone from here now!*

Lisha didn't stop. She put her hand up and signalled they were almost there but yes, she could do it.

He followed blindly, knowing he should pull her out, but apart from snatching her up, while she screamed insults, he had no way of doing it. He decided to trust her. She had been doing this for years and many times had come closer than this to death-defying situations. Because she was his sister, he figured he worried more. He breathed out and calmed as she pulled up hard again. He heard her pants rip she when she skidded on her hands and knees to the bomb. Rory dropped and, using superhuman speed, he had the weapon uncovered and turned to fend off the soldiers who were almost on their tail. He could see the shadow of guns and wished he had not been so stubborn and had brought Caitlin down with him. He and Caitlin had always been a team. They went everywhere together, but she had been gone a long time. Right now though, in situations like this, she was the only one with powers enough to get them out of this boxed-in situation.

He was annoyed she didn't seem hungry enough to want to be in the action and in turn, by his side. She had sat there and taken an order she once would have ignored. He wanted his Cait back and hoped leaving her behind would give her time to think. Annoyed at the way he was handling her return, he angrily reached for his knife and sword. He had never needed a gun and couldn't understand why others used them. There was no honour in them. He was ready, muscles flexed, breathing calmly. *Come on boys, time to dance!* Just as the criminal misfits were about to turn the last corner, he felt a hand on his shoulder. He spun around. *Done?*

Lisha nodded, and pointed to a hatch in the ceiling. Rory flipped open a disc and pulled out a rope with a hook. He attached the spool onto his belt and tossed the other end with the hook up to the roof cavity. After hitting the mark and checking it was secured, he wrapped an arm around Lisha, and let the mechanics pull them both up. Dangling quietly, they watched without breathing as the soldiers ran straight through, not even looking up.

'This way men,' a poorly dressed insurgent called. 'I heard something through there.'

Once alone, Rory smashed the trapdoor open with his fist. He lifted Lisha so she could get through before hoisting his own body up and out of the tunnel to where their horses waited.

The bridles. Rory snapped his fingers.

Lisha pulled one out and tossed it to him and placed the other over her own horse's head. They both lifted onto the saddle once it appeared. A couple of men sprang from the bushes, one with a shovel, and the other with a pick.

'You are the Rider, Rory.'

Rory nodded.

'I have a message for Jovis. We work with his brother. He is alive and is doing better now. He is proud of what his brother has achieved and passes on that when he becomes king, he will reward Jovis well for his dedication to keeping strong their family heritage. We were only just alerted to the bomb situation and have been sent by the future King to lend a hand. A bit late for that by the looks of it, but we can still help. Go… we will cover you.'

Ghost; get us out of here, back to the others… Fast! Rory gave the men a nod, and watched as they ran in the opposite direction, making a hell of a din, screaming and clanging the tools they held.

As the two Riders flew up and disappeared into a low-lying cloud, Lisha used hand language.

'That was too easy. It has to be a decoy for something bigger. They were old school NAVneutron bombs, nothing like what must have been used on Rocky's Ice Planet. Those things down there would have killed most of the population with the fumes and flames, but I doubt they'd even blow up one of those towers. Now they're disarmed I can feel a huge amount of explosive power coming from that direction.' She pointed out into space in the direction of Sedna.

I agree. I feel a mighty dark force, but more like a war zone. You're spot on, sis. It's coming from Jovis's Ice Planet. He was right when he told Caitlin they were after him. Let's go pick up the rest of the team and get moving. After our escape, the enemy down there will figure out our next move, and I'm sure they'll be on the NAVcom right this minute tipping off the bad guys we're coming for them too. Rory used his power to speed them up. Within seconds they had joined up with the waiting party. *Listen up team… that was a decoy to take our attention away from the real attack.*

Caitlin leant over in her seat and mouthed, 'Jovis?'

Rory nodded and held his finger to his mouth to hush her. *No talking, I think they're on to us and most likely guessed that the air attack didn't work. But it did give us cover while it was needed.*

The sound of another rocket launched from the ground below had Rory move them quickly. *Yep, they know where we are; time to get a wiggle on.* He opened a portal in the cloud and flew the team through. One by one they popped out into the airspace above Sedna. *Cait, is that the hideout where Jovis lives?* He motioned towards the far snowy mountain below.

She shook her head, and motioned to a flat area in the valley between two mountains further away.

What's that then? I'm picking up lots of heat.

She leant over the horse and studied it, turned to him and signed to him it was the cave where they found the hot spring.

Suddenly Lisha waved her hands, getting their attention. She motioned towards Jovis's secret fortress.

Are you picking up a bomb? Rory asked while taking them quickly to the site.

Lisha nodded and, impatient to land, was off the horse before its hooves touched the ground. Her hand waved madly for Caitlin and Rory to follow.

Stay with the horses. He left orders with the rest of the team. Once the bombs were disarmed, he wanted them fresh to track the enemy. Rory raced to catch up to both girls who moved quickly towards the fortress entrance. Cait thought she would need to put in the code but on arrival, the door was wide open. Peering in, Caitlin saw the elevator had been destroyed.

Rory stared down into the darkness over the top of the two girls' heads. *Of course, it has to be down there! Cait this is the only way to get below?*

She nodded.

It looks like we slide down that pipe, Lisha. Can you identify how many?

Lisha put her hand up and one finger.

Cait, head back to the others. Use your gut instinct to find the creeps doing this; my guess is they are definitely here. I can smell the revolting stench of evil from here. Leave our horses, and once Lisha disarms this bomb, we'll be right behind you. My guess is the mongrels are using this sabotage to scare the remaining royals into giving up the castle. If they think Jovis's brother is dead and now Jovis, this scare tactic might be enough to make them give up the kingdom and leave without conflict.

Caitlin gestured for him to come with her and let Zeke and Nathen go with Lisha as they always did. She was confused that Rory was working with Lisha now and not her. She hand-signalled... 'Are you still mad at me?'

Figure it's me you ran from. Don't want to crowd you on your first mission back. And also, Lisha was unsettled about this task. Unusual for her.

Caitlin gestured again... 'I need you more.' She dropped her lip and saw Rory grin at her for the first time as he tuned out from her while he sent a message to Nathen and Zeke. *Boys, come and escort Lisha. Cait and I are going after the culprit. Bree, get the horses ready with ropes to pull them out once the bomb is defused.*

In mere seconds the horses had flown towards them. With one

movement, Caitlin and Rory were up on Ghost and Shargan and had settled in the saddles. *Bree, no-talking rule still applies. When they are ready, they will tug, right boys?*

Nathen and Zeke agreed.

Men, get it done and come as quickly as you can. The mongrels are in this direction. I can still smell their filthy stench of hatred.

The boys both saluted, turned and slid down the pipe, one after the other to join Lisha.

Can you smell that, Cait?

She screwed up one side of her face and gestured towards the castle.

Rory already had them in flight, and they landed high up in the mountains overlooking a scene neither of them expected. Both dismounted.

The castle was surrounded. Thousands of warriors, men, women and creatures from many outer Oort cloud nations were ready to storm the castle. On the flat land that stretched out many thousands of acres, an army of half-breed man and beast marched together with burning torches. These flames were held high, ready to ignite a variety of cannons, both old-fashioned wood style and modern steel that they dragged along. Farther back, tripods were wheeled, the swinging wrecking balls big and heavy enough to smash down the high brick walls that prevented them from entering.

This looks like something out of an old black and white movie. Where the hell did Nitarn recruit these Stone Age fighting wackos from, a cave? Rory shook his head disgusted.

Caitlin put her hand on his shoulder to get his attention. Up so high and out of earshot to those below, she might have been able to speak quietly to Rory as they watched the sight below. Yet she was worried it might give their position away, so she used sign language. 'Nitarn's Ice Planet is on the edge of the solar system. Most these dark worlds would have no concept or understanding of how to use today's technology, even if it's given to them.'

Of course, he said. *That's why the bombs are old school. Because we have Nitarn locked up, they might not have access to his weaponry.*

She continued signing... 'That's my thought too. I believe they are still going ahead with the original plan for fear he will get out and punish them for not doing as he ordered.'

Rory agreed and turned back to the war zone when the churning of explosives in a launcher caught his attention. The puff of dirt, ice and flames exploded miles from the approaching enemy. *Idiots, the castle has started firing their weapons. At this rate, they will use all their firepower before the rebels even get within striking distance. It's not hitting anything. What are they thinking?*

'Trying to scare them off... Not really working is it?' she signed back.

Suddenly they both froze, as a loud explosion rang out from the direction where they left the rest of the team. The icy chill that ran up Rory's spine was the first clue something had gone terribly wrong. He shuddered, realising that these misfits of old-school-fools, had set up bombs to keep them busy, but that he hadn't considered that they were dodgy and unpredictable. They were fighting an ancient race, and modern thinking would not win this war. The team's magic and strength would be tested. *I should have stayed.*

Caitlin's eyes filled. She also had pain from her team members that shook her core and had her shudder. 'No Rory.' She wiped her eyes with the backs of her hands and kept signing. 'We both should have stayed.'

They mounted and were back at the location quickly. The area had collapsed, and a considerably large hole was where the fortress used to be. The horses had been saved by their armour, but thrown some fifty metres away. They were standing now and shaking off the shock.

Bree! Rory used telepathy to scream out loud to her. *Caitlin, can you hear heartbeats?* He asked as they dismounted.

She held up three fingers, pointed in the sunken dirt but kept listening.

Bree! Rory's face said it all; his sudden fear that the love of his life had been killed.

Suddenly the three fingers Caitlin held up, fingers he couldn't take his eyes from, turned to four.

Where? He shook her by the shoulders. She pointed to a slightly darkened mound a couple of metres from the horses.

'Go...' she mouthed, 'I've got this.' She pushed him and pointed towards Bree. 'Go...'

Caitlin had to use her powers to blow some boulders out the way and melt some massive blocks of ice before they could reach the trapped team members, so Rory took that moment to race to Bree's side. Before leaving, he pulled a warm NAVcover from his bag which was tied to the horse. *I'll just check she's okay!* Rory ran at full speed, but the thick snow slowed his pace, so he slid the last few metres to her on his knees. *Are you hurt, beautiful?* She blinked twice for no, but he knew she was in pain; he could feel her, never mind the telltale signs of bruised and broken skin on her arms and neck. After a quick examination of her limbs, he breathed out with a sigh when he felt no broken bones. With tender care, he wrapped her in the warm, waterproof skin. He saw she wanted to talk, tell him she was okay, but the no-talking order he gave kept her quiet. Instead, she gave him a weak smile. In shock, he expected no more... *Stay, rest. I'm going back to help Cait get the others out.* He had been torn about whether to stay with Cait until done or go and help his girl, but he knew life wouldn't be worth living without her. This made him suddenly see how much he loved Bree. The moment he thought she might be dead, he'd sent up a prayer that if the gods saved her, it was for him, and he'd sworn to make her his wife. When they got home, he was going to propose.

Back with Caitlin, Rory dug away the slurry of dirt and ice that she had blown away or melted while he was gone. He stepped back for her to clear more, and again her hand was outstretched. The steady stream of fire she ejected finally melted the last of the ice that had collapsed into the area where the Riders had tried to escape. It was on this third attempt, that Rory reached deep into the ice slurry and felt a hand, gripped it and pulled with all his might. Caitlin was under Rider magic, and when she wrapped her hands around Rory's waist, she felt arms go around her too. The heave brought Rory tumbling back on his butt, the action pulled the other three free. Out of the watery muck they came, wet, dirty but alive. None of them had let go of one another. Their friendship and trust had saved them.

Caitlin spun her head around to see who had helped. It was Bree. Battered and bruised, she was one who would never give up. 'Had to dig deep but you needed me.' She signed before her damaged body collapsed back in the snow.

Hugs and thanks, it's a luxury time does not permit. Back on your horses, team, we have work to do, Rory ordered. *Why that bomb exploded on you will be more evident to you when you see what Cait and I stumbled across. We are dealing with olden day weaponry. Here's hoping we get back in time before Nitarn's misfit army entirely destroys Jovis's castle with that prehistoric artillery they're using.*

Rory moved the horses before bums had even comfortably settled in the saddles. Bree hollered out in pain when she slipped to the side and almost fell off. The blast had also mucked with her judgment. *You right, Bree?* Rory worried for her and his sister. Neither looked well. Even so, he had to keep up momentum and move them to the portal and use its magic to help heal his team. *Nathen! Ride beside Bree until she gets her balance.*

He was there before Rory had finished speaking. Nathen was glad for the telepathy as he still couldn't hear a thing after the bomb went off.

Ghost; take the horses into that cloud to camouflage us. I'm moving us into the portal where I'll need your herd to assist with giving the team some healing. I don't want to drain Cait, she is going to need every ounce of her magic.

Suddenly they were in a cloud of stars. The glow around them was calming, yet they could feel their clothes drying. Nathen, Zeke and Lisha could hear again, and the bruising they all sported had lessened. Bree sat bright and refreshed. Rory patted his horse. *Good job Ghost!* He nodded, eyeing the team. *You guys okay now?* They responded by giving him thumbs up. Rory gazed out far in the distance. *Good, because our work has only just begun... Ready!*

They nodded.

Ghost; to the castle.

Rory stopped and had them hovering directly above the castle, high in the sky. With the naked eye, they would be nothing but specks, yet for them with their hawk-like sight, they could easily see the goings on below.

'What's the plan, boss?' Zeke rode beside him and signalled.

He scratched his head, shifted in his seat and chewed on his lip. *The way I see it, we have two choices. Go down and reason with them to leave, which we know doesn't work with ancients from worlds beyond the Oort cloud. Or,* he screwed up his lip while rubbing his forehead, thinking... *If Cait's up for it, we could try the Tartarus manoeuvre. Zap the enemy before they can damage the castle. I know Cait has the coordinates, so she could send them to the underworld. Let the bunch of thugs, thieves and killers plead their case with Hades. Have the God of the Underworld decide if they deserve a second chance. They won't be able to lie to him, and with their plea, he will either permit them to go back to their Ice Planets or stay where we put them as punishment.*

The team gave it the thumbs up.

Cait? Rory raised his brow and shrugged. *Leave it up to you!*

Caitlin used hand language. 'Hell yes. They just tried to blow up you guys, the only family I have. Not forgetting they are trying to kill my new friends and their families.'

I thought you, being the Goddess of Peace, would have fought me on such a move. Rory leant towards her, interested in her reply.

'I do this to protect the peace of all Ice Planets. This will keep other rulers far and wide from trying such a bold move, with luck, for many generations to come. Let's give it a go. I vote we save Jovis's remaining family and home. His fortress is gone, and he'll need to come back and live somewhere. If we rid him of Nitarn's scum and those who have slaughtered his parents and who have killed most of the royal bloodline, it will be safe for him to return. What's the worst that could happen? If I fail as the anchor and it's me that dies trying, geez, it might be worth the look on Jett's face when the reaper has me face court, next time it meets.'

Rory smiled. *Again, welcome back Cait. This you, the one who can see the funny side of everything is, who I have missed. Well, if you all agree, let's do this.* Rory communicated orders to his horse. *Ghost, move the herd into NAVstar configuration. Caitlin, hold Shargan steady. Once we're in place, Ghost will move Shargan to the middle of our formation. It's all you after that, Cait. When you have enough of our power, give me the signal, and I'll shut it off, okay.*

It had never been her job to spin, or chase death-stars, meteors and the likes across the sky like the other Riders. Her job was more controlled, and she was ready to prove to Rory she was still a crucial member of the team and deserved a place beside them. She nodded, serious and ready to battle the army below. She scanned the attacking enemy; they were almost at the brick wall boundary and past the point of no return.

After she was placed in position by Rory, she had a better view. The enemy had started to aim and fire off bags of impact explosive. Some exploded in the air, some met their target and fires were being put out in the village by the townsfolk.

She eyed Rory. He wiped his brow, a sure sign he was heating up, getting ready to power them up and move them into the final stage of this intricate manoeuvre. He was a good solid leader, confident and maybe a tad tough, but he had a side only she got to see. This was the side that saved her. She felt exhilarated to be back with this strong leader who had brought her from poverty and loneliness to the person she was today. She trusted his judgement and knew this course of action was a last resort for Rory. It bordered on dangerous if he got it wrong as it was not a tactic they had perfected. Yet she trusted this powerful, modern-day, superhero that had to control everyone's magic. He'd send it to her in short bursts and in just the correct amounts, as an overload would render her unconscious. They had practised this and many more manoeuvres in secret, but had never thought they would need it in this day and age. There wasn't a civilised sphere in the universe Rory couldn't talk down, but there was no reasoning with old-style, mob-violence. Taking the cave dwellers from the scene was the safest option, for everyone.

Rory moved her into position directly above the castle. This was the only way to protect the magnificent old building from the hammer effect of supercharged energy she would send forth.

CHAPTER THIRTY-EIGHT

Alpha Site Anger

A t the Alpha Site, the room had gone dead silent while staring at the reality NAVcom. Jovis was standing beside Axon and blinked at the technology possessed by powers he was now trusting to save his Ice Planets. An entire wall from roof to floor seemed to disappear, and they felt as if they were really in the war zone on Sedna, but Jovis was glad it was just smoke and mirrors. He would not have been able to contain himself from going in and being in the thick of it. Almost believing they were all standing on the ice surface, he watched helplessly as his fortress blew up. He cringed as the trapped Riders were dug free and sighed with relief when three of them were pulled from the elevator shaft alive. He was amazed as they flew into clouds and came out well, unscathed and ready for more action. And just now, he held still as Axon adjusted the NAVsatellite and moved the visual, taking them up high on a tall mountain so they could watch the battle going on below.

'How can this be happening? My home, all the family heirlooms stored within that fortress are gone, and now this.' Jovis was devastated that all he worked for was slipping through his fingers.

'Not all is lost, boss,' said Rocky, 'and don't go getting all cranky when I tell you, but Artisan and I hid your artefacts that night we came out of the spell and realised Nitarn was a crook.'

'Where?' Jovis's eyes were wide.

'We transported them to my world.' Artisan joined in the conversation. 'Don't worry,' he added as he saw the look in Jovis's eyes. 'They're safe in a cave.'

Jovis gave them a friendly nod. 'Should kick your arses for not telling me sooner. But glad I can always rely on my boys to look out for me.'

Although relieved the ancient royal treasure was safe, it didn't do much to lift his spirits while watching thousands of murderous delinquent thugs advance towards his castle, which was now under attack. His heart felt a heavyweight in his chest as he watched the Riders hover above the castle. He wondered how a team of six people, even with superpowers, could stop what was happening out there. His people were doomed, and all he could do was watch and wait until it was over. Even three more willing lads as he and his men would be could not stop that many savages.

'Where is Medusa?' Artisan put his hands on the top of his head in frustration.

In a mask of devastation and anxiety, Jovis shrugged.

Axon typed quickly on the device he held before pointing it towards the adjoining wall. Another screen flickered and a still frame of the cave where Medusa lived showed little. He twirled a knob on the control panel, which almost took them into the cave. And only seeing a short way in, they saw Medusa's tail, unmoving. He adjusted the light and they saw her tail sat in a puddle of green plasma. He shook his head when he turned to Jovis. 'Sorry buddy, Medusa is dead.'

Jovis showed no emotion and his face was like steel as Axon changed the image back towards the castle. Helplessly he watched as the last of his family, their royal bloodline, seemed bound to be slaughtered. He should have been there, but a part of him not only trusted Axon to stop this happening but knew he was right. He was the Prince of Sedna and had to survive to keep the royal heritage alive. He was his ancestors' only hope.

'What the hell?' Jovis squinted as the Riders formed a star shape, and Caitlin moved into the middle.

'Shush and watch,' Axon said in an edgy tone.

Jovis ignored him; he could see the team were doing something Axon was unsure of and he wasn't going to be bullied into shutting up. Magic was at play as the Riders were connecting with what looked like a blue live electricity charge that ran from Rider to Rider. The only one not involved was Caitlin. He turned to Axon. 'How can six people protect that castle? Even if they put a charge around it, you get it as I do, they'll run out of power. The enemy will eventually win. You might as well call them back now. I don't want them harmed trying to fight my war. Christ, Axon, they were almost killed just minutes ago. Rory is one tough commander. Didn't even give them time to breathe and now has them back on their horses, and fight ready.'

Axon sighed, knowing he'd been short. He wasn't quite sure what they were doing either but believed in them. He wished he could have been there alone, but had promised Cait he'd babysit. 'Look Jovis, this is what they do and that's all I can tell you. They put their lives on the line every time they hop on those horses. I know this is hard for you to watch but don't give up on them because it looks as if they haven't given up on you. Otherwise, they would have let Cait lose. Trouble is… she is so powerful her bombs would destroy not only the army but the surroundings of the castle and most of the town down there. It's not made of bricks so would burn easily in the attack.'

Jovis thought about that while he watched the team drop straight down but still in formation. It was quick and, by the gasps he heard from those used to watching them, it was something they very rarely did. After they pulled up, Caitlin dropped below them. When she stopped, she was visible and had been noticed by the enemy closest to her.

'What the hell are those idiots doing?' Calyx yelled.

'Never seen this battle configuration before.' Axon was just as bewildered.

Jett walked over and faced Axon. 'I believe it best that my brother and I go there just to make sure Glow is not harmed. We don't intend to break any laws by becoming involved and will stay out of sight, but do think we should be there to make a grab for Glow if anything goes wrong.' He saw Axon's eyes narrow with anger but continued to insist Calyx and he should be there. 'Hell, even you don't know what the plan is or what the intent. There are literally thousands of those thugs, and as Jovis said, they are merely six against... well, far too many if you ask me.'

Even as gods we would have to destroy everything at ground zero to fix that onslaught.' Calyx sounded furious.

'I swear... I'll lock the lot of you up in that blatzing chamber if you don't quit it!' He pointed to a glass-encased room. They had all been told earlier that this was a prism, and that if they interfered he would have the guards lock them in it for the duration.

Jett eyed Calyx. They knew once inside the room they were in their transporting abilities would not work. In the prism, they would not hear or see anything that was going on and be entirely in the dark. They had to suck it up for now and being under a signed contract, they couldn't go unless Axon gave the order. Jett folded his arms and stayed where he was, letting Axon know he wasn't happy with his judgement, not one bit.

Axon fumed at his persistence. 'I have faith in Rory. He will not allow harm to come to Caitlin. You men have no idea just how close their bond is; he saved her remember! He knows what her minders did to her growing up; saw it first-hand. He would never hurt Cait. Never! Now stand down or sit, I don't care which, but nobody goes, or they will deal with me. I'll be right behind you to drag you straight back here. Now shut up and let me watch.' Axon took a step to the side, ignoring Jett, and with folded arms, refused to discuss it further.

Jett huffed and turned back to the scene.

Once again silence fell. Jovis shut up too, amazed Axon would stand his ground with a god and live. If his friends didn't change his mind, Jovis knew he had no hope. He was blown away that Axon placed so much faith in his team, yet as he watched they showed no fear and looked game enough to face an onslaught of twice this size. Not wanting to end up in that room either, he had no choice but to stand beside the others and watch and hope the Cosmic Riders worked some kind of miracle.

Jovis glanced across at Jett, uneasy that he didn't hold trust in Rory as Axon did. He wondered if it was pure jealousy, because he also sure hated Rory at this moment for putting his girl in the middle of whatever was about to go down. Caitlin's trust in this Rory dude seemed unshakable, even though he was allowing her to be the one in the line of fire. *What a prick!*

Fireballs headed for Caitlin. She did nothing but sit still. 'Axon...!' Jovis called with a shaky tone, nervous for her.

'Wait!' Axon growled. He was just as tense, but his trust did not waver.

The five Riders began to spin in the one spot, and dazzling colourful sparks shot from each. Suddenly the sky crackled as the magic that ran between the team members intensified. The sound of a sharp crack snapped out, and lightning sparks discharged continually to form an electrical arc. The charge gathered in the centre of the Riders and shot down. Caitlin lifted her arms as her horse began to spin too. Faster and faster she went until she was almost invisible, and the explosives fired at her bounced off.

'Axon, they're magnificent. I'm so sorry I doubted them. I have never seen anything so powerful. Even if they do nothing more, this was amazing to see.' Jovis had such respect for Caitlin and this team he had never seen work together before. He had done the right thing signing up to have their protection. After this day he would always place his full trust in them monitoring and taking care of the sky security.

'So surreal,' he added.

'Holy shytzer.' Calyx put his hand to his mouth and bit on the side of his fist.

'What was that?' Jett called out as the sound of a massive bomb exploding rang out.

Axon put his hand up. 'Not yet! I will tell you when. Do not go until I say.' His strong command echoed in their ears.

As Jovis watched all six members now spinning, he wondered

what this would do. He was amazed they didn't get dizzy and fall off their horses, yet this spinning top effect they had created was kept in perfect formation. 'Oh wow,' he almost whispered with wonderment when what looked like rapid lightning bolts shot out from Caitlin's spinning form. The sliver of light met its mark. The attack on the enemy was as effective as if fifty machine guns were being fired all at once. As the enemy was hit, they dropped on the spot, lifeless, not a movement to be seen. The bursts of light caused instant separation from their mortal forms. The souls floated to meet the ferryman of the underworld.

Not a fire burst or any harm came to the castle or the village. Caitlin's aim, even while spinning, was impeccable. 'Who are these people?' Jovis blinked twice in disbelief.

Everyone else in the room clapped and high-fived each other, but not Jovis and Axon; they hadn't moved. Axon spoke without shifting his gaze from the screen.

'They are my team, the best-goddamned Riders in the universe.' Axon grinned. 'And they are all grounded when they get back here for not telling me they'd been working on this secret new manoeuvre.'

Once the army was gone, and the threat to the castle ceased, Caitlin and the team above slowed and stopped spinning. Caitlin pointed, and hand signalled Rory. He squinted to see where and nodded, putting his thumbs up.

'What now?' Jovis asked. 'What did she say?' He scratched his head as they took off. Sign language he knew, but that made no sense to him, though it must have meant something to Rory. He had them fly into a low-floating cloud and disappear out of sight.

Axon kept watching while he spoke. 'Cait spotted Aravik and Loray. Rory has to move fast or lose the trail. The heat they give off dissipates quickly and this is what he tracks.' He put his hand up and clicked his fingers.

A voice spoke. 'We're on it, chief. Tracking them in 3-2-1...'

The castle scene on the screen Axon still stared at flickered. The stars and planets whizzed past as if they were flying high and fast in space. 'Got them!' Axon called out, 'at 2.4 right, speed 1,000

NAVlights and slowing.'

Jovis couldn't see anything but lights flashing past at an incredible speed.

'Stop! You're there,' Axon called out again.

'Got it chief, they've landed,' the voice responded.

Jovis glanced around the room, interested to see who spoke. A panel of space researchers sat above them. Three men and two women looked through a glass panel that had been invisible until now. It was the youngest of them speaking.

'Where?' Axon moved closer to the screen. 'Not familiar with this Ice Planet.'

They didn't answer straight away. Then the voice came over the speaker very controlled, but not happy. 'It's Nitarn's homeland, the Ice Planet Ixon. Sorry chief, this doesn't look good. The Riders have just landed and are surrounded by armed combat soldiers.'

'I can see. Shush! I want to hear what's being said.'

Taken by surprise, the Riders had been pulled from their horses and were face down on the ground. Jovis was mystified as to why the Riders hadn't put up a struggle. He was sure his boys could have taken them on, *well... without their guns,* which led him to believe the Riders were not bulletproof. He would have thought after what he just witnessed that the Riders were capable of protecting themselves from every kind of flying missiles.

Jovis had his fists closed. 'Punch him Cait,' he yelled at the screen when Aravik personally pulled Caitlin off her horse.

Aravik held Caitlin's arms behind her back as he pushed her in front of Loray. 'Is this the brazen bitch you were just cussing for ruining everything? Tell me, as I want to kill the culprit first.'

Loray sneered at him, her lip curled. 'She's mine! I've had to live with that horrid whining cow for weeks. Little miss, oh-I can't-cook-or-clean. She's as useless as they come. What happened out there, no way she would have instigated as she cons everyone to do her dirty work. I know for a fact she couldn't fight her way out of a wet paper bag. She is one annoying waste of space, and right now I want to rip her conniving blatzing heart out.'

'Hear that little lady? Loray wants to play with you first. I'm looking forward to seeing a scrag fight. Blatz, having two bitches locked in a catfight turns this package right on.' He grabbed his crotch and shook what he held. He pushed Caitlin face first into the slushy mud. 'This should be fun. Do a good job of entertaining me, Loray, and your loins will feel my thunder later.' He signalled the men with guns to back off and give them room. The rest of the team were dragged out of the way and tied to nearby trees.

Caitlin sluggishly got to her feet. 'A man like you should enjoy a wager then. Let's see, if I beat your bitch, you let my friends go, and I will show you how a real woman parties with a man like you,' she mouthed off.

Back at the Alpha Site, they watched intently. There was not a sound, not even loud breathing as they concentrated to hear every word.

Axon threw his head back and laughed, wiping the tears quickly from his eyes so he could watch. 'Sorry guys, but this is a side of Cait that only rears its red head when she gets really mad.' He turned to Jett. 'It's the side I got when Rory and I dared to keep her from going to you.' He turned to Jovis. 'And the attitude I got when I tried to stop her going back to stay with you and Artisan.' He smiled and pointed to the screen. 'Men, meet the Cait I fell in love with.'

Back on Ixon, Aravik slapped his leg. 'The darnedest thing is I've never had a true redhead. Give it what you got, Red. I've got twelve fat inches that appreciates that bet.' He grabbed at himself again.

Caitlin turned for just one second. 'And I'm just the girl to teach you how to use it, big boy. Now keep it in your pants until I sit this whore on her backside and show her some goddamned manners.'

'Grrr!' Loray ran for her, so riled up her face was red with fury. 'You're dead, you lazy lying bitch!' she screamed.

Caitlin waited until Loray's outstretched hands were almost on her shoulders. With one swift movement, she somersaulted backwards and kicked hard into the chest of her attacker. Loray was knocked backwards and into Aravik's arms.

'Couldn't fight her way out of a wet paper bag you said.' He lifted an eyebrow and pushed her back into the circle the guards had created.

'She's been fooling everyone, the lying scum!' Loray hissed.

He shrugged. 'You called it.' He leant against a tree trunk. 'Don't let me interfere with your fantasy of ripping her heart out.'

'That was before I found out she's nothing but a lying cow who just goddamned busted a couple of my ribs.' She sneered at Caitlin. 'I want her dead... Kill her!' she yelled at the rebels surrounding them.

Aravik put his hand up, irritated. 'No! Now finish the blatzing fight, Loray. Prove you're the one worth keeping... or so help me!'

'Kill me! You pig-headed snot wipe! Nitarn will kill you!' she screamed.

'Nitarn is not in charge anymore, I am. Go!' His arm shot out towards Caitlin. 'Or you'll wish it was you dead.'

'Pig.' Loray spat out some blood.

Caitlin knew the penny had dropped at last. This was the outcome Caitlin hoped for, and it hit Loray hard. She had been used but had made her bed, and would be undoubtedly killed if she didn't do as commanded. Now Loray had been put in her place, hating Aravik enough to testify against him, Caitlin had her sights on the instigator of this entire operation; the one who called the shots. He had destroyed property, affecting many lives. He'd involved and had killed armies from many other worlds. The death toll was the worst they had ever encountered. He deserved the highest penalties for such crimes. Death was too good for this evil mind, so before the cuffs went on, she had a score to settle. She turned to Aravik. 'Hey stud, if she won't fight me for the freedom of my friends, why not you? Or are you scared of a little redhead?' She put her hands on her hips. Her hair had unravelled, and she gathered it in one hand, tossing the copper locks over her shoulder with attitude.

Back at Alpha Site, Jovis swore at Axon. 'Are you going to stop this nonsense, or am I? Doing a backflip won't help her fight this vicious prick. I've seen him train, know his capabilities as a warrior. Ask Rocky.'

'True,' Rocky said, 'he was the best we had.'

Axon shook his head. 'She is the best I have. Now settle down. I won't warn you again.' He turned back to watch.

Jovis wished to wipe the smug expression from Axon's face. He glared at Jett and Calyx who stood with arms folded, expressionless. *No help there!* They were as pissed as he was but obviously knew their place with this overbearing blatz that was happy to watch his own wife get the hiding of her life. *Maybe he's like Aravik and gets off on it, too!* Jovis was so mad he could hardly breathe, but he couldn't leave. He didn't want to break the trust of these people who had saved his kingdom. Yet he loved Caitlin and didn't think he could stay and not do something if Aravik laid a hand on her. He was worried sick for her, and sweat poured down his face from his brow as the action continued on the Ice Planet of Ixon.

Aravik hadn't answered, just stared at her arrogance. She took another angle to tick him off further. 'Well stud, I'm waiting. I mean I can see you like to keep the women around you in their place. You must be busting out of those britches to slap the smugness off my face. Let me ignite the fire down there.'

'You couldn't handle a man like me, twinkle toes. That move is old school. Hell, I learnt that at preschool. You wenches are useless, only good for one thing as far as I can see. Not really worth the effort unless I get something out of it.'

'I promise, you'll get more out of it than you bargained for and just the way you like it. No weapons, only fists. I'll give you something that might really get you hard. Because let's face facts, we know what you look like, who you are and now, where you live. You'll have to kill us or risk us coming back in numbers. So what's say we have a bit of fun first?'

'It is true. As much as you're entertaining, I will have to kill you, Red.' He kicked off the tree trunk and walked towards her. He slapped Loray across the face as he walked past. It was so hard it knocked her into some guards standing near. When he faced Caitlin, he smirked. 'Want some of that, sugar?'

Caitlin shot out her hands so fast it caught him off guard, and his instinct had him back away from the assault. Her hit was direct and aimed to hinder his response; the attack prevented him from mustering up the normal superhuman strength to fight back. The playing field now even, she advanced on him, one fist after the other, her small hands dug deep into his solar plexus. He lost breath and buckled over quickly. She stood over him. 'That was for trying to kill my teammates. I will let the law decide your fate for what you did to Jovis and his friends.'

He knelt with arms wrapped around his waist. 'Kill her, kill them all!' Aravik choked out, and coughed.

The rebel army aimed their guns at Caitlin and her team. 'Hell No! Do not... even think about firing those weapons.' She stood with her hands out. 'Just try, and I swear you'll be in the cell right next to these two losers. She heard the cocking of mechanism, and with a loud clap of her hands, she threw one hand up high as if holding something. As she did so, the rifles were reefed out of the army's hands and held up high above their heads. Now unarmed, the rebels continued to fight, pulling knives and other combat weapons from their pockets and darting for her.

'You have to be kidding, really!' She couldn't believe she was giving them a chance to give up and stay out of prison. She showed them the power she had yet they still questioned her authority. With her free hand not holding the guns, she opened her palm and let out short, sharp bursts of power to knock the guards away. They kept coming. Unless she killed them, which was against all she stood for, she had to keep fighting one handed. The problem was she was getting tired. If she had a moment, she could look around to see where the safest place would be to store the guns until they left.

'Anytime you want to step in and help out, would be good.' She glanced at Rory and spotted his look. 'I knew you lot were playing possum... payback for leaving the group, right? Well, you've had your fun, so come join the fight. Rotten sod!' She had caught him grinning.

Rory nodded and began to power up the team. They glowed brightly. The ropes fell from them and, free, they sprang to their feet. From their belts they pulled out a choice of weapon, jumping straight into combat. The army became thicker.

'Where are they coming from?' yelled Caitlin.

'Can't see,' called Bree who was the farthest away.

'Keep them from Cait, so she can finish teaching that creep some goddamned manners,' Rory called out. The team formed a circle around her.

Aravik's body quickly recovered and he turned to grab Loray, who for some reason had not moved. She looked dazed and wore a blank expression. 'You're coming with me.' He shook her.

Caitlin felt him ready to transport out. 'Not so fast!' She held out the hand she had been fighting the guards with and from it, ejected a glowing force which encircled Loray and Aravik. This magic she'd learned from Nitarn. He had used it to prevent her from leaving his side. Fear for her well-being had helped fight this power, and winning it over allowed her to keep it within. It was fitting that she now used it on his very own people.

Without having to battle with guards, Caitlin's thoughts were able to slow down enough to help her get rid of the guns being held out of reach. The hand she held in the air clenched into a fist. This grouped the firearms together high above her head, which sounded out like metallic crashing when they smashed together. Opening her fist, she made a throwing motion. The guns went flying and landed in trees a considerable distance away. She didn't want to destroy their only means of protection, but it would be a while before they were found and gathered. She and the team would be long gone by then.

Still holding the prisoners in the new magic, her walk towards Aravik and Loray was confident. She was back and feeling good.

Her swagger was enough to make Rory stop fighting for just a second and watch. He was glad she had her magic back. He acknowledged she needed some tweaking, but she had grown intellectually since he saw her last and once again, held her own. This final test wasn't to give her a hard time as she may have thought, but rather to help her regain the confidence he felt she lacked. The Cait he knew would never have hung back when he ordered her to. She would have argued and gone with him and Lisha to disarm the bombs on Artisan's Ice World. Caitlin was a skilled Rider, and he couldn't have been prouder of her performance. She and her horse were working well together. The beating she gave Aravik had more impact by using Shargan's magical armour around her delicate hands. This made the blows stronger than most men could manage. He was amazed she had learned to do this, and would be sure to ask her how when this was over. Knowing she was okay now to be left unsupervised, he turned back to his new opponents as they charged towards him, thinking he was off guard. He smiled... *as if*. Their fists and knives were met with his fists and chains. Rory left them utterly disappointed when it was them that copped a firm fist in each of their faces. His long arms were always an advantage. One by one, he took down the many that had run at him once they thought he wasn't watching. Some went down two at a time. Two met with his chains. They were tossed some metres away. Both landed with a crack against the very tree where Rory had been tied. 'Fitting justice,' he called out before the two rebels he just took down fell into unconsciousness.

'These men are pouring out from the ground like ants.' Nathen picked up a rebel and gave him one last punch. 'Night-night!' He tossed him aside.

'I want those two behind bars,' Rory bellowed to his team over the noise. 'Hold the sympathisers back from Cait. She's almost done.'

Caitlin secured the prisoners before speaking. Aravik and Loray sat cross-legged with hands secured behind their backs. Caitlin knelt. 'No good struggling, Aravik, the chains are from the Angel of Peace himself. You will never break them, and they will leave a nasty scar if you keep that up. The lock has just alerted the angel, and he is on his way.'

'Bullshytz, what blatzing angel?' Aravik scoffed. 'There's no such thing.'

Caitlin stood up. She suddenly illuminated and put her arms out. 'Stop!' She called out. Her voice was so incredibly melodious all fighting ceased. Those with arms up ready to attack dropped them by their sides and turned to her. Rory and her Rider friends were surprised, but had expected the Goddess of Peace to emerge at some point and do something big to stop this war. They had never had to leave so much hatred behind. And the way they kept coming, they thought they would have to.

'I am the Goddess of Peace.' Her voice rang out, forcing all who stood before her to stop and listen. 'I will turn a blind eye once only, so hear me now, lay down your weapons and walk with me in my light or face the consequences of these actions here today by me and me alone.' She glowed brighter to show further authority when still hearing whispers. 'They call me Glow Girl.' She lifted off the ground just as an angel would. One by one the enemy soldiers went down on one knee and bowed to her.

She landed back on two feet and walked through them, touching some. She lifted the chins of others to look at her. Those few stood and followed her back to the front of all those who bowed before her.

'All eyes on me!' She had them look up. 'Your Ice Planet is now free of all tyrants and evil rulers. As for a leader, these few have been chosen by me as your council of Ixon until a new ruler is chosen. These men and women of the council will work directly with Jovis, the newly appointed Prince of the Ice Planets. I will leave it up to Prince Jovis to choose a new ruler. I am confident he will find a most suitable replacement who will give this world much light and happiness. Until then, no decisions are to be made without the deliberation and authority of these chosen on this night. If you go against the council, know this, that second chance I am awarding for loyalty to me will be revoked, and you can instead answer to Hades in the underworld.'

She turned her attention to her team. 'These men you currently battle against are your friends, and you will fight with them never more. They wish only the best for your homeland, and are the same team who will help the prince to bring order into your current darkened existence, while new technology is introduced to give you light. They are known as the Cosmic Riders, the peacekeepers of celestial spheres. Get to know them well as you are now under their protection against those who mean you or your families harm.' Caitlin glowed and heard them gasp. She held out her arms. 'Do you accept my terms for this new life I give to you, your family and your friends?'

CAITLIN II

The crowd mumbled.

'Can't hear you!' Her voice echoed with force, and the defining pitch had many cover their ears.

'Aye!' they yelled collectively. Many close to the Riders shook their hands and introduced themselves.

Caitlin waited for the chatter to die down. 'Before you go back to your homes and families, I want you to meet my boss, Zoren, the Archangel of the Heavens. He has come to give proof we are serious in our undertaking of Ixon. Zoren has come to take these prisoners of war to the dungeon where Nitarn is safely secured. This is why I say you need never worry about your safety again.' She pointed upwards.

The sky lit up brightly in the darkness of this poorly run world. The glow was so light, most shaded their eyes. Zoren entered the atmosphere and looked magnificent with his huge white wings that glowed so brilliantly. This was not a normal ending to war, but out in this galactic darkness where only death waited, Caitlin was going to make sure these people believed there was more to life than war and hatred. News of light and angels would travel to many. Hope and peace would end many wars. This she had felt they needed more than any other form of goodwill. She communicated this to Zoren and suggested his arriving in such glory would give them divine belief to be the key to the future wellbeing of not only this world but all these inhabited dark Ice Planets. He had agreed.

Zoren made a hand movement, and a glowing birdcage structure encased Loray and Aravik. This, the glowing angel picked up effortlessly by the top. With a sweep of soft, white feathered wings, he flew off with them, zapping out of sight. The heavenly being left a feeling of peace and love in hearts that had long ago darkened with greed, hate and anger.

While the crowd watched Zoren, the team had mounted their magical rides, and the six of them and their horses were glowing brightly. The sudden light and glow were not what the onlookers expected. They gasped and held hands to their faces in awe of what this night had brought to them. Instead of death and further despair and hatred, they were calm, warmed by forgiveness and a promise of a new tomorrow. Sour thoughts turned to delight.

Caitlin spoke for the last time. 'Now go home to your families and count your blessings that I allowed you this chance to be with them. Live a good life and remember, we, the Cosmic Riders of the heavens and peacekeepers of your worlds, will be watching you.'

They flew off leaving the darkness behind as they vanished out of sight.

* * * *

Axon turned, looked up through the windows and praised the Alpha Site researchers for the excellent feed. 'Good job guys. Switch it off and give us some privacy.'

Jovis sat slowly in the chair he had leaned on, flabbergasted and unable to find the right words to apologise to Axon. He knew, while they had no clue, his team were unbelievable. But more than that, he had been honoured by one he honoured. Did he deserve it? He thought not.

The others joined him at the table where barely a word was spoken. Axon sat opposite with Calyx and Jett. All three gave Jovis time to digest what Caitlin had bestowed upon him. He had the title he wished for, had fought for and had hated all of them for not acknowledging. He was finally granted royal status for all to recognise and in front of the Archangel of the Heavens! He knew from the nod of approval he gave to Caitlin on how she handled matters, it had been stamped with his permission.

'I can't believe my brother is alive. I'm stoked we were able to hear those men so clearly. But even more so that Cait has left me in charge of Ixon. I don't know what to say.' Jovis eyed Jett. 'Are you okay with her doing this? I thought you were king over all these worlds as well, so how do we make this work?'

Jett grinned. 'I'm stoked with her choice, Jovis. I did wonder how Glow was going to make it work between us and this is perfect. You have legal title over the Ice Planets until you can bring them up to Dwarf Planet status. The standard for them, you, Calyx and I can draw up and have it signed off by Axon. This will free me up to concentrate mostly on the Dwarf Planets that come online. I can help them fine-tune any issues of hardship they still face, and not neglect my other duties to the underworld.'

'But there are hundreds of Ice Planets out there! It's a big job. I will need help.'

Calyx motioned towards Artisan and Rocky. 'You have two very capable and trustworthy friends. Cait would never have expected you to do this alone.'

'He's right boss, we'll help,' said Artisan.

'Count me in or else.' Rocky didn't wait to be asked. Caitlin had shown him how worthy he was in Jovis's eyes and it would never be questioned again. The three of them were the real deal, mates always.

'Cait must have a lot of faith in me, in us...' He glanced at Artisan and Rocky. 'She's given us such an honourable standing in the universe. I'm still getting used to the idea. It's going to be huge.'

Axon put down his NAVcom, finding it strange he had not heard from Caitlin. 'You have Calyx, Jett and me to help with the hiccups. But from what Cait tells me, you'll do just fine, especially now she has put the fear of her return into them. That news will travel fast, and by the time you get to your first round of visits, the heads of state will look forward to your visit, and not hers.' He grinned.

'That was for sure, one very classy mission. I will never doubt Cait's abilities again. That is one fine woman you have there, Axon.' Jovis sat back, feeling better about Axon and wishing now to get to know him better.

'Yes, and if you men are happy, maybe she might come home and spend time with me.' He was surprised by their answers.

'She sure has put the spring back in my step with this latest move.' Jett nodded, looking pleased. 'Guess it's time she left us all to settle into a routine with her team and Axon, well for a week, anyway.'

'Hear! Hear! to that!' Jovis leant over the table and high-fived Jett. 'Next weekend at your house isn't it?'

'What's this?' Axon looked surprised.

'Well, Cait's a step ahead of you, Axon. She has already organised our visitation rights. There is a get together with us all next weekend. So I guess I can wait until then to catch up with her if you want us... me included... gone before she returns.' Calyx was reluctant to appease.

Axon chuckled. 'Shytzer, I give up. You're all welcome to come over home and visit any day of the week. Just leave without her, is all I ask.'

They all burst out laughing, but finally agreed to let him have a wife for a while. None of them knew what the future was to hold. Axon did wonder if his wife had manipulated this course of conversation from wherever she was right now.

* * * *

Rory led the team towards the next portal. He had one stop on the way home, and that was to drop Caitlin off with Axon. Once the most important woman in the universe was safe, he would be free to pop the question to the most important woman in his life, his girlfriend. Bree was beside him. He was happy she was there, and her smile gave him goosebumps. He had nearly lost her and for now, wanted her close. *Good job guys. Caitlin, well done!* Rory communicated.

'Permission to speak privately?' Caitlin was able to speak now the threat was over.

Sure, come up front where I can hear you. Bree honey, can you drop back? Nathen, keep my girlfriend company while I talk to Cait. It was unusual for Caitlin to request a chat while in transit.

Caitlin gave him a nervous smile. 'Rory, we need to discuss my Rider status and it has to be now.'

He closed his mouth.

She took a breath and continued. 'The work I did back there was to calm things down and hopefully, it lasts a few years or so because things are about to change. You see... I'm pregnant. Axon and I are going to have a baby.'

'Does he know?' Rory squeaked out, surprised.

'He would never have let me come if he knew.'

'Caitlin, this gift happens to very few immortals. I wouldn't have let you come either. This was a huge mission, what if something had gone wrong?'

'It didn't. You see, I knew Zoren was there. He watched over me and it was he who tossed me the special chain when no one was looking. It rendered them helpless. It helped me to ease up and rest a bit. This allowed me time to concentrate on calming the army.'

Rory's eyes were wide. 'Shytz Cait, Axon will be cross if he finds Zoren and I knew before him. Well, I'd be peeved if it were Bree. But apart from that, wow, a mum, my little girl is all grown up. Congrats kiddo!' He smiled. 'Love to give you a hug but a bit hard with wings between us.'

'Thanks, Rory. I'm scared but happy.'

'How far along?'

'Best guess about six weeks.'

'You haven't seen a doctor?' His eyebrow went up.

She grinned. 'Dr Zoren. You know he knows everything. He spoke to me out in the garden telepathically before you picked me up earlier. He gave me the option of not coming on this mission but did say he couldn't foresee harm coming to me. That was all I needed to know, and I was thrilled to join you guys today. I had to give it a shot to keep the peace for many years to come, because you know I have always said I want to be in my baby's life full time. So I had to fix it, so I only go on missions with you guys. That way bub can come.' She grinned seeing his look.

But Rory did understand. Her upbringing was frightful, and she would want much more for her own child. 'So, you saw the softer side of Uncle Zoren, and he is okay with this.'

'I told him, you and I would make it work.'

'And we will. Together.' Rory was over the moon she wasn't giving up as a Rider. Just tossing aside the stealing thieving lot of planets rulers, who kept taking his Rider mate.'

Caitlin grinned and nodded. 'Knew you'd have my back and Zoren has too, he also promised to keep this quiet until I tell Axon. You get why though, right? I didn't want him charging in all worried and ruining my plans today, to end the war.'

'He's going to be shitty you told me first.' He chuckled happily because she had.

'You're my family, Rory. I will always tell you everything first.' Caitlin teared up.

'You're my family too, and I miss you like crazy when you're away for too long. Geezers, the babies not even here yet and I'm already starting to feel like a proud bloody grandpa.' He chuckled.

'Will you mind working with me while I'm fat?'

'I've seen you at your worst and at your best, Cait. You're a blessing in my life… as if a fat stomach would worry me. I'm just so excited for you. This is your chance to live your younger years through your own child. Enjoy every minute, Cait. You deserve this more than anyone I have ever met.'

Tears ran down her cheeks. Only Rory would understand why she needed to be a hands-on mum, and she loved knowing they were that close he would help her still do what she loved doing most, being a Riding. 'Thanks Rory, only you would get why.'

'You're leaving now aren't you?' He saw her glowing.

She nodded. 'Tell the others after you get home. Axon will know by then.' She chuckled as his eyebrows raised and looked around.

'Zoren's here, isn't he?'

'He's ready to take me now. He doesn't want me harmed until I am checked out thoroughly and given the doctor's approval everything is okay. Love you guys! See you soon.' She called out to them all, as Zoren flew down, his massive wings sounded majestic in the emptiness of space. With a gentle movement, he swept her into his arms and took a smiling Caitlin from her horse and transported her away.

I'll explain later, guys. We're heading home to celebrate. Rory communicated to the team.

The others had no idea what, but they would first be toasting his engagement to Bree when he proposed on the way home. After, knew they'd be proud as punch when told they are going to be uncles and aunties to Axon and Caitlin's baby when it arrived. He liked the title *Uncle* rather than *Pa*, but he'd brought Cait up and to stir him she would give him the *Pa* title anyway. You couldn't wipe the smile off his face. Life couldn't get any better than this. *Yep, let's go home!*

The roar of excitement he heard would get louder after the news... the best news ever.

A baby Rider was coming.

Personal Message

Thank you for purchasing my book.

If you enjoyed it, please take a moment to leave me a review at your favorite book retailer?

To discover more about the
Magical Cosmic Collection and my other books
visit:

www·debbiebehan·com

Author of YA Fantasy Fiction.

Regards,

Debbie

Also Available in
Paperback and eBook

Magical Cosmic Collection
Book One

CASSANDRA
GODDESS OF HARMONY
Paperback: 978-0-9954205-0-2

Magical Cosmic Collection
Book Two

CAITLIN
GODDESS OF PEACE
Paperback: 978-0-9954205-2-6

Alina Eternal
Paperback: 978-0-9954205-3-3